"Do you remember how I touched you?"

His voice dropped lower, to the tone of a confession. "Your skin was so soft, like the petal of a rose. The roses are in bloom at Montague, and every time I smell them I think of touching you. And kissing you. In my mind I have kissed you a hundred times, in a hundred different ways."

Claudia didn't breathe, afraid she would break the spell between them. She'd never guessed that she plagued his thoughts as completely as he plagued her own. Never guessed the effect those revelations would have on her. It took a conscious effort not to move, to keep herself from melting into his arms.

He could be toying with her, testing her resolve. In her mind she repeated everything he'd said, but couldn't recall a single word that rang false. She felt an overwhelming urge to touch him. She felt an urgent need to surrender to his kisses and to admit that she wanted nothing so much as to be in his arms. . . .

Bantam Books
by Elizabeth Elliott

THE WARLORD

SCOUNDREL

BETROTHED

Betrothed

Elizabeth Elliott

BANTAM BOOKS

New York   Toronto   London   Sydney   Auckland

BETROTHED

A Bantam Fanfare Book / October 1996

ISBN 0-553-57566-X

Published simultaneously in the United States and Canada

Bantam Books are published by Bantam Books, a division of Bantam
Doubleday Dell Publishing Group, Inc. Its trademark, consisting of the
words "Bantam Books" and the portrayal of a rooster, is Registered in
U.S. Patent and Trademark Office and in other countries. Marca
Registrada. Bantam Books, 1540 Broadway, New York, New York 10036.

PRINTED IN THE UNITED STATES OF AMERICA

OPM   10 9 8 7 6 5 4 3 2 1

To Jennifer Pattison Hall,
for her tireless crusades against
the heathen Schedules.

Very special thanks to Mr. C. H. Ostfeld of Milan,
for all Italian translations that appear in this text
and for his heroic rescues of sleeping hands
and children's songs.

Betrothed

1 &

Guy of Montague rode into Lonsdale Castle as if he owned it. Atop a massive black warhorse, his armor glittered so brightly in the midday sun that those who cheered his arrival shaded their eyes as he passed by them. A score of knights in blue and white surcoats rode behind him. The knights' lances rested in holsters near their stirrups, the tips pointed skyward with a long, fluttering pennant tied to each end; the white wolf of Montague on a field of midnight blue.

Guy surveyed all he could see of the castle. The massive gatehouse with its twin barbicans and double gates looked well kept, and the outbuildings before him were freshly painted. The six-story keep that sat atop a raised knoll in the center of the castle seemed in good repair as well. Guy had yet to meet Baron Lonsdale, but already he could tell that the man knew the value of a properly run fortress. Apparently Baron Lonsdale knew the value of many things, including the run-down keep he intended to sell to Guy for a king's ransom.

Evard de Cordray, Guy's second-in-command, rode up beside him. He'd removed his helm to reveal dark hair and pale green eyes that also scanned the bailey. " 'Tis a fine welcome, is it not, my lord?"

"A promising start, Evard." Guy looked at Lonsdale's high stone walls, which blocked the cool summer breeze. The sun beat mercilessly on his armor. Guy removed his own helm and tucked it under one arm. In response, the crowd sent up a roar of approval. He shook his head and sighed. "They act as if I just presented them with a trophy."

"You have." Evard cast a wary glance around them, although none were close enough to hear their conversation over the clatter of hooves and armor and the din of the crowd itself. "Their baron will become a rich man as a result of your visit. Each of them will prosper from their overlord's new-found wealth."

Guy looked out over the crowd, at faces filled with the excitement of the moment, at many broad smiles that could be a reflection of greed. He felt like a fat pig being led to the slaughter. "For the price their baron asks, one would think I meant to buy Lonsdale itself."

"You have an army strong enough to reclaim Halford Hall," Evard said in a quieter voice. "Why bargain with a man you do not trust?"

Guy shook his head. "War will not ease Halford's suffering. If I can settle this without bloodshed, so be it."

Evard nodded, but presented another concern. "I still think it a mistake to ride into Lonsdale with but a score of knights at your back. You are vulnerable, baron."

"I have weighed the risks, Evard. Lonsdale knows he will have his own war should he take me prisoner. My death begets nothing but bloodshed. It is in his best interests to be a congenial host, for he will get what he wants most. Gold." The black warhorse began to toss its head, and Guy loosened his hold on the reins, aware that the beast could sense his tension. "In the unlikely event that he should employ some treachery, the odds are still weighed in our favor. I have no doubt that our spy knows as much about this fortress as Baron Lonsdale himself."

" 'Tis an advantage," Evard agreed, without much enthusiasm.

Guy turned his attention forward again and saw the stained glass windows of a large chapel. "Make certain the men are quartered together," he told Evard. "You will stay with them to make sure they do not partake too generously of Lonsdale's hospitality. No wenching, and no more than a sober measure of wine or ale."

"They will be aggrieved to hear that, my lord."

"They will be aggrieved if they—" Guy lost his train of thought as his gaze moved to the shadowed doorway of the chapel. In the darkest recess of the doorway was an ominous vision of some sort, the pale oval of a woman's face floating suspended in the shadows. The vision moved forward and he sighed with relief. The woman was indeed a whole person. She was also staring at him.

He watched her watch him, a little surprised that she didn't seem distracted by the noisy procession. She held her hands clasped at her waist, her expression so serene that he felt his own tension begin to slip away. As they drew closer to the chapel, her features became clearer. He was still too far away to tell the color of her eyes, yet they looked hauntingly familiar. Where had he seen those eyes before?

They were her only remarkable feature. Her hair was a plain, dark chestnut color, the slope of her nose not as dainty as he preferred, and her cheekbones too high and sharp to flatter the roundness of her chin. He stared openly, trying to summon a word to describe her. Few would call her pleasing or even pretty. Those terms were too earthy to describe a face such as hers. He stared harder.

Exquisite.

That word came very close. "Breathtaking" was a more apt description. He wondered that all in the bailey didn't gape at her, dumbfounded by such perfection. Not that he would know if others stared or not. He couldn't take his eyes from her. No matter how common or mismatched her features, they somehow combined to create the face of an angel.

The portcullis slammed shut behind the procession with a resounding clang that broke her strange hold over him. He forced his gaze lower to examine her dull green gown. What that gown contained lacked the religious inspiration of her face. Indeed, that part of her would tempt any man to more earthly thoughts. The high neckline emphasized the lush curves of her breasts and the tattered yellow ribbons around her waist made him want to place his hands there to see if they would encircle her as easily. The skirt flared down forever, an indication that her legs would be long and probably well-shaped. Then he noticed her thick braid, that the tail of it ended somewhere past her knees. Unbound, the hair would cover her like a cloak.

He found himself glad to be seated atop a horse. Standing upright, the wave of lust that struck him would have sent him to his knees. The face of a Madonna, a body meant for a man's hands, and hair to tempt a saint to sin.

"Baron?" Evard repeated himself twice before Guy answered.

"Find out who she is, Evard."

"Who?" Evard asked.

They rode past the chapel, and Guy had to turn his attention forward again or all within the bailey would remark upon the direction of his gaze. The reins drew tighter within his gauntlet, and the horse tossed its head in protest. The woman's regal bearing and fine clothing marked her a lady, probably the wife of a Lonsdale knight. It didn't matter. He had to know who she was. "The woman on the chapel steps. Dark hair and a moss-green gown. Learn everything you can of her."

Guy spurred his horse forward, no longer anxious to meet his host. He wanted to reach the keep where their spy awaited, where Evard could find out more about the woman in the bailey.

"You will not attend the mass to celebrate Baron Montague's arrival?"

Claudia Chiavari tugged another weed from the bed of herbs, then looked up to smile at the young friar. Her soft voice carried the lyrical tones of her native Italian. "Nay, Friar Thomas. I attended mass this morning."

That wasn't the entire reason she wouldn't attend the special mass, but more of an explanation than she would give any other. Friar Thomas seemed to understand her when she spoke his difficult Norman language. He didn't ridicule her accent, nor shun her as did many at Lonsdale. The English were a suspicious lot, distrusting of anyone different from themselves. In her five long years at Lonsdale Castle she'd learned to understand the Norman language, yet she spoke only when spoken to and kept her answers as short as possible. The Norman words sounded right to her, but others said her accent made them hard to comprehend. She hated it when she had to repeat herself, slower, louder, again and again. They made her feel a fool.

Friar Thomas never asked her to repeat herself, and he always seemed interested in what she had to say. It didn't take long before Claudia considered him a friend, although she knew their friendship would be a short one. He'd arrived at Lonsdale little more than a fortnight ago on his way to the shrine of Saint Andrew. Like many pilgrims, he had decided to extend his stay and do odd jobs in exchange for the food and supplies he needed to continue his journey. Each afternoon he came to the chapel gardens to help her pull weeds.

"And the feast afterward?" Thomas asked. He brushed off his hands then pushed back the cowl of his homespun robes to reveal brown hair the color of his eyes. "The middle bailey looks like the grounds of a fair. There are tents set up around the tables where minstrels and entertainers of all sorts will perform. Will I see you at the feast, Lady Claudia?"

She bent over her work to hide her scowl. "Nay, I will not attend. I must finish my work in the gardens this afternoon."

"The weeds will still be here after the feast."

Claudia said nothing.

"Did your uncle forbid you to attend?" he asked.

"He fears I will embarrass him in front of his guests, that the Montagues will think him related to a half-wit." She kept her head bent and concentrated on her task. Despite her thick leather gloves, she worked cautiously around a stubborn thistle so the sharp spines would not scratch her arms. "I did not want to attend anyway. The feasting grounds will be crowded and noisy, and many will be drunk by nightfall. I prefer the quiet of the gardens, where none will disturb me."

" 'Tis said Guy of Montague often travels abroad, my

lady. I doubt he will consider anyone a half-wit because they are not English. 'Tis a shame your uncle is not so enlightened."

Her eyes widened over the anger in the gentle friar's voice. Before she could remark on the oddity, he gave her a small bow.

"If you will excuse me, Lady Claudia? I must attend mass."

Claudia watched him walk around the rose arbor that stood in the center of the gardens, then to the gate that lay on the other side. With a sigh, she turned toward a clump of rosemary, then hunched down to pick at the endless supply of weeds. She did prefer the gardens. None would bother her here. Not that anyone would bother her at the feast. The people of Lonsdale avoided her whenever possible and that suited her just fine. She shook her head to shoo away a fly that was intent upon circling it. Stupid fly. Stupid *English* fly.

Next, a bee appeared on the white flower of the clover she wanted to pull. She sat back with her hands propped behind her and waited for the insect to find nectar elsewhere. Any sensible bee would join the drone of others that created a steady hum in the apple trees at one side of the gardens. The trees were so laden with blossoms that they looked like giant snowballs against the tall outer wall of the castle. The rare English sun shone bright above her, and she closed her eyes, then tilted her head back to let it warm her face. The scent of herbs and apple blossoms perfumed the air. England was not all bad, she decided. She might even marry an Englishman someday, a man like the one who had ridden into Lonsdale that morning.

Her eyes popped open and she returned to her work with renewed vigor. She was not some pampered English maid who could loll about a garden, her head filled with fanciful thoughts. She'd spent a good portion of her day trying to forget Baron Montague, ever since she watched him ride through the gates. Her curiosity had landed her in trouble again, for she would not be plagued by these thoughts if she had tended her chores as she should have that morning. But she had heard so much about Baron Montague that she wanted just a glimpse of him.

From everything her uncle said about Baron Montague, she had expected a man in his middle years, fat with the bounty of his wealth. Yet Baron Montague looked no more than a half dozen years older than herself. The armor probably made him appear more imposing than he would be without it, but when he removed his helm, she could tell the armor was no more than a reflection of what lay beneath. Even from a distance she knew that he was the handsomest man she'd ever laid eyes upon. His dark brown hair looked flecked with gold in the sunlight. His eyes were dark as well, keen with intelligence as they swept over the crowd. His face was all sharp planes and perfect angles, classical, she thought, like the statues of her homeland. When she looked upon Guy of Montague, she knew that this was what God intended when he created man.

She'd even deceived herself into thinking he returned her bold stare before she realized he could be looking at anything or anyone in the vicinity of the chapel. More than a score of people stood before her on the chapel steps, all waving their arms or bright scarves. Why should he notice one insignificant woman who stood in the shadows of the doorway?

That reasoning didn't affect the force that drew her forward, an irrational urge to do whatever she could to be closer to him. The sound of the portcullis as it slammed shut had brought her to her senses just moments before she would have made a spectacle of herself. Aye, she would have looked a fool if she'd rushed forward to skip along the edge of the crowd after him, as foolish as the silly, giggling group of wenches who did just that. A few of the bolder ones did all but juggle cats to gain his attention. He'd paid them as little heed as he'd paid Claudia.

"Sono belli questi giardini."

Crouched down near a patch of tarragon, Claudia startled at the sound of the deep voice. She shot to her feet and spun around to search for its owner, even as she wondered who within Lonsdale Castle could speak such flawless Italian. She found the answer under one of the apple trees. Baron Montague stood there, one arm draped over a low-hanging branch. Her mouth opened for a moment, then closed again. He'd made a remark about the beauty of the gardens. She couldn't think of anything to say, other than an admission that his armor did not do justice to his muscular build. His casual pose displayed his long, lean body to perfection. She pressed her lips together.

He pushed away from the apple tree and took several steps toward her. His dark blue clothes emphasized the strong lines of his body as well as his wealth. He wore slouch boots and leather breeks dyed the exact shade of his richly quilted tunic. Pearls were sewn at the cross-point of each quilt, a pattern that made the fabric appear an evening sky scattered with stars. At his waist, sapphires the same dark blue color as his clothing glittered along the hilts and sheaths of his dagger and sword. Only his eyes were a different shade of blue. They were the color of a warm, southern ocean.

The leopardskin sash he wore over one shoulder made a fitting emblem of his power. Like the big cat, there was an exotic air about him with just a hint of the dangerous animal that lay beneath the refined exterior. Even the tawny streaks of gold in his hair lent a deceptive warmth to his appearance.

"Very beautiful," he went on, still speaking Italian. Something in his eyes gave the impression that he spoke of her, not the scenery around them. His gaze flickered over her, and she had the feeling he did not miss much in that quick inspection. Dirt and grass stains marred her skirts, and her green gown looked tawdry at best compared to his fine clothing. She felt like a child caught playing in mud puddles.

She responded in her own language, delighted by the opportunity to speak it aloud. "Where did you learn Italian, Baron?"

He smiled, and Claudia knew she'd never seen a smile so handsome. It made her feel warm all over. His words carried just the barest trace of a Norman accent, his voice deep and silky. "I visit your country often, little one. I learned the language long ago." He glanced around them, a casual glance that missed nothing. "What are you doing here all alone? The feasting will start soon. Will you not join the others?"

How did he know she was Italian, or guess to speak the language in the first place? Claudia supposed it must be the foreign look about her that Uncle Laurence often remarked upon, the look of her father. She glanced toward the chapel. The mass couldn't be over so soon, yet the angle of the sun told her that almost two hours had passed since Friar Thomas departed and she could hear the distant sounds of voices as people made their way from the chapel. "The feast will not start without you, my lord. And I did not think to see you today without Baron Lonsdale and his entourage at your side. I could ask the same questions of you."

" 'Tis impolite to throw a man's questions back in his face. Will I impress you with my fine manners if I answer them?"

Claudia heard herself giggle. She never giggled. What was wrong with her? She schooled her features into a dignified expression that would befit any lady. "You may try."

He seemed amused by her attempt to maintain her composure. His smile grew broader when she lifted her chin at a haughty angle. "I told your uncle that I wanted a few minutes alone to reflect upon the uplifting message of Bishop Germaine's sermon. Your uncle appeared impressed by my bent toward religious contemplations."

Claudia felt her breath catch. "You know who I am?"

"Aye, Lady Claudia. I know that you are Baron Lonsdale's niece." He gestured toward the marble bench that sat beneath the rose arbor. "Will you sit with me?"

She took an involuntary step backward. "I—I have work to do."

"Your uncle gave all within the castle permission to leave their duties for the feast. The meal might not begin until I arrive, but I would wager that the festivities are already under way. By your uncle's own words, you are now released from your duties until the morrow."

Claudia bowed her head and tried to take as much time as possible to remove her gloves while her mind searched for another excuse. "I do not wish to intrude on your contemplations, Baron. I must leave."

"Some might think it odd if they saw you leave the gardens just now."

"What do you mean?"

He shrugged, a small gesture of dismissal that made her aware of the breadth of his shoulders. "This could appear an arranged meeting between us."

"I must leave now, before anyone thinks any such thing!" She began to make her way from the herb plots. "No one will think anything amiss if I leave you to your contemplations so soon after you entered the gardens."

"I have been here longer than you think, lady." His words brought her up short.

She twisted her gloves between her hands and cast a worried glance toward the gate. "My uncle will be furious if he discovers that I tarry here with his guest. That is, we have no chaperon. This is improper."

"One of my men guards the gate even now to make certain no one disturbs my meditation." He started to walk toward her. "Come sit with me, Lady Claudia. I promise that none will know of your presence." She began to back away from him until he came to a stop and extended his hand. "I have no mind now for religious thoughts, and I would enjoy your company. Give me a few moments of your time, then I will leave you in peace with none the wiser of our accidental meeting."

She bit her lower lip and stared at his hand. If the baron had a man posted outside the gate, that meant her uncle had one posted there as well. Uncle Laurence would want to know the baron's every movement inside the fortress. Word would surely reach her uncle if she left the garden before the baron. She didn't take the hand he offered, but she did make her way to the bench and sat down. No good could come of this, yet it wasn't fear that made her heart beat faster. It was the man who walked toward her.

He sat beside her without asking permission, his movements smooth and unhurried. "I was surprised when I did not see you at mass. Tell me you are not a pagan, or excommunicated for some dire reason."

"I attended mass this morning," she informed him in a prim voice. Her brows drew together in a frown. "You looked for me at the mass?"

"I searched for you everywhere." He said that with such ease that she felt certain he teased her. He studied her face for a moment and seemed to read her thoughts. "You do not believe me?"

The exaggerated look he gave her was one of such wounded feelings that she smiled, aware that she smiled into the face of danger. This one could charm snakes, did he put his mind to it. "You cannot search for someone you do not know, Baron."

"I know more about you than you might think. You are only half Italian, on your father's side, and your mother was Baron Lonsdale's sister. Five years ago, you and two brothers came to England after the deaths of your parents. Your brothers left soon after, but you remained at Lonsdale and earn your keep as a seamstress. 'Tis all I know of you at present, yet I would like to know more. Much more."

His gaze moved over her face and settled on her mouth. Probably because it hung wide open. She snapped it shut. "How do you know so much about me?"

"It is in my best interests to know everything I can about Baron Lonsdale and his family. I came here to make a contract with your uncle, and I never enter into a contract without knowing all I can of who I bargain with." He propped his hands at the edge of the bench behind him and stretched out his legs to cross them at the ankle. He looked every inch a nobleman at his leisure. "What would you like to know about me?"

"What would I—" She took a deep, steadying breath. "I have no need to know anything about you, Baron. Perhaps you should have this conversation with my uncle."

"Ah, but I am here with you now." His roguish grin made her pulse race. "Are you not the least bit curious? Is there nothing you wish to know about me? I will answer any question you pose."

"Why would you pay so much for a keep worth so little?" The question left her mouth before she could think better of it. She shouldn't question him at all, but now that she had, she grew bolder. " 'Tis said you intend to purchase Halford Hall, that my uncle asked a fortune in gold florins, yet you agreed to his price without hesitation. Why would you agree to such a poor bargain?"

He looked away from her and studied his boots. She could tell from the downward tilt of his lips that he had little liking for the question, but true to his word, he answered it. "Halford belonged to Montague a long time ago. My father signed it over to your grandfather when I was still a boy. My mother grew up there, and I want Halford Hall under Montague rule once more."

"You are sentimental about your mother's childhood home?" The notion that this powerful man might be sentimental seemed incredible, yet she could think of no other reason he might want a keep so insignificant. "You wish to honor your mother's memory by reuniting your estates?"

He seemed to find some grim amusement in her observations but it soon faded. "I wish to save my cousins from starvation. They still reside at Halford and will not leave their land. Your uncle's stewards tax and tithe all that Halford can produce, then they claim every beast and bag of grain we send them. My people grow old with ease at Montague, while my mother's people starve each winter. Your uncle guessed right enough that I would hear of their plight. He even sent word to Montague that he would be willing to part with Halford. For a price. I expected him to ask twice what he did for

Halford Hall, and I would have paid it to see this business at an end."

Claudia couldn't believe he'd answered the question in the first place. She'd never expected him to reveal so much. "You should not tell me this, Baron. My uncle would delight in this information. It is not in your best interest to tell anyone within Lonsdale so much."

"I feel I can trust you, Claudia." He said it so surely that she felt an odd glow of pride. "I also know that you and your uncle are not close. Why does he dislike you?"

The glow of pride died a quick death. She began to brush at a few smudges of dirt on her gown. "My grandfather arranged my mother's marriage to a man Uncle Laurence never liked. He says I am the image of my father in looks and temperament." She concentrated on a grass stain, unable to look him in the eye but willing to repay his honesty. "I do not speak your language as well as I should after five years in this country. My uncle says it offends him even when I speak, for he must hear my father as well as look upon him whenever I enter a room. 'Dislike' is a mild word to describe what my uncle feels for me."

He said nothing for a long time. She'd probably disgusted him by blurting out her family problems.

"Your life here must be very difficult, Lady Claudia."

His voice was so soft, so very gentle that she wanted to cry. She forced a smile instead and gazed out over the gardens. " 'Tis not so bad. Lonsdale is a large fortress, and I can avoid my uncle's company most of the time. Indeed, there are days when I believe he forgets I exist."

"You must see him at mealtime each day."

"Oh, nay. Ofttimes I eat in the kitchens, or else in my chamber." Her smile dimmed. She was making herself sound pathetic. She didn't want this man's pity. "I prefer to be alone. There are so many people within the castle that I feel lucky to have a chamber I can call my own. I like to work in this garden as well, for only the priest and immediate family are allowed its sanctuary without permission." She pointed toward the wall beyond them. "I helped plant those vines three years ago. Soon they will cover the wall. I plant and tend the herb plots each year as well. The work I do here is very rewarding."

"But you would rather live somewhere else?"

That remark made her think of her brother, Dante, of the fine Welsh keep he mentioned in his last missive. If all went well with Dante, someday she would have a garden of her own, in a home where she could be happy again. "Yes, I would rather live somewhere else."

He startled her when he placed his fingertips beneath her chin and turned her face toward his. "Do you have a suitor, Lady Claudia? Some man who longs to make you his wife?"

She laughed aloud. "Nay, Baron. I doubt any man in England longs for one such as me. Most can understand no more than one of every three words I speak, and I am beyond the age when most maids marry." She shook her head and held her hands with the palms upward to show them empty. "Most men long for a wealthy heiress, but what you see here is my dowry. Only a fool would wish for such a wife."

His expression grew more intense. "I am well acquainted with a fool."

She didn't know what to make of that strange remark, nor what to do when he gathered his legs beneath him and moved toward her. "What are you doing, Baron?"

"I would like you to call me by my given name." He leaned closer, his eyes as deep and mysterious as a fathomless sea.

Panic rose fast inside her. She slid away until she sat on the edge of the bench, but had to lay her palm against his chest to hold him at bay. "You should not look at me this way, Baron!"

"Guy." He captured her hand beneath his and held it against his heart. "My name is Guy."

The moment he touched her hand, Claudia forgot why she'd placed it there in the first place. She felt dizzy and disoriented, as if every thought had suddenly emptied itself from her head. He continued to move toward her, yet she didn't realize his intent until his lips touched hers. And still he watched her, with eyes that had somehow turned to blue fire.

Claudia didn't know what to do. She closed her eyes. That didn't help. The dizzy, ringing sensation in her ears grew stronger. She couldn't seem to maintain her balance, yet now she couldn't open her eyes, either. If one strong arm hadn't wrapped itself around her, she would have fallen off the edge of the bench. She was soon surrounded by his warmth. His lips began to move against hers, brushing back and forth but never leaving her, pressing closer and closer until her mouth was moving with his and against it at the same time. She found herself focused entirely on the feel of his kiss, the hard, masculine lips that somehow managed to be soft at the same time. No man had ever kissed her, although she'd sometimes wondered what it would be like. Now she knew. It was like being drunk on thin air. She wanted it to go on forever. It seemed as if it would. She wanted—

She was sitting on his lap!

Claudia stiffened and tried to push away from him. First she would have to unwrap her arms from his neck. How did they get there? How did he manage to kiss her in the first place? She placed her hands on his shoulders and shoved backward as far as his arms would allow. "Baron! Y-you forget yourself!"

"Guy," he murmured, pressing one last, lingering kiss against her lips. He lifted his head and looked into her eyes, as if he were searching for something. At last he smiled. "You must learn to call me 'Guy.'" She tried to scoot off his lap, but his grip on her tightened. "Hold very still, Claudia."

"Release me, Baron."

He shook his head. "Never."

She tried not to panic. He'd turned into a madman. A lust-crazed madman. That was the source of the strange light in his eyes. Before they kissed that light had fascinated her.

Now it frightened her. She lifted her hand and slapped him, not hard, but hopefully hard enough to bring him to his senses.

Guy blinked once very slowly. When he opened his eyes again, they no longer burned with passion. He looked confused. "Why did you do that?"

"Why did I—" Claudia pressed her palm to her own cheek and released a shaky sigh. He was wooden-headed as well as crazed. "I thought it might return you to your senses, Baron. You did not come here to kiss me."

He lifted one hand to her temple and his gaze moved to the stray wisp of her hair that he rubbed between his fingers. "I suspected rightly enough that you wanted to kiss me. There seemed no reason to delay the matter."

Claudia pulled the lock of hair from his grasp and tucked it behind her ear in one harsh movement. He looked as if she'd just slapped him again. "I don't know why I let you kiss me, but it will not happen again. What we did—what you are doing now is—is sinful."

"Perhaps." He didn't look the least disturbed by the possibility. "Perhaps not. You are right about Halford Hall. The bargain does seem unbalanced in your uncle's favor."

"What do you mean?"

He was staring at her mouth again. His voice sounded distracted. "I must discuss the matter with Baron Lonsdale before I can tell you anything more." He shook his head as if to clear his thoughts. "Indeed, I have said too much already."

A feeling of dread settled over her. "My uncle will be furious if you refuse to go through with the contract for Halford. You are in his fortress, Baron. Within his power. If you think to refuse his offer, you would be wise to make that refusal from the safety of Montague. Make any excuse you wish to leave the fortress, but do not speak a word of what you have told me to anyone else while you are within these walls."

"I am not the fool you must think me, Lady Claudia. Baron Lonsdale expects a bargain that will make him a wealthy man. In that, he will not be disappointed." He stood up and brought Claudia to her feet with him. His hands rested on her hips, his hold on her far from intimate, yet the firm pressure made her skin tingle. Everywhere. "Was that your first kiss?"

He did know how to make her head spin. This man could exasperate a saint. More likely, he was related to the Devil. She didn't know what made her answer the foolish question, yet he seemed pleased when she did. "Aye."

He lifted her hand and pressed another sensuous kiss against her wrist. "Good. I hoped I would be the first." He glanced toward the path that led to the bailey, and his mouth became a straight line. "I must leave you, Claudia. 'Tis unlikely we will have another opportunity to speak alone again before tomorrow." His lips brushed against hers in a kiss so brief that it was over almost before she realized it began. "Do not kiss anyone else until then. I want you to save your kisses for me."

She supposed she should offer some argument to that rude order, or at least inform him that he would never kiss her again. She would have said just that if he hadn't already turned around and stalked away from her.

2

"**Y**ou must tell me what is afoot, my lord. Baron Lonsdale looked furious when he retired from the feast." Evard paced the length of Guy's bedchamber. He rubbed his temple with steepled fingers, a habit that manifested itself only when he was nervous. Very nervous.

"I *must*?"

Evard paused long enough to rake a hand through his hair. "Did I say must? I meant it as a request, of course. Your brother bid me protect your back, yet I deem that task impossible when I never know where your back is turned. You would drive a lesser man to strong spirits, milord."

Guy inclined his head as if to concede Evard's opinion. Although they were the same age, at times Evard tended to treat him as a younger brother, one who must be guarded even from his own ways. It didn't matter that Guy knew exactly what he was doing every moment of his life. Evard's orders came from Kenric of Remmington, and Evard treated an order from Kenric as he would an order from God himself. If Guy were a less religious man, he would wonder if Evard knew the difference between the two.

It was Guy's half brother, Kenric, who had worried that Guy's sword arm was growing rusty in his odd pursuit of trade. He had sent Evard to Montague to oversee the castle's defenses and to hone Guy's fighting abilities. Evard rarely saw battle in his three years' service as Guy's knight, nor did he supervise the defenses of Montague Castle as Kenric intended. Most of Guy's battles took place at bargaining tables with merchants in far-off lands, yet the powerful merchants Guy dealt with proved as dangerous as warlords in their own way. Few hesitated to see a throat slit or a suspicious accident befall a man if they stood to gain. An entire army of merchants would gain from Guy's demise, and Evard had proved his worth and loyalty in ways Kenric had not imagined.

Rather than address his knight's concerns, Guy shifted on the trunk he sat upon to pat the stone wall behind him. "My back is to this wall, Evard. You can relax."

"Your back is to a Lonsdale wall," Evard retorted.

"It seems solid enought to me." Guy picked up the goblet of wine he'd just poured and gave Evard a salute. "Although I daresay our spy told you enough about this fortress that you now know every crack in its walls, every chink in its defenses. You have worked out a plan with our spy?"

"Aye, but 'tis madness that we need such a plan in the first place. If you would—" Evard halted in midstep, his gaze on Guy's hand. "Did Stephen taste your wine before he brought it here tonight?"

"You know he did," Guy answered. "My squire samples all my food and drink."

Evard strode across the room and threw open the door to the chamber. A blond-haired lad of about fourteen lay on a pallet spread before the door. The sleepy look in his eyes fled when he spied Evard and he bolted upright.

"Did you taste Lord Guy's wine?" Evard demanded.

Stephen nodded. "Aye, Sir Evard. There is naught amiss with my lord's drink. No smell of almonds or bitterness to its taste, nor any other polluting sign you taught me to watch for."

"Very good, Stephen. You do your duty well." Evard rewarded the boy with a solemn nod before he closed the door.

"Your worries are misplaced." Guy took a long drink of the wine, then set the goblet on the trunk. "Lonsdale will not get any of his gold until Halford is safe in my hands. He needs me alive to accomplish his scheme."

"We are within Lonsdale Castle," Evard reminded him. "And not all poisons are meant to kill. The effort it would take to make you a prisoner here is laughable. 'Tis unlikely we would find Lonsdale's ransom demand so humorous."

"A ransom would gain him nothing but a war," Guy said. "Soon he will realize that I will not be persuaded from my course, that he will gain all he wants if he but agrees with me."

"What is your course, my lord? What did you say to make Baron Lonsdale leave the feast in such a foul mood?" Evard offered a possible answer before Guy could respond. "You are well within your rights to demand every beast and ration of grain we sent to Halford these past years. Is that your intent, to demand more than the keep itself?"

"Aye, I would have more than Halford from Baron Lonsdale." His gaze moved to a point past Evard and he recalled the image of Claudia's face when he kissed her. "She has eyes the color of emeralds."

"A woman?" Evard looked confused for a moment, then his eyes widened. "Do not tell me—not the niece. My lord, please do not tell me that you intend to make Lonsdale's niece your next mistress."

"Very well. I will not tell you." He smiled at Evard's horrified expression, but did not let him suffer long. "Actually, I thought she might make a more suitable wife."

Guy wondered if he'd rendered Evard speechless at long last. The knight's eyes were round with shock, and his mouth worked up and down in silence.

"I have to marry sooner or later," he went on. "I always pictured a wife more the image of Kenric's fair-haired Lady Tess, but I never considered the benefits of a wife such as Lady Claudia. Our trade depends upon the Italian merchants. My dealings with them will be that much smoother when they realize I have taken one of their own as my baroness. When they journey to Montague, she will make them feel at home. She might even gain me greater acceptance into their circles when we journey to Venice."

Evard finally managed to find his voice. "You have lost

your mind! Baron Lonsdale will beggar you when he learns you would make a marriage."

"I doubt Lonsdale has any idea what it would take to beggar me," Guy replied. "However, he could name almost any amount as the dower and she would be worth the price. Think it through, Evard. Her father was an Italian, and that makes Claudia an Italian in the eyes of the law. The Venetians will not allow outsiders to traverse their southern trade routes. With Claudia as my wife, I could purchase ships in her name and increase our trade tenfold." The thought of Claudia as his wife brought to mind many images, but none involved Italian merchants or ships. He tried not to grin. "At this moment, Lonsdale knows nothing more than my intention to draw out the negotiations. Tomorrow morning during the stag hunt I will tell Lonsdale that I want Claudia as compensation for the outrageous sum he demands for Halford Hall. He will counter with another exorbitant demand for the dower, and we will settle on an amount that will make him more than happy. The betrothal can take place tomorrow afternoon."

"I can scarce believe you are the same man who professed not a fortnight ago to be in no great hurry to marry. Now you would tie yourself for life to a woman whose uncle is little more than a blackmailer?" Evard shook his head. "You have concocted many mad schemes in my years of service with you, but this is the maddest."

"Have you known one of my schemes to fail?" Guy demanded.

"Nay, but many came so close that I did picture us both in shrouds."

Guy gave up his effort to convince him of the plan's merits. He stood up and indicated that the conversation was over. "See if you can manage another meeting with our spy tonight and relate what I just told you."

"Aye, my lord." Evard began to walk toward the door, but hesitated when Guy called out to him.

"Just one more thing, Evard." Guy unstrapped his

swordbelt and placed the weapon near the bed. He unsheathed his dagger as well, intending to place it under his pillow, but first he pointed the tip toward Evard. "Watch your own back, my friend. Lonsdale needs me alive. You, he might find more useful dead."

Hours later a thump roused Guy from his sleep. His hand reached for the dagger almost before his eyes opened, but he could see nothing in the pitch black that enveloped the chamber. He listened for another suspicious sound, but felt too groggy and disoriented to concentrate. His eyes slid closed and sleep soon reclaimed him.

A strange dream began to take shape. He was being carried as he'd seen wounded men be carried from the battlefield; one man gripped his legs while another lifted his shoulders. Odd that he didn't feel any pain, odder still that they were not on a battlefield. They were in a hallway of some sort, narrow and musty-smelling. He could see the outline of a third man ahead of them who held a rush torch aloft to guide their way, yet he couldn't focus on the flames. They danced and hissed together in constant patterns of fuzzy motion. He looked at the arched ceiling and experienced a floating sensation, a weightlessness that made him think he could fly if he put his mind to it. The stone blocks that formed the archway raced by faster and faster until he became dizzy and closed his eyes.

"Remove their clothing."

The voice came from far away. The man spoke again several times but he couldn't make out the words, then a long silence descended. He no longer felt weightless. His limbs seemed made of lead. He couldn't move, didn't want to move. What an odd dream.

It got better. He rubbed his cheek against something warm and soft that smelled of flowers. The something shifted beneath him.

"Mm."

A woman. He had been so long without one that now he

was dreaming of them. He would have to remedy that situation soon. His remedy had green eyes and long, long, long dark hair. He rubbed his cheek against the soft surface again, hoping she would make that same sweet sound. He smiled when she did.

His eyelids felt weighted with lead. He could barely open them. When he finally accomplished the small task, he was surprised to see the gray light of dawn through the window. Strange, but the window seemed in a different place than it had last night. That did not matter. Not while his head rested upon the curve of a woman's breast. Claudia's breast. What other woman would he conjure up in his dream?

His heart began to beat harder. Very little in his life happened without plan and purpose. Even when events seemed to occur at random or beyond his will, their reason became clear in time. Omens were signs he never ignored, and this dream was a sure omen. Claudia was the true reason he came to Lonsdale Castle. She would be his bride.

Aye, it all made sense, even her presence in this dream. It was a sign that she, too, knew her fate and accepted it. She had sealed their fate that afternoon when she returned his kisses with a passion that set his soul on fire. He'd wanted to take her then and there. Now that he knew she would be his, he was content just to hold her. He drew her into the circle of his arms and pressed his body against hers. His hand traveled the length of her slender back and he realized that she was naked. Gloriously naked. So was he. The groan he heard was his own as he pulled her closer. Then he wanted to look at her.

He propped himself up on one elbow, amazed that it required such an effort and disconcerted that the room felt unsteady, as if they were on the rolling deck of a ship. He focused on Claudia's face easily enough. She was asleep. Her thick lashes looked like delicate fans against her cheeks, and he reached for her face with an unsteady hand. Soft as the petals of a rose. His fingers trailed down her neck so clumsily that he ventured no farther than her shoulder. He wanted to impress her with his lovemaking, seduce her with the skills he'd learned through years of experience, yet his body wouldn't cooperate with his mind. Christ's bones. She wasn't even awake.

"Claudia."

Her lashes fluttered as if she, too, had trouble opening her eyes. She moved closer to him and rubbed her face against his chest as a small kitten might. "Mm."

The affectionate movement had an immediate affect. Heat flooded through him, lust tempered by a wave of tenderness. "Claudia, wake. Up," he added, as an afterthought. Nothing he tried seemed to work quite right in this dream.

He pushed that worry aside when he felt her turn in his arms. Her eyes were luminous as she looked up at him, so green that the pupils were no more than small pinpoints of light in the center of priceless emeralds. A fanciful thought, but he imagined he could glimpse her soul in those eyes as well. She was a creature of the shadows at Lonsdale, always on the fringe of a crowd, lingering in doorways and beneath darkened arches, just out of reach and all but out of sight. He would bring her into the sunlight again, draw her forward into his life as effortlessly as he drew her into his arms tonight. He would make her smile.

His finger traced the outline of her lips, but they did not curve into the expression he wanted to see. He would have to work harder for that reward. His fingertips trailed across her cheek and he marveled at the softness of her skin, even as he made an unsettling observation. She looked serene, but she didn't look happy. He vowed to fill her life with smiles.

He pressed his lips against her forehead to seal his vow. She was still staring at him when he drew back. She lifted her hand and touched his mouth, a slow, steady exploration, as if she wanted to memorize the shape of it. Her fingertips moved to the rough surface of his cheek and her nails made a small scratching sound against the stubble. He couldn't breathe.

Nay, he'd forgotten to breathe. He filled his lungs with air, then slowly released it. Her delicate brows drew together, as if she were puzzled by his reaction to her touch. He turned his head and captured one of her fingertips between his lips for a provocative kiss. Her eyes widened with surprise as she drew her own deep breath.

He caught her hand before she could pull it away and turned the palm toward him to brush feathery kisses along the sensitive skin, the bones of her wrist small and fragile in his big hand. He brushed his thumb across the area where the skin moved in a steady reflection of her heartbeat, fascinated for some reason by the rhythm. He kissed her wrist again and flicked his tongue across the pulse point, pleased by the shudder he felt run through her. Next he pressed her palm against the center of his chest to let her feel the erratic beat of his own heart, then leaned down to capture her lips for a long, deep kiss.

The kiss started out just fine, but something did not feel right. She didn't respond as she had in the gardens. Her lips became lifeless, passionless. He lifted his head and saw that her eyes were closed again. She had fallen asleep, the stubborn wench. This was his dream. She could at least cooperate.

Another thought made him frown. Perhaps he couldn't make love to a dream. The blood pounded in his ears so hard that he couldn't concentrate. He closed his eyes and tried to gather his muddled senses. A wave of dizziness struck so hard that his stomach protested its violence. The pace of his heart and breathing quickened, but this time from alarm rather than lust. Something was wrong. Very wrong. What was that pounding noise in his ears?

"What are you . . . Oh, my head!"

His eyes opened and he watched Claudia hold one hand to her forehead, her eyes squeezed tightly shut. She released small puffs of breath that ruffled his hair and seemed to brush at the fog that encased his thoughts, the haziness that blurred his vision.

This was no dream.

He jerked himself upright but had to stop and clap his hands over his ears. A hot burst of pain shot through his skull and set black spots before his eyes. The sound of his heartbeat became a deafening roar in his ears. The wine! Dear, God, they'd poisoned the wine after all.

He thought of Stephen, who had drunk the fouled brew as well, then of Evard and the rest of his men as he murmured a one word prayer for their safekeeping. If he died—

Even as that thought crossed his mind, the pain in his head subsided. He still felt off-balance, but no longer close to death. Either he hadn't drunk enough of the poison to kill himself or the poison was meant to incapacitate rather than to kill. His eyes narrowed as he looked again at Claudia.

She sat up with the sheets tucked beneath her arms, and held both hands to her head. Was she also drugged, or was she mimicking him to make it appear that way? He clenched his jaw. "Get out of my bed!"

"Your bed?" She tried to meet his gaze but her head weaved from side to side and she finally placed one hand over her eyes and clutched the sheets with the other. "Baron, you are in *my* bed."

He glanced around the room. "Christ!" She was right. Another wave of dizziness caught him off guard. He closed his eyes in an effort to regain his sense of balance. The pounding noise that had plagued him since he awoke suddenly ceased, just as he realized it came from someone banging a fist against the door. The sound of a muffled voice came from the other side.

"Break it down."

His first instinct was to protect Claudia. He reached automatically for his sword, but it wasn't in its usual resting place next to the bed. This wasn't his chamber. Why would his sword be here? And why would he be in bed with Claudia for any reason than to be discovered? The pieces of the puzzle fell together with sickening ease. With a curse, he searched for something to cover himself. He found all the clothes he wore the night before on the floor. He'd worn only a loincloth to bed last eve. Why would his clothing be here and not in his chamber with his damned sword?

More incriminating evidence, came the silent answer. No one would believe that he'd ventured here near-naked. Even as he pulled on his breeks, he noticed that the clothes were flung about as if he'd undressed in great haste. Clever bastards.

He no more than had his pants in place when the door burst open. A half dozen Lonsdale soldiers pushed through the opening, followed by Baron Lonsdale and Bishop Germaine. The soldiers wore Lonsdale tunics and light armor, yet Baron Lonsdale and the bishop still wore long sleeping shirts and dark robes.

"So *this* is how you repay my hospitality!" Baron Lonsdale glared at the bed where Claudia clutched at the sheets to cover herself. "You seduce my niece under my own roof! You will pay for this, Montague, and pay dearly." He turned to the bishop. "I thought the night guard made some mistake when he reported that Montague came to my niece's chamber, yet you are my witness to this foul truth."

Guy felt an immediate urge to defend himself physically from the lewd charge, even as he realized that it was Lonsdale's opening move in this game. The strategy. He had to remember his own strategy, to shake off the malaise that still held his mind and body in its grip. His hands clenched into fists and he concentrated on deep, steady breaths. Thank God he'd drunk no more than one ration of wine. Another goblet and he would be in a stupor right now. He needed his wits to avoid a misstep that might cost his life. "Where is my squire?"

"I am here, my lord." Stephen made his way around the soldiers and stepped into the room. The young man wore a worried expression, but he bowed low to Guy. "These men came to your chamber and demanded you be awakened. I did not know—That is—"

"Never mind, Stephen. Did you see anyone enter my chamber last eve? Or leave it?" He frowned when Stephen shook his head, even though he had expected that answer.

Stephen looked alert, but perhaps they'd drugged him as well. "Wake Sir Evard and bid him join me."

Baron Lonsdale clapped one hand on the boy's shoulder. "Nay, I think not. You have no need for your second-in-command, Lord Guy. The boy stays here."

Guy shrugged as if unconcerned. He reached for his shirt and continued to dress, one eye on Lonsdale. The room swayed at a dangerous angle as he performed the mundane task, and he concentrated all his effort to appear unaffected. He could not afford any display of weakness. "What drug did you use, Lonsdale? I did not come here of my own will, and know well enough that one goblet of wine could not render me senseless."

"Are you trying to deny the evidence?" Lonsdale looked incredulous. He turned to Bishop Germaine. "You are witness to these lies, Bishop. 'Tis obvious to all that this man seduced an innocent lady with lies told just as smoothly. I demand retribution, yet I am a man of God. I will let the Church guide my actions in this matter."

Guy almost smiled at the bishop's eager effort to appear surprised. Then he thought of the part Claudia had played in his betrayal, and the urge to smile disappeared. Thank God he'd retained enough sense to keep his mouth shut, to share his foolish plans with none but Evard. Had he really thought her so honorable that she wouldn't betray him? A woman worthy enough to be his bride?

He did smile then. At his own stupidity. He felt robbed, betrayed by his own misguided instincts. Baron Lonsdale's fury seemed trifling in comparison.

"This does not warrant bloodshed," the bishop began. He crossed his arms over his generous girth and stroked his chin. "Only a woman's husband has the right to take her innocence." His dark gaze flickered toward Guy. "You do owe Baron Lonsdale reparations, Lord Guy. 'Tis my judgment and that of the Church that marriage shall be the reparation."

Guy crossed his arms in a gesture that mimicked the

bishop's stance, mocking and challenging at the same time. "And if I do not agree with your judgment?"

The bishop shrugged. "Then I shall concede judgment to Baron Lonsdale. Think hard on your decision, Montague. As a guest at Lonsdale you are within Baron Lonsdale's power, and at this moment you are the man who wronged his niece. You may find my judgment more to your liking."

"I see." They were a simple lot, Guy decided, to plot such an obvious trap. Simpler still to believe they would snare him with it. "How long do I have to make my decision?"

"We will have your answer by tomorrow morning," said the bishop. "None will say you came to your decision in haste." He paused as he would in sermon, to let the importance of his words take hold. A marriage performed by a bishop, with the groom given a full day and night to accept or deny his bride. It would be a hard marriage to annul. "I am sure you will do what is best for everyone, Lord Guy."

"There will be no marriage without a betrothal contract," Lonsdale broke in. "I will not be denied the dower. The marriage cannot take place until the dower is in my hands."

"And what dowry will you provide for your niece?" Guy's voice dripped with sarcasm, but Lonsdale paid it no heed.

"Halford Hall will be her dowry," he retorted. "I will provide nothing more than that. The dower will be twice the gold we agreed upon for the sale of Halford."

Guy looked at Claudia. "Somehow I suspected as much."

"He will remain confined until the ceremony can take place," Lonsdale told the bishop, "else his men may think to spirit him away. Indeed, I believe it wise if his men were to set their camp outside my walls rather than within them."

"That decision is yours to make, Laurence."

Lonsdale gestured toward the guards. "Take him to the gatehouse tower and place him in the ransom chamber. Make sure of our guest's comforts, but he is to carry no weapons and a guard will be at his door at all times. Rouse his men and send them on their way. They may return after the marriage."

Guy spared another brief glance at Claudia. Silent tears

rolled down her cheeks, and her face looked as pale as the sheets. If this was an act, she was good at her craft. "I would inform my second-in-command of your, ah, decision," he said to Lonsdale. "You may find my men more cooperative if their orders come from Evard de Cordray."

"As you wish. Your second-in-command will be sent to meet with you in the ransom chamber." Lonsdale gave him a mocking bow. "We will await your decision, Baron."

Claudia watched four of the soldiers lead Guy away, stunned to immobility by everything that had just transpired. Not that she would want to go anywhere stark naked. She had an awful fear that her uncle might order just that. Her breath caught in her throat when he called one of his soldiers forward.

"Send a carpenter to repair this door. I want a bolt fashioned on the outside and a guard posted there to ensure that my niece does not leave this room for any reason. See that someone brings her food twice a day."

"Aye, my lord." The soldier bowed then hurried away to carry out his orders.

Lonsdale turned to Claudia, his gaze dispassionate. "You will remain here until the marriage can take place, and you will not make trouble of any sort. Do you understand me?"

She bowed her head so he would not see her anger. She had never particularly liked her uncle. Now she hated him. He had drugged her with some foul poison the night before, as surely as he'd drugged Guy. Now he was telling her to go along with Guy's betrayal, to become a part of this filthy plot. She could barely speak the words. "I understand, my lord."

"Excellent." He turned to the bishop. "I must see that Montague's men leave the castle as I ordered. If you will excuse me, Bishop?"

"We must talk further of this matter," said the bishop.

"Very well. Let us meet after the nooning meal in my solar, if you find that convenient." Lonsdale's tone said he did not look forward to the meeting. The bishop looked displeased at being put off for so many hours, but he gave Lonsdale a sharp nod.

The men left soon after, although one soldier remained in the hallway to stand guard at the broken door. He stood so that he faced Claudia, staring at her in a way that made her skin crawl. She pulled the sheets closer and looked away when he began to pick at what few teeth remained in his mouth. Her nightshift lay on the floor, so she tugged the sheets free of the mattress, then wrapped them securely around her. Another of her uncle's shows of kindness, to leave her naked as a strumpet with his man set to watch her. Perhaps the soldier at the door was the one responsible for her state of undress in the first place. That thought made her shudder in disgust.

Rather than retrieve the nightshift, she walked to her clothes chest and pulled out a chemise and saffron-colored gown. Her grip on the sheets remained painfully tight, aware of the soldier's gaze upon her every move. Thank heavens for the garderobe in her chamber. The tiny room would provide the privacy she needed to perform her morning ablutions and repair a few shreds of her pride. Not that her pride would ever be fully intact again after this morning's work. She used her chemise to blot up the last of her tears and stepped into the small room to dress.

A carpenter had started work on the door when she emerged from the garderobe. A tray of food that sat atop the clothes chest held bread and cheese along with a mug of thin ale to break her fast. She pulled up the sewing stool next to the chest and started to eat. She would need her strength for what lay ahead. She glanced from the carpenter to the stonework around the fireplace. The lack of mortar along the crevices of certain stones was almost unnoticeable.

When she first arrived at Lonsdale her brothers had teased her about the hours she spent exploring every inch of the castle, but she remembered her mother's story that there were secret hallways within the walls, that only the eldest son could be told of their location and the concealed doorways that led into them. But Claudia knew how to find them.

The secret passageways were the source of her troubles, the means by which Baron Lonsdale carried out his plot. Of that she was certain. Much more remained a blur. She could recall nothing more than flashes of the men who brought Guy to her bed, the half-formed images of shadowy figures and blinding torch light. It seemed a passing nightmare until she awoke to the gray light of dawn and seductive caresses. Guy had made her forget that anything might be wrong. Being with him felt so very right. His hands touched her and stirred to life emotions long denied in the years she spent at Lonsdale, feelings of tenderness, of being loved and cherished. For that brief, shining moment, she had lowered her guard and responded to him with all the love she kept bottled inside, the part of her that no one else wanted. Guy wanted her. She gave him her heart.

Then the illusion came crashing down around her. She should have realized sooner that what seems too good to be true never is. Like as not, Guy had not realized who he was in bed with, or would even care if he did know. He had simply responded as he would to any naked woman wanton enough to return his kisses. She felt very sorry for herself. Then she got angry.

Was that all she was to be allowed in this life, a brief glimpse of happiness? To be given that one small taste of what might be, then to have it snatched away forever was a cruelty she had never imagined. If she did nothing she would be tied for life to a man who despised her, to a man who could visit even greater cruelties upon her.

The emptiness she felt inside was a bottomless pit, as black and cold as it was numbing. She would survive, just as she had survived the many deaths in her family. But she would never be the same. Each person she loved took a part of her heart when they left her. Guy took a part she had never known existed.

She forced herself to swallow the tasteless food and washed it down with the last of the ale. The carpenter had finished his job and tried the latch several times to make sure it worked. He spoke to the soldier in hushed tones, then doffed his cap and departed. She carried her tray to the doorway and handed it to the guard.

"A wench will bring your supper at dusk," he told her.

"Please ask her to bring a bucket of water as well."

He scowled at the request, but gave her a curt nod and closed the door. She heard the bolt slide into place.

Hours later Claudia wedged herself further into the crevice, certain that a woman smaller than herself or a child had designed the secret passage behind the solar. In the long morning she spent alone in her chamber, a plan began to take shape in her mind. At first she thought to make her own escape from the fortress. If she could reach London she could begin her search for her brother, Dante, yet a woman could not make such a journey alone. The forests were filled with wild beasts and the roads preyed upon by robbers.

Baron Montague had many well-armed men outside the walls of Lonsdale. Even they might seek to harm her if she stumbled across them, for they surely held her responsible for their baron's plight. If she helped Guy escape as well, he might provide the escort she needed to London. It would be much more difficult to free them both, yet without him she would never reach Dante. She could do nothing until nightfall, but in the meantime she decided to learn what she could of her uncle's plot.

She turned sideways in the passage and prayed. This would not be a pleasant place to get stuck. She would not even think about the possibility of rats.

The walls could become no tighter when the passage opened into a small, square chamber, lit by small eye-level cracks on three sides. Even here she could smell the strong pomander that Uncle Laurence used to scent his clothing, a cloying mixture of ground cloves and balsam that he favored for reasons known only to himself. The sound of his voice echoed in the chamber, and she leaned toward one opening, then looked into the solar.

Her uncle stood near the fireplace with one arm propped against the mantel. His blond hair had turned a yellowed shade of white with age, but his pale blue eyes still reflected an alert, devious mind. He wore a long burgundy and gold tunic, the colors of Lonsdale, and he rested a mug atop the buckle of his sword belt.

Bishop Germaine sat in a high-backed chair before the fireplace. She could see little more of him than the top of his gleaming bald head, but she could hear his words clearly enough. "What have you involved me in, Laurence? I would stake my life that what you told me this morning is not the whole of it."

"Do not fret," said Lonsdale. "I will pay you well for your part in this."

"Aye, that you will," he agreed, "but I will know all of my part, not some hurried explanation when I am half awake and roused at dawn. And you may cease your insistence that Montague seduced the girl. We both know that is not the truth."

"We will both be wealthy men," Lonsdale insisted. "With the Church's decree that Montague marry my niece, he will know he has no choice in the matter. The dower will be paid, and the marriage will take place."

"And a war will soon follow," added the bishop. "You cannot think that Montague will not exact retribution for this deception. What possessed you to concoct this hoax?"

Lonsdale raked one hand through his hair, his tone impatient. "He knows something is amiss with Halford Hall. I showed him the articles at the feast yesterday, but he said he wanted more time to consider the matter. If he did not suspect some trickery, he would have signed the articles then and there. I will lose everything if he discovers Halford is not mine to sell."

"What are you talking about?" the bishop asked. "Halford is not entailed to your estates. You are free to dispose of the property as you wish."

"Nay, you are wrong. My father had the old Baron Montague sign Halford over to my sister, Catherine. He wanted to tie one of her children to English soil, and Catherine bequeathed the keep to her daughter. Halford Hall is not mine to sell. I hold it only in wardship for that unnatural daughter Catherine bred." He paused to take a long drink from his goblet, then wiped the back of his hand across his mouth. "The articles I showed Montague are a forgery. As my overlord, the king holds the true articles to Halford. Those at Lonsdale who knew the truth of the matter are dead, and even if the king learned of Halford's sale I doubt he would recall its true ownership. It is no great estate, of importance to no one but Guy of Montague. Even my niece is ignorant of her rights to the property."

Claudia braced her hands against the walls of the chamber. All the miserable years at Lonsdale swam before her eyes, the slights and insults, the jibes that she was nothing but a destitute, unwelcome relative, a burden who must work long hours to earn her keep or go hungry. She was an heiress! And each year she labored, Uncle Laurence collected the wealth of her inheritance until he turned the people of her keep into beggars as well. If the wall were not standing between them, she would have plunged her dagger into his heart. Or been sorely tempted to try.

"He must have noticed something amiss with the forged articles," Lonsdale went on, a petulance to his voice that one would expect from a boy rather than a grown man. "I had to act before Montague discovered the truth."

"You were ever rash," said the bishop. "Always the first to charge into a battle with no thought of what would happen when you left your army behind. I can tell you what will happen this time. Montague will exact his retribution the moment you set him free. An annulment will be his first order of business, then he will return with his army and lay siege until he starves you out. Did you give no thought to that?"

"I want the gold he promised," Lonsdale said defensively. "With twice that amount, I can raise an army of mercenaries to keep Montague at bay."

"And take in a pack of blackguards who are as like to

seize Lonsdale as they are to guard it." The bishop shook his head. "Nay, you must accept my counsel in this matter or suffer the consequences. If we are successful, I will take half the gold you receive from Montague."

"Half!" Lonsdale sputtered. "I would give you a generous share, of course, but *half?*"

"Admit the truth, Laurence. You will have nothing without my help." He waited until Lonsdale gave him a grudging nod, then he leaned back in his chair. "Well, now. The first thing we must do is convince Lord Guy that I will not take sides in the matter, that I am acting only on the facts presented. I will offer to hold the marriage properties at the monastery for safekeeping, and will assure him that nothing will be distributed to either party while the marriage is in dispute."

"Excellent! We will lure Montague into a false sense of security. He will go along with that plan much more readily than he would with my demand to deliver the dower into my hands." Lonsdale's hopeful expression faded. "But nothing will change when he finds out I have the gold. The marriage could even be declared invalid if he discovers your part in the plot, the dower forfeit."

"He will never discover my part, nor live long enough to know that we split the gold between us."

The bishop's clear intention to murder Guy did not seem to startle Lonsdale. He made a dismissive gesture with his hand. "Oh, aye, I thought of murder right enough, but I am not so rash that I cannot see the finger of guilt pointed right back at me. I would hang sure as sin."

"Not if we make it look the work of another, one who would appear to have ample reason to murder her new husband."

"Claudia?" Lonsdale's eyes widened with disbelief, then the light of understanding. "Of course! My God, John. 'Tis perfect!"

"Aye," the bishop agreed. "We will give him a fortnight to deliver the dowry, then I will perform the marriage. Montague's men will enter the fortress the next day. You will tell them you witnessed the bedding ceremony, and their lord is well and truly wed. Do what you can to encourage their belief that he has made the best of the bargain and accepts his bride, that the couple prepare as you speak to depart for Montague Castle. We will send one of Montague's own men to fetch him from his chamber. There they will find the baron's throat slit, with your niece's dagger nearby."

A dark sound came from the bishop that might have been a chuckle. Her uncle wore a smile that grew broader with every word the bishop spoke. "The cry will go up and several of Lonsdale will step forward to say that Claudia plotted to seduce Lord Guy into marriage. Then I will tell them of her dead brother, Roberto, and the reason she has to hate all Montagues. We will give her to Montague's men to hang the next morning."

"They will question her," Lonsdale pointed out.

"They will be in a rage. We will hand them Claudia. I doubt she will last an hour in their keeping. They will not believe anything she babbles in that half-English of hers. Even if some suspect her innocence, they will hang her anyway in their vengeance. Then we may tell the king that Montague's own men served justice, that they did accept and execute the murderess. Once Claudia dies, we will be beyond the law."

"There are Montague's vassals and family to consider," Lonsdale mused. "Most especially, his brother. Kenric of Remmington is not a man to accept his brother's death so lightly."

The bishop waved his hand to dismiss the matter. "One does not challenge the word of a bishop without great cost, and his bastard brother has no reason to interfere. He will gain all of Montague when his brother dies without an heir. It will be in his best interest to let the matter rest. He will have his brother's lands and estates, and we will have his brother's gold."

Claudia knew she had to leave the chamber before she

became ill. She backed into the passageway with both hands clamped over her mouth. She made a vow her uncle and the evil bishop would never know, one that she would make true or die in the effort. These would be the last tears she shed within Lonsdale.

3

Claudia pressed her back against the wall of the gatehouse and held her breath. She glanced down and nearly cursed aloud. The two brass goblets she held gleamed like beacons in the moonlight. She thrust them under her dark cloak and watched the shadowy figures of two guards walk across the bailey. They passed less than a dozen paces from her hiding place as they made their way to take the midnight watch in the west tower. Only the sounds of the guards' footsteps disturbed the silence of the bailey, and those faded away soon enough. She ventured forth once more.

With the goblets balanced in one hand and the leather flagon of wine tucked into the crook of her arm, she reached for the latch to the gatehouse door. The leather hinges made a small creak and she opened the door just wide enough to slip inside. Darkness greeted her in the passageway, along with the pungent smell of tar and pitch that was stored in the bowels of the gatehouse, kept ready in case of siege. Uncle Laurence might need those defenses soon if her venture tonight proved successful.

With her free hand held against the wall to steady herself in the dark, she felt her way along the damp stones until she came to the base of a staircase. A rush torch at the top of the steps cast its dim, flickering light down the stairwell. There she hesitated. Once she ascended this staircase, there would be no turning back.

She was his only hope.

Guy was her only hope as well. Those thoughts gave her the courage she needed to climb the stairs, to lean around the corner and peer down the deserted passageway at the top of the steps. If only she had discovered a secret passageway in this part of the castle. A hidden passage or two would be a comfort right now.

Her slippers made no sound as she walked the length of the flagstone hallway to the next set of stairs. Behind one of the wooden doors that lined the passage she could hear someone snoring. More than a score of soldiers were assigned to gatehouse duty, and if her luck held, all were asleep behind those doors. If not, the wine she carried should take care of any soldiers set to guard the prisoner. There would be only one more place where she might encounter opposition to her plan—outside the chamber on the floor above her. She had visited the chamber once before and knew it to be a luxurious prison, built to hold noblemen captured in tournaments or battles until their families paid their ransom. Tonight it held a man marked for death.

She had always known Baron Lonsdale was a despicable, greedy man. Until today, she had never guessed the depths to which he would sink. Her own uncle would put her to death without second thought for a murder not yet committed, or hang her just as easily if he discovered this night's plot. She would rather take her chances with Guy of Montague. The humiliation she would feel at seeing him again would be nothing compared to her guilt if he perished at Lonsdale's hands. Yet even if she managed to drug Guy's guards and free him from this prison, she could not be sure he would agree to her plan for their escape. He might balk at the idea of taking a woman along on such a dangerous journey, or doubt that she told him the truth of her uncle's cold-blooded plan. Her hand went to the collar of her cloak, to the hard lumps hidden beneath the cloak's draped hood.

After the servant delivered her meal that evening, she had spent a precious hour sewing her mother's emerald necklace into the cloak, the last piece of wealth that she and her brothers had smuggled away from their home in Italy. The rest had gone to purchase the armor and warhorses Dante and

Roberto needed to ply their trade as mercenaries. Roberto had wanted the necklace as well, but Dante insisted that Claudia hold it for safekeeping, that she should have something for her dowry in the event that her brothers could not regain their rightful wealth and estates. Rather than a dowry, tonight it might buy her freedom.

She pushed aside those musings when she reached the landing and walked around the corner. Sputtering flames from the rush torches on either side of the guard's well kept the shadows in constant, eerie movement. The guard's station was empty, and the door to the ransom chamber stood half open. Her brows drew together in a frown. The guard must be inside the chamber. Why, she didn't know, but this unexpected turn might be to her advantage. Perhaps she could sneak up on the guard from behind.

Careful not to make any sound, she set the goblets and flagon to one side of the hallway then drew the small dagger at her waist. She would never have the courage to actually harm the guard, but hopefully she could bluff him into thinking otherwise. She forced herself to take one step closer to the chamber, then another. She drew one last steadying breath and stepped into Guy's prison.

Only the torches outside the door lit the large chamber, but what she could see of the room appeared empty. Her heart did not slow its mad beat at that realization. She pushed the door wider and took another step forward. Her voice sounded no more than a shaky whisper. "Baron?"

A movement from the corner of her eye made her turn to the right and she took a startled step backward. Guy stood in the shadows along the wall, dressed in the same clothing he wore to the gardens, but now he wore a cloak as well. Seeing him again brought back a flood of memories, none of which she anticipated. Her gaze moved along the line of his jaw and she recalled the feel of his cheek, rough with a day's growth of beard. She looked at his lips and remembered how they felt beneath her fingertips, how he had drawn one of her fingers into his mouth for a kiss that sent shivers down her spine.

He took a step toward her. "Give me the knife, Claudia."

She looked down at the forgotten dagger in her hand. It did not seem important at the moment and she ignored the order. "Where is your guard?"

"The guard is dead," he said in a low voice, "as you will be, if you do not give me that knife this instant."

He meant it. She tried to suppress a shudder, and refused to look around the chamber for evidence of the dead guard. Tonight Guy looked nothing like the man who kissed her in the gardens, the gentle, teasing suitor who told her to save her kisses for him. Nor did he appear the tender lover of her hazy dreams. At the moment he looked capable of great violence, his big body tensed and ready to strike out. There was not a doubt in her mind that he would carry out his threat if she did not obey him.

"You think I would try to harm you with this puny dagger?" Perhaps it was the memory of the man behind this cold exterior that made her sound braver than she felt. She shook her head and handed him the knife hilt first. "I came here to rescue you, Baron."

"Did you really?" He tucked the dagger into his belt then looked beyond her into the hallway, still on his guard, his tone sarcastic. "I suppose your uncle and his soldiers lay in wait to catch the lovers as they flee?"

" 'Tis not a trick." She wished there was some way to convince him that she did not lie. She had only the truth to persuade him. "I know you have little reason to believe anything I say, but I did not play a willing part in your betrayal. My life is in as much danger as your own. We must be away from here before we are discovered."

" 'We'?" He shook his head. "You are a clever little cat, always ready to land on her feet. If you were not a part of this plot you would be made a prisoner. You would not be allowed to traipse around the gatehouse in the middle of the night to pay me a visit. Tell me where the soldiers wait for us."

"No one waits for us," she said. "I came here alone. After they took you away this morning, my uncle did lock me in my chamber. He thinks he is the only one who knows where the secret passages lie, the passageways that allowed them to bring you to my room last night even though I bolted my door from the inside. Did you not wonder how you left your chamber without your squire's notice?"

He lifted one shoulder in a dismissing shrug. "He was probably drugged as well."

"Nay, they took you through the passageways. I was drugged as you were." She felt a blush warm her cheeks at the memory of finding herself naked and in bed with him, yet she could not afford to dwell on those thoughts. "This afternoon I made my way into those same passages to a spy hole behind the solar and heard the whole of their plot. My uncle thought you changed your mind about Halford, that you did not intend to go through with the contract. He concocted this scheme to get even more of your gold. Bishop Germaine thinks to gain your confidence by offering to hold the marriage portions in safekeeping at his monastery, but he will insist that the marriage itself must take place. The day after the wedding your men will find you dead with evidence that I murdered you. My uncle and the bishop will then split the gold between them."

Guy didn't show the shock or horror that she expected. He smiled, but the expression lacked any trace of warmth. "You weave a worthy tale, lady. Do you think I am some gullible squire to be taken in by such nonsense?"

" 'Tis truth," she insisted. His hardened expression did not change. To tell him any more of the plot against them would be a waste of breath. He would never believe her, never trust in her again. She could not blame him. There was only one truth he could not ignore. "The bishop himself drew up a betrothal contract and with his signature it became valid. The Church will not allow you to marry another while a prior contract exists. Even if you escape tonight, you may be sure that my uncle will petition the Church and delay any hopes you have for an heir until you pay him off. 'Tis common enough to blackmail wealthy men by claiming a prior contract, and this one will have the seal of a bishop upon it. If you take me with you, I will swear before any priest or even the king himself that you were betrayed by my uncle. With both of us as witnesses to the facts, the contract will be made invalid."

His gaze flickered toward the doorway then returned to her face. "Somehow I find it hard to believe that you would betray your own family. Surely your uncle will give you a portion of the gold if you remain silent on the matter."

"He will give me to your men to hang!" She pressed her lips together. Anger would gain her nothing when reason alone had so little effect. She took a deep breath. "As of today, the only family I acknowledge is my brother, Dante. His last missive arrived from London nearly a year ago, but if I can find him I know he will take me in."

"I thought you had two brothers. Why look for this Dante if he is so hard to find? Why not go to the other?"

"My oldest brother died many years ago. Dante is all I have left." She lowered her gaze to the floor. If Guy discovered the name of her eldest brother, he would never consider her request. She hurried on before he could ask any more questions about Roberto. "If you help me escape, I would hire a company of your men to help me search for Dante. I have a necklace that belonged to my mother. In London I can sell the necklace to pay your men. Perhaps there will be enough to compensate you for your trouble as well. You will be free of me soon enough, and free of any claims my uncle might try to make. 'Tis the easiest way to rid yourself of me for good."

"Nay, 'tis not the easiest way," he mused. He folded his arms across his chest, then rubbed his chin. "Many of the problems you present would go away if you were to die."

Claudia backed up a step, even though she doubted he would carry out that foul threat. He was bluffing. Wasn't he?

He continued in a firmer tone. "If I find out that—" A shadow fell between them and Guy lunged toward her. *"Nay!"*

Claudia tried to flee his attack. Before she could move, something large and solid struck the back of her head. Guy's alarmed face swam before her, then everything went black.

"Christ! I thought you meant to cleave her in two!"

"I have apologized twice already, Baron. When I returned from the guard walk I saw her standing in the doorway with her back to me. I knew you saw me there, and I mistook your words for an order to kill her. Had you not called out at the last moment, she would indeed be dead. She was lucky to take no more than the broadside of my sword to her head."

"I meant to frighten her into telling me the truth, not to murder her."

"Aye, well, we both know that now, although you may soon wish the mistake was uncorrectable. She is dead weight. You will never manage your way down the wall with her tied to your back. I say we toss her over the side and be done with the problem. At this time of night, no one will hear the body land."

Claudia awoke in time to hear that vile announcement. The hushed, male voice sounded familiar. Or were there two? It took another groggy moment to get her bearings, to realize she lay in a careless heap atop one of the gatehouse towers. Her eyes popped wide open when she realized who might be the most likely candidate to get tossed from the tower wall.

"I will not have the blood of a woman on my conscience. In any event, what if she awakened halfway down? Her screams would rouse every soldier in the garrison."

"I'll slit her throat first," came the matter-of-fact answer.

Claudia's hands went to her throat in a protective gesture.

"Damnation," the throat-slitter continued. "She is awake."

A cloaked figure loomed over her. As she sat up and pressed her back to the tower wall, the clouds that obscured the half-moon drifted away. She had intended to bolt to one side, but found herself startled to immobility by what the moonlight revealed. "Friar Thomas?"

The realization that a holy man wished to slit her throat shocked Claudia more than she thought possible this night. Friar Thomas was such a gentle, soft-spoken man. He was her friend!

The friar ignored her pointless question and looked to his right. "Now what do we do?"

Claudia's gaze followed the friar's and she saw a man standing a few feet away, his attention on a rope he had secured around one of the raised stone sections between the tower's crenels. Guy's face looked harsh and forbidding in the moonlight. After a quick test of the knot's strength, he tossed the long coil over the side then turned to give her a scowl as dark as the friar's. "You have a choice to make, Lady Claudia. Either you follow me down this rope with a gag in your mouth to ensure a measure of silence, or our good Friar Thomas here will see you over the side without benefit of either gag or rope. The choice is yours."

Claudia didn't care for either choice. Going over the wall meant hanging by a rope at least fifty feet above the jagged rocks that formed the base of the castle. She could scarce climb a stepladder without getting dizzy. Heights terrified her. On the other hand, so did the thought of Friar Thomas slitting her throat.

"Th-there is a bolthole. We need not climb down this wall." She gritted her teeth together to keep them from chattering.

"Aye," Thomas sneered. "A bolthole with a soldier assigned to guard that passage during the night. But you knew that already, did you not?"

Claudia stared at Thomas openmouthed as another realization struck. "You speak Italian. All this time—"

Thomas made an impatient gesture with his hand. "Only someone who knows your language could understand a word you speak in ours." He turned to Guy. "The watch will pass this way again in less than an hour. 'Tis insanity even to consider taking her with you. Let me make the decision for her."

"I will cause no trouble! I swear!" She looked from Guy to Friar Thomas. The long dagger he held made her blurt out her decision. "I will go over the wall!"

Guy took a step toward her. "Give me your hand."

She took an unconscious step backward. "W-why?"

His brows narrowed. "Never argue with men who would rather slit your throat than set you free, lady. Give me your hand."

Claudia could not hide the way she trembled, but she extended her hand. Just as he reached forward, she snatched her right hand back and extended her left. She favored her right for most tasks and might not find herself so hampered if he intended lasting damage.

Guy made a sound of disgust. In one quick movement, he grasped the long sleeve of her gown and gave it a sharp tug. The sleeve ripped free at the shoulder and came away in his hand. "Turn around."

Claudia stared at the sleeve he held. What did he mean to tear from her next?

Guy seemed to read her thoughts. He made a sound of impatience. " 'Tis to gag you. Turn around!"

She obeyed the order, but soon rethought her docile compliance. With her back to the baron, it would be an easy matter to slit her throat, and a quiet task once he had her gagged. Her knees buckled and she gripped the tower wall to right her balance. The makeshift gag came down over her face. She tugged it off her nose just as he made a tight knot at the back of her head, then he spun her around by the shoulders to check his work. She assumed the curt nod meant he felt satisfied that the strip of cloth would keep her quiet. He kept one hand on her arm and all but dragged her to the crenel where he had tied the rope. He looked over the side, then leaned back to look at her skirts.

"You will break your neck," he predicted. Before she could guess his intent, he drew a dagger and knelt before her.

He grasped the hem of her gown and the dagger sliced through the fabric to a point well above her knees. He resheathed the dagger just as she gathered her wits enough to make a muffled sound of protest. "Thomas will lower you over the side of the wall. Get the rope between your legs before he lets go of you." He turned to Friar Thomas. "Cut her throat if she hesitates. Cut the rope if she makes a sound on the way down."

On that loathsome note, he stepped into one of the crenels and disappeared from sight.

Friar Thomas's hand clamped down on her arm and he moved toward the crenel to watch the baron's progress. His voice sounded distracted. "I hope you are stronger than you look, lady. 'Tis a long climb down, a sore strain on a lady's arms when they have lifted nothing weightier than a needle."

If not for the gag, she would have informed him that she was stronger than he assumed. She hauled a dozen heavy buckets of water to the bathhouse each night, for she refused to bathe in water dirtied by another. It seemed her obsession with cleanliness was about to prove a valuable trait.

"He made it to the bottom." Thomas pulled her forward until she stood before the crenel, then he whispered in her ear. "One sound, lady. One whimper, or one false move, and the rope will not hold you. Do you understand me?"

Claudia gave him a frantic nod. She braced her hands on either side of the crenel and stepped into the opening. The moonlight revealed the craggy rocks far below and the shadowy figure of a man. Baron Montague looked the size of an ant. She kept the moan of fear locked inside her throat. The rope that extended down the wall lay at her feet, beyond her reach in the narrow opening. How did Guy manage it? How would she manage?

Thomas solved that problem for her. His hand clasped her arm in a fierce grip while the other pushed her forward. In that moment she knew why they had gagged her. He meant to throw her over the side after all.

This time she couldn't contain her muffled cry of terror.

She clawed at the stone crenel with her free hand, but her balance was lost. She pitched forward, a slow, falling motion that seemed to take forever, but ended almost before it started. Her heart slammed against her chest with a force equal to the one that jerked her in a half circle to face the outer wall of the tower. Thomas's grip on her wrist held fast. She said a hasty prayer of thanks that he did not intend to murder her after all, cut short by an overriding instinct to secure her dangling weight.

Thomas lowered her enough to grab the rope, then eased her left hand downward until she could grasp the slender lifeline with both hands. He even continued to hold her by the arm until she managed to get her knees and slippered feet around the rope through the vicious slash in her gown. Uncertain when Thomas might change his mind about her fate, she gave him a choppy nod and he released her.

She couldn't move.

Her hands felt frozen around the rope, her legs as well. If she moved, she would fall. If she did not move, Thomas would cut the rope from inside the wall. She wondered if she would be lucky enough to faint before the fall killed her.

"You made it this far." Thomas's voice sounded surprisingly gentle, yet she could not look up to see his expression. "The rest is easier. Just grip the rope with your feet and move one hand at a time."

Claudia tried to take a deep breath, but even her chest felt as if it were trying to wrap itself around the rope. She focused all her attention on the stone wall straight ahead and on the movement of her left hand as it eased lower. She let her feet slide down a few inches of the rope as well. Her right hand let go of the rope just long enough to move below the left, then she repeated the motion, again and again, until she thought it would never end. Her arms ached, her legs ached, even her bones ached from the fierce effort. And she thought a few buckets of water would prepare her for this task?

This was hell. Thomas had pushed her and she just didn't remember the fall that had killed her. Whatever sins she committed in her life, she had been damned to climb down this rope for eternity.

Someone grabbed her ankle. A smothered sound of relief came from behind her gag. Guy. She released the rope and fell on top of him. They both landed in a heap, although he managed to cushion her fall.

"Christ's bones, you are heavy!" He pushed her away and stood up.

If he thought she might try to escape him, he didn't appear worried by the possibility. He drew a dagger from his waist and cut a length of rope several feet long, then he gave the remaining rope two sharp tugs and kept his attention focused high overhead. From her seat on the ground Claudia watched Friar Thomas pull the long rope back inside the wall. She wanted to stay there for a very long time, mayhaps even kiss the solid rock beneath her. In another week or so, she might be able to walk again. But she had made it this far, and would not return to the fortress after this much trouble to escape it. She scrambled to her feet and swayed once before she steadied herself.

Guy turned to face her, the short rope lying across his upturned palms. "Give me your hands."

Not again, Claudia thought, but this time the order was for both hands. He meant to bind them. When she obeyed his order, he hesitated. For a long moment he stared at her hands, then he looped the rope around her wrists and secured the binding. He didn't knot the rope as tightly as she had expected. Indeed, the rope seemed almost loose around her wrists. She glanced down and saw how much her hands shook.

He had noticed as well. " 'Tis over, Claudia. You are safe now."

Safe? Aye, from the danger of falling, mayhap, but now she faced a threat just as perilous. She looked at the baron's face and knew he must have realized how ridiculous his words sounded. He scowled, then pulled her hood into place.

"Keep your head down. Your cloak is dark enough to

blend with the rocks, but the moonlight could reflect your face enough that a guard on the wall might notice."

She nodded and bowed her head. She could not look him in the eye any longer, to see what the moonlight reflected in his face. The pity and trace of regret in his eyes were nothing she wanted. Once they were safely away from the castle, she would try again to explain this colossal misjudgment of her character and offer payment to hire a company of his soldiers to escort her to Dante. Wherever *he* might be. She had to keep her faith that the emeralds would buy her that information as well.

4 &

"*Stop* squirming." Every muscle in Guy's body tensed, his patience strained to the breaking point. Claudia sat sideways in his lap rather than astride the warhorse, with her cloak arranged to hide the slash in her gown. She had wriggled around every moment of every hour since they left Lonsdale. He could not take much more of it.

When they met his knights in the forests outside Lonsdale, he didn't think he would mind sharing his mount. He had exchanged a handful of words with Evard, then lifted Claudia to her seat before him. As the bright moon that guided their flight gave way to the rose-colored streaks of dawn, the hip that once felt soft and supple now seemed solid as a rock against his groin. She shifted position again. "Can you not sit still?"

"My legs fell asleep."

It took him a moment to realize the gag should have prevented her from answering his question. He jerked her hood aside. "When did you pull that down?"

A wide yawn delayed the answer. Her still-bound hands rose to form a steeple over her mouth, then dropped again to her lap. "Soon after you put me on this beast. You had no need to gag me in the first place, Baron. I would be the last to raise an alarm."

He didn't know why it irritated him that she spoke in Italian, but it did. "You will speak in my language, or not at all."

Her lips parted, then closed again. She lifted her chin in the air and looked pointedly away from him. She tugged her hood back into place, too.

He scowled at the back of her head. "You will never learn to say the words correctly if you do not practice the language aloud."

Her head tilted sideways as if she considered this logic, but she remained silent. Evard rode up beside him. "Our soldiers await, Baron."

Guy followed the direction of Evard's gesture. The wide valley before them lay blanketed in morning mist, the air scented by dew-fresh meadows that lay beneath the fog. The valley belonged to Halford, while the ridge across from them marked the edge of Montague lands. On the ridge, a thin column of smoke rose above the treetops.

"And my cousins?" Guy asked.

"I sent a messenger to Halford before we returned to meet you outside Lonsdale, a different messenger than the one I sent to Montague. Each had orders to fulfill the other's duty if one did not return to this ridge by dawn. The signal fire means both were successful."

As usual, Evard left little to chance. Guy nodded his approval. "When we reach the ridge, the men and horses may rest while I meet with my cousins. You will stay with Lady Claudia."

The cold look in Evard's eyes when he glanced at Claudia revealed what he thought of that duty. Their flight from Lonsdale had required few words. Evard had not asked whether Claudia came with them of her free will or against it. He saw now that Evard regarded her as a captive. He supposed the rope that bound her wrists was a sure indicator. "See that the men know my wishes."

"Aye, my lord." Evard knew his overlord's tone of dismissal, and he allowed Guy to take the lead once more.

Guy studied the thin ribbon of road that led into the valley, more like a path made just wide enough for carts with deep ruts from those conveyances and the rains that must turn the sloping road into a river. He loosened the reins and let the horse pick its own path down the incline as he considered his "prisoner."

He could almost believe the wild tale she had spun, for he had indeed given Baron Lonsdale reason to believe the sale of Halford was in jeopardy. There was also the fact that they had encountered no opposition to their escape other than the guard at his door. Either Claudia was telling the truth or Lonsdale wanted him to escape. Claudia herself provided the reason Lonsdale might allow him to leave the fortress. As long as Lonsdale held a betrothal contract signed by the bishop, Guy could not marry another. That contract would provide a safer means of blackmail for Lonsdale than a forced marriage. Yet why would Lonsdale allow Claudia to escape with him? Or did Lonsdale allow nothing at all?

He fought the urge to believe Claudia, the deeply ingrained instinct that she was telling the truth. In the past his instincts had never failed him, but he was vulnerable where she was concerned. He wanted to believe in her too much to allow himself that luxury. Never again would he put himself into a position to be played for a fool.

Claudia broke into his thoughts. "I am to be your prisoner?"

"Are you talking to me, or to my horse?"

She turned to look up at him. "I no talk—" She drew a breath that made her nostrils flare. "I do not talk to horses. Will you make me a prisoner, or allow me my freedom?"

She spoke in a deliberate voice, making an obvious effort to be understood. Guy found that he liked her sultry accent. He had to concentrate on what she said, rather than on the way she said it. "I will decide your fate when we reach Montague Castle."

She did not look satisfied with the answer. "Am I tried and condemned already in your mind?"

Her words carried the rhythm of a caress rather than a barb. The affect on him was startling. And unwelcome. "You would be wise not to press me, Lady Claudia. 'Tis been a long night, and my mood was not the best when we began this journey."

Her lips puckered into the beginnings of a pout, then she

turned her attention forward. The snub annoyed him. She did not behave much like a woman who had plotted against him. She had either ice in her veins or an impressive streak of courage.

They began to cross the valley, and the fog soon engulfed them. He made his way toward the ridge by the muted sunlight to the east rather than by sight of the ridge. The fog muffled the sounds of the men and horses behind them as well, and made him feel as if they were alone together. He found himself thinking about what he would do with Claudia if they were truly alone.

Her treachery should have destroyed whatever lust he had felt for her. Now he discovered that was not the case. He became aware of every inch of her that pressed against him, the floral scent that did not belong entirely to the meadow flowers, and the heady scent that was Claudia's alone.

He lowered his head until his cheek almost brushed against the side of her hood. He was obsessed with her, felt every part of her swaying gently against him in the saddle. Could she truly be as soft as he remembered? She would have to be naked before he knew for sure.

He lifted his hand to rub his tired eyes, and his arm bumped her head by accident. Claudia's hands disappeared inside her hood and she groaned just as she began to slump forward. His arms tightened around her even as she caught herself. "Are you all right?"

She moved her head from side to side, her hands fisted against her forehead. "My head hurt. Hurts. The back, where Friar Thomas hit me. He is the one who hit me, no?"

"Aye." He felt a rush of guilt. He should have checked before now to make sure her skull was not fractured. With one arm wrapped around her waist to steady her, his other hand searched the back of her head until he found the large knot, and she cried out.

"Hush," he murmured. "I will not touch it again." He tried to part the hair around the bump. "Did it bleed?"

"Nay. 'Tis but a lump and a headache. It will heal itself in a few days."

He frowned. How in the world would she know? Still, she had not complained of it before now. "Is your headache worse than before?"

"It will pass."

He pressed her for a more thorough answer. "Did you feel faint before now?"

"Aye, when we first set out, many times I felt faint. Now the spells are not so many."

That had to be a good sign, he decided. "Lean back in my arms until this one passes." He added an excuse when she looked wary of the offer. "I do not want you to fall off the horse."

She leaned back until his arm supported her shoulders and head, then she closed her eyes and he felt her body begin to relax. She lay in his arms as trusting as a child. A very foolish child. When she tucked her hands beneath her chin and burrowed closer to his chest, he realized she had fallen asleep.

How could she sleep?

She wore a gag around her neck, and a rope bound her wrists together. For all she knew, he might change his mind at any time about slitting her throat. She should be on her guard, not asleep, for God's sake. She was indeed a fool. A soft, warm fool who smelled good, too.

Guy rolled his eyes. He had been without a woman too long. Nothing else could explain his ridiculous obsession with this one. On the other hand, the urge to finish what he had started in her chamber was a logical one, he supposed. He'd wanted her more in that moment than he had wanted anything in his life. His body reacted immediately to the memory. He gritted his teeth and tried to concentrate on the horse's direction.

The ground began to rise again, and they emerged from the fog. A treeless gap along the ridge overhead revealed the distant figures of mounted soldiers. Montague soldiers. They were safe now, on Montague land.

Sometime while he held her the land had wakened around them, the birds mostly, with their cries and twitters, and the hum of an enterprising insect here and there. The fog would burn off fast now that sunlight blazed into the valley. Even the woods they passed through seemed less forbidding than those on the ridge behind them.

"Claudia, wake up." A half-remembered warning surfaced that a deep sleep after a blow to the head sometimes proved fatal. He gripped her shoulders harder. "Claudia!"

"Mm." She rubbed her cheek against his chest.

He made his voice sharp, angry. "Claudia. Wake up."

Her eyes fluttered open and she met his gaze. Her lips curved into a smile that made his heart do strange things inside his chest. It returned to a more normal beat when the smile disappeared. She sat up with a start, looking guilty. "I did not mean to sleep."

Her regret did not change the fact that she had. A prisoner who slept in her captor's arms. What was he to make of that? "We will reach the main force of my soldiers soon. Give me your hands."

"Why?"

"Just give me your hands." He untied the knots that bound her, noting that she struggled to sit straighter in his arms. When she was free, he examined her wrists for signs of chafing. "There," he pronounced, "no lasting damage."

"May I remove this?" She looped one finger through the makeshift gag around her neck.

He inclined his head.

She lifted her arms to untie the cloth, and her cloak parted and fell to her sides. First he looked at the slender bare arm that lacked a sleeve. Next he watched the dark brown fabric of the gown stretch tight across her breasts as she went about her work. He showed no reaction until the third time her elbow accidentally jabbed him, this time in the nose.

"Be careful!"

"Sorry," she mumbled. The sleeve came away from her neck and disappeared into a pocket of her gown. She drew her cloak forward again until she was covered from neck to toes.

The road leveled out, and he pushed the horse to a canter. Nearly a hundred soldiers awaited them at the clearing. Guy brought the horse to a sliding stop near his two cousins. He did not relish the thought of what he must tell them.

When a squire came forward to hold the horse, Guy swung down from the saddle, then he lifted Claudia by the waist and set her on the ground. He continued to hold her until she loosened her grip on his arms, an indication that she could stand on her own. Another horse trotted up beside him, and Evard dismounted.

"Tell the men to break their fast," he ordered Evard. "We will stay here an hour or more. Have a squire prepare a bag of rations and tie it to my saddle. When I am done with my cousins, I will eat with Lady Claudia." He nodded in her direction. "Guard her."

Without another glance at Claudia, he turned and stalked off toward his cousins.

Claudia looked from Guy's departing back to his second-in-command. Evard de Cordray folded his arms across his chest and stared back at her. His stance seemed to dare her to challenge him. She looked around the clearing and realized that most of Guy's soldiers stared at her as well. If she'd had any notion to bolt for freedom, she would not get far. Where did they think she would go? Into the woods, to take her chances with wild animals? She would rather take her chances with the civilized ones.

Evard called a soldier forward and relayed Guy's orders while Claudia sought out their source. Guy stood near the edge of the ridge with two men who must be the cousins he and Evard spoke of, too far away for her to hear their quiet discussion. The cousins lacked any resemblance to Guy, and they appeared much older. One had steel-gray hair with a wooly beard; the other was black-haired and clean-shaven. There was a leanness to their builds and the lines of their faces that spoke of hard living. Her gaze wandered in the other direction and she spied a small elm tree with soft-looking grass beneath it.

"May I rest beneath that tree?" she asked Evard. The knight's brows drew closer together, but he did not reply. She repeated the question.

Evard tilted his head to one side, his frown even deeper. "I cannot understand you. Say it again. Slower."

Claudia gritted her teeth. She pointed to herself, then to the tree. "Me—sit—there!"

Evard shook his head. He pointed to the ground, then answered in a voice loud enough to startle his horse. "No, stay here!"

Claudia affected a blank look. "Parli più forte per favore. Non ti sento bene."

"You heard him just fine the first time." Guy spoke from behind her. She spun to face him, but he didn't look at her as he remounted. "And the horses would bolt if he spoke any louder."

Claudia glanced over her shoulder to gauge Evard's reaction to Guy's translation. A dull red blush stained his face. She didn't realize Guy had moved his horse closer until he reached down and lifted her onto his lap. She scrambled to grasp the edges of her cloak together so his men would not see her ruined gown. The long slash up the front might give them the wrong impression about how it came to be there.

"I will speak with Lady Claudia alone," Guy told his second-in-command. He nodded toward the forest to the east and Claudia noticed that the road they followed reentered the woods in the same vicinity. "There is an old oak tree about three hundred yards from the entrance to the forest. I do not wish to be disturbed unless the watch spies Lonsdale soldiers in the valley below us."

"Aye, my lord." Evard gave Claudia a pitying look, as if he thought something dire awaited her.

Guy spurred the horse forward.

The patches of blue sky became fewer as they rode into the forest, until the sky disappeared entirely beneath leafy branches that grew thicker and taller. These were ancient woods, with oak trees as big around as a watchtower. Smaller trees that would seem impressive in an open field struggled to find the sun amidst the neighboring giants. Even the grass ceased to grow, replaced by a carpet of moss that muffled the hoofbeats against it. A damp odor lingered in the air, a smell of things long dead, yet fresh at the same time.

"Why must we be away from the others?" she asked, still taking in their surroundings.

Guy grunted by way of reply.

She glanced up at him, but his gaze continued to sweep over the forest, searching, probably for the oak tree he mentioned to Evard. Why did he want to be alone with her? Surely there was nothing of a romantic nature on his mind. He didn't even like her. If he meant to harm her, there was no reason to leave his soldiers. They would not lift a finger in her defense. Perhaps he was looking for a place to abandon her. He could not bring himself to order her death, but leaving her alone in this forest would amount to the same thing. "You will not abandon me here, will you?"

"Nay, Claudia. I will not abandon you." His expression was unreadable, but she sensed that he told her the truth.

The sunlit leaves turned this entire, isolated world a glowing shade of green. She held up one hand to examine the strange new color of her skin, knowing it was but a trick of the light, yet fascinated by it just the same.

One could find sprites and fairies in woods such as these. After dark, ghosts and goblins. Careful to make the gesture unnoticeable, she crossed herself then said a silent prayer to ward off evil. A raven screeched at the same moment, then took sudden flight from a low-hanging branch above them. She clutched at Guy's tunic and cowered closer to him.

"We stop here, please? They will no hear us." A raven

was the worst sort of omen. Nothing good awaited them here. Her hands turned to fists when he shook his head.

"We are almost there."

"Where is 'there'?" she demanded. "Every tree in this place looks the age of time!"

"There." He pointed in front of them.

Claudia's gaze followed to an oak that looked the parent of every tree around them. It rose from the forest floor like a mighty fortress, its roots the roads that lead to the tower, the sprawling branches its own strange sky of green clouds. She felt a sense of awe as they drew closer. If magical creatures lived in the forest, this would be their home. She did not think they should disturb them. "What is this place?"

" 'Tis just a tree. I discovered it years ago, when I was a boy." He seemed to notice her apprehension. "What did you think it was?"

She shook her head, distracted by a black circle on the ground between two of its massive roots. "Something started a fire at its base!"

"Something?" He laughed aloud. "You think this a place of spirits?"

"You think it not?"

That made his smile fade. He dismounted and helped her down, then removed a length of rope from the saddle to hobble the horse. "Wait for me by the tree. I will return as soon as I tend the horse."

She shook her head. "I will help you."

"I need no help to tie my horse." He handed her the bag of rations from his saddle. "Wait for me here."

She supposed it would behoove her to obey that order. It would do no good to anger him. He led the horse away but she somehow ended up standing behind him as he tended the animal. He nearly stumbled over her when he turned around.

His hands grasped her shoulders to steady her and he held her at arm's length. "I told you to wait by the tree!"

She glanced over her shoulder, hesitant to turn her back

on the fortress-tree. "I am not all that hungry. Can we not continue our journey?"

"We have been in the saddle all night. An hour's—" He held her chin in his hand so she could not cast another wary glance over her shoulder. "You are afraid of this place, aren't you?"

She didn't care if he thought her a coward. Great knots in the trunk of the tree looked like twisted faces, the faces of poor souls who had wandered too close to something they should avoid. She gave him a frantic nod.

He took her hand and began to walk toward a hollowed-out area formed between two of the tree's enormous roots. She began to tug against his hand. "Come, Claudia. I want to show you something."

She didn't have much choice but to go along with him, since he held her hand in a fast grip. He didn't release her until they reached the base of the trunk. He looked along the bark in front of them as if searching for something.

"Ah. Here it is." He pointed to a smooth section of the trunk that was level with his shoulders. Someone had stripped away a portion of the bark, and she could still make out the initials G. M. in the weathered carving. "Guy of Montague. I think I carved those letters when I was no more than eight or nine." His tone turned boastful. "I made this tree mine long ago, and all the woodland sprites and spirits do bow to me as their overlord."

Claudia found a reluctant smile. "You make light of me."

"That was my plan. Is it working?"

His teasing tone caught her off guard. Uncertain how to deal with the abrupt change in his mood, she tried to change the subject. "You came to this forest alone when you were so young?"

"Nay, my father liked to camp in the clearing near the ridge when he rode to his outlying properties. He let me explore the forest as long as I took a page along, most often a page named Thomas."

Claudia's eyes widened. "Would this page now be a humble friar?"

"Nay, the humble friar would be a respected knight in my service." He smiled at her expression, and she made a conscious effort to close her mouth. "I am not such a fool that I would ride into Lonsdale knowing nothing of the place or its people. Thomas served me well in his role of friar."

" 'Tis a sin to mimic a man of God." If Thomas had masqueraded as an ordained priest, that would be a serious matter indeed. But a friar? She had to admit that his plan was clever. "You were wise to have a spy within Lonsdale. I did not know about the guard at the bolthole. My plan would have failed."

The shadow of a frown crossed his face, then he turned to retrieve their bag of food. They settled between two of the tree's large roots to share their meal of bread and dried beef with a leather flagon of wine. Guy sat cross-legged with his back resting against the root. He had unbuckled his sword belt and propped the weapon next to his side. Claudia made her own seat across from him, arranging her ruined skirts to preserve her modesty. She had not thought to bring her sewing kit on this journey and hoped she could borrow one when they reached Montague. She had no coin to purchase a new gown.

"You asked me earlier about your fate." Guy sank his strong, white teeth into a strip of beef and tore a piece free. He watched her as he chewed. After he swallowed, his words sounded unhurried. "In all honesty, I am not certain what to do with you."

His unwavering attention made her self-conscious. She tried to be dainty about her meal, rather than wolfing the food down as she would like. The long ride had restored her appetite for some strange reason, and she was starved. She gave the chunk of bread in her hand a wistful look, but made herself offer a suggestion. "If you will allow me to hire a company of your men, you need do nothing more. I told you the truth last night. Before I leave for London I will make a statement before your priest about the events that took place at Lonsdale. You will be free of me, Baron."

"I am not so certain I wish to be free of you."

Claudia's hand stopped halfway to her mouth. "What do you mean?"

"You could go before another priest and say that I had forced you to lie to mine. There is also the fact that you want me to send you to London with a company of my men when you have no coin to pay them." He shrugged one shoulder. "You will forgive me if I question the wisdom of such a bargain."

"I will not misspeak myself, and I *will* pay your men!"

"I have yet to see this necklace you intend to barter," he said. " 'Tis doubtful any bauble is worth a company of men."

"The necklace will fetch enough to pay your men, and I have told you already that it is sewn into the lining of my cloak." She drew one side of her hood away. "You see? If you will return my dagger, I will cut open the stiches and show you the necklace."

He made a small gesture with his hand to dismiss her request. "I doubt you realize the expenses you face, lady. I would not trust a woman's safety on the road to London with any less than a knight, three archers, and two men-at-arms. The archers will charge you threepence a day, the soldiers eight, and the knight twenty. Count on no less than tenpence each day for the cost of meals and lodgings at inns along the way—if you are fortunate enough to find an inn each night, with stables and feed for the horses. You must also take a serving woman along to vouchsafe your reputation, and she will cost you a ha'pence per day. The journey to London will take you three weeks if the weather holds, then you must quarter this small army of people once you reach the city. In London, lodgings of a suitable size for your company start at sixteen pence per night, with the cost of meals and stabling doubled." He gave her a meaningful look. "And that is where you intend to begin your search?"

"I did not realize the daily cost." She picked at the piece of bread she held. "It sounds a small fortune."

"Aye, and no one will step forward to volunteer for your company unless I guarantee their pay. They are my people, and you will be indebted to me, not to them. How many coins will your necklace fetch?"

"I have never bartered for coin." She had felt certain the emeralds would fetch more than enough for her search, yet the array of numbers he spewed out and the expenses she had not considered made her less and less certain. "My brothers told me the necklace was valuable, but they did not mention its worth in gold or silver."

Guy smiled and shook his head. "A London jeweler would think you a gift from heaven."

"You think a jeweler would try to cheat me?"

"Have you never dealt with tradesmen?" He rolled his eyes when she shook her head. "They will rob you blind."

"Perhaps I could make do with just a soldier or two, then—"

"Nay."

"But I—"

"You are my responsibility now," Guy interrupted. "You will remain at Montague. I will give you a fair price for the necklace, and send one of my knights to search for your brother. I intend to petition the Church to have the bishop's edict set aside, yet that could take months. You will not leave Montague until I can settle the issue to my satisfaction."

She wanted to rail against his arbitrary decisions about her life, but on the whole they made sense. Guy dealt with many merchants. He would know the value of her necklace. She trusted him to give her a fair exchange for the emeralds far more than she would trust a stranger in a strange town. "Sending a lone knight does sound less costly than going to London myself," she mused. "How much will it cost each day to feed and lodge this knight?"

"Never mind that," he said. "What part of London does your brother live in?"

"I am not certain. He did not make mention of his lodgings."

"What trade does he pursue in London? Most tradesmen live within the same districts."

"He is a knight, not a tradesman," she said.

"Who is your brother's liege lord?"

"Well, as to that, I am not certain he calls any man his liege." She took a bite of bread and took her time to chew it. "Your king hired his sword, but I do not think a knight must swear his allegiance under such circumstances."

Guy lowered his chin and raised his brows. "Your brother is a mercenary?"

"Aye. 'Tis a noble profession for landless knights who wish to make something of themselves," she said defensively. Guy's droll expression said he thought otherwise. "King Edward promised Dante a fine keep in Wales for his efforts. If he is not in London, I am sure to find him in Wales."

"You are more likely to find him in a grave." He pressed his lips together. "I did not mean to be so blunt, but 'tis the truth of the matter. Mercenaries do not live long lives. They are paid well because a nobleman will not risk his own knights in whatever task they are hired to accomplish. 'Tis a dangerous—" He stopped and stared straight into her eyes, his own widening. "*Christ!*"

She gasped when he leaned forward and grabbed her by the arms. "What—"

"By all the saints, I am a fool!" His gaze raked over her then returned to her eyes. "I knew you looked familiar. Your eyes—I have seen them before." He gave her a small shake. "Tell me the name of your oldest brother."

"Roberto," she answered, her voice a frightened whisper. Just saying the name aloud brought back a flood of memories: the oldest brother she had always looked up to, the embittered man he became after their parents' deaths, and most of all, his own dishonorable death. This was what she dreaded from the moment they met, the truth she knew Guy would learn sooner or later. She had foolishly hoped for later.

"Aye, Roberto of Ravenna." He released her in an abrupt movement, as if he could not bear to touch her. "Another mercenary brother, one who took his blood money from the king of Scotland, did he not?" His lip curled in disgust. "If I had known you were the sister of that bastard—"

"He was *not* a bastard!" Her hands turned into fists, smashing the bread she held into hard lumps. "Roberto paid a high price for the mistakes he made in his life, but he was not a bastard."

"Mistakes?" Guy gave her an incredulous look. "He was an assassin! He tried to kill my brother and his wife, and I am the one who made it possible. That foul worm you call a brother insinuated himself into my company at court, told me some far-fetched tale about losing his lands in Italy, then he asked if I could gain him a place in my brother's army. God help me, I did as he asked." His eyes narrowed and he leaned back, his posture deceptively relaxed. "Do you know what it feels like to have your own brother suspect you of plotting against him?"

"Surely your brother did not—"

He held his fingers against the bridge of his nose and closed his eyes. "Be silent, Claudia."

She bowed her head and remained silent. He hated her. Before he did not trust her, but he seemed to accept the possibility that she was telling him the truth. Now he despised her. He would always despise her. And she was his prisoner. The future looked very bleak indeed.

"Poisoners, blackmailers, assassins, and mercenaries," he finally muttered. "Did I miss anyone in your family? Perhaps a thief, or a defrocked priest?"

She shook her head without looking up. The words hurt, as he surely meant them to hurt. She hoped he would abandon her, that he would get up and simply walk away without a backward glance. What did it matter if she was alone and unarmed? A trifling problem in the face of all others.

"Are you crying?"

She shook her head again. The movement made two fat

tears splash onto her hands. From beneath her soggy lashes, she saw him reach for her. "Please do not touch me."

His hand wavered, then fell away.

"I do not like to cry. I especially do not like anyone to watch me indulge in such a childish display." She didn't know why she tried to explain herself. Why should he care? She rubbed the fallen tears into her hand. "If you wish to leave me here, I will understand."

The hiss of steel against steel made her heart skip its beat. Her heart stopped beating altogether when she looked up.

Guy had drawn his sword.

5 ❧

Claudia gasped. "I—I did not mean—"

"Silence!" Guy hissed, his voice little more than a whisper as he rose to his feet. "We are not alone. Stand up, but do not make any sudden moves." He held his hand toward her, palm up, but kept his attention focused over her shoulder. "Use my left hand as a stirrup. I am going to hoist you onto the branch above me."

" 'Tis a boar," he said when she hesitated. "I must get to my horse, Claudia. Do as I say!"

She followed his orders without question. He crouched down to catch her foot in his hand and lifted her without any noticeable effort. She swung one leg over the wide branch just a few feet above his head, then made certain her cloak did not tumble down to blind him.

Guy began to take measured steps toward his warhorse, his attention on a felled tree that lay a few hundred feet away. The trunk was splintered by a long-ago strike of lightning, and a clump of new shoots formed a tall bush of sorts at its base. Its branches moved in a way that could not be caused by the wind in the still forest. Just then the horse whickered, a startled, nervous sound. The leaves of the bushes stirred, then Claudia heard a low grunt.

Guy spoke in a low, steady voice without looking at her. "Do not make a sound unless the beast charges before I reach the horse. If it charges while I am still afoot, scream for all you are worth."

She knew why he gave that order. Uncle Laurence and a company of his knights had stumbled across a boar last summer when they were hunting deer. The knights repeated the tale for weeks afterward. Boars were unpredictable beasts that would turn and run as often as they would stand and charge. Once provoked, a boar could take down a mounted knight. It had taken a half dozen men on horseback armed with spears to bring the beast to ground. Guy's sword would not protect them.

The horse neighed, a frightened sound that meant it caught the scent of the boar. The sound of the jangling curb chain and shank rang out like a bell in the still forest. The brush rustled as the boar moved forward.

She saw the snout first, hooked with long, curved tusks. Then the head appeared, and the entire beast itself ambled out from behind the bushes, its stance a clear challenge. Her heart thudded hard against her chest. The boar looked even bigger than the one her uncle and his men had brought back from their hunt, its massive bulk covered with coarse brown hairs. Its small, beady eyes moved from the horse to Guy, and it snorted again.

When Guy came within five paces of the horse, the boar trotted forward a few steps and came to an abrupt halt, its jerky movements a warning or a challenge. The closer Guy drew to his horse, the more agitated the boar became. Claudia wondered if the beast waited until it could attack both Guy and the horse at once.

"Hold." Guy gave the command in a hushed voice. The single word brought the horse's skittish movements to a halt, and it stood still and silent. He closed the distance to the horse in one long stride. His sword sliced through the rope hobble in a single stroke, even as the boar began its charge. Claudia clapped one hand over her mouth to stifle an involuntary scream.

The warhorse did not move until Guy leaped onto its back. He spurred the horse into a charge to meet the boar head-on. A moment before the sharp tusks would have gouged into the horse's chest, he gave an unspoken command and the horse gathered its haunches and leaped into the air.

They cleared the beast, even though it lifted its head and

tried to rake the horse's belly. Enraged by the near miss, the boar squealed and turned in pursuit. Surprisingly, when the boar reached the bushes, it shuffled to a stop. Guy slowed the horse to a trot then turned to face his foe, moving the horse in a wide path around the felled tree as he worked his way toward Claudia.

The boar watched his every movement. As soon as Guy closed the arc of his path, the boar began to paw at the ground. Guy came within twenty yards of the fortress-tree when the boar charged again. This time Guy galloped toward the road that led toward his men.

Claudia watched him ride away. She kept waiting for him to turn around. He *would* turn around. Surely he was not so cruel that he would abandon her. Not here, with a wild beast ready to devour her. But that was exactly what he did. He disappeared from sight, then even the sound of his horse's hoofbeats faded away.

He was gone.

The boar had also watched Guy's departure, but now turned and trotted toward her perch in the tree. Once beneath her it stopped to investigate the scattered remnants of their breakfast, eating everything it found. The animal was so close that she could hear every snuffling breath it took, every grunt it made. She buried her nose in the crook of her arm to escape its musky scent. Every once in awhile it stopped rooting long enough to glance up at her, as if to remind itself of her presence. Each look from those flat, emotionless eyes was a clear warning that it would kill her, given the chance.

At last the boar returned to the felled tree and began to dig around one of the downed branches. Her heart began to slow its frantic beat.

How could Guy leave her? She was alone and defenseless, without a horse or even food. What hope she nourished that he might still return for her died a little with each passing moment until she stopped watching the spot in the forest where he had disappeared and propped her chin on her crossed arms.

"I hate this tree," she muttered. The boar glanced up at the sound of her voice, but soon returned to its snuffling. She would have to wait until it lost interest and wandered away. Hopefully, a very long distance away. And then what would she do? Once she climbed down from this branch, where would she go? What other animals would she encounter?

He had really abandoned her. So much for knightly honor, the duty to rescue any lady in distress. So much for courage in the face of danger, the coward. So much for—

The sound of hoofbeats interrupted her thoughts, faint at first, then they grew louder. One horse could not make so much noise. The boar let out a long series of grunts and shuffled back to its post by the bushes.

Guy and his warhorse reappeared on the path, followed by a dozen soldiers on horseback. They all carried lances. The grim expression on Guy's face didn't change when he glanced up at her. He didn't return her smile, but that mattered not at all.

He had come back for her!

She looked at the boar and her smile faded. One cloven hoof tore at the mossy earth, and it made a loud snort each time its hoof struck the ground. The danger was far from over.

The men fanned out in a semicircle and lowered their lances. They drew to a halt when they neared the fortress-tree, and Guy glanced up at her. "Stay where you are, Claudia. Do not come down from there until I tell you it is safe."

As if she needed to be told as much. She nodded anyway. "Aye, Baron. I am in no hurry to leave my perch."

A faint smile touched his lips, then disappeared when he turned his attention to the bushes. The boar leaped forward then came to an immediate, jarring stop, a challenge to those who invaded its territory.

"I would rather we faced a boar with spears," Guy told his men, "yet your lances will serve well enough in the open ground. If it bolts to the side, swing your lance up and over when you turn lest you unhorse the man next to you. Have a care for the branches overhead as well. If the attack is straight on, the three nearest the charge will use lances. Everyone else move in with swords or we will end up skewering each other. Understood?"

The men voiced their assent, then followed Guy's lead and began to move forward again. Guy rode in the center of the company, a length ahead of the men around him. Claudia bit her lower lip. Riding before his men meant he made the most likely target. Was that his intent?

Whether he planned it or not, that was the result. The boar gathered its weight on its haunches and charged forward. The horses broke into a gallop at the same moment. Claudia's fingernails dug painfully into the bark, but she kept her attention on Guy as the boar headed straight for him.

The animal swerved at the last moment, and the tip of Guy's long lance glanced off its side. The slash from the lance did not stop or even slow the boar. It continued to head straight for Guy and his warhorse. Guy dropped his lance, and she realized that he held a sword in his other hand. In one blur of movement, he leaned low in the saddle with his sword extended. Another lance grazed the animal's left side, but it was the lancer on the right who found a vulnerable purchase between the boar's rib cage and haunch, an instant before the beast's tusks would tear into Guy's warhorse. That piercing blow made the animal stumble, then the lance snapped. The animal flailed its short legs then regained its balance, still looking as deadly as ever, still intent on Guy.

"Evard, Simon! Lances!" Guy gave that order as he wheeled his horse around. The warhorse bucked, then kicked its hind legs out in a flash of ironclad hooves. One hoof connected with its target and stunned the boar, but at a cost. The horse screamed as a long tusk raked into its hindquarter. Two more lances drove into the beast at the same moment, one into its neck in a blow that brought it to ground. Once more it struggled to its feet, this time with less vigor, and another lance appeared to strike its chest dead-center. The animal screamed long and loud.

Claudia turned her head and took deep breaths, trying to erase the bloody images from her mind. She couldn't block the shouts of the men as they moved in for the kill, nor the eerie, almost human death cries of the beast. She wanted to scream as well.

The boar quieted at last, and Claudia lifted her head to search for Guy. He had dismounted, and another knight held the reins while Guy examined the damage done his horse. A slash of bright red blood streaked down from a wound to its back haunch, and the animal made restless movements as if to escape the pain. From the corner of her eye she saw the other soldiers as they tended their own horses and the fallen boar, but she refused to look in that direction.

"You may come down now, lady."

The voice startled Claudia. She looked sideways and saw Evard. He was still mounted, his horse standing beneath the tree limb while he twisted in the saddle to look back at her. He gestured to the animal's rump, then held up one hand. "Step onto my horse's back, then I will lower you to the ground."

She glanced toward Guy, then back at Evard.

"The baron must tend to his horse," he told her. "Surely you do not wish to remain up there?"

Claudia shook her head. She eased her legs off the branch, then more of her weight, until her feet touched down on the horse's broad back. She was surprised but thankful that the animal remained so still. Evard held her arm to steady her as she slid to the ground.

"Thank you for coming to my rescue," she told Evard, careful to speak slowly so he could understand her.

"You owe the baron your thanks, my lady." He would not meet her gaze, and seemed to look anywhere but directly at her. "For coming to your rescue, at least."

She didn't dwell on his odd reply. Another dizzy spell caught her off guard, most likely a result of being stretched out for so long on the branch then suddenly standing upright. She covered her eyes with one hand and steadied herself against the horse's rump with the other. Evard was dismounted and at her side in an instant.

"Sit here for a moment, Lady Claudia." He led her a few paces away from his horse, but she refused to sit down.

"I will be fine in a moment," she assured him.

"What is wrong with you?" Guy asked, as he walked up behind them.

Evard turned to face him, his voice accusing. "She is faint from her ordeal. I will stay with her."

Guy looked from Evard to Claudia, then back again. "Nay, I do not think that is wise. Send someone for the others. We will continue our journey from here, but first I want Francis to tend my horse. Tell Stephen to ride double with another squire, and I will take his mount."

Evard gave him a curt nod, but did not move from his place by Claudia's side. "I did not think you were one to abuse defenseless women," he said in a low voice, then he turned and stalked away.

Claudia stared after him, shocked that he would speak to his overlord in such a tone, and baffled as to where he came up with such an idea.

"Will you be all right?" Guy asked.

"What did—" She thought better of questioning him when she looked up and saw his scowl. "Aye. The spells do not last. This one has passed."

"Good." He walked past her and retrieved the sword belt he had tossed aside when the boar first appeared. "Cover yourself before the rest of my soldiers arrive."

She remembered then that she had thrown her cloak over her shoulders to get the bulky garment out of the way. She gasped and pulled the edges forward until it covered her tattered gown. Guy ignored her as he examined his sword belt for damage, then strapped it around his waist. She glanced around the clearing and realized that all his men watched them. A few looked away to avoid her gaze. Others talked quietly among themselves. It was obvious that she and Guy were the topic of their conversation.

No wonder Evard acted so strangely. Her gown was ripped to shreds. Guy had removed his sword belt and weapons. It did not take long to realize the conclusion his men made of those facts. Her face felt on fire. She turned her back on the men and held out one hand to stop Guy before he could walk past her. "Your men—They think—"

"I know what they think."

"You must tell them it is not truth!"

He looked grimly amused by her distress. "Why should I?"

"You would have your own men think you so dishonorable?" She shook her head. "You saved my life, Baron. I would not have anyone think you any less noble than you are, much less your own men."

"What about your own reputation?"

"What about it?"

"Many will believe that I ravished you no matter what I say to the contrary. It will not matter if I order my men to silence. There will be whispers among them, and those whispers will spread. When they journey to tournaments or to court, the gossip will spread beyond Montague." He folded his arms across his chest. "You are ruined, Claudia, and there is nothing I can do to alter that fact. Does that not concern you more than my own noble reputation?"

"Nay," she said honestly. "At Lonsdale I told you the reasons I am unlikely to marry, and this is but one more. I knew when I asked you to take me on this journey that most would consider me ruined as a result. I am in your keeping without a servant or tirewoman to vouchsafe my reputation." She shrugged her shoulders. "It seemed a small price for freedom, indeed, for my very life."

He stared down at her, then slowly shook his head. "I cannot decide if you are the most cunning woman I have ever met or the most guileless."

She gave an impatient sigh. "Will you explain to your men that they are mistaken in their beliefs?"

"I will tell Evard the truth of the matter," he conceded,

"but he is probably the only one who will believe there is not more to the tale. The story will spread faster than the truth. The more one denies gossip, the truer it becomes in many minds."

He was right. To insist upon the truth would only make the lie that much more believable. And the story would spread beyond Montague. She didn't care what the English thought of her, but one opinion did matter. If Dante heard the gossip, he would be furious. She didn't want to think about what he might do if he heard the lie before he heard the truth. "I worried that something like this might happen, and I tried to keep my gown covered for just that reason." She stared at the ground. "I am sorry, Baron, but I am grateful you did not abandon me after all."

"Believe me, Claudia, a little gossip is the least of my concerns." He tilted her chin up with one finger. "Did you really think I would leave you here?"

She lowered her lashes. The gentleness of his touch felt almost like a caress, a temptation to move closer to his warmth into the sheltering safety of his arms. She took a deep breath to rid herself of those fanciful thoughts but caught his scent instead, the faint, masculine smell that she missed when they were apart. Until that moment, she hadn't realized that she had missed him.

"Claudia?"

She took a shaky step backward and kept her gaze glued to the ground. "Aye, Baron. I know you despise me as much as you despise my family, and I myself suggested you abandon me. I thought you took that suggestion to heart." She steeled herself to meet his gaze. It wasn't so hard. His eyes were as warm and welcoming as his touch. She could stare at him for hours, remembered well enough what it felt like when she thought she would never see him again. "Rather than abandon me, you saved my life. I will prove myself worthy of the efforts you made on my behalf."

"Will you indeed?" His voice lacked any trace of sarcasm.

He sounded curious. "And how do you intend to prove yourself?"

"I will make certain you are free of me," she said. "And—and I will do everything I can to see that you get Halford Hall for a fair price."

Both dark brows rose. "And how do you intend to accomplish that?"

She had said too much and tried to retreat to safer ground. "I do not know yet, but I will do what I can."

"The men are ready to move out," Evard said from behind her.

She turned around and noticed that the other soldiers had joined them. She had been so intent on her conversation with Guy that she didn't hear their approach.

"Set a half dozen men to make a litter," Guy ordered. "We shall dine on roast boar tomorrow. Have Stephen make room in a baggage cart for Lady Claudia. 'Tis too long a journey to burden his palfrey with two riders." He turned and walked past her without another word.

"I will see that you are made comfortable," Evard said, scowling as he watched him go.

"You are kind," Claudia murmured. She knew the reason for his scowl, but decided it was not her place to interfere with Guy's men. Evard would learn the truth soon enough from his overlord, then he would likely turn his scowls in her direction once more.

Evard motioned toward a two-wheeled cart that had pulled up beside them. A squire sat atop the gray gelding, which eliminated the need for a driver.

"There might be enough space near the quivers." Evard pointed toward a stack of arrows at the center of the cart. Armor and weaponry crammed every available inch, but Evard started to climb into the cart. "I will stack the bows upright to make enough room."

"Evard!"

Claudia glanced up to see Guy order Evard to the front of the procession with a gesture of his hand.

"You must excuse me, my lady. Young Jack here will help you get settled. We will stop to water the horses in about an hour when we reach the stream on the other side of the forest. I will check on you then to make sure you are comfortable."

The baggage cart proved cramped, but Claudia did not complain of her small quarters. She managed to make enough space in the cart to curl up and sleep. It wasn't comfortable. In fact, she thought it impossible to sleep in such a position until she woke up late that afternoon and realized she had done just that. She felt as if she could sleep forever. Every muscle in her body ached, and her head felt as if good Friar Thomas had taken a mace to it, the wretched man.

Rather than days, it seemed as if a lifetime had passed since she and Thomas had talked in the chapel gardens. Her whole life had changed from the moment she met Guy, along with the way she looked at everyone in it. The gentle friar was a spy and a knight, her uncle and a man of God would hang her to gain a few bags of gold, and the man she would dream about forever would probably forget her existence the moment he was rid of her. On top of all that, Guy spoke aloud the fear she had harbored for months. There was more than a small possibility that Dante was dead.

She untangled her leg from a crossbow and struggled to sit up. Self-pity would accomplish nothing, and she pushed those grim thoughts firmly aside. She had awakened because of the shouts from the soldiers who accompanied her, the calls to open the gates, then the cries of greetings. By the time she gathered her sleep-muddled senses they were inside the walls of a castle, a castle that must be Montague. The bailey they passed through looked larger than any at Lonsdale, with well-kept outbuildings along the walls and a few buildings that stood on their own. As orderly as the place looked, it smelled awful. The cart drew to a stop and she discovered the source of the foul odor. The cart had pulled up next to the stables.

Three young men dressed in brightly colored tunics stood

before a mound of soiled straw, and each leaned on a pitchfork. It took her a moment to comprehend that they were cleaning the stables in such fine clothes. A punishment for some boyish prank, no doubt, for they were too well dressed to be serfs.

She turned to survey the other castle folk who had halted their work to watch the procession of Baron Montague's soldiers. Everyone in the bailey wore clothing too fine for the tasks they had set aside. Two women stood next to a vat of boiling tallow, dressed in simple but costly cambric frocks. A man with a bundle of wood slung over his back wore dark green hose and a matching tunic of woven linen. She looked from one building to the next, at the dozens and dozens of people gathered there. No one wore simple smocks or roughspun tunics, and their clothing looked every color of the rainbow. Where were the serfs and villeins? Even freemen could not afford the clothing these people wore.

"You are to come with me, Lady Claudia."

She turned toward the voice. A soldier stood near the back of the cart. He extended one hand to help her down, but had to wait while she picked her way around the stack of bows. He took her hand just long enough to steady her as she stepped down from the cart, then he turned and walked toward the front of the procession. Most of the soldiers led their horses toward the stable or gave directions to young boys who hurried forward to hold the reins of their mounts. The boys could not be stable lads, for they wore clothes fit for a squire. Surely there could not be so many squires in one castle, and what squire would serve a simple soldier?

Claudia forgot her questions when she caught sight of Guy. He stood by his injured warhorse with Evard and Francis. He didn't acknowledge her in any way, but his gaze never left her as she followed the soldier toward the keep. She didn't know what to make of the way he stared at her. For a time she stared back, until she nearly ran into her escort when he paused at the stone steps that led to the keep. She felt a blush warm her cheeks and made a more concerted effort to watch where she placed her feet.

The soldier led her up the steps of the massive keep, then through the great hall. They hurried through the hall so quickly that she caught little more than a glimpse of long silk banners that hung from the ribbed crossbeams and costly stained glass windows. The walls were covered with colorful tapestries, the walls themselves whitewashed, with every arch and colonnade painted in bright colors and intricate patterns to look like Moorish mosaics. Most astonishing of all, the tables were draped with cream-colored linen. Did Guy expect his king to pay a visit?

"This way, Lady Claudia." The soldier gestured toward a winding staircase, then led the way.

Claudia held one hand against the wall to steady herself so she could crane her neck to gape at the great hall until it disappeared from sight below them. The soldier led her to the end of a long hallway where a door of stout oak stood open. He indicated that she should step inside.

"The baron bids you await him here, my lady. He will join you after you are refreshed from your journey."

Claudia wondered if the room was a guest chamber or a prison, even as the soldier closed the door behind her. It looked neither. She turned in a half circle to stare at the strange room. The place appeared to be a nest of pillows and curtains. Large blue satin pillows with gold tassels were piled before the fireplace. A large bed dominated the wall next to the fireplace. Its blue brocade bed curtains matched the coverlet, with more brocade pillows stacked near the headboard. Both the headboard and footboard were carved to resemble waves. She had never seen anything like it.

Her gaze moved away from the bed to a window seat padded with blue cushions, to the pillows stacked on top of the pads that were blue and white striped. A table and two chairs with wide arms stood near the window, simple in their design compared to the bed, and several trunks rested along the outer wall. To her left, the room had been partitioned with dark blue curtains so sheer that they seemed to float with every slight breeze that entered through the window. Somewhere behind those curtains she heard the sound of splashing water. Two ladies made their way around the curtain, a brunette dressed in a gown of pale yellow with a pumpkin-colored bliaut, and a blond who wore a gown the colors of roses and cream. Both carried buckets, and they dropped a quick curtsy to Claudia. She was the only lady she knew who would carry a water bucket. These two did not seem the least offended by the lowly chore.

"Greetings, my lady," said the blond. "My name is Lenore, and this is Mary." She gave Claudia an expectant look that met with silence, then she turned to Mary. "Fetch a trencher of hot food from the kitchens. 'Tis certain the lady will want a hearty meal after her journey."

"You are servants?" Claudia asked, as Mary left the chamber.

"Aye, my lady." Lenore sounded surprised that Claudia didn't know this. Her faint blond brows formed a frown. "The baron sent a rider ahead to give our steward instructions about your arrival. The steward said I am to be your tirewoman, if you have no objection."

Claudia could not believe that Guy went to so much trouble or that Lenore was a tirewoman. "But your clothing." She made a sweeping gesture with her hands. "Everyone's clothing. Is the baron so rich that he dresses his servants in clothing fit for lords and ladies?"

"Clothing?" Lenore looked puzzled, then her dark brown eyes traveled over Claudia's cloaked form. Her face brightened. "Oh, aye, the steward said you would need clothing as well. I have new garments laid out by your bath."

It seemed obvious that Lenore didn't understand Claudia's question. She would have to remember to speak slower.

Lenore gestured toward the filmy blue curtain. "The water should be cooled by now. Would you like to bathe, my lady?"

"Aye." A bath sounded heavenly. Claudia felt as if someone had dumped a bucket of dust on her while she slept in the baggage cart. Even her teeth felt gritty. She followed Lenore around the curtain, but came to an abrupt halt at the sight that greeted her. An enormous marble square occupied one corner of the partitioned area, with two marble steps that led to the hollowed-out oval at its top. Steam rose from the water that filled the oval. It looked very much like a Roman bath. In England?

Lenore must have noticed her astonished expression. "The baron had this made last year. Look." She pointed into the water. "It has a cork stopper at the bottom. When the plug is pulled, a cistern carries the water outside the wall. That saves the trouble of emptying the tub by bucket."

"Very ingenious," Claudia mused, unaware that she spoke in Italian.

"Forgive me, my lady." Lenore twisted her slim hands together, work-roughened hands that could not disguise her station as a servant the way her clothes did. "The steward did not tell us you were Flemish. If you would prefer, I can send for another who can speak your language."

"I am Italian," Claudia said, slow enough to be understood. "What made you think me Flemish?"

"I just assumed—" Lenore's brows drew together in a frown. "All foreigners at Montague are Flemish. The baron brought master weavers and their families from Flanders five years ago to teach us their trade. Many learned their language as they learned their craft." Lenore looked distraught. "I can do little more than count to ten in their language, and I do not speak any Italian."

" 'Tis not a sin," Claudia chided. The girl acted as if she had just confessed one. The people of Montague were as unique in their thinking as they were in their dress. What an amazing place. "And I would rather speak your language. I am told I need the practice. Tell me when you do not understand what I say. Sometimes I say the words too fast."

"Aye, my lady." Lenore smiled again, but the smile faded when Claudia shed her cloak. "Your gown! 'Tis—ruined."

"I think I can sew it, if you can find me a needle and thread." Claudia hung her cloak on a row of pegs near the tub, then bent to examine her slashed skirts. The tears looked fairly even.

"You cannot wear that gown again. 'Tis fit for naught but the fabric of a quilt." Lenore moved forward to help untie the side laces of Claudia's gown. She nodded toward a dark blue garment that also hung from a peg. "The gown I brought you might be a little large, but now that I have seen your size I will have the seamstresses alter a few others. By tomorrow you will have gowns that fit. The baron would be vexed if we let you wear this rag."

"Do the Flemish weavers make all the clothing for Montague's servants?" Claudia asked.

"Oh, nay, my lady. Most of our clothing comes from the apprentice weavers and dyers." Lenore pointed out an almost unnoticeable section of her skirt where the fabric had drawn into a nub that ran the length of the gown. "We fashion our clothing from the flawed fabric. 'Tis often no more than an uneven weave or a dye that fades. The baron could sell these fabrics as well, but he says Montague must have a reputation for producing only the finest. Baron Montague knows what he is about, for nobles of many countries vie for Montague brocades and patterns. 'Tis said some at court scoff at the baron's penchant for trade, but all of Montague prospers as a result."

Lenore had continued at her task while she talked. Now she seemed to wait for Claudia's opinion of the baron's trade. Claudia stepped into the tub and sank into the water with a weary sigh. The tub was so large that it felt as if she were afloat in a sun-warmed pond. She took the sponge and scented soap that Lenore offered and began to scrub her tired, bruised body before she lost the ambition. "Those at court must be jealous of your baron. Few live with such luxuries. Do many chambers have baths such as this one?"

Lenore wore a puzzled expression, and hesitantly asked Claudia to repeat herself. She listened very carefully the second time and a look of comprehension brightened her features. She smiled and shook her head. "Nay, my lady. Only the baron's chamber has such a tub."

"The baron's chamber?" Claudia repeated dumbly, even as comprehension sank in. Of course this was Guy's chamber. The rich furnishings, the bath . . . She stood up in a cascade of water but nearly fell down again in the slippery tub. She sank to her knees and gripped the edge. "I must dress, Lenore. Quickly."

uy slipped in to his chamber like a thief. It was his
own fault that he had dreaded coming here tonight,
to the one place at Montague that should offer a
welcome respite from his duties and responsibilities.

The room looked welcoming enough. A small fire blazed
in the hearth to chase off the evening chill, and a brace of
candles cast a golden glow all around the table. The cozy
setting turned cool where the ghostly light of a full moon
spilled through the window, the figure that stood there a
contrast of light and dark. Her gown was the color of the
night sky, her face bathed in pale moonlight. Claudia stood
so still that she might be a statue, a study of fragile, feminine
beauty.

The last two days had proved she was far from fragile.
She had displayed a streak of courage that would befit any
man. Or courage that would befit any fool. What a puzzle she
was. When he mulled over what he knew of her in a calm,
logical fashion, there was no question in his mind that she
was as devious and plotting as the rest of her family. Whenever he was anywhere near her, he started to recall little
things that didn't make sense, small pieces of the puzzle that
would never fit.

Without a doubt, part of his indecision stemmed from
the physical attraction he felt toward her. A man would have
to be dead to remain unaffected by her beauty. Yet the other
part came from her character itself. He had known plenty of
scheming women along the course of his travels, and she
displayed none of their traits, nor the traits of any treacherous
man, for that matter. She all but exuded innocence and hon-

esty, with an unexpected air of sophistication about her as well, the hard-earned knowledge that the innocent did not often fare well in the world.

"Why did you bring me to your chamber, Baron?" She spoke without looking at him, as if she had known of his presence the entire time he stared at her.

Her calm manner irritated him. Any sensible woman would be crying and near hysterics. An enterprising woman would be trying to seduce her way into his favor. This cool, collected approach was a much more effective spur to his conscience than tears or coy glances. Saint Claudia was the last woman he wanted to face right now. He had hoped for passionate, sensual Claudia, sensible Claudia, *reasonable* Claudia. He did not have the patience to deal with a saint tonight. He should have installed her in another chamber until he had managed a decent night's sleep. "I thought you might like a measure of privacy for your bath and meal. The bathhouse and great hall offer little."

Her eyes widened in surprise, then narrowed as she looked him over from head to foot. His hair was still wet from his own bath and he wore a white shirt and tan breeks that he had borrowed from Evard. "I find it hard to believe that you would give up the luxury of your chamber to a prisoner."

"You see the proof before you," he said. "And you are not exactly a prisoner here."

"Then what would you call me?"

"I called you a guest in my missive to the king." The sudden uncertainty in her eyes brought a surge of satisfaction. Two could play the role of saint. "I also asked him to give my messenger any information that might help locate your brother."

"You will help me find Dante?"

"Aye, but you need not sound so hopeful." He clasped his hands behind his back and looked beyond her through the window embrasure. Wisps of a lone cloud curled around the moon like bony fingers, a gypsy's crystal ball where he could read the future. "Mercenaries do not live long lives in the service of the king. Most are lucky to survive a year, much less four or five. There is every likelihood that my messenger will return with news of your brother's death." He waited for some reaction, anything to indicate that she understood her situation. Her silence made him feel churlish for speaking so plainly. "I do not mean to alarm you, but I think it wise to consider all possibilities. Have you given any thought to what you will do if Dante is no longer alive?"

"Dante is fine." She nodded to emphasize her opinion, but her clenched fists belied the certainty of her words. "He is a brave and valiant knight, and none can best him on the field of honor."

He was not about to point out that the king's enemies rarely showed up on the field of honor. "Your brother Roberto was also a mercenary in the service of a king, and you know his fate."

" 'Tis not the same," she insisted. "Dante is nothing like Roberto. He would never do anything so dishonorable."

"You think the king of England has fewer enemies than the Scottish king? That he sends his mercenaries on assignments any less deadly?"

"He is alive, I tell you." She gave him a regal look that would befit any queen. "He will return for me."

He could see it then, the crack of fear in her armor, and the means to open her eyes to the truth. "Are you trying to convince me, or yourself?"

Her haughty expression faltered, then she turned her head in a sharp movement to look out the window. An oppressive silence descended over the room. Even the fire ceased to crackle and the candle flames burned lower, as if caught by a sudden lack of air.

Her rigid shoulders began to relax and he sensed a change in her, as if a wall she had tried to build around her had suddenly crumbled. Her voice came to him low and soft, the solemn tone of a confession.

"Dante sent messages every few months with the merchants and minstrels that travel to Lonsdale, but last summer the messages stopped." She lifted her chin to gaze up at the moon, speaking more to herself than to Guy. "I told myself that the roads are dangerous and the routes his messengers take are uncertain at best. A lost message or two would not be uncommon. Then I thought he might be in Wales. His last message said the king had granted him the right to crenelate in Wales, that he would depart within a few months to build his fortress. No one travels between Lonsdale and Wales, and there would be none to carry his messages. I clung to that hope, even though I knew in my heart that he would not leave England without telling me. I could not bring myself to consider the possibility that he might be dead. When we were children, Dante was always there when I needed him. He promised to return for me." She looked up at him, her eyes a reflection of her pain. "I should know by now that promises are nothing but false hopes."

She fell silent, and Guy found that he had moved toward her, drawn by an almost physical need to comfort her. He stopped just a pace away, determined not to reveal any more of his weakness for her than he had already. Yet standing so close to her, it was hard to think of anything but the scent of sandalwood that his soap had left on her skin, the familiar smell that mingled with her own scent to become something new and exotic. It was as if he had left his mark on her already. His hands began to tingle, but he resisted the urge to reach for her. "What about your father's family? Is there anyone in Italy who would take you in?"

She shook her head. "My father's relatives will not welcome me. They made up many lies when my parents died so they could claim my father's wealth. We cannot return unless Dante . . ." Her voice trailed off, then she released a deep sigh. "I cannot return to Italy."

He felt a stab of guilt that she had no one to turn to, guilt because that knowledge brought with it a sense of triumph. Aside from her traitorous uncle and a brother who was probably dead, he had almost wanted to hear that there were no others who might claim her. Things between them were much simpler this way. He placed his hands on her shoulders, turning her to face him.

The thick crescents of her lashes lifted and he stared into silver-green pools that possessed their own mysterious undercurrent, a force that drew him closer even though he didn't move. He had thought all day about what he would say at this moment, the way he would say it. Now it seemed wrong. Very wrong. He forced himself to say the words anyway.

"Let me take care of you, Claudia." His fingertips traced the curve of her cheek to rest beneath her chin, an unplanned caress and an invitation. "I will give you the bride's price your uncle demanded for our false betrothal. You will never want for anything."

Her brows drew together in an uncertain frown and she took a step backward. "You need not pay me, Baron. I said that I will help free you of my uncle's claims. I do not sell the truth, but give it willingly."

The words formed a sudden image of Claudia giving herself to him just as willingly, not for coins, but because she followed the dictates of her heart. His tongue felt suddenly clumsy and he had to concentrate on what he was saying. "That is not why I would give you the coins, Claudia. 'Tis what I intended to pay for Halford Hall, but now I will seize the estate as retribution for your uncle's treachery. In the months it will take to break your uncle's claims on me, word will spread that you are here without a guardian or relative to protect your virtue. Regardless of what happens between us, you will be marked unchaste." His gaze dropped to the lush curves of her lips. "Gold might not buy happiness, but it does buy short memories. People will overlook a great deal if you have wealth of your own."

She gave a small gasp and pulled free of his grip. "You would make me your mistress?"

He couldn't deny the truth, but he sought to make it sound less harsh. "I will not make you do anything, Claudia. I will protect you while you are at Montague, no matter what happens between us."

"But you would have a great deal happen between us, is that it?" She folded her arms across her chest and glared up at him. "Only whores take gold for their favors, and I am not a whore."

"I did not say that you were." It took a considerable effort to maintain a patient, reasonable tone. He wasn't entirely successful. "We are betrothed, for God's sake. None who have a wish for a long life will dare call you a whore."

"Then what will they call me when you have our betrothal declared invalid?"

She had a point. Fortunately, she had already provided him with an answer. "You said yourself that you did not care what people thought of you. Have you changed your mind?"

Her chin rose another inch. "I care most what I think of myself, and I will not sell my soul for a bag of gold."

"Women sell themselves into marriage every day. I daresay you would accept my bargain willingly enough if I offered the gold as your dower." He clamped his mouth shut too late to stop the damning words.

"Your gold cannot buy my virtue, Baron." Her eyes narrowed. "I will not sell myself for gold, no more than I would sell myself for the title of 'wife.' "

He had expected a certain degree of reluctance, but he had also expected some amount of gratitude. Instead she scorned his generous offer, made him feel perverse for making it. His patience was at an end. "Everyone has their price, Claudia."

"You really believe that, don't you?" She sounded more amazed than offended. The look of pity in her eyes was his undoing. She thought to shame him for his belief in the truth.

"Nay, I do not believe that everyone can be bought," he said. "I know it for a fact. The day will come when you will learn that lesson as well. Being the selfish beast that I am, I would rather you learned that lesson from me rather than from some rogue who would turn you out without a pence to your name." He watched her eyes grow wider as he spoke but he couldn't seem to stop himself. "I want you to be my mistress. Is that what you want to hear? That I am guilty of lust?"

Her hands dropped to her sides, as if she just realized that she had pushed him too far. "I do not want to hear anything of the sort."

"You are just as guilty," he charged. "You would have given yourself to me willingly the morning I awoke in your chamber." She shook her head in frantic denial and backed away until the window seat stopped her retreat. He advanced on her. "You cannot deny the attraction between us, Claudia. I felt it from the moment I first laid eyes on you."

She sat down in an abrupt movement, and he dropped to one knee in front of her, as much to block any escape she might think to make as to be closer to her. He captured her hands, his grip firm yet gentle, and his voice dropped to a seductive murmur. "There is no reason to deny what we both want, no reason to deny the inevitable."

She snatched her hands away as if he had burned her. "I was drugged when they put you in my bed! I cannot be held accountable for any impressions I gave you that morning."

"And in the garden? What about the impressions you gave me then?" His hands moved to her waist, fitting them to her slender curves. "Look me in the eye and tell me that you did not enjoy being in my arms, or that my kisses repulsed you."

She bit her lower lip and looked away. Her silence was an answer in itself. He knew her price then, knew just as certainly that it was a price he would never be willing to pay. His hands dropped to the seat on either side of her. "I will not marry you, Claudia."

"I have never deceived myself into thinking you would want me for your wife."

He didn't believe her. How could she not know that marriage was his intent before her family dictated otherwise? He had all but dropped to his knees in the gardens at Lonsdale to pledge his troth. If not for her uncle's interference, he would have done just that the next time he saw her. Nay, she knew he had wanted her for his wife. Best she learn now that what she wanted could not be. He would not give her any more false hopes, but he tried to make his voice gentle. "You know that a marriage between us is impossible. I am not fool enough to put myself in thrall to your family, and mine would think me possessed if I married Roberto of Ravenna's sister. My brother would probably slit your throat the moment he laid eyes on you," he exaggerated. "Kenric is not known for his forgiving nature, and he will not believe your innocence in the plot to betray me at Lonsdale. He might accept that I have made you my mistress, but he would never accept you as my wife."

She gave him a sharp glance. "Do *you* believe in my innocence?

His heart began to beat harder. Any man in possession of his senses would believe her guilty. He sat back on his heels and raked a hand through his hair. "Aye, Claudia. I believe you are innocent, in more ways than I would like."

"What do you mean?"

"I mean that you do not seem to comprehend what can happen to women with no home or family they can claim, no money of their own, and a tarnished reputation. Your innocence will not protect you from the world, but I can." The disillusionment he saw in her eyes made him hesitate. Did she think him too noble to lay claim to her, that he would worship her from afar like some lovesick courtier? She was within his fortress, within his rights to possess with or without her permission. She would have to accept the fact that he was just noble enought to want her in his bed willingly rather than by force. Never by force.

What if marriage was the only price she would consider? He tried to push that thought aside. It was too impossible to consider, a thought fit only for a besotted fool. He made himself say the words that needed to be said, rather than words they would both regret. "I cannot give you my name, but I can give you my protection. Let me take care of you."

She bowed her head and remained silent. He listened to the sound of his breathing, slow and steady just as he forced it to be, his attention focused on the small pulse that he could see beating at her temple, the wayward curl that always escaped her braid to rest against her cheek. He wanted to see that hair unbound, to feel it brush against his skin. He wanted her not only for the pleasure she would give him in bed, but for the pleasure of knowing that he possessed something rare and exquisite, something no other man had known. Of all the bargains he had made in his lifetime, this one seemed the most important. Why didn't she answer him?

She looked up at that moment, as if she had read his mind. Her eyes sparkled like jewels, shimmering with unshed tears, but her voice betrayed none of her emotions. "Your offer is very generous, Baron, but I am afraid I cannot accept. Unless your messenger returns to Montague with news to the contrary, I must believe that my brother is alive. God willing, that will come to pass. If Dante discovered that you made me your mistress, he would probably slit *your* throat the moment he laid eyes on you." She gave him a humorless smile. "Brothers can be meddlesome, can they not?"

Guy wanted to argue the point, but couldn't think of anything that would sound reasonable.

"In the meantime," she went on, "I think it best if I earned my keep at Montague as I did at Lonsdale. I am considered an accomplished seamstress, and with all the cloth your weavers produce it seems that Montague would have more need for seamstresses than most."

He counted to himself, not daring to speak until he reached ten. "I will not make you into a servant."

"And I will not let you make me into a whore."

"Christ! I will not—" He clenched his jaw. He had offered her security for a lifetime, and she made him feel some sort of despicable monster. So he wanted to bed her. He would stake his life that she wanted him just as badly. The way she touched him, the way she had kissed him. There were times when she looked at him as if she could devour him whole.

This was not one of those times.

He stepped back to rethink his strategy. She would not listen to reason. Perhaps a different sort of persuasion was in order. He turned on his heel and paced to the bed, then sat down to remove his boots.

"W-what are you doing?" she asked.

"I have been two days without rest and I am in no mood to argue. If you wish to be a servant, then fine. Be a servant. I will not ask you to perform duties other than those you can accomplish with a needle and thread."

One boot thudded to the floor then he began to tug on the second, his attention focused on the task. Claudia glanced at the door. "I would be happy to earn my keep in such a manner, Baron. If you will tell me where I might find the servants' quarters, I will leave you to your sleep."

"You are welcome to sleep with the servants," he said, with a dismissive gesture toward the door, "however, I should warn you that gossip spreads faster than a draft in this castle. By now my people have heard the story of what happened at Lonsdale and of our journey here. If you leave this chamber, they will assume I have tired of you already, that you are free to bestow your favors upon another. After all, they will learn soon enough that I was forced into the betrothal, if they do not know already." His gaze swept over her from head to foot, insolent on purpose. "Most soldiers consider wenching a sport, you know. The more you resist, the more they will pursue you. And I am not so sure they would heed the refusal of a servant as readily as they would a lady." He gestured again toward the door. "Of course, you are free to test the truth of my words."

Claudia frowned. She hadn't considered all the implications of being labeled a servant at Montague, or anywhere else for that matter. No wonder he thought her naive. There was no help for it. He had no way of knowing that she didn't need his protection. If Dante didn't come for her, she would sell Halford to Guy herself. The gold he had offered her to be his mistress was more or less her own money already. The wretch. He didn't waste any time trying to take advantage of her circumstances. And to think she had intended to tell him the truth about Halford, that the keep would be his if he simply married her. He seemed to want Halford badly enough that he would probably do it. She would not marry him now if he begged her. All he wanted from her was a quick tumble, a meaningless affair. What a fool she had been.

Guy nodded toward the pile of pillows before the hearth. "That is probably the safest bed you will find in the castle. I have slept there myself on occasion. The rug is thick, the pillows are soft, and there are extra blankets in that chest next to you."

"You expect me to sleep *here*?"

He made a noncommittal grunt as he pulled off his shirt. "I have given you my word that I won't ask anything more of you than seamstress duties, and I promise that I will not ravish you in your sleep. Unless you doubt my word and my honor, I suggest you resign yourself to these quarters."

"But I couldn't possibly . . ." Claudia's words died on a faint whisper. She stared at his bare chest, at the light sprinkling of hair that tapered down toward his flat stomach, then disappeared beneath the waistband of his pants. Her mouth felt suddenly dry. The foreign, male contours of his chest fascinated her, stirred an irrational urge to trace the ridges and hollows with her fingertips to memorize each line.

"Ah, I almost forgot." Guy padded across the room and opened the door, treating her to a view of his back. He was sleek and masculine everywhere she looked. She found the sight no less mesmerizing than his front and had to force her gaze to the doorway. His squire sat on a pallet in the hallway, readying his own bed. Guy nodded a greeting. "Tell Roland and Herbert that they need not stand guard at my sister's old chamber tonight or any other. Lady Claudia will not be sleeping there."

"But I would prefer to sleep there!"

The boy ignored her objection and hurried to carry out the order. Guy closed the door and turned to face her. "That chamber is for guests, Claudia. Servants are not allotted private quarters, nor guards to ensure their privacy. Two soldiers earn more in one day than a seamstress earns in a week."

She pressed her lips together. If she had kept her mouth closed in the first place, she would be headed to her own quarters right now, to a real bed rather than a nest on the floor.

He pointed to the brace of candles on the table as he walked toward the bed. "Snuff those wicks before you retire for the night."

His hands went to the waistband of his pants and Claudia realized that he intended to undress in front of her. She jumped up and hurried to the table, her back toward the bed as she blew out the candles. She didn't move from her place even when the smoke from the extinguished flames burned her nostrils. Her hands gripped the edge of the table so tight that her nails would leave marks. When she heard the bed give beneath his weight and the sound of rustling covers, she released her breath in a slow sigh and opened her eyes.

The moonlight cast pale shadows in the room, while the hearth created a cozier glow near Guy's bed. She could see him clearly, his arms propped behind his head and his eyes closed. She had slept half the day in the baggage cart, yet fatigue weighted her bones like lead. He hadn't slept at all. No wonder he was so abrupt. If only she could blame his ugly offer on something so simple as a lack of sleep.

She glanced at the chest that held her bedding. Did he really expect her to get a moment's sleep in this chamber? She walked to the window seat, resigned to a long vigil.

Claudia snuggled deeper under covers that smelled of sandalwood, adrift in a warm sea of satin. Someone nudged her shoulder.

"Lady Claudia?"

The voice was no more than a whisper, but Claudia

opened her eyes. There was a face hovering just inches from her own, enormous cow-brown eyes framed by blond hair. She screamed.

Lenore scrambled backward on all fours like a startled crab. Her head banged into the bedpost and she came to an abrupt halt.

Claudia sat up and pushed her hair over one shoulder, trying to get her bearings. She couldn't recall falling asleep the night before, but felt certain she didn't leave the window seat. Guy must have carried her to the pillows and covered her with the satin quilt. That realization brought a vague sense of relief. Being a light sleeper, she would recall if he tried to ravish her. He had kept his promise.

She glanced at Lenore. The girl's eyes were wide with fear.

"Th-the baron asked me to attend you." Lenore righted herself and glanced toward the door. "I will leave if you do not wish me here."

Claudia shook her head. "Forgive me, Lenore. You startled me." She gave the maid an encouraging smile. "Why are you here?"

"I am to be your tirewoman, Lady Claudia. The baron bid me attend you."

Claudia's smile faded. "The baron did not tell me that servants were accorded servants of their own."

"Milady?"

"Never mind." Claudia lifted a stray lock of hair and blew another out of her eyes. "If you have possession of a comb, you will find me grateful." She stood up and began to right her bedding, piling the pillows into a neat row before the hearth. Lenore hurried over before she could start folding the blankets.

"Did you fall out of bed?" Lenore averted her eyes when Claudia gave her a sharp glance. "Forgive me, Lady Claudia. I did not realize he would make you sleep on the floor like a lowly squire."

"He did not make me sleep on the floor," Claudia replied, before she thought better of her answer. Why did she feel compelled to defend Guy? Lenore did not need to know anything more of her sleeping arrangements than that.

Lenore packed the blanket away, a touch of excitement in her voice. "May I have the soldiers bring your trunk in now?"

"I have no baggage," Claudia told her. She tried to brush some of the wrinkles from the blue daygown she had slept in. The linen was hopelessly wrinkled. She looked up to see a shy smile on Lenore's face.

"The gowns I told you about yesterday are altered to your size, along with chemises and other garments. The baron said to make certain you have everything you need." The girl crossed the room then opened the door to exchange a few words with someone who stood on the other side. She opened the door wider and two soldiers entered the chamber carrying a very large trunk between them. Lenore showed them where to place the trunk, then she turned to Claudia when the door closed behind the soldiers. "The seamstresses worked late into the night to make the alterations. I think you will be pleased with their efforts, my lady."

Lenore lifted the trunk's lid and inclined her head toward the opening, inviting Claudia to look inside. Claudia crossed the room in slow strides. Lenore's obvious excitement stirred a sense of dread. She did not want to be any more indebted to Guy than she was already, yet she couldn't contain her curiosity.

The first thing that caught her eye was an exquisite set of silver combs and a matching mirror. She leaned down to brush her fingers along the mirror's handle and the delicate filigree, carved to look like entwined vines that blossomed into etched roses on the back of the mirror. There were flowers and vines along the spines of the combs as well.

"They are beautiful," Claudia whispered, lifting the mirror from the trunk. She turned it over to look at her image, then frowned at what she saw there. "I wish I could say the same for my reflection."

Lenore studied her with a critical eye. "We will have you looking yourself again in no time."

"I fear that is not much of an improvement." Lenore ignored her sarcasm and helped unload the seemingly bottomless trunk to show her the treasures inside—chemises, stockings, gowns, bliauts, and even slippers—far more clothing than Claudia had left behind at Lonsdale. She stared in silence as Lenore presented one item of clothing after another.

"Where did all these clothes come from?" Claudia asked.

"From the cast-off bolts, of course." Lenore draped a deep green bliaut over the back of the trunk, then dragged out a gown the color of summer grass that would match it, holding the gown by the shoulders for Claudia's inspection. "The seamstresses used the measurements from your ruined gown to make the final alterations. The fabrics all have small flaws of some sort, but most are hardly noticeable. I hope you will not mind."

"Nay, I will not mind," she murmured.

"The baron also mentioned that you like to sew," Lenore went on. "He asked that I take you to the storerooms so you might choose a few bolts of fabric for your use, then we can visit the seamstresses to gather threads and needles. The baron said that he would very much like a new tunic or two, sewn by your hands." She looked ready to say more, but pressed her lips together instead and stared at the floor. After a silent moment she glanced toward the door, as if afraid someone might be eavesdropping, and her voice dropped to a conspiratorial whisper. "Many people are asking questions about you, my lady. Are—are the rumors true?"

Claudia shrugged. "I have not heard the rumors, so I could not say."

"One of the soldiers told me that you tried to trick the baron into marriage." Lenore's face turned a deep shade of red, but she managed to continue. "He said the baron was falsely accused of bedding you at Lonsdale Castle, that his revenge was to kidnap you and make it truth." She cast a nervous glance toward the bed. "Yesterday I thought you were here of your own free will, Lady Claudia. It is not like the baron to—to—" Lenore bit her lip and fell silent.

Claudia considered the girl with a thoughtful frown. Yesterday she had told Guy that she didn't care what his people thought of her. Now she discovered that was not true. She did care, and strangely, she cared what they thought of him. Her presence in his chamber made it pointless to proclaim her innocence, but she could put a stop to part of the rumor. "I am here of my own free will, Lenore."

The girl's face dissolved into a smile. "I told them the baron would not be so heartless."

Claudia found it grimly amusing that Lenore would rather think her a harlot than the baron a ravisher of women. "Will you show me to the storerooms, Lenore? I am looking forward to seeing more of the castle."

7

uy turned down the hallway that led to the solar, a stack of ledgers tucked under his arm. The solar was a large, airy room with a row of tall windows that faced the south wall. The windows provided plenty of light to review his accounts, a tedious task he never looked forward to, but it was an excuse to avoid his chamber and Claudia. He had never considered himself a coward, but today he had to revise his opinion. He had all but fled his chamber that morning, a coward's retreat, to be sure. He was always so sure of himself, so confident in his ability to control everything in his life. Claudia had turned it upside down.

What plagued him most was his indecision. Should he treat her as the enemy and a prisoner? An unexpected guest? A servant? What he wanted most was to treat her as his mistress. She didn't seem the least inclined to allow him that simple solution. Her own desire and the fact that everyone thought them lovers already did not sway her, nor did the promise of wealth and security for a lifetime. Then again, he obviously hadn't happened upon her price, the thing she wanted badly enough to come to him willingly. He had made it clear that marriage was not an option. What did she want from him?

He pushed open the door to the solar, lost in his thoughts until he stepped on something soft where there should be only flagstones. A length of deep green brocade lay beneath his feet.

"That will look better as a tunic than it does as a rug."

His head shot up at the sound of Claudia's voice. She was crouched down on her hands and knees over a length of white samite that she had laid on top of a Persian rug at the far end of the room, a pair of shears in her hand. The pose displayed her rounded bottom to perfection. One of the ledgers he held tumbled to the floor.

He stepped off the brocade and bent to retrieve the ledger, his gaze fixed downward as he steeled himself for another tantalizing glimpse. By the time he looked up, she had pushed herself upright to settle onto her heels. "What are you doing here, Claudia?"

"Lenore showed me the buildings where your seamstresses and tailors work. There was no room for me there, and the light is better here than in your chamber. I find it strange that you agreed Montague needed another seamstress when you have so many."

She bent over her work again and his grip tightened on the volumes he held. Her gown was the color of a fine Bordeaux wine, a heady drink that offered a pleasing bouquet and rich subtleties in its flavor, perfect for a man of discriminating tastes. What her gown contained offered the same. He could get drunk just looking at her. It took almost more effort than he possessed to tear his gaze away from temptation.

He walked to the long table that sat beneath one of the windows and placed the ledgers there. "You wished to earn your keep, and I would value a tunic sewn by your hands." His words sounded harsher than he had intended and he tried to soften them. "You may also sew gowns for yourself, if you wish."

She shot him an inscrutable look over one shoulder. "As of this morning, I have more gowns than I ever owned at Lonsdale. I have no need for more, Baron."

Was she displeased by his generosity? Aye, another tactical error on his part. So much for plying her with gifts.

"As you wish," he murmured. Retreat seemed the wisest course for the moment. He pulled a stool up to the table and opened the first leather-bound volume.

Soon all the ledgers were open and the top of the oak table disappeared beneath a sea of parchment. His quill scratched a steady rhythm across one of the pages, his large hand as adept at wielding a pen as it was with a sword. Then Claudia began to hum. She probably wasn't aware of what she was doing, but her deep, sultry voice reached across the room like an invisible caress. He recognized the song, a favorite among the gondoliers in Venice. It brought to mind moonlit nights under a warm Italian sky.

He could well imagine himself in a gondola on such a night, reclined against the plush seats with Claudia in his arms. The long lists of numbers turned into dark canals sprinkled with stars. He could almost hear the water lapping around them, the gentle rocking motion of the boat, the scent of roses when she leaned closer to give him a taste of her lips. He closed his eyes and the image became clearer, the imagined caresses more potent.

The song came to an end and his eyes drifted open. The tip of his quill rested against an open page, the white goose feather seeming to point to the middle of a small, black sea of ink. He lay the quill aside with a curse and reached for the blotter, knowing the damage was irreparable.

"Ah, what a pity." The soft words spoken so near his ear made him nearly leap from his seat. Claudia laid one hand on his shoulder as if to calm him. "I did not mean to startle you, Baron. I only wondered what makes you scowl so much. You have frowned at these books since you opened them."

He glanced over his shoulder and quickly turned back to the ledgers. She couldn't know that her breasts were in the most direct line of his vision. He felt like a deviant for noticing. His fingers felt suddenly damp and he glanced down. The ink had soaked through the blotter cloth. He wiped the ink from his fingers as best he could and tossed the cloth aside. "Do you read?"

"Aye, but I did not mean to spy."

"There are no great secrets here," he assured her. "Only puzzles."

"Puzzles?"

He swept his hand toward the stacks of ledgers. "Great

twisted puzzles within puzzles. These are the records of all sales and trades made by my agents over the last three months. 'Tis the story of each bolt of fabric that left Montague during that time."

She leaned closer and he felt her breath caress his cheek. "Will you tell me one of these stories?"

At that moment he would have told her anything she wanted to hear. He gritted his teeth to prevent just that. Instead he turned to the first page of the ledger in front of him. Perhaps she would grow bored with the details of his business and leave him alone. If nothing else, the dizzying array of facts and figures was sure to confuse her. Then she would leave him in peace.

" 'Tis only one story, really, made up of many parts. In April I struck a bargain with one Baldassare of Venice to trade a shipment of brocades for three hundred gold florins, one hundred eighty bolts of lace, fifty kegs of glass beads, and two stones of ground saffron."

He flipped through the pages of another ledger to its beginning. "Here one of my agents traded five kegs of the glass beads to a Norse merchant for three score pelts of ermine. A score of the pelts were traded to Alfred of London for twenty gold florins, and the remainder to a nobleman in Burgundy for five hogsheads of wine. The wine was sold to the earl of Marly for sixty-three florins." He glanced over his shoulder to gauge her reaction, but he couldn't tell if her expression of interest was feigned or genuine. He couldn't seem to look away from her. "That was a fairly uncomplicated trade. Others involve goods traded from this shipment along with previous shipments of cloth. Those trades are harder to trace, but I assign portions of the value of each trade so I will know the final price of every bolt of fabric in gold florins."

She rested one hand against the edge of the table to take a closer look at the ledgers. "Why?"

"For many reasons. My clerks keep accounts of all coins spent and I make sure the balance reported by my treasury clerk agrees with the amount my agents report. All know that

I balance the accounts myself, and that tends to keep honest men honest." Rather than continue to stare at her profile, he pretended an interest in a spot of ink on one of his fingertips and rubbed it against his thumb. "The profit of each trade also helps me decide if I want more or less of the goods involved in a future bargain."

She reached over his shoulder and tapped an entry with one slender finger. "You gained twenty-three more florins from the sale of the ermine pelts that you traded for wine than you did from the ermine pelts alone. Does that mean you will increase your trade with the nobleman in Burgundy?"

He glanced down at the ledger, startled to realize she had calculated the amount correctly. "Perhaps, but I must also consider the cost of each trade. Pelts require much less effort to transport than hogsheads of wine, yet if a ship is nearly empty on its return voyage from Italy, that would make a profitable cargo."

"I see." She looked distracted by something she saw in one of the ledgers. She pointed toward the page of a ledger that sat farthest away from her and he felt the soft swell of her breast brush against his shoulder. The heat of her penetrated his shirt to warm his own body, and he reacted instantly to that innocent touch. He released a silent breath and tried to concentrate on her words rather than her tempting nearness.

"That entry should be thirty-two bolts of lace rather than twenty-three, else the sum will not total one hundred and eighty." She gave him a sharp glance, then her gaze became evasive, as if he had caught her doing something she shouldn't. "I could be wrong, of course."

He scanned all six of his agents' ledgers and picked up his quill to write down each reference to the bolts of lace. There were seventeen references in all, and the sum was nine bolts short of what it should be. He turned to look up at her. "You calculated this in your head?"

She gave him an uncertain nod.

"How did you know that this was the entry in error?"

"You will think me strange if I tell you."

"Humor me."

" 'Tis the only unequal trade." She gave him a wary glance, then pointed at the first ledger. "Here twelve bolts were involved in three trades that totaled sixteen florins. In this trade, forty-two bolts resulted in a profit of fifty-eight florins." She continued to rattle off the final profit of the other bolts. When her finger moved to the reference in question, a small, triumphant smile curved her lips. "This one is wrong because the value of these bolts is listed as thirty-one florins. When you average the profit of the other bolts, that is almost the exact value of thirty-two bolts, not twenty-three."

"My God." And he had thought to confuse her? He couldn't believe what he was hearing. "You calculated the *average* price of each bolt in your head?"

She nodded. "You should expect a profit of four florins for every three bolts of lace."

She was right. He had already added the amounts in his ledger, but the book was turned now to a different page. He decided to test her. "What is the profit for all one hundred and eighty bolts?"

"Two hundred and forty florins, more or less."

"If I received five florins for every three bolts rather than four, what would my profit be?"

"Three hundred florins, of course."

He leaned back in his chair and tossed his quill aside. "Of course."

"I knew I should not have told you." She released a small sigh. "You think me strange."

"I think you amazing. Who taught you mathematics?"

"My father said I had a natural talent with numbers." She sounded defensive. "The tutors he hired for my brothers taught me as well."

"I take it you excelled." He studied the play of emotions that crossed her face while he waited for her answer. She was good at hiding her thoughts, but he had learned to read closed faces long ago. Right now she was thinking that she had told him too much already and wondered how he would use that knowledge against her. He wondered what her life was like at Lonsdale to make her fearful of revealing something so harmless.

"Aye."

He drummed his fingers along the table top, then stood up. "Have a seat."

Her eyes reflected confusion. "Why?"

"You were right when you said I do not need another seamstress." He gestured toward the chair. "If you truly wish to earn your keep at Montague, I would rather you ply a quill than a needle."

"You want me to be a clerk?" She sounded appalled by the prospect.

"You find a clerk's position more objectionable than that of a seamstress?"

"Nay, 'tis not that. I would enjoy such duties, but women are not allowed to act as clerks."

"But you are not just any woman, Claudia. At the moment you are my betrothed." He shrugged her concern aside. "No one will object."

"Not even you?" She arched one brow. "If honesty is the reason you balance your own ledgers, then why would you trust me with the task?"

"You have no reason to cheat me." He pulled up a stool and sat down beside her, then reached across the table for a ledger. "Come. We will work together so none can accuse me of shirking my duty. The ledger in front of you is mine, the others belong to each of my agents. I will locate the trades while you record them in my ledger. Does that seem a reasonable plan of attack?"

She smiled and picked up the quill. "Aye, Baron. Very reasonable."

Three hours later Claudia was still smiling, even as she shook her head. "Nay, Baron. You are being unreasonable."

Guy's scowl would befit any five-year-old denied a sweet.

"There is nothing wrong with allowing a ship to return empty upon occasion. I need not show a profit on every venture."

"Yet you never show a profit on your Flemish journeys," she pointed out. " 'Tis odd that you continue such worthless voyages. You will not take any of their bolts in trade, which means you would rather show a loss than return to England with a profitable cargo of Flemish silks and brocades. That does not strike you as being a bit unreasonable?"

"Nay," he insisted. "You do not know these Flemish merchants. They are quick to buy the exotic goods we carry from Venice and the southern ports, knowing they are goods we gained by trading Montague bolts. Yet they must always point out that were it not for the Flemish weavers I employ, my people could not produce such fine cloths. They constantly rub my nose in the fact that we do not have nine hundred generations of weavers in residence, that we are little more than upstarts. It pleases me to take their gold, but I would not carry a bolt of their cloths in a ship of mine if they paid me to do so."

"Nine hundred?" She knew it an exaggeration, but couldn't resist baiting him. All afternoon he had displayed a shrewd head for the staggering array of facts and figures related to his business, yet he grew sullen and terse whenever the trades involved Flemish merchants. It was telling that he referred to his people as 'we,' including himself in their number. She suspected he would not be half so insulted if the Flemish jibes did not involve those sworn to him. And that made him a rarity among noblemen, a lord who offered more than his sword in his pledge to protect his villeins. He considered them worthy enough to defend their reputations. "The Flemish give you half the gold you would receive if you traded for bolts of their fabrics instead, then sold the Flemish cloths in England."

"Do you presume to tell me how to manage my affairs?" He folded his arms across his chest, his blue eyes lit with challenge.

She inclined her head in gesture of subservience, made

mocking by her smile. "Nay, Baron. I presume to tell you when you are being pigheaded. Your agents are paid by commission and you would punish them because you dislike Flemish merchants. That is unfair."

His hand made a rasping sound as he rubbed his chin. The shadowy stubble on his face emphasized the lines there, the creases in his cheeks when he scowled. "They do not complain."

"Nor would I, if I thought you might turn me out if I did."

The corners of his mouth curved into a lazy smile. "So my agents think me a tyrant, but you know better, that I would not turn anyone out for such a minor offense?"

She shrugged her shoulders. "It would seem that way. I have just complained."

"It may surprise you to learn that my agents have good reason to fear my ire." He said nothing more to enlighten her on the matter, but instead looked toward one of the windows. "The hour grows late. Will you join me for evening meal?"

"Join you?" she repeated dumbly. No one had ever asked her to join them at a meal. She wasn't certain what the invitation implied.

"Aye. Join me. I would have you sit by my side."

She didn't know how to respond. He wanted her to sit at the head table where all would see her, where all would know that he truly considered her a guest. "Why are you being so nice to me, Baron? I thought we agreed that I would be nothing more than a servant at Montague, yet you provide me with a new wardrobe, a servant of my own, duties I enjoy, a place of honor at your table." She gave him a wary look. "Why?"

He placed a hand over his heart, as if offended by her suspicions. "Do I need a reason to be nice to you?"

"Most people have a reason whenever they are nice to me," she countered. Last night she had feared he would try to seduce her into his bed. Today he behaved as though the thought would never occur to him. He was all courtesy and smiles. It was worse than a seduction. Their easy camaraderie the last few hours had relaxed her guard. Now it made her nervous. The attraction she felt for him could too easily become a complicated friendship. She would rather dislike him. "If I join you for dinner, will you allow me to sleep in a different chamber tonight?"

"Ah, a bargain," he mused. "So you have your own reasons for being nice to me. Would that be why you suspect *my* motives?"

"The thought just occurred to me," she said. He had some devious reason for conferring such a sign of favor. She just couldn't perceive it when he was being so charming. "I will join you at dinner tonight without condition, if you place no conditions on my presence there."

"You have a suspicious mind, Lady Claudia." He studied her for a moment in silence, then nodded. "Very well. Without condition. You have my word."

Guy propped his arm on the back of Claudia's chair and leaned over to whisper in her ear. "I swear to you, this is not what I intended."

"Is it not?" Claudia's smile felt brittle. This was exactly what he had intended when he invited her to the evening meal, she was sure. She forced herself not to lean away from him, to keep herself from showing a reaction to anything that happened around her.

The great hall swelled with the sounds of the meal, laughter and conversations, minstrels and singers, the occasional yelp of a hound that strayed too close to the tables in its quest for scraps and got a smack for its efforts. The food smelled delicious. Servants and squires served a staggering variety of meats, fruits, and sauces flavored with costly spices. Claudia wouldn't mind if the entire meal consisted of plain porridge. She remembered to take a bite of food now and then, but she could taste none of it.

If there were any questions that remained about her virtue, this meal put them to rest. Guy displayed her before his people like a prize, her place in the seat his wife should occupy nothing more than a cruel parody. Everyone within the hall recognized the gibe. It wasn't how often Guy's people stared at her that bothered Claudia. It was the way they looked at her. The men stared long and hard, some curious, others lewd and leering. The women pretended to ignore her and looked away whenever she caught them staring at her.

The people of Lonsdale had scorned her when she first arrived in England, treated her to ogling of a different sort, yet in many ways the same. She had learned to ignore them, to retreat inside herself without displaying any outward signs of cowardice. She didn't belong at Lonsdale, no more than she belonged at Montague. Everything these people took for granted—friends and family, a home and security—were as foreign to Claudia as their language. She could learn to survive among them, but she would never truly fit in. Rather than bow her head to shield herself from the rude stares, she lifted her chin and gazed out over the room.

First she chose the color blue, the color of Montague. She began by counting every occurrence of the color in the great hall, making a mental tally of where she spied the color, in a jewel, gown, cap, pennant, painted arch. Perhaps she should divide her count into—

"Are you listening to me, Claudia?"

She turned in Guy's direction. "Twenty-three?"

A blush warmed her cheeks and she bit her tongue. No wonder he looked confused. Her count of blue tunics was not the answer he wanted. What had he asked her? "Forgive me, Baron. Did you ask a question?"

"Aye." He gave an impatient sigh. "You have just answered it. As a rule, I prefer to speak to someone other than myself."

Her gaze slid back to a tall man with a blue feather in his cap. "I did not mean to ignore you, my lord."

"You are ignoring me now." He found her hand beneath the table and gave it a firm squeeze. "What are you doing, Claudia?"

The touch of his hand surprised her and she gave him a startled glance. "I beg your pardon?"

"What are you doing?" he repeated. "You answer my questions with numbers, and I have watched the king look upon swineherds with more warmth than the looks you give my people."

"I would rather have them think me aloof than know how—" She pressed her lips together.

His scowl deepened. "We could have our meal in the solar or my chamber if you would prefer."

"And undo your efforts to display me as your mistress?" She smiled and shook her head. "After your many kindnesses, I would not wish to appear so inhospitable."

"I did not invite you to my table to put you on display. You would sit by my side tonight if you were my betrothed in truth."

She lifted her wine goblet and took a delicate sip when she would rather consume every drop in one swallow. Numbing herself with wine would accomplish nothing except to make herself look more the fool. Still, that small taste of fine burgundy seemed to loosen her tongue. "I know as well as they do that I am the last woman you would marry. Just as they know that I share your chamber willingly, if Lenore is the gossip I suspect. This morning I put to rest a rather disturbing rumor that you forced me to share your bed as revenge for my part in your betrayal at Lonsdale." Her smile turned sickly sweet. "I would not want your servants to think badly of you, or see your reputation suffer because of me."

Guy stood abruptly, an intense blue fire in his eyes as he gazed down at her. The hall grew quiet.

"What are you doing?" she whispered.

He didn't answer. Instead he looked out over the hall and held up his goblet. "I would have you raise your drinks and your voices in a toast." He turned to Claudia. "To Lady Claudia, who risked her life at Lonsdale Castle to save mine."

Her name echoed from the lips of everyone gathered in

the great hall. Claudia couldn't have been more stunned if Guy had slapped her. "Why did you do that?"

He took a drink of his wine, then lifted her hand to press a chaste kiss against her cold fingers. His eyes didn't leave her. "I would not have my people think badly of you, or see your reputation suffer because of me." He sat down again, his expression solemn. "In truth, I simply told them to treat you with respect, or they will answer to me."

"I did not hear you say that."

"What is said and what is heard are often two different things." He watched her closely, as if searching for something in her face. "I would not have you hide in the shadows at Montague as you did at Lonsdale. You will find friends among my people if you give them a chance to know you."

She turned her attention to her meal and reached for a bowl of mint sauce, then slathered the green goo on a slice of mutton. "I am not very good at making friends. Indeed, I have made no friends since I left Italy. Most English think me odd because I do not speak as they do. They have trouble understanding what I say."

"I can understand you just fine." He motioned his squire, Stephen, forward and helped himself to the platter of roast beef the boy carried. "I told you it would help to speak our language more often. And my people are more accustomed to foreigners in their midst than those at Lonsdale. You will not be ostracized because you are not English."

"Perhaps." She wondered what it would be like to have friends again. Not that she intended to make any at Montague. That would only make leaving more difficult. Life was much simpler without entanglements. Uncle Laurence had done her a favor by making certain she had no friends at Lonsdale, no one she would miss when she left, no possessions of any account to regret leaving behind, not even a pet. Her departure from Montague would be the same. No friends to miss, and no regrets.

She looked at Guy and knew that was a lie. What had

filled her thoughts before he came into her life? What had she seen when she closed her eyes?

She couldn't recall. He rode into her life and it would never be the same. Even this night would become a memory, the look in his eyes when he toasted her, the sound of his deep voice, the way he smiled at her. Small memories to tuck away like keepsakes. But would they be memories of a happier time, or reminders she would rather forget?

The signs did not bode well that these would be happy times at Montague. They would mark a change in her life, of that she had no doubt. Was it too much to hope that a change in her life might just once be for the better? Guy's offer came to mind once more, and she knew the answer to her question. His money would not buy her happiness, no more than selling herself to him would buy his affections.

She glanced out over the great hall again, taking in all the obvious marks of his wealth and power. For a man of the world, he could be remarkably unenlightened at times. Why couldn't he understand that her refusal had nothing to do with the gifts he offered or the price he would pay? It was the price he demanded that would always make her turn away when she wanted nothing more than to feel his arms around her, to experience the breathtaking magic of his kisses. She would lose a piece of her heart when he tired of her. She had precious little of it left to lose.

Everyone has a price, Claudia.

Those words would echo in her mind forever. He was wrong about that. It was the price he demanded that was too high. Guy would pay for his pleasure with gold. She would pay for hers with her soul.

A murmur went through the crowd, and Claudia's gaze went to the double archway where a richly dressed knight entered the great hall, his black cloak pushed over one of his broad shoulders to reveal a matching black tunic and hose, and a pair of tall boots that ended midthigh. He was armed to the teeth. One hand rested on the hilt of his sword to keep the sheathed tip from striking the floor as he strode forward. He wore not one but two deadly misericords on the right side of his sword belt, with another, shorter dagger at his waist. His long strides revealed the hilt of a fifth weapon strapped to his thigh, almost hidden by his boots. This was a man who expected to find trouble.

He drew to a halt before Guy and gave his lord a low bow. When he straightened, Claudia glanced at his face, to take in more than the vague impression of brown hair and dark eyes. Her mouth dropped open. "Friar Thomas."

"Lady Claudia." Thomas smiled and gave her a look bolder than any she recalled from Lonsdale, the look of a man who might be trying to decide what she wore beneath her gown rather than the darting glances of a pious friar.

She was too startled to take offense. Other than the color of his hair and the shape of his eyes, it was hard to believe that this man and Friar Thomas were one and the same. The robes had made the friar look lanky and awkward. She glanced once more at his build and saw no trace of awkwardness, only the long, lithe body of a man who knew how to use the weapons he wore so casually. Even his face looked different, his plain features made more handsome by an air of self-confidence and a wolfish grin.

She looked at Guy and found him watching her already, a dark look in his eye. "There are things I must discuss with Thomas. I will have Evard escort you to my chamber."

"But—"

"I will likely retire late tonight," he interrupted. "Do not wait up for me."

He turned to Evard, who sat at his left, and gave him instructions to escort Claudia to his chamber, then to post a guard outside his door. Claudia wondered if the guard was to keep others out or to keep her within. None would be foolish enough to enter their lord's chamber without permission, so that answer seemed obvious. She lifted her chin and bid him good night with a stiff nod.

Guy watched Claudia leave the hall, certain she was offended by his abrupt dismissal. He didn't care. He wanted to hear Thomas's report before she did, to decide what he would tell her of the events that had taken place at Lonsdale after their escape. He was annoyed by the appreciative glances she gave his knight. His gaze moved to Thomas, more annoyed to see the knight watching her departure as well.

"Have a seat, Thomas." He gestured toward Claudia's empty chair, then took a long drink of wine while he waited for Thomas to make his way around the table.

"'Tis good to be home again, my lord." Thomas sat down and motioned a servant forward to bring him a trencher of food. "I am famished. My squire and I rode hard from Lonsdale and stopped just long enough to water the horses." He reached across the table to pull several platters of meat closer to his trencher.

"I would hear word of the situation at Lonsdale before you fill your mouth with food."

The cold tone of Guy's voice made Thomas set his knife aside. He gave his trencher a wistful glance, then turned his attention to Guy. "You are about to be married, my lord."

8

Claudia was asleep when Guy returned to his chamber late that night. He had told her not to wait up for him, but he felt a stab of disappointment anyway. She lay amidst the pillows in front of the fireplace, wearing the same dark blue gown she had slept in the night before. The light from the fire cast a reddish sheen to her unbound hair, a tempting sight that drew him forward. Her skin reflected the golden colors of the flames, one hand tucked beneath her cheek, while the other rested upon a length of emerald-green brocade, a silver needle still held in her outstretched hand.

She had tried to wait up for him. He smiled and unstrapped his sword belt to place it next to the bed, then he knelt beside her.

She was no less beautiful asleep than awake. Last night he had spent hours staring at her, so tired that his eyes were nearly crossed, yet not so tired that he could deny them such a pleasing sight. For some reason he hadn't noticed until now how long her lashes were, that they nearly grazed her cheeks. His hand hovered next to her face before he realized he had reached out to touch her. He hesitated.

He had the right to touch her. Thomas confirmed that the Church had indeed given its blessings to their union through the dubious actions of Bishop Germaine. They were betrothed, yet that was not enough. Not for Claudia, anyway. Not when she knew he intended to break the betrothal. Rather than brush his fingertips along her cheek, he reached down to take the needle from her limp grasp, smoothing his fingertips along the lines of her hand, then turning it over to trace the small callouses on her palm. It was not the hand of a helpless lady who expected to be waited upon by others, but one that could scale a castle wall when the occasion warranted. Or wield a quill with more skill than most of the clerks in his hire, or sew a tunic for a man who forced her to sleep before his hearth like a common hound. Little wonder she rarely smiled.

He wanted nothing more than to cherish her, to shower her with gifts that would make her happy. She had but to open her arms to him and he would make her one of the richest women in England. She had frowned over his gifts, and smiled most when he insisted she help balance his ledgers. Most galling of all, she seemed more inclined to be a pauper. His generous offer had offended her.

He might admire her determination to guard her virtue if he didn't know the fate she faced without wealth of her own. And more to the point, if he didn't ache each time he looked at her. She didn't want his gifts, she didn't want his gold, and she knew they could not marry.

Yet there were times when he caught her staring at him with such blatant longing that his bones felt as if they were melting. Those looks revealed far more of her thoughts than she knew, and far too much of her character for his peace of mind. A passionate virgin. That was just what he needed in his chamber each night.

He settled back on his heels and rubbed his chin. There was no doubt in his mind that marriage was her price. Was that really so impossible? Thomas had told him enough of what had happened after they left Lonsdale that he was convinced of Claudia's innocence. If she were truly as innocent as she seemed, was it fair to hold her responsible for the actions of her uncle and brothers?

His family would hate her, but they did not have to live with her. They might accept her in time. Not that it mattered if they never accepted her. His marriage was his own affair. Only the king could object to his choice of brides, and with the Church all but forcing the issue, an objection from that corner seemed unlikely.

That left only the dower. It would be a cold day before he paid her uncle one florin to marry Claudia. He didn't relish the thought of paying the brother, either, if Dante turned up alive, for he was surely cut from the same cloth as Roberto. That problem would take a little more time to work out.

He stood up and walked to his bed, feeling half dazed. The notion of making Claudia his wife was not nearly as appalling as he thought it would be. The thought was not the least bit appalling. It made perfect sense. He did not need a marriage made to forge a political alliance, nor the lands and coins of a bride's dowry. He needed heirs. He pictured a child with bright green eyes, then rolled his own.

This obsession with Claudia needed to come to an end. Why couldn't she be sensible and just agree to be his mistress? That was the easiest course for them both. No ties, no commitments. When they tired of each other, they could simply go their separate ways.

He climbed into bed and turned onto his side, his gaze drawn to her once more. Her face was turned away from him, but he studied the pattern of waves in her hair, how the firelight caught each swirl in a perfect, seemingly endless sea of mahogany. Most women wore their hair braided at night, but not Claudia, much to his delight and dismay. Right now he would like nothing more than to run his fingers through those silken tresses, to wrap his hands in it until they were bound together by her hair.

He closed his eyes in an attempt to banish the image, but that only brought more vivid images to life. How many more restless nights would he be forced to endure? She had slept untroubled and untouched for two nights in his chamber. Already it seemed like two hundred. Soon he would be willing to promise her anything to have her in his bed, not for just one or two nights, but for the two hundred he had already imagined.

He rolled onto his back and frowned at the ceiling. It seemed unlikely that he would tire of her that soon. He might not ever tire of her.

That was a foolish thought. Of course he would tire of her. No woman could hold his interest or attention for more than a few fortnights.

His eyes drifted shut and he began to dream of green-eyed babies.

Claudia dreamed of rats.

She was on the ship that had brought her to England, a barque that carried wines and spices and as many passengers as the captain could cram into the crowded cargo holds. And rats. A great many of them. Roberto and Dante slept on either side of Claudia to protect her from the creatures that came out at night. Not the ones that crawled, but the ones that walked upright. It was impossible to protect anyone from the rats.

The rats were everywhere, scurrying about in the open as if they owned the ship, crawling over and around anything in their way, occasionally sinking their sharp teeth into an exposed hand or ankle. She had felt the shiver of small clawed feet scamper over her blankets each night, but she could never grow accustomed to the rodents' presence as the others seemed to. She hated that ship. She hated the rats even more.

In her dream she heard the disgusting noises they made, smelled their dank, musky scent that had fouled the cargo holds, and felt the quicksilver weight of the rodents dart over her legs. She even fancied that she felt one tugging at her hair. It was just a dream, of course. Somehow she was conscious enough to know that she was in Guy's chamber, that the ship's rats couldn't possibly be here. If she could just wake up a little more, the rats would go away.

She opened her eyes and breathed a sigh of relief when she saw the faint outline of the hearth in Guy's chamber. Half-waking dreams were the worst kind, for they tended to mix fantasy with reality. Even knowing she was in Guy's chamber, the presence of the phantom rats seemed to linger. She could almost smell the horrid beasts. Then she felt something tug at her hair, a very real tug that had nothing to do with her dream. At the same moment, she saw the silhouette of a rat against the dying embers of the fire as it scurried across the hearth.

Guy bolted upright at the sound of Claudia's scream and grabbed his sword. His gaze searched the shadowy lumps of pillows before the fireplace, but the shrieks seemed to come from different parts of the darkened room. Then he heard the ropes creak beneath the mattress as she leaped onto his bed.

"Santo cielo! Via! Vattene!"

The shrieks that followed made it nearly impossible for Guy to listen for sounds of an intruder. He moved closer to Claudia's vague figure but kept his back to her, to protect her from the unseen threat. His sleep-dulled senses struggled to find the words to ask her what was wrong. "Ma che ti prende?"

His squire burst into the room before Claudia could answer. Not that she seemed inclined to do anything but shriek.

At least Stephen proved more helpful. He carried a sword in one hand, a rush torch held high in the other. Guy scanned the corners of the room and found it empty.

"Grazie a Dio! Toglieti dai piedi!" Claudia looked as if she had gone mad. She clung to his bedpost with one hand and shook her long hair with the other, all the while performing some wild dance on his mattress. "Ho un topo nei capelli!"

He caught a glimpse of frantic green eyes through the mahogany cloud of her hair before she gave the heavy mass another vigorous shake.

"Un topo! Oddio un topo!"

"A rat?" He felt a grin curve his lips until she let out another wail.

"Toglimelo dai capelli!"

He dropped his sword and knelt next to her on the bed, pulling her down in front of him. He had always wanted to bury his hands in her hair, but not to search for a rat. Or a mouse. Or whatever she felt was tangled in the silky tresses. She calmed down the moment he touched her, held herself still and silent while he ran his hands over her head, then he gathered her hair at the nape to sift his fingers through its entire, amazing length. He repeated the process, not to search for a nonexistent rodent, but because he couldn't seem to help himself. It was like holding a river of satin. He felt her shiver and only then remembered to reassure her.

"There is not a rat in your hair, sweetheart." He motioned to his squire. "Light the brace of candles, then you may leave us, Stephen."

"Aye, my lord."

Guy continued to stroke her hair while Stephen carried out his order. It seemed to calm her. It didn't calm him one bit. His heart began to beat harder, and each breath felt more labored than the last. Stephen left and he couldn't stop touching her, couldn't stop combing his fingers through warm silk.

"Did you find anything?" she asked.

"Hold still," he murmured. Her hips shifted once more between his knees and he scowled at his hands, glad she could not see them tremble. He continued to work at her hair, gently untangling it, secretly trailing the ends over his bare legs.

He was sick. He had stooped to sneaking his pleasure from her. What torture would he dream up next? A horsehair shirt? Nay, that would be a minor discomfort compared to the brush of her hair against his skin. It would have to be something more drastic to surpass this torture. The rack, perhaps. He looked down at his hands, startled to realize they had turned to fists in her hair. He made a conscious effort to unclench his fingers.

"I swear I saw rats in this chamber." She looked over her shoulder, her face flushed from embarrassment, or her earlier exertions, or perhaps both. He felt a guilty rush of excitement as he watched the enticing rise and fall of her breasts beneath her blue gown. "I saw one on the hearth, and felt another in my hair. The nasty beast was trying to make a nest there. And I am sure I felt a third run across my legs."

She shuddered, and it seemed the most natural thing in the world to pull her onto his lap and into his arms.

Claudia had other ideas. She braced both hands against his chest and tried to scoot away. "Per l'amor del cielo!" Her eyes widened to the size of saucers. "You are naked!"

"I am not naked." He tightened his grip on her waist, although there was no need to restrain her. She sat as still as a statue.

"You look naked to me," she insisted.

He was not about to stand up to let her examine the loincloth he wore. At the moment, that would probably alarm her more than thinking him naked. "You have nothing to fear from me, Claudia. You are frightened and I would comfort you, if you let me. Nothing more."

Where did that promise come from? He was beyond sick. This bordered on insane. He took several deep breaths and wondered if she had any idea how tightly he held himself in check, how his control could slip through his fingers as easily as her silky hair.

She gave him a wary look. "I do not need comforting, Baron. Those loathsome rats simply startled me. I am not afraid of them."

He found himself smiling at the blatant lie. "Truly? Then is it some sort of Italian ritual to dance around a bedpost and toss one's hair about when one sees a rat?" He rubbed his chin, his tone thoughtful. "I suppose that would scare off any rat."

Her eyes narrowed. "Perhaps I was a little disturbed at the thought of a filthy rat tangled in my hair. Anyone would be startled after waking up from a sound sleep to find rats crawling all over them." She nodded, as if to confirm her opinion. "Aye, I was startled. Your home is so fine that I did not expect it to be infested with rodents. Now that I think upon the matter, I do not remember seeing any cats inside the keep. 'Tis little wonder rats roam so freely. I will visit the dairy barns tomorrow to find a nice tabby for your chamber, and these rats will be—"

"Nay."

"—gone within a day or two." Her brows drew together into a puzzled frown. "Even if it does not actually catch anything, rats will not stay where—"

"No cats. I cannot abide the creatures."

"Surely a cat is more tolerable than filthy rodents. Cats are clean and quiet, and they—"

"I said, no cats. They are sneaky, conniving creatures found most often in the company of witches." One dark brow rose. "You are not a witch, are you?"

"A witch! How could you—" She studied his face for a long moment. "You are afraid of cats?"

"I am not afraid of any scrawny feline."

"Aye, you are afraid of cats," she insisted. "Why else would you live with rats?"

Guy glared down at her. "I do not live with rats. I tolerate them. If you must know the truth, cats make me ill."

"I see."

"'Tis truth. They make me sneeze. My eyes itch and water, then they swell to the size of eggs."

Claudia burst out laughing. His indignant expression made her cover her mouth to muffle her laughter, but that didn't seem to appease him. "I am sorry, my lord. 'Tis just the thought of eggs where your eyes should be . . ." She started to giggle.

Guy's scowl faded into a sheepish grin. "You will not repeat that to anyone. I would not have my men know that I could be brought low by something so insignificant as a common cat."

"My lips are sealed, Baron."

She drew a line across her lips, and his gaze followed the path of her finger. He stared at her mouth, a dark look in his eyes. "Aye, they are."

He wanted to kiss her. The knowledge sent a sharp stab of heat through her. She wanted him to kiss her, to feel the same delicious rush of excitement she had felt in the gardens at Lonsdale when he held her in his arms and caressed her mouth more than kissed it. But he hadn't been naked then, nor in his bed. He began to lower his head.

"What news did Thomas bring?"

He hesitated, his brows drawn together as if he needed a moment to comprehend her question. "No news I did not expect. We are betrothed."

His mouth moved closer to hers. She grasped for some subject that would distract him, her own thoughts muddled by his obvious intention. "I, ah—ahem. That is to say—" His warm breath felt like a caress against her face. In another instant, he would be kissing her. "Sewing. Yes, that's it. Did I show you the fabric I chose to make your tunic? I will need to measure you to make sure it fits." His hands tightened on her waist. He didn't look the least distracted. "I-I also removed the necklace that I sewed into my cloak. Will it be safe in my clothes trunk, or do you have a strongbox where I could place it for safekeeping?"

"The necklace will be safe in your trunk."

"Would you like to see it?"

He shook his head.

"You wanted to see it when we stopped in the forest. Now you may." She gestured toward her trunk. " 'Tis right there. Perhaps you could tell me its worth in florins so I could begin to make plans for the day I leave Montague. I have no notion of its value, but my brothers gave me the impression that the necklace would allow me to live in some measure of comfort if they could not see to my needs. Surely it should fetch enough to see me settled in modest lodgings in London, if I manage to journey there with less than an army. And yesterday I noticed that your agents trade jewels on occasion. 'Tis likely they could strike a better bargain with a buyer than I. Do you think one would accept my necklace on commission?"

Guy released a long sigh and his hands fell to his sides. "Fine. I will look at your necklace, but I can only guess at its worth. The price of anything depends on how badly the buyer wishes to possess it."

She wondered if there was a double meaning somewhere in that statement, but she didn't take time to reason it out. She scrambled off Guy's lap and went to her trunk to fetch the necklace. While she dug through the layers of clothing, she took deep breaths to calm her racing heart. That was a close call. Another moment on his lap and she would have kissed him, regardless of his wishes in the matter. Not that he looked ready to object. She would wager every emerald in her necklace that he wouldn't make any objection at all. The wretch.

Nay, she was the wretched one, she decided. At least Guy was honest about what he wanted. She couldn't bring herself to admit that it was cowardice that kept her from his arms, the sure knowledge that he would someday abandon her.

"Well?"

She gave a guilty start. Her hand closed around the necklace and she pulled it from the trunk. Holding it carefully in both hands, she turned to face him, then released a sigh of relief. He had donned a pair of breeks while she searched for the necklace. That did nothing to diminish the impression his bare chest made on her senses, but the breeks helped. She did not think she could manage anything that remotely resembled a conversation if she had turned around to find him still naked. He was seated on the edge of the bed, and her gaze followed the line of corded muscles in his neck, then moved lower to study his broad shoulders. Her voice sounded distracted. "Here it is. I could not remember which corner I placed it in."

Guy stared at the necklace a long, silent moment, then motioned her forward. "Let me take a closer look."

She crossed the room to stand before him, the gems strung between her hands like a sparkling green web. The larger stones were cut into faceted oblongs. Strings of smaller emeralds were square-cut and set in an unbroken line on three different strands, each strand braided around the chain that held the oblong stones. There were an even score of the large emeralds. She had never bothered to count the small ones.

Guy reached out to lift a section of the necklace, one oblong gem held between his fingers. "These emeralds are—rather large."

"'Tis a gaudy piece," she agreed. "Perhaps someone would see more potential if the stones were unset. The gold chains and mountings would surely be worth something melted down. Or do you think it would attract a buyer as it is?"

"Few could af—" His mouth became a straight line. "There would be more expense to free the stones and melt the mountings. My agent, Harold of Milroy, has an eye for gems. I will ask his opinion of the matter when I next speak with him." He gathered the necklace in his hands and scowled. "This is not quite the trinket I imagined, Claudia. It would be best to keep it in my treasury under lock and key." He gave her a sharp glance. "That is, if you trust me to keep your necklace safe."

"You are not a thief, my lord. I would trust you to keep anything of mine in safekeeping. Well, almost anything," she amended, thinking her heart would not fare so well as the cold, lifeless stones in his hands. She began to release her hold on the necklace, but he caught one of her wrists.

"I have asked you more than once to use my given name when we are alone. I will agree to commission this necklace to one of my agents, if you will agree to call me 'Guy' on occasion."

She stared down at her wrist, where his thumb rubbed against the pulse point. "Must you bargain for everything—Guy?"

"Aye. 'Tis a habit ingrained in my very marrow, one that serves me well enough." He turned her hand over and draped the necklace across her open palm. "Why don't you return this to your chest for tonight, and tomorrow I will take it to the treasury."

There was a mysterious undercurrent in his eyes, a look that promised he had not forgotten his intention to kiss her. Claudia all but dragged her feet as she returned the necklace to its hiding place in the trunk, feeling his gaze on her the entire time. After she closed the trunk lid, she made her way to the fireplace and retrieved the tunic she had started to sew. She turned in a slow circle, searching for the needle.

"Look on the mantel," Guy said.

She headed toward a glint of silver and the strand of green thread that trailed down from the mantel. "I am sorry I disturbed your sleep, Baron. You may return to bed if you wish."

"May I?" His voice was a deep, lazy drawl, what she imagined a hungry wolf might sound like if it could speak. "And what do you intend to do?"

"I thought I would sew for awhile, if you do not mind a little candlelight by the table. I do not think I could get any sleep tonight on those pillows."

"You could sleep in my bed."

"Ouch!" She jerked her hand away from the mantel and the needle came with it, stuck into the end of her finger. She plucked the needle out, then pressed the tip of her finger to her mouth to suck away the sting.

Guy patted the bed. " 'Tis a fine, soft mattress. I promise that no rats will bother you here."

She arched one brow. "I see something far more dangerous than a rat sitting on your bed right now."

He smiled. Claudia lowered her gaze to the floor to avoid its affect on her. "I had nothing more in mind than a good night's sleep. What did *you* have in mind?"

She walked away from him and took a seat at the table, making a great show of settling her wrinkled skirts just so. "I intend to sew until dawn, then I will find Lenore and ask her to show me the herb gardens. I know many fine recipes to tempt a rat to his doom."

"A witch's potion for yon rats?" he asked, a teasing note in his voice.

She refused to be baited. "Nay, a simple mixture of yew, apple seeds, and certain flowers. My mother taught me all she knew of herbals and vigors. There is nothing she could not cure nor kill."

"She must have taken lessons from your uncle." His grin faded, then disappeared entirely. "I am sorry, Claudia. That was a thoughtless remark."

"Actually, you are not far wrong. Mother said she learned what she could from Uncle Laurence so she could protect my father when they were betrothed. She feared Uncle Laurence might try to poison him before the wedding could take place." Claudia expected to see shock on Guy's face, but he listened without showing any visible change of emotion. His silence encouraged her to continue the story. "After her marriage, she met an alchemist in my father's hire who taught her even more of the poisoner's art. My father had many enemies, men who were known to use poisons as a means of dealing with their rivals. Mother insisted that my brothers and I learn all she knew of poisons, and the cures for them." She stared across the room, seeing a place very far away. "In the end she could not save herself nor my father. Uncle Laurence says my father was cursed, that he passed that curse to all of us. Sometimes I wonder if he is not right."

She wasn't startled to feel Guy stroke her hair, even though she didn't see him cross the room to stand next to her chair. His hand grazed her shoulder and moved down her arm, then he lifted her forgotten sewing and set it aside. He took her hands and gently pulled her to her feet.

She avoided his gaze for as long as she could, not wanting to see pity in his eyes. When he tilted her chin up to force the issue, she didn't see pity, but something closer to anger. "You are no more cursed than I am, Claudia."

"Think on what has happened since you met me, Baron. I have brought you nothing but trouble. How can—"

He placed his fingers over her mouth. "I will tell you what happened. I met a woman whose beauty took my breath away, who managed to look a vision even in a grass-stained gown with a dirt-smudged cheek. Each day that followed revealed some new part of her: courage, a quick wit, startling intelligence, honesty so rare that I still distrust it at times." He lifted her hand and pressed his lips against the fingertip she had pricked with the needle. "You are not cursed. You are only indulging in a little self-pity. Which is fine," he added, when she started to draw away. "You have not had an easy time of late. But do not let that pity control you. Yesterday is done and cannot be changed. Let it go, Claudia. Life is today and the next."

"You make it sound so simple."

"Nay. 'Tis a complicated affair. But dwelling on past misfortunes does not make life any easier." His expression hardened. "My own father let the past control his future, and he, too, called himself cursed. That belief blinded him to the good in his life. He saw only what was wrong with everything and everyone around him, never what was right. When one expects nothing but misfortune, those expectations tend to bear fruit."

"You have cured me of feeling sorry for myself," she said in a soft voice.

He seemed to mentally shake himself and gave her an apologetic smile. "You must think me morose beyond bearing."

"I think you are patient and kind." *And a great deal more*, she added silently.

"Compliments?" The light of amusement returned to his eyes. "Now I know you are overtired. You need to sleep, much more than you need to sit up all night. The rats are probably too frightened by your screaming to return for at least a fortnight." His fingers tightened almost imperceptibly around her hand. "Come to bed, Claudia. I swear that sleep is all I have in mind. Bring your quilt if you like, and sleep on top of the covers. I will not be able to rest if I know you are sitting up, starting at every small sound."

"I would not start at every sound." She knew that was a lie, but hoped it sounded convincing. This latest offer was as tempting as every other he had made. And he had always kept his word. They would do nothing more in his bed than sleep. She looked toward her unappealing bed on the floor. "I would not like to disturb your sleep any more than I have."

"Good." He released her hand to retrieve her quilt, then tossed the satin cover on the bed. "Make yourself comfortable. I will douse the candles after you are settled."

Claudia hesitated. This was a bad idea. There was no way to back out of it now without looking cowardly and distrustful of his motives. She stared at the bed. It looked enormous. She could pile the quilt between them and they would still have plenty of room on each side, but that would appear suspicious on her part. Her feet felt made of lead as she forced herself to take a step forward, then another. She folded the quilt in half and placed it on one side of the bed, then climbed between the two halves, making sure her skirts stayed modestly in place. She brushed her cheek against the pillow and breathed deep of Guy's clean, masculine scent that clung to the linens, then released it very slowly, savoring the forbidden pleasure. The mattress was indeed soft. It was her body that felt as stiff as a board.

Guy doused the candles one by one until the room was blanketed in darkness. The embers of the fire had turned to ash while they talked. Through the window, the clouds obscured whatever light might linger from a moon that set hours ago. Her eyes were useless in the pitch-black room, but her other senses tried to compensate for the loss. Her heartbeat sounded deafening, her rapid, shallow breaths as loud as they might be after a hard run. Somewhere in the distance a dog or a wolf howled, a lonely, plaintive sound that made her shiver. The smell of snuffed candlewicks drifted to her just as she felt the bed shift beneath Guy's weight, then the rustle of covers as he settled beside her.

Every nerve in her body tingled, as if she radiated some invisible force, a sixth sense that focused itself on the man next to her. A good foot separated them, but she felt his every movement, as if they lay touching each other, heard each deep, steady breath as if her ear were pressed against his chest. Sleep was as far from his mind as it was from hers. She would wager any amount on that sure bet. The silence between them became intolerable. "You did not tell me that I had a smudge of dirt on my cheek."

His tone was alert, with no trace of sleepiness. "What?"

She wished she could see him. "I knew there were grass stains on my gown the day we met, but you should have told me if my face was dirty."

"Ah, that." His voice reflected the smile she could not see, and she knew that he was lying on his side to face her. She turned toward him, seeing nothing but inky blackness, imagining the incredible blue color of his eyes. "It was a very well-placed smudge, too charming to let you wipe off yourself. I brushed it away when I kissed you."

The memory of his kisses made a tendril of warmth uncurl inside her. She sounded breathless. "I do not recall that."

"You cannot recall my kisses?" His voice was deep and seductive. "Do you not remember how I touched you? How I held you in my arms and caressed—"

"I remember," she whispered.

His voice dropped lower, to the tone of a confession. "Your skin was so soft, like the petal of a rose. You smelled like roses, too. And sandalwood. The roses are in bloom at Montague, and every time I smell them I think of touching you. And kissing you. In my mind I have kissed you a hundred times, in a hundred different ways."

Claudia didn't breathe, afraid she would break the spell between them if she made the slightest sound. His revelations were as shocking as they were thrilling. She had never guessed that she plagued his thoughts as completely as he plagued her own. Never guessed the effect those revelations would have on her. It took a conscious effort not to move, to keep herself from melting into his arms.

"Few men would admit such thoughts," he went on, "especially to the object of their affections. That kind of knowledge tells a woman that she has a certain power over a man, an element of control. I always swore that I would let no woman control me in any way, yet I have never thought about a woman as much as I think about you, never wanted a woman so much that I dream of her when my eyes are wide open." The bed shifted as he rolled onto his back. "I control everything in my life with an iron fist, Claudia. Everything but you."

She waited for him to say something more, to tell her how he intended to gain control of her. He remained silent. Did that mean she truly had some unbreakable power over him? Something he knew he couldn't control?

He could be toying with her, testing her resolve. In her mind she repeated everything he had said, but couldn't recall a single word that rang false. She felt an overwhelming urge to touch him, to surrender herself to his kisses once again and admit that she wanted nothing so much as to be in his arms. But she also knew the price of his kisses. Her lip hurt, and she tasted a coppery trace of blood from biting it too hard. How could she agree to his terms, knowing they would destroy her?

The shadow of Guy's profile began to take shape as the misty gray light of dawn filtered into the chamber. Her eyes strained to see his face, wanting to watch him sleep, but her eyes slid shut just moments before she would have realized that Guy was awake.

He had waited to hear some response to his declarations, waited for what seemed like hours, perhaps days, hoping for some sign that she was ready to end his suffering. She remained maddeningly silent. The chamber turned from gray gloom to cheerful gold as the sun rose higher on the horizon. He turned to look at her. She lay facing him, her lips gently parted, sound asleep. How could she sleep just an arm's reach away from him, *knowing* how much he wanted her? His body was so tense from forcing himself not to reach for her that sleep was impossible. What possessed him to talk her into his bed with the promise that he wouldn't touch her? He was insane, for this was sheer madness, a torture he wouldn't wish on his worst enemy.

He glanced toward the pile of pillows on the floor, wondering if he might find an hour or two of sleep there. He pushed the covers aside, but Claudia began to stir at his movements and he grew still. One hand smoothed over his chest, as if to make sure he was still there. He tried to ease away from her and she moved her whole body closer, using his waist as an anchor to pull herself to his side. She released a soft sigh.

Guy groaned. The weight of her arm was like a brand against his belly. He wanted to fling it away from him. He wanted to wrap her in his arms and crush her against his chest. If he moved so much as a finger, he was lost. "Claudia."

She didn't answer. The covers tangled around her legs, but she managed to nudge her knee up and over his own. Her forehead pushed against his arm, as if she were trying to burrow beneath it.

"Claudia, wake up." Little wonder his voice sounded strained. It matched every muscle in his body. She nudged against him once more. Somehow his arm ended up around her and his shoulder became a pillow. Soft, warm puffs of breath swept across his chest, tickling the hairs, reminding him of a brush fire as it swept through a dry meadow. Her body was the live coal, and he was the tinder. "Sweet Christ, Claudia. Wake up this instant."

Her eyes fluttered open, jewels that caught and reflected the morning sunlight. She stared at his face as if seeing him for the first time, examining each feature, then she looked into his eyes and he watched sunlight turn into green fire. He was lost.

Her lips parted and he waited for the words that would set him free; *I am yours*, or a simple *take me* would do just as well.

"I . . ." She fell silent and he barely resisted the urge to shout *Say it!* She wet her lips and he followed the movement of her small, pink tongue the way a hawk would watch its prey. "You—you may kiss me, if you wish."

He ground his teeth together and clenched his jaw. Oh, he wished all right. "Nay."

"Nay?" she repeated. Her eyes widened.

Any other time, he would have smiled at her obvious disappointment. Now he concentrated on slow, deep breaths, on making his voice sound more substantial than a harsh croak. "You may kiss *me*. If you wish."

She rose up on one elbow to stare down at him. God, she was going to do it. His breath caught in his throat.

"Why?"

"Why what?" he managed.

"Why must I be the one to kiss you?"

He could hardly breathe, much less think. And she thought he could talk about what he wanted her to do? She was going to drive him mad. "I would not have you say afterward that I seduced you."

"Oh." Her brows drew together in a puzzled frown. "After what?"

"You cannot be *that* naive. You are in my bed, Claudia. What do you think will happen if I kiss you?"

She started to blush. "Could you not manage just one kiss?"

"I doubt you would allow that." He shook his head, amazed that he could think at all, much less with any degree of sense. "You would sigh your little sighs, and your body would be all soft, welcoming warmth beneath me, and you would make me promises without speaking a word."

"I would not." Her breathless denial lacked the force of conviction. She couldn't seem to meet his gaze, and stared at his mouth instead.

"Aye, Claudia. You would." He decided to give her a dose of her own medicine. He wet his lips in a slow, seductive movement and watched hers part on a soft sigh. "You would because you want me to touch you, to kiss and caress you, to hold you in my arms and make love to you. I want the same thing, but I will not make your decision for you. If you ask me to kiss you again, you know the consequences." He took a deep, unsteady breath. God, let her ask for a kiss. "Say you agree to my terms, or you must leave my bed."

Her eyes were like mirrors, reflecting her every thought. Temptation, desire, and . . . fear. Why was she so afraid of him?

"You said I could sleep here."

He knew the keen taste of defeat. She had made her decision. He could see it in her eyes. That only inflamed his passion-starved body even more. "Then I will leave. 'Tis my mistake for inviting you to my bed in the first place." God, how he wanted her. He tried one last time to convince her. "You know I will never do anything to hurt you, Claudia. I would cherish you, if you let me."

The fear in her eyes disappeared, leaving only a sadness so deep that he felt its ache inside him. Her voice was no more than a whisper. "For how long?"

He didn't have an answer. No one had ever asked him such a question. It was insulting.

She had every right to wonder.

She lowered her lashes and drew away, her hand trailing across his chest as if she were reluctant to lose that last contact with his body. He didn't try to stop her.

How long?

He began to wonder himself. Would a month be enough to sate his need for her? A year? A lifetime? Nay, no woman could hold his interest that long. He was not some besotted court fop who would pledge undying devotion to his ladylove. He remembered doing just that the summer he turned sixteen, the year he met Lady Jennifer of Pattison Hall.

Lady Jennifer was a widow two years his senior, with an air of worldliness he found irresistible. He had thought her the most beautiful creature alive. Her husband had died in tournament the year before, and she had journeyed to Edward's court to find a new husband. Guy had every intention of winning that title. He wrote her sonnets and sang them beneath her window each night. He followed her wherever he could and ran errands so silly that he knew full well that she was toying with him. He didn't care. There was no task too menial that Lady Jennifer might ask him to perform. Apparently, he was the only one at court who hadn't known that Lady Jennifer would never marry a near-penniless youth who had little hopes of inheriting a title. Her betrothal to the earl of Saint John's was announced while he was busy braiding ribbons into the mane of her palfrey. He had made a complete buffoon of himself.

That was the first and last time he had ever fancied himself in love with a woman. It was a humiliating lesson, but he had learned it well. What he thought of as love was nothing more than infatuation. It didn't matter that what he had felt for Lady Jennifer paled next to the bone-deep desire he felt for Claudia. Given time, every infatuation came to an end. Did Claudia expect him to lie and say that it would not?

He supposed she did. Claudia had rolled to her side to face the opposite wall, so far away from him that he wondered how she managed to balance herself on such a thin edge of the mattress. She didn't move or make any sound, but he would stake his life that she was crying. Aye, if he leaned over her, he would see great crystal tears rolling down her cheeks in an endless river.

She glanced over her shoulder. "I thought you said you would leave."

She wasn't crying. She didn't even look the least bit upset. Wasn't he worth crying over?

Aroused beyond bearing, and now kicked out of his own bed. He glared at the back of her head.

The thought of her sleeping the day away where he could not sleep at all grated on his nerves. He rose in one swift movement and reached for the clothes he had shed the night before. "You will help with the ledgers again today. Meet me in the solar in three hours."

She answered in the prim, saintly voice he was beginning to hate. "As you wish, my lord."

9

"Your hands are too delicate for this task, my lady." Thomas took the basket of foxglove from Claudia's lap before she could object.

Lenore giggled.

Claudia shot the girl an irate glare, but Lenore had her head bent over a basket of yew, pretending to be busy at her task. Lenore seemed to find Thomas's constant meddling in their task a great source of humor. Claudia found them both annoying. She sat between the two on a long stone bench in Montague's sprawling gardens with baskets of colorful flowers spread all around them. The flowers were deceptive in their beauty, the poison Claudia would make from them one of the most deadly known. The rats of Montague were about to meet an untimely end.

She was almost thankful for the infestation, for it gave her a meaningful task to occupy her time. Mindless sewing would let her thoughts dwell on Guy far too often. Helping him with his ledgers would be even worse. Already she dreaded the hours she would spend with him in the solar, knowing his nearness was a drug as potent as the one she intended for the rats. The hours she spent in his bed proved that much.

Waking up in a man's arms was a delight she had never guessed existed. Not just any man's arms, she amended. Guy's arms. Only Guy's. Now and always, there would never be another. That knowledge only made it harder to resist temptation, the urge to surrender to her own weakness.

He would use her, then cast her aside.

That was all that kept her from disaster. Guy's words

weakened her, his touch tempted her, his logic made her doubt her own convictions, but in the end she could never forget that he was a man, subject to a man's fleeting lusts.

For years she had listened to her brothers tell women all manner of beautiful lies to coax them into their beds. Roberto's actions didn't surprise her, for he had always done as he pleased with little thought to consequences, but the string of broken hearts in Dante's wake made her realize that men were much alike when it came to women. They savored the thrill of the chase. Once victorious, men soon lost interest in the prize and sought another, making more false promises, telling more lies.

Guy didn't lie to her. He pointed out lies she would tell herself. She had asked for his kisses and he had refused. Not because he wasn't willing, but because he knew her better than she knew herself. This morning she had wanted nothing more than to be possessed by him, to learn all the secrets a man and woman could share. Afterward she would have assuaged her guilty conscience by telling herself that he had overwhelmed her senses, that he had taken away any choice she had in the matter. And that would give her the fuel she needed to harden her heart against him, to protect herself from the careless pain he would inflict when the day came that he rejected her.

Why couldn't he be a man and simply lie?

"Hai delle belle mani, donna Claudia." Thomas gave Lenore a cursory glance, then his gaze returned to Claudia. His heated stares made her uncomfortable. Her friend the friar was no longer. Thomas the knight was a different man entirely, one whose gaze raked over her with an unwelcome familiarity. With his knowing smiles and easy, self-assured manner, this Thomas made her wary.

She glanced down at her hands and wondered how he could think them beautiful. His fingers wrapped around her wrist in a gentle grip and he turned her hand over then trailed his fingertips over her palm. Her hand became a fist and she tried to pull away. "They are common hands, Sir Thomas. Quite suited to perform this common task."

She had replied in his language, but he seemed determined to converse in hers. "Invece sono belle, delicate e femminili."

A deep voice responded to Thomas's shameless flattery. "Bugiardo."

"*Liar?*" Thomas sputtered. He jerked around to find the source of the insult. Guy stood in the arched stone entry to the gardens, his arms folded across his chest, one shoulder propped against the archway. His relaxed stance was at odds with the dangerous light that glinted in his eyes. Thomas flinched and dropped her hand. Claudia smiled.

Guy held up one hand and turned it over to examine his nails. "What are you doing here, Thomas?"

Thomas rose to his feet and gave Guy a courtly bow. "I am helping Lady Claudia gather herbs and plants for a potion she intends to make."

"It looks to me as if you are picking flowers." Guy polished his knuckles on the shoulder of his dark blue tunic. "Why are you not on the practice grounds?"

"I trained earlier this morn with Evard, and I am to lead the south patrol this afternoon. I did not think I would be missed for a few hours." Thomas shifted from one foot to the other. "If you will excuse me, my lord, I will return to the practice grounds."

Guy didn't excuse him. His silent, inscrutable stare seemed to make Thomas nervous. The air between the two men crackled with tension.

"I meant only to renew my acquaintance with Lady Claudia," Thomas went on. "We worked together in the gardens at Lonsdale on many occasions. I did not think you would object if I joined her here."

"Did you hear me make an objection?" Guy's tone was deceptively friendly, his smile dangerous.

"Lenore was with us the entire time. Nothing of an unseemly nature took place." Thomas glanced over his shoulder. "Is that not right, Lenore?"

Lenore gripped her hands together and gave him an awkward nod. That did little to ease the worried expression on Thomas's face. Lenore looked downright frightened. Claudia patted the girl's trembling hands. "Calm yourself, Lenore. You have no reason to fear your lord's anger."

Thomas and Lenore stared at her as if she spoke in a language they could not comprehend. Perhaps her accent had confused Lenore, but why would Thomas look so baffled?

"You are speaking of Lord Guy?" Thomas asked. His mouth snapped shut as if something had escaped it that should not. He cringed at the sound of Guy's soft laughter.

"Lady Claudia knows I am possessed of a mild temper, Thomas." Guy's expression lost some of its humor as he focused on Claudia. "Aye, she knows I would not be more than mildly annoyed if I told her to meet me in the solar but instead find her in the gardens."

"You said four hours," Claudia pointed out. "I have plenty of time before the hour I am to meet you in the solar."

"I said three hours, and you are late."

"You said four."

Lenore caught Claudia's hand and gave it a squeeze, but Claudia ignored the silent warning. She stood up and set her basket aside, then brushed the wrinkles from her skirt. "You know what I wish done with these plants, Lenore. I will join you later." She turned to face Guy. He still stood in the archway, the lines of his face so taut that they looked carved from stone. "I am ready, my lord."

He inclined his head in a mocking bow and extended his hand. As she walked forward, he issued orders to Thomas. "You may indulge your newfound love of gardening by helping Lenore in Lady Claudia's absence."

"Aye, my lord." Thomas sounded miserable.

Guy's hand closed around hers, not in the crushing grip she had anticipated, but in an almost gentle hold. Drawing her forward, he wrapped one arm around her waist to lead her toward the keep, his manner tender and loverlike. He leaned down to murmur in her ear. "And I do not think you are ready for anything I have in store for you, Claudia."

A shiver of apprehension trickled down her spine. She caught a flash of blue fire in his eyes, then his gaze moved forward to survey the path before them. Why was he so angry?

A line of tall arbors separated the path from the gardens, the wall of greenery broken by evenly spaced archways that led to different sections of the gardens. The south wall of the keep rose before them, dark and forbidding. Just before they reached its massive ironclad doors, Guy turned and led her through one of the archways.

"Where are you taking me?"

"Perhaps I did say four hours. That means we need not rush to our work with the ledgers." His thumb brushed back and forth along her spine, and his splayed fingers seemed to caress her waist. "There is something here that I would like to show you."

He continued forward. More tall arbors separated this section of the garden from the others. The path that ran in straight, precise lines began to curve in lazy, random circles around wooden trellises that were fashioned into clever shapes. Clumps of rosebushes around the base of the trellises were trained to cover the frames with their greenery. They passed a giant green sword dotted with yellow roses, its tip pointed skyward, then a knight fashioned of scarlet roses and his lady fashioned of a pale golden pink, then he led her up a small wooden drawbridge and into a miniature gatehouse.

A stone bench awaited them inside the mock gatehouse, set against the outer wall of the garden. Overhead, dozens upon dozens of vines intertwined to form a bushy green canopy strewn with white roses. Dappled spots of sunlight painted the air with bright beams of gold. Claudia felt as if she had just stepped into an enchanted cottage. Guy stood deep in the shadows, then he took a step toward her into a narrow ray of sunlight that bathed his handsome face in a warm, golden glow so bright that she was tempted to shade her eyes.

"This is what I picture each time I smell roses." His voice held no trace of his earlier displeasure, or, perhaps she had simply mistaken this rigid expression for anger. Now she recognized the banked fire in his eyes for what it was. Desire. A very fierce desire, from the looks of it.

She flinched when he reached toward her, then felt foolish when his hand rustled the vines above her head and reappeared holding a single perfect rose the color of snow. Her hand moved automatically to accept the flower, but he held it away from her and shook his head.

"I think of these flowers whenever I see you." He lifted the rose to breathe deep of its scent, stroking his upper lip with the petals, then he held the flower out to brush the velvety bloom along her cheek, beneath her chin, across her lips. "My memory tells me that you are softer than this flower, but there are times when I begin to have doubts." He rubbed the petals between his fingers until they drifted to the ground like warm snowflakes. The ruined bud followed their descent, but his hand remained extended in midair, hovering next to her face. "Will you let me prove the truth of the matter?"

She felt herself nod, held captive by the smoldering fire in his eyes. His fingertips trailed across her cheek, as light as the stroke of the rose petals, following the same path beneath her chin and across her lips. This time he lingered there, testing the shape of her mouth. She fought down a strange urge to stroke his fingers with the tip of her tongue, to taste the roses she could still smell on his hand, to taste Guy.

As if he could read her thoughts, he drew one finger along the line between her lips. Her lips parted and she heard his sharp intake of breath, or, perhaps it was her own. His hand stilled, his gaze intense as he stared at her mouth, as though he performed some task that required great courage.

The temptation was too great. She touched the tip of her tongue to his finger, amazed when he swayed slightly. Their gazes met and she saw the oddest look in his eyes, a look of helplessness. This was the power he spoke of, the control he gave no other. It was a heady feeling, one that made her grow bolder. She drew the tip of his finger into her mouth and caressed it with her tongue, as though she were licking sweet honey from his finger rather than the taste of roses.

"Sweet saints." The whispered words were as much a prayer as a curse. His eyes widened but he didn't move, didn't look away from her. Or couldn't. She felt the heat of the fire she had started inside him reach out to warm her as well, a flame that swirled in lazy circles through her veins, curling in an ever-tightening coil inside her stomach.

At last he drew his hand away, groaning as though it were painful to do so. His breathing sounded rapid and shallow. So did her own. For a long moment he just stared at her, then he captured her hand and drew it to his lips. Fear flashed through her, and a quicksilver rush of desire as she realized that he meant to inflict the same torment.

He cradled her slender hand between his much larger ones, his voice harsh with desire. "Thomas did not lie. Your hands are indeed beautiful."

His lips brushed across the back of her hand, then her fingertips. He kissed each one in turn, taking the very end between his lips and stroking each tip with his tongue. Claudia felt her legs begin to tremble, and knew what it was to feel helpless. She heard the whimper of a small animal, then realized with a start that the sound came from inside her. "Oh, Guy."

He gave her a dark look, and even managed to smile around her index finger. "Oh, Claudia."

He kissed her palm, then her wrist, then pushed her sleeve up to press a line of erotic kisses along the inside of her arm to her elbow. Then he stopped.

Somehow she found herself standing within the circle of his arms. His lips moved and she had to concentrate on the words they formed. His mouth was so beautiful, so masculine, so very sensual.

"Right here, right now, all I ask from you is a kiss." He cupped her face, rubbing his palm in a slow circle against her cheek. The flame inside her licked higher, even as his hand drew away until only his fingertips stroked her cheek. "A kiss, Claudia. Grant me this boon and I will give you—"

She pressed her fingertips against his lips before he could start to bargain with her. Just this once there would be no bargains between them, no promises made or broken. She drew her fingers over his lips, marveling that they could be so firm yet soft at the same time. "Kiss me."

He lowered his head very slowly, his gaze holding hers until their lips met, then she closed her eyes. His warm breath coaxed her lips to part, as though he were a breath of sunlight. She gasped at its brilliance. All the tense muscles in her body relaxed at the same time, but she did not tremble or lose her balance. He held her safe, his arms wrapped around her as securely as the rose vines all around them. She could feel the strength in him, the power that was his now and could crush her with its will, yet he held it in check, coaxing her closer to it, tempting her with the notion that he might share that part of him.

His kisses became caresses, each one deeper, more erotic; sandalwood and exotic spices, the spices of a man's desire. His tongue traced the outline of her lips, then retreated, then returned again for more of the torment. He made a sound deep in his chest, that suggested impatience, and she finally recognized the invitation. She touched her tongue to the corner of his mouth, then drew it slowly over his upper lip. He pressed her against the length of his body, as if to teach her that he was hard everywhere she was soft. She shuddered, the lesson learned.

His mouth taught her the meaning of carnal. He took a full taste of her, his tongue stroking and teasing until she felt light-headed, then he drew the tip of her tongue into his mouth and began to suckle as he had one of her fingertips. She collapsed against him.

They were kneeling on the floor of the mock gatehouse.

She couldn't recall how they came to be in that position. She had lost all control of herself. Nay, she was still losing control. Summoning the last of her willpower, she tilted her head back, then to one side, desperate to escape, desperate to save herself.

"Guy." His name sounded more a harsh croak than an actual word. He was kissing her neck, the most sensuous kisses she had ever imagined. "Please. You said . . . only . . ." She tilted her head back again. Surely his lips were leaving brands against her skin. When she looked in a mirror at her reflection she would surely see burns all over her neck, each the perfect shape of Guy's mouth. "You said . . ."

What had he said? For that matter, what was she talking about? Her hands tangled in his silky hair, drawing him closer, but his lips slid away and he pressed her head against his shoulder. Her arms were still around him, their bodies pressed together. He felt like a powerful stallion, winded after a long run. It could only be her imagination, but for a moment she thought he was trembling as much as she was. His arms tightened around her as if trying to prove her mistaken.

"I cannot kiss you again," he murmured. His voice sounded as harsh as her own and he rubbed his cheek against her ear, a caress to smooth the roughness of his words. "Sweet Mother of God, I am lost. Do not let me touch you again, Claudia." His hand cupped the back of her head and he held her even closer, a silent denial of his own orders. "Not unless . . ."

She had not thought it possible, but his body grew harder against hers, all warm, deadly steel. Her own body responded in kind and she tried to lift her head, but he held her fast. His unspoken question frightened her. Given her response to his kisses, she was afraid of her reply.

"Do not answer," he whispered. "I know it already. I can feel it in you as surely as I feel your passion." The restraining hand on her head curved into a lover's caress against her hair. "Roses. I should have known better." He took a deep, unsteady breath. "Return to Lenore. Now, before I change my mind. Before I try to change yours with more kisses."

" 'Tis not that I—"

"God in heaven, Claudia. Do not argue with me now." He took her shoulders in a firm grip and thrust her away from him, his gaze averted, unable to bear the sight of her. "Leave me."

She stumbled to her feet. Tears blurred her vision, but not enough that she couldn't see the look of disgust on his face. Disgust with her or with himself, she wasn't certain. Mostly with her, she imagined. She turned and fled.

"Where is she?"

The two soldiers who stood before Guy took a step backward. The shorter man looked around the bailey, as if searching for the best path of retreat.

"W-we have not seen her, Baron," the other managed.

"And Thomas?" Guy demanded. "If that miscreant—"

"Lord Guy!" Evard rode through the gates of the lower bailey and held up one hand to hail Guy.

As Evard rode toward him, Guy dismissed the two soldiers with a flick of his wrist. "You have found her?"

"Lady Claudia?" Evard asked. "Have you misplaced her?"

"Do not taunt me," Guy warned. He began to walk toward the stables. Evard turned his horse and followed. "We had an ar—a discussion that upset her earlier this morn. I have searched for her to no avail. She is not in the gardens, nor my chamber, the solar, or the seamstress quarters. 'Tis likely she mistook something I said to her and fled the castle. We must mount a patrol to—"

"She did not leave the castle, my lord."

Guy stopped in his tracks. "You know where she is?"

"Aye." Evard swung his leg over the saddle and dismounted. He motioned a boy forward from the group of squires who stood near the stables, watching the baron's anger from a safe distance. The boy looked to his friends for encouragement, then started forward.

"Perhaps you would rather have this conversation in a place less public," Evard suggested.

"I wish to know where my—" Guy clenched his jaw. "I want to know where she is, damn it."

Evard handed the reins to his squire and gestured toward a set of gates. "I will take you to her, Baron."

"Through the upper bailey?" Guy asked, even as he fell into step beside Evard. "What is she doing in the upper bailey?"

"She is not in the upper bailey. 'Tis simply the quickest route to where we can find her, and the most private." He gave Guy a disapproving look. "You are making a great fuss over a lover's quarrel, Baron. Your people will begin to think that your mistress has you under her spell."

"I do not give a damn what they think," Guy growled. "Perhaps it should occur to someone that she is a valuable prisoner, that keeping her within these walls greatly affects my future."

"Aye, there is that," Evard agreed. "Yet some are curious about why she would cry when the lord who holds her sends her away from him, when that lord later appears frantic to find her. 'Tis fine fuel for gossip."

" 'Tis you who are too curious for your own good." Guy gave Evard a sideways glance. "She was crying?"

Evard nodded. "I found her behind the chapel. Several soldiers saw her flee there, but were afraid to follow. More to the point, they considered your reaction to the news that they had followed her, so they sent for me."

Guy's hands became fists. "Was Thomas with her?"

"Thomas?" Evard repeated. "Why should Thomas be with her?"

"I found them together in the gardens," Guy bit out. "That miscreant son of a—He was trying to seduce her. Beneath my nose, he was wooing her with smooth flattery, courting her, by God, in my own gardens."

Evard digested that for a moment. "All know Lady Claudia is your mistress, Baron. None would dare suppose to take your place. But I have heard talk already, and none of it from Thomas, that many intend to compete for her favors when she no longer shares your bed. I would wager that Thomas seeks nothing more than her friendship for the time being, so that she might turn to him when you tire of her."

"I will not tire of her!" The words shocked Guy more than they seemed to shock Evard. They sounded suspiciously like the truth. He shook his head to clear it of such a strange thought.

Evard didn't respond to the outburst. His expression remained calm.

Guy scowled and released his hold on the front of Evard's tunic. "I will cut off the hand of any man who touches her."

"None doubt that, Baron." Evard rubbed his temple. "Yet even I have wondered what will become of her when you settle the dispute with her uncle."

"Nothing will 'become of her,' " Guy snapped. "Her uncle will not want her back. She will remain at Montague for as long as she wishes. When and *if* she leaves here, she will have wealth of her own, enough that she need not barter herself to any man."

Evard's voice was little more than a whisper. "As you would have her barter herself to you?"

"You tread dangerous waters, Evard."

"Aye, and I am just fool enough to wade deeper." He fanned his fingers across his forehead to rub both temples. "You would send her from Montague with nothing to protect her but your gold, and that will only make her a prize."

"What do you mean?"

"I mean that you have not thought through your plan, unless it is your intent to sacrifice her to the first man who takes a notion to force her before an altar. She has no family to protect the fortune you would give her. There are knights throughout England who would cut a dozen throats to get their hands on such a bride."

"She will have soldiers in her hire to protect her."

"Soldiers can be bought," Evard pointed out. " 'Tis even possible that one in her hire will take it into his head to marry her. A man has but to swear before a priest that he was intimate with her, and she will have no choice in the matter."

Guy fell silent. Evard was right. A wealthy, unattached woman was a prize that impoverished knights dreamed about at night. The gold he would give Claudia would be a stone around her neck. Christ's bones, she already possessed a fortune greater than the one he intended to bestow upon her, and she could wear that around her bloody neck as well. The emeralds alone would keep her in lavish comfort for the rest of her days. Or keep any man in comfort who forced himself upon her as husband.

His scowl darkened.

Evard seemed to read his thoughts. "Lady Claudia needs a husband before she leaves Montague, my lord. A man who will not rob her blind. I have never asked for any rewards in your service, but now I ask you to promise Lady Claudia's hand in marriage. To me. I do not ask for a bride's price," he hurried to say. "She is a lady born and bred, and as a knight, I am sworn to uphold the honor of any lady."

"And I am not?" Guy's voice was low and deadly.

"Nay, my lord. 'Tis plain to all that your rank and title prevent you from doing what is right by Lady Claudia. None would expect you to wed a woman forced upon you. I would take her freely, without an eye to her fortune or her past."

"You would, would you?" Guy folded his arms across his chest. Stalwart Evard, smitten by a woman. Who would have guessed? Had it been any woman but Claudia, he would have laughed. "Are you in love with her?"

Evard's brows drew together. "I have not spent enough time in her company to say with any certainty."

"You would know," Guy said. "I had but to lay eyes upon her and I knew—"

What had he known? His mouth snapped shut and he looked at Evard without seeing him. He lusted for Claudia, nothing more. Yet, if he wanted nothing more than her body, why didn't he simply bed her and end both their torment? He could feel her desire for him in every touch, every look. She wanted him, but she didn't want the terms he would impose upon her, the label of mistress rather than the title of wife. Or, was there more to it than that?

He turned and continued to walk toward the keep, lost in his own thoughts. Thoughts of eyes as rare and mysterious as her emeralds. How had her mother come by such jewels? He had believed that he knew all he wanted to know of her family. There was much more to know. Her past might shed light on the present, on why she asked for kisses, yet refused to allow their natural conclusion. Surely she realized that she meant more to him than some passing fancy.

For how long?

Her words came back to haunt him. She didn't know, any more than he had known until this moment, that he wanted more from her than physical pleasure, more than an intimate interlude that would end in a few months. For the first time, he allowed himself to think of the day when they might part, of what would become of her. He could not imagine a day without hearing the soft, sultry sound of her voice, of smelling roses and finding himself completely distracted by her scent, by the gentle sway of her hips, the soft brush of her hair against his skin. Her smiles alone were worth a king's ransom.

He would send her into a world where a hundred men would be eager to snatch up what he had tossed away so carelessly. They would not care if she ever smiled. Aye, he knew what would become of her. But what would become of him?

"My lord?" Evard placed a hand on his shoulder. "You are going in the wrong direction."

"What?" Guy came to a halt and looked around him in confusion. He was standing on the path that led to the doors of the keep. Where else would she be?

Evard pointed to another path that led around the east

wall of the keep. "Lady Claudia is in the kitchens. This way is quicker."

"Oh." His brows drew together in a frown. "What is she doing in the kitchens? Does she now intend to make herself into a serf?"

"Nay, my lord. She said she promised to join Lenore there to help her mix a poison." A hesitant smile appeared on Evard's face. "Not for you, I hope?"

Guy gave him a look of disgust. " 'Tis for the rats. It slipped my mind that she was about that task. I should have started my search by looking for the servant."

"She did seem intent on helping Lenore," Evard said agreeably. "I hope her poison proves effective. The rats run rampant in this place. 'Tis rumored that you even had a few visit your chamber last eve."

"Is there anything you do not hear?"

"Very little goes unremarked within these walls, especially when you are involved, Baron, as well you know."

"Then remark this, Evard. You will pass along the well-founded rumor that any man who looks upon Lady Claudia with a glimmer of anything more than the loyalty and fondness of a vassal for his lady will meet the full force of my displeasure. In short, I will make his life a living hell. Any man who touches her in lust will greet hell in person. She is mine by rights of betrothal, and mine alone. Do I make myself clear?"

"Aye, my lord." Evard smiled. "I knew you would see reason."

"I have not seen reason since I met that woman."

"But you still intend to marry her?"

Guy's eyes narrowed. "Was it your intent all along to goad me into admitting as much?"

"Aye," Evard admitted cheerfully, oblivious to Guy's scowl.

"You argued against the match at Lonsdale, and you just pointed out that I should not let myself be forced into marriage."

"Paltry arguments, were they not?"

"My brother's arguments may carry more weight when he learns the whole of her family." Guy had informed Evard of Claudia's relation to Roberto on the ride to Montague, and the reminder wiped the grin from Evard's face. "Claudia is nothing like the vermin she is forced to call kin, and I would not have my family shun her because of them. Kenric and his soldiers will arrive within the fortnight to help me lay siege to Halford. I would have him meet Claudia before he learns that Roberto was her brother."

Evard looked uncertain. "He may recognize her, as you did. Very little escapes Lord Kenric's notice."

"I want to be the one who tells him. Is that clear?"

"Aye, my lord."

"Good." Guy turned on his heel and began to walk back toward the gate to the middle bailey.

Evard hurried after him. "You are going the wrong way again, Lord Guy."

"Nay, 'tis the right direction for the moment. If I saw Claudia now—" He shook his head to free it of thoughts of what he wanted to do to Claudia and with her at that moment. "I need to consider my course with care before I speak with her, for she has a way of twisting my words. I must endeavor to chose the right ones."

"*Baron!*" A mounted knight waved to them from the bailey gates and spurred his horse forward. The charger slid to a halt before the two men, its great hooves slicing long, brown gashes into the cropped grass. The rider's expression made both men reach for their swords. "Alfred just returned from afternoon patrol with a bolt from a crossbow in his back. He could tell us nothing before he fell unconscious, and the surgeon holds little hope. Sir Thomas and the rest of his men are still missing."

10

*H*e was leaving her.

Claudia watched Guy's squire dress him for war, remembering another time when she watched her brothers don their armor to ride away from her.

They had never returned.

She gripped her hands together until the knuckles turned white, her back held so straight against the wooden chair that it ached. Guy would return. Montague was his home. It was foolish to think he would ride away and never come back. Nothing could prevent him from returning to his fortress. Nothing except an arrow such as the one that killed his soldier, or a sword, or mace, or lance.

Her hands began to tremble. Why did he submit her to this torture, to the misery of watching him leave? In the kitchens she wouldn't know of his departure until he was gone, wouldn't be forced to imprint these images of him in her mind, dreading the thought that they might be the last. After the way they parted in the gardens, why had he sent for her?

A fat tear splashed onto her hand. She gasped and brushed it away, determined that he would not see her cry. He had probably noticed anyway. His gaze rarely left her as Stephen worked to encase his body in padded leather and chain mail. Would he gain some pleasure knowing that she cried for him? She glanced up at him through spiked lashes. He was scowling.

"Stop crying, Claudia. I will find Thomas and bring him home. Like as not, he is in pursuit of whoever attacked them."

She blinked once very slowly. He thought she cried for Thomas? She felt a twinge of guilt that she had forgotten all about Thomas, that he and the rest of the missing patrol were the reasons Guy meant to leave her. She looked toward the window. " 'Tis nearly dusk. Should you not wait until morn when you can make a fresh start?"

"Nay, I know the route he intended to travel, and the moon will be nearly full tonight. If my men are wounded, I would not leave them in the wilds of the forests all night."

She pictured every demon that lived in the woods, some creatures she knew were real, most she could only imagine. Nothing would convince her uncle to leave the safety of his fortress at dusk. Why should Guy be so noble?

His loyalty to his missing men was another trait she wanted to hate but couldn't. She recalled how she had felt while stranded in the forest, thinking he had abandoned her. His men would know better, sure in the knowledge that Guy would search for them. That must be a comforting feeling.

"Make sure my horse is ready, Stephen. I will join you soon in the stable."

"Aye, my lord."

The squire departed, and Claudia forced her gaze to remain on the floor. They were alone. She had an overwhelming desire to fling herself into his arms, to pour out everything in her heart before it was too late.

It was a ridiculous urge. He would probably return before dawn. There was no pressing need to tell him anything. He didn't want her to touch him, or to kiss him, or show any other sign of her affections. This morning he had ordered her to leave him. She could do nothing but sit in miserable silence and watch him leave. Was this some sort of punishment?

She heard him walk closer and found herself staring at his boots. He took hold of her hands and drew her to her feet. She stared at his chest, at the white wolf of Montague that was embroidered on his blue surcoat. If she wrapped her arms around his waist, her head would rest against that fierce-looking beast. It seemed appropriate that the emblem covered his heart, one ruthless predator atop another.

"I am your betrothed, Claudia. It displeases me to see you so distraught over another."

What was this obsession he had about her feelings for Thomas? Only one man held her affections, and he stood before her. Was he blind? She supposed he must be. She was not about to enlighten him.

He brushed his fingers beneath her chin, forcing her to meet his gaze. "I would rather carry the memory of your smile with me."

"Then do not leave," she whispered. "Send another in your stead."

His jaw tensed as he studied her face, his eyes searching hers. "Your tears are for me?"

The uncertainty in his voice crumbled her flimsy defenses. She threw her arms around his waist and pressed her cheek against the wolf, a creature that could devour her whole. The sharp metal links of his chain mail bit into her skin but she didn't care. She wanted to hear the steadying sound of his heartbeat, but his armor made that impossible. She heard only her own, pounding an uneven rhythm in her ears.

"Please, Guy. Do not leave me." She held him tighter, but his hands remained slack at his sides. His lack of response only made her more desperate. "I will agree to anything you wish, if only you will not leave. I cannot bear it!"

Oh, God, she was making a fool of herself. A complete and utter fool. He stood stockstill, no doubt shocked by her hysterics, at the very least, disgusted by them. Before he could answer her besotted plea, she tore herself away and spun toward the door. His hand plucked at her sleeve, but her sudden flight must have startled him too much to give chase. He called out just as the door slammed shut behind her, cutting off the sound of her name.

❦

Guy did not return by dawn. Nor did he return by mid-morning when Lenore coaxed Claudia to the kitchens to bake the rat poison they had made into sweetened wafers. They spent most of the afternoon tucking the wafers into small crevices, high ledges, and any other out-of-the-way place that only a rat would find. Still, Claudia asked Lenore to warn everyone of the danger. The girl's eyes lit up at the opportunity to spread that bit of information and doubtless a few tidbits of gossip at the same time.

Without Lenore's company to distract her, Claudia wandered through the castle to the walkways that ran along the outer walls, anxious to avoid Guy's chamber or the solar, knowing the memory of his presence was too strong in those places to let her do anything but worry about him.

Evard came upon her on the walkways an hour later. "I did not realize you left your maid's company, my lady. Would you mind mine?"

She interpreted the polite comment as a warning that she was not to be alone in the castle. Seeing nothing wrong with that edict, she inclined her head. "Nay, Sir Evard. I would welcome your company, for I hoped to speak with you today." She looked out over the high battlement walls, her arms propped up on the smooth stone, her chin resting in her hands. The countryside unfolded below her like a beautifully worked tapestry, but she had eyes only for the roads that led to Montague, watching for any movement or cloud of dust on the horizon that would announce Guy's approach. It seemed much longer than a day since he left, longer than a day since she made a fool of herself with lovesick declarations. Last night she had lain in Guy's big, empty bed and whispered all the things she wished she had said, practiced them aloud until they sounded just right. Now she would gladly swallow her pride for the opportunity to say them to his face.

"My lady?" Evard prompted. "You wished to ask me something?"

"Ah, yes." Her gaze returned to the road that led into the forest. "Does your baron have a violent temper?"

"Lord Guy?" Evard sounded incredulous. "Nay, my lady! What would make you think such a thing?"

"Lenore and Sir Thomas acted very strangely in the gardens yesterday morn when Lord Guy grew angry." She gave Evard a sideways glance. "I would say they looked afraid of him."

Evard considered this for a moment. " 'Tis likely you saw wariness rather than fear. The baron is not a cruel or unjust lord, but his punishments to those who displease him are swift and long-remembered."

"What do you mean?"

"Lord Guy knows each of his people," Evard said, "well enough to know which punishments will prove most effective. A few months ago, Lord Guy discovered that one of the chandlers had gambled away the guild dues of his apprentices. He ordered the apprentices to collect the chandler's earnings for a fortnight while the chandler went to the dairy barns for the same length of time to serve as a milkmaid."

Claudia wrinkled her nose, unimpressed. "That does not sound like much of a punishment to me. Most barons would flog such a man to dissuade him from future gambling."

"The chandler is deathly afraid of cows, my lady." Evard's smile grew broader. "Lord Guy does not beat nor maim his people, yet you will see influences of his temper everywhere if you know what to look for, or, what not to look for. 'Tis rare you will find any drunkards at Montague, for they know they will be wakened at dawn the next day to clean garderobes." He tapped his chin and looked skyward. "And I once knew a young knight who charged into a skirmish with a band of mercenaries, anxious to prove his worth and bravery to the baron, yet in his haste he left the men in his charge without a leader. For a month afterward, Sir Thomas was awakened an hour early each morn, ordered to arrive an hour early for each meal, and sent to his bed an hour early each night. 'Tis likely Thomas recalled each of those dull hours when he faced the baron's anger yesterday." Evard shook his head. "Nay, Lord Guy is not a violent man, but many on the receiving end of his judgments would call him devious."

"Little wonder his clerks do not complain," Claudia mused, intrigued by Evard's insight into how Guy's mind worked. Devious, indeed. "If the baron were displeased with me, what do you think his punishment would be?"

Evard looked baffled. He gave her a helpless shrug. "I could not say, my lady."

Claudia propped her chin on her hands again and gazed out over the forest. "I think he might delay his return to Montague an entire day, knowing I worry about him every hour of that day." Her voice turned almost hopeful. "That could be the reason he has not returned yet, don't you think?"

A long silence passed between them. "If you say so, my lady."

Three days later, Claudia knew that Guy's prolonged absence from Montague had nothing to do with an imagined punishment. No one spoke their fears aloud, but she could see the worry on every face.

"He will return today," Evard said. He pretended to contemplate the abacus that sat on the table in Guy's solar, sliding the wooden beads back and forth in a random pattern. "My hunches are rarely wrong, and I have a strong hunch that this is the day he will return."

Claudia wished he would find something else to occupy his time. The abacus beads clicked together in an annoying rhythm. She wanted to toss the stupid instrument out the window. Instead she continued to sew. Her silver needle moved steadily through the white samite. Four thousand, three hundred and eighty-seven stitches, eighty-eight, eighty-nine. A few more rows of embroidery and the tunic would be complete, a tunic sewn with hands frantic for anything that would keep them busy, sewn for a man who would probably never wear it.

She forced herself to speak her worst fears aloud. "My

uncle would demand a ransom if he had captured Lord Guy. We would have word by now if he were a prisoner. I—I do not think he will return, Evard."

"There could be any number of reasons for the baron's delay," Evard said. "Lord Guy can hold his own in any battle, and he rode from Montague expecting to find trouble. He is not likely to fall prey to a trap."

" 'Tis surely some trickery of my uncle's that lured Guy away from Montague," she insisted. "Each night I try to prepare myself for the worst, to imagine . . ." She rearranged the tunic across her lap to hide how badly her hands began to shake. "The people within this fortress will hold me responsible."

"You are letting your imagination run away with you," Evard said, an uncustomary harshness in his voice. "By Lord Guy's own orders, I will protect you with my life, Lady Claudia. None here will harm you."

She gave him a sideways glance. "Who will become baron here when news arrives of Guy's death?"

Evard scowled and looked away. She had wondered if Guy had told anyone about her brother, Roberto. Now she had the answer. Evard could not protect her if Guy's brother, Kenric, became Montague's baron.

"You have little faith in your baron's abilities, lady."

"Nay, you are wrong. I have great faith in Lord Guy's abilities. He is the one who made me consider all possibilities when I would try to hide the truth in false hopes." She bowed her head. "And he is not my baron, Evard. Only those sworn to him may claim the protection of his name. An illicit betrothal will not protect me."

"This is foolishness, Lady Claudia. I, too, am worried by the baron's absence, but I am not ready to order his shroud sewn. I know him too well." The abacus abandoned, Evard began to pace. He raked his hands through his hair until it fair stood on end. "Lord Guy is like a cat, always landing on his feet."

Claudia felt a humorless smile tug at her lips. "Guy does not like cats."

Evard made a sound of impatience. "I feel a need for fresh air, my lady. Will you walk with me along the curtain walls?"

She knew why he made the suggestion. They had walked the curtain walls each day near dusk, both using the excuse of fresh air and the fine view, both straining to see any sign of Guy's return. There was no longer any need to keep watch, for there would be no sign this day, or any that followed. Still, she could not push that last thread of hope aside. She set her sewing aside. "A walk sounds like a fine idea, Evard. There are clouds on the horizon. Why don't we go now, before it rains?"

"I would rather you stayed."

The sound of the deep voice made her heart stop beating. Even as she turned toward the sound, she told herself that it was nothing more than her imagination. She had conjured the sound of Guy's voice in her head because she wanted to hear it so badly. Last night she had sworn she heard him call out to her, yet she awoke to an empty bed, her arms clutching the pillow that still held a faint trace of his scent. Perhaps it was his ghost calling out to her, trying to answer the tearful pleas she made each night that he return to her. Aye, why wouldn't he haunt her as thoroughly in death as he had in life? She took a deep breath and slowly lifted her gaze from the floor.

Her imagination summoned up a perfect image of him as well. Guy stood in the doorway of the solar, one broad shoulder propped against the doorjamb, dressed in the same clothing as the day he left. Ghosts were not supposed to smile, but Guy was smiling. He pushed away from the door and moved toward her, his arms outstretched as if he meant to enfold her within them.

His image wavered, and the entire room seemed to shift beneath her feet. She tried to take a small step toward him. Guy and the room itself suddenly disappeared as everything went black.

❦

"—nothing but worry since you left."

"—sleep? She looks—"

Snatches of the conversation penetrated Claudia's hazy senses. A few words here and there, but she gave up trying to make sense of them. They blurred into the deafening sound of rushing water. Or was it a high-pitched wind? The sound seemed to come from inside her head, that realization coming just as the sound started to fade.

"Send up a tray of food. Something filling."

"Aye, my lord."

Guy and Evard. Why would she dream of them talking about food? Then she remembered her vision in the solar. She wanted to snap her eyes open to see if the apparition remained, but her eyelids felt made of stone.

"Claudia?"

She wanted to weep. How often had she hoped to hear her name on Guy's lips just once more? It sounded so real. At last her lashes fluttered open and she feasted her eyes on the sight of him. He looked real, too.

"Claudia? What is wrong?"

She realized dimly that she was in Guy's bed. He sat on the edge and leaned over her. His brows drew together as he studied her face. "Why are you looking at me that way?"

She could only imagine her expression at that moment. She gathered her muddled senses along with her courage, then extended one finger and poked his shoulder. Rather than the thin air she had expected, he felt solid. She sighed her relief and wrapped her fingers around his wrist. Reassuringly warm, and very solid. "You are not dead."

His worried expression dissolved into a slow smile. "You needn't sound so disappointed."

The teasing words cut to the quick. "You find some humor in my grief?"

"My God." His smile disappeared. "You really thought I was dead?"

Guy's image turned watery as tears filled her eyes. That

seemed the only answer he needed. He gathered her in his arms, cradling her as gently as a child. He had shed his surcoat and most of his armor somewhere between his arrival in the solar and the time she awoke in his chamber. Her head rested against his padded leather gambeson, the suede warm and soft beneath her cheek. He smelled of armor and horses, and beneath that, his own comforting scent.

"Do not cry, sweetheart. I am here now. There is no need for tears." His words only made her cry harder, but he didn't seem to realize their effect. When she continued to cry, he began to slowly rock her in his arms, as if he wasn't aware of what he was doing. His voice dropped to a husky murmur. "Hush, love. You are breaking my heart. How could you think I would not come back to you?"

Her answer was a broken sob. He must think her an idiot. She didn't care. She cried not only for her fears of the past few days, but for everyone she had loved and lost, for the overwhelming relief that Guy was not among their number. She pressed herself closer to his chest, wishing she could press herself so close that he would become a part of her, a part she could always keep safe.

" 'Twas no more than a roguish band of merce—ah, thieves and reavers," he said, when her sobs faded to hiccups and sniffles. "Thomas had no idea they had murdered his messenger. He and his men gave chase to the north, thinking we knew their intent. It took us a full day to catch up with the patrol, then another to herd the outlaws they had captured to the stockades at Carlisle. With more than a score of criminals in my care, I had no wish to reduce my number by sending a messenger back to Montague. I suspected you would worry, but I had no idea how much." She felt his lips at her temple, a kiss as much as a caress. "I swear that I will always come back to you, Claudia. Always. Never doubt that."

She wanted to believe him. How easy it would be, even knowing that it was a lie, well intentioned, but a lie just the same. Dante had made her the same promise.

Yet Guy was here, and he was safe. She had been granted

the gift of time. Time to fall more deeply in love with him, to surrender her heart completely. This was but a taste of the grief she would know if she allowed him any closer, yet the past days had also taught her the bitter taste of regret. Guy once said that she lived too much in the past, but he was wrong. She lived too much in the future, living for what might be rather than for what was. There was no longer any doubt in her mind that she was meant to be in his arms, whether for a day or a lifetime. Her heart belonged to him already. What else did she have to lose?

Perhaps the price he demanded was not so high after all. She glanced down to where his hand rested against her hip and traced its outline with the tip of her finger. He smoothed his other hand over her hair, long, soothing strokes that made her sleepy. She savored each one, the achingly sweet gentleness of his touch. She wanted to stop time somehow, to stay within his arms in this chamber, just the two of them, forever.

Someone knocked on the door.

Neither of them moved, but Guy released a deep sigh. " 'Tis our meal. Are you hungry?"

She shook her head, hoping he would ignore the knock.

He brushed a kiss against her forehead, then shifted her weight onto the bed. "You look thinner than when I left. I think you will feel better if you eat something."

The door opened at Guy's order and Stephen entered, carrying a tray laden with food. As the squire took the tray to the table, Guy walked behind the curtains that divided the room, then returned a moment later with a small linen towel.

"That will be all," he told Stephen. "Have water heated for my bath. I will let you know when I am ready for it."

The squire bowed, then departed. Guy crossed the room and handed Claudia the towel. "Dry your eyes, sweet, and we will share a meal together. We have much to discuss."

His gaze swept over her and the appreciative look in his eyes gave her a good idea of what he wanted to discuss. She dabbed at her eyes and nose, suddenly anxious to avoid their meal. She wasn't ready to put her feelings into words, or to hear any new bargain he might try to make with her. The bargain was made already.

"I would dine in my robe if you have no objection," Guy said, even as he unlaced his gambeson. "These clothes smell of my horse, and I am heartily sick of that beast's company." He tossed the tunic aside and began to unlace his shirt as well, but stopped when he realized she was watching him. A spark of desire lit his eyes and his hands dropped to his sides. "Our food grows cold."

" 'Tis ham and bread from the midday meal, my lord." She stood up and set the towel aside, her gaze locked with his, but she made no move toward the table. Food was of little interest. What she hungered for stood before her. " 'Tis cold already."

"Then we should not let it grow too warm," he said, even as he reached for her. She went unresisting into his arms, but he shook his head. "There are things we must talk about, Claudia."

She laid her fingers over his lips. "I have yet to give you a proper welcome home, my lord. You once said that I could kiss you if I wished."

His arms tightened around her, yet he remained silent until her fingers slid away from his mouth. "Guy," he murmured. "I would have you call me by—" He stopped in midsentence and cupped her face between his hands, his touch almost hesitant. "Do you know what you are telling me?"

She managed to nod. "You said that I must be the one to kiss you, that you would not make my decision for me." Her gaze dropped to his mouth. "I have made my decision, Guy."

"You are distraught," he said, his voice uncertain. "I have no wish to take advantage of you."

She turned her head and placed a kiss in the center of his palm, strangely pleased to hear the sharp intake of his breath. The affect she had on him made her bolder. She leaned closer to him, sure in the knowledge that what she was doing was right. "Will you deny me?"

His fingers splayed wider, stroking her face and neck. "How can I?" he whispered. "You have the face of a saint, yet you awaken the sinner in me each time I look at you. Each time we touch."

He did not wait for her kiss. He covered her mouth with his, not hard or punishing, but no less than possessive. His hand cradled the back of her head as he deepened the kiss and she drank in the taste of him, returning his kiss full measure. Her fears began to fade away, fast replaced by the warmth of desire. All the longings he had awakened the first time he touched her stirred to life again, longings made stronger with each kiss and caress that taught her the meaning of passion. An uncontrollable force inside her yearned to learn more. If it was sin, she knew why there were so many sinners.

One strong arm wrapped around her waist, the feel of his powerful body and the circling protection of his arms all that mattered in the world. This was what his eyes promised each time he looked at her, the fire that would burn out of control when she surrendered to it. They would burn together. She didn't care.

His hand slipped lower to caress her hips with startling familiarity. He made a sound deep in his throat and his arms tightened around her, lifting her higher until her feet no longer touched the floor. He held her so tight that she could barely breathe, yet it was instinct that made her secure her dangling weight. She lifted her legs to wrap them around his waist. Her wide, gathered skirts made it an easy task, yet she was unaware until that moment of how intimate the position would be.

Guy tore his mouth away from hers, and she felt him shudder. His forehead dropped to her shoulder, as if she were the one who held him up and not the other way around. He began to nuzzle her neck, then the curve of her ear. "Take care, Claudia. You will have me on my knees."

His deep voice vibrated through her, a caress she hadn't known possible, a flash of lightning that struck deep inside her. Her hands tangled in his hair to pull him closer, seeking the center of the storm itself. The room tilted and she realized he had knelt on the bed to lay her down against the pillows, yet they were still joined as intimately as when they were standing. She couldn't seem to let go of him. She shifted restlessly beneath him. His hand went to her hip, his grip firm enough to hold her still. "Easy, love. I would not have this end before it begins."

Her brows drew together, her voice uncertain. "I am too wanton?"

She shifted her legs as if to move away. His arm wrapped around her hips to keep her from moving. That only brought him into closer contact with the warm, soft core of her, the few layers of clothing between them not nearly enough to shield him from her heat. Yet Claudia looked worried, as if she were doing something she shouldn't.

Guy tried to give her a reassuring smile. It wasn't his most successful effort. "Nay, sweetheart. There is no such thing as too wanton where you are concerned."

She started to wriggle again, another belated attempt at a more modest position. His groan made her stop.

"You make a face each time I move," she whispered. "If it is not my brazenness that displeases you, then what?"

She really had no idea of the exquisite torment she was putting him through. He wanted to laugh. He would settle for the ability to take a few deep, steady breaths. "I like you brazen, even more than I like you wanton." He stroked her cheek with the back of one finger, annoyed to see his hand tremble. " 'Tis I who am too impatient. I want to be gentle with you, introduce you slowly to the pleasures we will share."

She seemed to mull this over. The ache in his loins became nearly unbearable. That was nothing new. He had spent the last four days in a near-constant state of arousal. How often had he daydreamed of the time when he would hold her in his arms again, of all the erotic things he wanted to do to her? The fantasies haunted each hour of the nights he had spent apart from her. The reality made the fantasies seem tame in comparison.

If there was any hope of slow, gentle lovemaking, he needed to regain control of himself. That would not happen while cradled between her thighs. He resolved to roll away from her, perhaps pace around the room a few times, yet he was captured by the feel of her soft body beneath his, the sight of her kiss-swollen lips, the glittering green of her eyes. She had an effect on his senses that he had never experienced, a newfound awareness that focused itself entirely on the woman in his arms. His skin burned everywhere their bodies touched. Every color seemed brighter, from her crimson lips to the burnished mahogany of her hair. Her cheeks were the color of pale, pink roses, and the smell of those delicate flowers came to him along with another faint aroma that made his nostrils flare. He drew a deep breath to savor the heady scent of her arousal.

His gaze drifted lower, to the enticing swell of her breasts. A frown creased his brow when he realized the gown must lace up at the back or the sides. He needed to remove her gown, wished he had thought of that before he found himself in this position. Perhaps he would ask her to undress while he watched, envisioned the sight of her standing before him as she stripped herself bare. His hips arched against her of their own accord, returning his thoughts to the present, very pleasurable state of affairs. The gown could wait.

"I like to touch you," Claudia said, in her soft, sultry voice. "There are times when I want so badly to touch you that it hurts not to." She lifted one hand to his face and brushed her fingertips along his cheek. When they moved over his lips and down his neck to his chest, he felt as if she had raked a live coal over his skin. He tried to focus his concentration, to comprehend what she was saying. "You do not seem impatient to me. I think you are the most patient, gentle man I know."

Patient? *Gentle?* He felt like a wild animal, ready to devour her whole. To hell with her gown. His mouth came down hard on hers, even as he tried not to hurt her. Her lips were bruised already from his kisses. They would soon be swollen even more. His body moved with a mind of its own, all touch and sensation. One hand trailed down her leg to slip beneath the hem of her skirt, then smoothed a slow, delicious path up again, over the sensitive spot behind her knee, along a sleek thigh. He wanted to lean back to see if her legs were as long and shapely as they felt. He couldn't stop kissing her. His hand decided to test the curve of her bared hip instead, finding her softer than anything he had imagined. She was all but naked beneath him.

A low growl filled the air, a warning of the beast she stirred to life inside him, one that intended to claim her as its prey. He had never made such a sound in his life. It should have terrified her. Amazingly, she didn't seem to notice. Her tongue darted between his lips in the same sensual play he had just taught her. He let her have her way as long as he could withstand the provocative invitation, then he returned her thrust and dominated once more. Her hands moved over his shoulders and back as if searching for something she could not find. He knew what she searched for, what her body sought by instinct. He vowed to deny his own needs until she found that magical place. Her hands clutched at his shirt as if she meant to rip it from him, and he heard himself groan again. She was a passionate creature, his Claudia.

His Claudia. She was truly his now, would always be his. He hoped the thought would help cool his blood. That didn't happen. She began to tug at his shirt again. He reached behind his neck to grab a handful of the shirt and pulled it over his head, vexed that he had to break off their kiss to do so.

Their gazes met, and he saw a glimmer of uncertainty in her eyes. He waited for her to brace her hands against his chest, to protest his unbridled urgency. Her hands went instead to the laces at the side of the gown, her fingers made clumsy by their trembling. She made a small sound of frustration, then gave up the effort. Her arms wrapped around his neck, pulling him down to her sweet, waiting lips for a kiss that made the soles of his feet tingle.

He had braced himself for hours of wooing and seducing. Her passionate response aroused him more than he had thought possible. He was the one being seduced. She responded to him as if she were starved for his touch, answering each caress with a sigh or small moan of pleasure. It suddenly occurred to him that she had been deprived for years of even the smallest show of love or affection. Little wonder that she craved his touch, that her hunger manifested itself in her passion. The knowledge only made him more determined to make up for those years of loneliness, to cherish her. He had to regain control of his senses to do either. His lips moved to the slender column of her neck, unable to resist his own need to place a sensuous kiss at the base of her throat before he drew away and braced himself on his elbows above her. "Claudia, I—"

She shook her head, her eyes frantic. "Do not leave me."

Her fear battered at his resolve. He had to comfort her. What he had in mind was not the comfort she needed. She was a virgin. He had to remember that fact and not confuse her need for love with his own need, his own lust. She whispered one final entreaty. "Please."

His hand already worked at the fastenings of his breeks, before he realized what he was doing. Even as his mind told his body to stop he freed them both of their garments just enough to fit himself to her, the hard steel of his flesh cradled against the very softest part of her.

He had spent the last four days planning this moment, sure in the knowledge that he would give her every pleasure imaginable. His hips circled against hers and his lovemaking very nearly ended then and there. Sweet saints, he could not do that again.

"Claudia." Her name was almost a plea, yet he knew that she could no longer stop him, even if she had a mind to. Nothing could stop him. Not unless one could die from too much pleasure. It seemed a possibility. His heart beat so hard that he expected it to burst from his chest.

He managed to focus his gaze on her face, to watch the play of emotions there: shock, desire, innocence, and awe. He wondered if his own thoughts were as transparent, even as she began to nod. He meant to ask her if that gesture was mere coincidence, or if she truly knew what he was thinking. She arched her hips, mimicking his movements. He whispered his own final entreaty. "Forgive me, love."

Her body was a miracle of welcoming warmth and virginal resistance. He wanted to shout his joy. He wanted to murmur sweet endearments. He couldn't speak a word.

Her nails bit into his shoulders when he met the proof of her innocence and that small flash of pain cut through the last tattered shreds of his control. He drove into her, feeling as if he were the one untried, driven by his eagerness to make his possession of her complete.

Her soft, feminine cry set him on fire. The incredibly tight sheath of her body was made for his. He held himself as still and unmoving as stone, hovering on the very edge of sweet oblivion. She held him, gripped him, in small reflexive movements that made him dizzy.

He did no more than arch his hips against hers and his world collapsed. His body moved beyond his control, slow, smooth strokes that were both beginning and end. He squeezed his eyes shut and watched one star after another explode in the darkness. It seemed to go on forever.

It ended so abruptly that he almost collapsed on top of her.

uy opened his eyes and discovered Claudia staring back at him. Somehow he had managed to roll onto his back, and she now lay on top of him. Rather than relax against his chest as he hoped she would, she had braced herself on her arms to gaze down at him. Her elbows dug painfully into his ribs. More disturbing than that, she looked shocked. He dimly recalled a shout, and sincerely hoped it was nothing blasphemous. At the moment he didn't have the strength to apologize for anything, not for the swift loss of her virginity, or the abrupt end of their lovemaking. As soon as his heart started to beat again, he would reassure her that everything would be much different next time, that he could indeed be patient and gentle.

She began to slide toward his side and his grip on her hips tightened. "Give me a moment, love. Just rest now."

"I cannot," she said, her voice oddly strained. "My skirt is trapped beneath you."

He felt her tug on the garment and realized she was right. With her skirt pulling her one way, his hands and body the other, she could not be the least bit comfortable. He turned to his side and gently separated their bodies. She lowered her lashes and started to rearrange her skirts. Those small, fluttering movements brought a wave of realization.

"Christ." He hadn't even undressed her.

Her quick, darting glance made him realize that he had spoken aloud. The glimpse of pain and uncertainty in those emerald depths made him scowl. So much for cherishing her, for letting her touch and caress him to her heart's content. He waited for her to look up at him again, but she kept her eyes hidden beneath the thick fringe of her lashes. He had just found more pleasure with her than he had known possible. Claudia looked ready to cry.

Guy scowled as he rearranged his own clothing. He had taken enough women to his bed to know his skill as a lover, yet he had failed to please the woman he wanted to please most. Now that he thought about it, he couldn't recall failing at anything that truly mattered. Until now. He had never lost control so completely. What did she do to him? "This did not happen as I planned, Claudia. Forgive me."

Her lashes lifted and she gave him a puzzled look. "You are sorry we made love?"

"Nay, of course not. I am only sorry that—" He pressed his lips together. It occurred to him that she was still inexperienced in the ways of men. She wouldn't have any idea what he was talking about if he tried to explain his regrets. "Never mind. We will have that discussion another time. I would rather hear how you feel. Did I hurt you?"

A deep blush turned her cheeks the color of roses. " 'Twas not so bad."

A smile tugged at his lips and he placed his hand on her waist for a small caress. "A man lives on tenterhooks, waiting for the day he will hear his betrothed say his lovemaking was not so bad."

She stiffened beneath his hand and the glow in her cheeks faded. "I would rather you did not jest of our false betrothal."

"I said nothing in jest." Guy mentally kicked himself. Nothing had gone as he planned since his return. Nay, since he met her. Still, his voice softened as he spoke the words he had intended to say before he left Montague. "We are betrothed in truth, Claudia. I will not set our betrothal aside, nor will I set *you* aside. We will be married as soon as I can make the arrangements with Montague's priest."

He waited patiently for one of her beautiful smiles. She had wanted marriage from the start. This news would make her smile for a week.

Claudia frowned. "Why?"

"Why?" he echoed. "You want a reason?"

"Aye." Claudia wanted to be certain she heard him right. She was stunned as much by his sudden declaration as by what just transpired between them. She had known from the beginning that lovemaking would only deepen her feelings for Guy, and strengthen the bond between them. He possessed her, body and soul. She belonged to him as she would never belong to another. Did he feel the same sense of completion?

Something instinctive told her this was not a decision he had made in the throes of passion. Wariness fast replaced wonder. "Under the circumstances, a reason for your sudden change of heart seems a sensible request."

"There was nothing sudden about it," he said defensively. "I gave the matter a great deal of thought these past four days. It never occurred to me that you would demand an accounting of my decision." He arched one brow. "By law, I am accountable to none but God and the king."

"What reason do you intend to give God and your king?" Claudia could almost see his mind work fast and furious behind his mask of arrogance. He was trying to think up a good lie. She gave him an expectant look and waited.

"I thought you would be happy." He sounded downright sullen. "You made it very clear that you would rather be my wife than my mistress."

"I would rather have lovely blond hair than this mousy brown, but I should also have a question or two should that amazing change ever come about."

"Who dared compare your hair to a mouse?"

"I did." She released an impatient sigh. "You are trying to distract me from my questions, Baron."

"Guy," he prompted.

"Very well, Guy. Why this sudden wish to marry a woman who was not fit to bear your illustrious name just four days ago?" She propped herself up on one elbow to look down at him. "And have you considered that I might have no wish to marry into a family that will hate me?"

Guy rose onto his elbow as well. "You *will* marry me. No matter the reasons. Your uncle named me your betrothed, and that gives me the right to name you my wife. I will not relinquish that right to any man who happens along, nor let any other man have what is mine."

"There seem to be no other men who want me," she said in a quiet voice.

"I want you." He gave her a look that dared her to argue that fact. "As I tend to have excellent tastes, you may be certain there are others who want you as well."

Her gaze moved over his face feature by feature, from the set angle of his jaw to the lowered storm of his brow. She wondered how many people he had terrified with this expression. It had the opposite affect on her. How strange that his anger could make her feel protected and safe. Stranger still that she would like nothing more than to smooth his troubled brow with gentle kisses. She shook her head. He could distract her without speaking a word. "So you would marry me because you are a possessive man, and you view me as a possession?"

"I said nothing of the sort," he retorted. "You make a habit of twisting my words."

"I did not twist anything. You cited no reasons other than possessiveness," she pointed out, then she waited again for some other explanation. Guy remained stubbornly silent. He was hiding something from her. Something important. Then it came to her, the only reason he would suddenly wish to marry her. "You found out about Halford."

He gave her a sharp glance. "What did I find out about Halford?"

"You know well enough." Her chest felt as if something very heavy pressed against it. She wondered if he had received a missive from his king. Uncle Laurence had worried that it was only a matter of time before Guy discovered the truth. And now he had. A small glimmer of hope that she hadn't even known existed died inside her. "Just as I know why I am suddenly fit to be your wife."

"What are you babbling about?"

She searched his face for some sign of guile. No wonder he could strike such profitable bargains. He was very good at hiding any trace of guilt he might feel at taking such blatant advantage of her emotions. "How did you find out?"

"I tire of this riddle, Claudia." He didn't raise his voice, but the threat was unmistakable. "Explain yourself. Now."

"Halford Hall," she said. "You decided to marry me because you learned it was part of my dowry."

He said nothing for a very long time, his gaze locked with hers, his eyes the color of blue ice. For the first time, she felt a twinge of fear. "You intended to let your uncle sell me something that was not his in the first place?"

"I did not know it was mine," she protested. Oh, Lord. He hadn't known. And she had enlightened him at the worst possible moment. "I learned of my dowry the same day I overheard my uncle's plot to murder you. My grandfather signed Halford to my mother as part of her dowry, and she, in turn, to me. Uncle Laurence hoped to gain your gold before you learned the truth."

"You have known the truth since we left Lonsdale."

The accusation stung, yet it was his silent reproof that made her ashamed, his knowledge that she hadn't trusted him. "It seemed a good truth to keep to myself. You would have forced me into marriage had you known."

"Would I?" He leaned back and his gaze flickered over her, quick and dismissive. "You seem to know my mind very well."

She lifted her chin. "I know you are a man determined to get what you want at any cost. You meant to pay a fortune for Halford when it cannot be worth a tenth of that amount. You refuse to sell Flemish bolts of cloth because you do not like their merchants. I refused the fortune you offered to become your mistress, yet now I should believe that you intend to marry me when I am in your bed willingly?" Just stating her reasons aloud made her sure of her convictions. She gave him a firm nod. "I know your mind well enough, Baron. You will go to amazing lengths to have your way."

"You are right, of course. Had I known of Halford Hall, I would have kidnapped and married you the moment we rode through the gates of Montague. 'Tis obvious I have proved myself a ruthless knave in your eyes since then."

"You are being sarcastic."

"Am I?" His smile sent chills down her spine, a perfectly civilized smile that managed to look predatory. "In truth, I am only guessing at the thoughts that made you decide to keep this news from me. Why don't you enlighten me? Was it fear that I would rob you of your inheritance? Revenge for taking you from your snug home at Lonsdale? A pleasant surprise you were saving for just the right moment?"

She lowered her gaze. "I intend to sell you Halford at a fair price."

"And just when do you intend to make this sale?"

When would she learn to keep her mouth closed? Sensing that anything she said would only make him angrier, she shrugged her shoulders.

"You own nothing more than a piece of paper, Claudia." He shook his head, as if she should already know what he told her. Oddly enough, the lines around his mouth indicated irritation more than anger. "Halford belongs to whoever controls its walls. Your uncle's men are there now. My men will be there soon enough. Did you think I would pay for what I had gained already by conquest?"

What could she say? That she hadn't thought that far in advance? In the silence that followed, Guy seemed to read her mind. He rolled his eyes. "Do you aggravate me on purpose, or is it a natural talent?"

Claudia wisely ignored the question. "Will you punish me for not telling you about Halford?"

"Nay." He raked one hand through his hair, still scowling. "But you should have told me sooner."

"I realize that now," she murmured. She had badly misjudged him and he knew it. The urge to comfort him overcame her wariness. She reached out and laid her hand on his cheek. "Are you terribly angry?"

"I am not angry, but I am more than a little annoyed." He looked sideways at her hand. "Is this your attempt to placate me?"

"Aye." She smoothed her fingers over his forehead, then rubbed his temple. Her lips curved into a shy smile. "Is it working?"

The corners of his mouth twitched upward. "Aye."

She traced his high, sharp cheekbone and the line of his jaw. He urged her hand lower, along the corded contours of his neck to his collarbone. The banked fire in his eyes burned brighter.

"I am in need of much placating. Or will be," he qualified. "I want to know what other 'good truths' you decided to keep to yourself."

Her fingers swirled small circles toward his heart. She would much rather explore the interesting planes and ridges of his chest than argue. "I cannot recall anything."

"Tell me about your parents."

Her hand stopped moving. What had he learned about her parents? She decided to test the waters before she blurted out something else she would regret. "My parents?"

"Aye, how did your mother happen to possess such valuable emeralds?"

"The usual reasons," she murmured. "My father was a wealthy man. He liked to give my mother pretty gifts." She explored the shape of his breastbone with the tip of her finger. This might not be such a bad time to tell him the last of her family secrets. Not that there would ever be a good time. He would find this secret even more sordid than the one that involved Roberto. She bit her lower lip and remained silent.

"If your father was so wealthy, how did you and your brothers find yourselves so destitute?"

"My father's family conspired to seize our wealth when my father died. My brothers and I were forced to flee our home with nothing more than we could carry." She smoothed her hand over his shoulder. "Are you certain you are not angry about Halford?"

He wasn't to be distracted so easily. "How did your parents die?"

That was the question she had dreaded. She drew a deep, unsteady breath. "You will not like the story."

"I wish to hear it anyway." He tilted her chin up and waited until she met his gaze. "Give me your secrets, Claudia. You can tell me anything and it will not affect what I feel for you."

"What *do* you feel for me?"

He shook his head. "Your story first."

He couldn't know what he asked. Claudia focused her gaze on a point just past his shoulder, seeing images of her parents. Her father had always seemed larger than life, tall with dark hair and piercing green eyes, yet she always remembered his smiles. Her mother looked delicate in comparison, with the fair hair and blue eyes of the Lonsdales. Claudia recalled only worried frowns from her mother. Her parents were different from one another in their temperaments, but Claudia never doubted their love for their children and each other. Their family was the most important thing in all their lives. They never said anything critical of one another in the presence of outsiders, and family secrets were just that: secrets told to none other. Yet Guy had a right to know of her family if he truly intended to make her a part of his. She closed her eyes and pictured the sunlit villa where she grew up, the endless vineyards and olive groves, and in spring, the scent of almond blossoms.

"The trouble began when my father's sister, Giovanna, married the son of a neighboring nobleman. The two families were often at odds over a rivalry that began so many generations ago that no one can even remember how it started. Some thought a marriage might help ease the troubles between the houses."

"I take it that did not happen?"

She opened her eyes and stared at his chest, longing to

rest her head there to listen to his comforting heartbeat. "Nay, Giovanna became her husband's means to an end. You see, Lorenzo wanted much more than a Chiavari bride. He wanted everything the family possessed. As soon as Giovanna bore him a healthy son, Lorenzo devised a plan to seize control of everything."

"He laid seige to your home?" Guy guessed.

"Sieges are not as common in Italy as they are here," she informed him. "Lorenzo employed a much more cowardly means to achieve his goal."

Now that she had started the story, it seemed almost a relief to tell him. She had foolishly hoped that Guy would never ask about her parents, but then again, she had never thought he would ever ask her to marry him. She knew now that marriage to Guy was but another tantalizing glimpse of what could never be. Learning that Roberto was her brother should have turned him away, but that was a matter that involved their brothers and not either of them directly. What she intended to tell him affected her irrevocably. It would affect Guy as well. He would never want her after she finished the tale. Not even as his mistress.

If she remained silent on the matter he might come to care for her, perhaps even to love her. Then she would hurt them both when he discovered the truth and sent her away. It was too late to spare her own heart, but she could not bear the thought of hurting him with her silence. She plunged into the worst of the story.

"My father had no other siblings, but he had three healthy heirs. Lorenzo was too clever to have us all murdered, for he knew none would believe him innocent of the crime. Instead he poisoned my father. He had spies employed as servants in our home to carry out the crime, then those same spies stepped forward to swear that my mother and her alchemist had plotted and carried out the murder. Lorenzo used his marriage to my aunt to proclaim himself our guardian and his men took my mother away the day after my father died. A fortnight later, we learned that she died of the tortures they inflicted because she refused to confess."

Claudia struggled to bar the images of those gruesome days from her thoughts, closed her mind to all but the words themselves. Her voice sounded almost devoid of emotion. "The alchemist proved more cooperative. They tortured him until he begged for death, until he knew his confession was all that would release him from the pain. He swore before a council of priests and magistrates that he had been my mother's lover for years, that he fathered all her children, and that they murdered my father so they could marry."

She wet her lips and recalled the pressure of Guy's mouth against them. In the eyes of the Church she was the daughter of a murderess. Guy would never want to kiss her again.

"Lorenzo petitioned the Church to have my parents' marriage annulled on grounds of adultery," she went on. "The pope himself signed the decree, and my brothers and I were declared bastards. Roberto and Dante did all they could to convince the Church of my mother's innocence, but Lorenzo had planned too long and too carefully. His son was named my father's closest legitimate male relative and sole heir. Dante and Roberto decided we should flee to England when one of my servants died from drinking a goblet of wine meant for me. It was Lorenzo's way of telling us we would never be safe if we remained in Italy."

With the tale ended, a deafening silence fell over the room. Claudia waited for Guy to roll away from her, or express some other sign of aversion as soon as he recovered from his shock. Then again, perhaps he would not care that the Church marked her a bastard, that she would be required to confess as much to his priest before they married. If they married. She forced herself to meet his gaze. His icy expression put a heartrending end to the dim hope that he might still want her. His gaze moved over her face as if he searched for something.

He reached out to brush his thumb across her cheek. "Have you no tears for your parents and brothers?"

"They are a sign of weakness. I learned to control them."

"Yet you wept for me."

She lowered her lashes, unable to look him in the eye any longer. "I—I seem to have no control when it comes to you."

"It grieves me to see you cry, but I would not have you harden your heart any more than you have already. There is no need." Before she could guess his intent, his hands were at her waist, then he drew her into his arms. The kiss he pressed against her forehead was infinitely gentle. "You made yourself strong to survive and learned to depend upon yourself and no one else. Am I right?"

"You are not far wrong," she murmured. Actually, he could not be any more right. She didn't know what to make of this show of tenderness. The story of her family should have repulsed him. "You realize that there are those who consider me a bastard? The daughter of a murderess?"

"Aye." Guy sounded no more concerned by that revelation than he would had she told him the skies looked like rain tonight.

She chewed on her lower lip, almost afraid to ask her next question. "Then you will abandon this crazed idea of a marriage?"

"Nay." He answered with enough force that she leaned back to look at his face. Other than the slight lowering of his brows, she could see nothing to reflect his thoughts.

"Barons do not marry bastards," she pointed out. "Not unless they are the king's own. You will—Why are you smiling?"

" 'Tis your choice of words that make me smile." He leaned toward her for a sweet, lingering kiss that made her forget about his smile and everything else for a moment. All too short a moment. He drew away from her but pressed his fingertip against her lips as if to seal his kiss there. "I do not care what some might call you, for I know what you are. And I know what you will be. Soon none will dare call you anything but 'baroness.' "

"Why are you so determined to marry me?" she whispered. "You cannot wish to align yourself with what is left of my family. My dowry is worthless, for you intend to seize that property either way. What gold my necklace might fetch will not affect your wealth by any great measure. Still, you insist on marriage. Why?"

"Can you not guess?"

She gave an exasperated sigh. "I just gave you the reasons why I cannot. The only other possibility is lust, but that cannot be the reason because you know I will come to you willingly, without the promise of marriage."

"You will?" He sounded amazed, even though he managed to keep a straight face. "You will sate my lust willingly?"

"Who twists whose words?" She pushed against his shoulder. "Will you tell me your reasons or not?"

"Hm." He gave her a considering look. "I think not. That does not seem my wisest course at the moment. You said yourself that you know how my mind works. The answer will occur to you soon enough."

"You need an heir?" she tried, even as she shook her head. "You could have your choice of brides. You do not need to marry me to get your heir."

"Perhaps I require an heir with green eyes," he teased. He took her hand and placed it on his chest. "This is the quickest path to your answer, Claudia. Where you will find what you are looking for."

"I will find the answer by touching you?" Her mouth turned downward. "Then lust is the reason after all."

He just smiled and shook his head. "Do you like to touch me?"

"I have told you that I do," she answered, wondering at the sudden change in him. The remote look in his eyes had disappeared, leaving the man she liked best. He should be scowling, raging at her for keeping her secrets for so long. Instead he smiled and teased her. She would never understand how his mind worked.

His fingers tugged on the laces at the side of her gown. "I like to touch you, too."

"What are you doing?"

"I want to look at you." He leaned over her to use both hands on the laces, trapping her hip beneath his arm. The simple weight and warmth of his body stirred an immediate response in her, a longing for more of him. Even his voice caused a tingling of sensual awareness. "I want to look at all of you."

She tried to push his hands, but he brushed hers away as if nothing more bothersome than a fly disturbed his concentration on the task. Giving up the useless effort, she leaned back and cupped his face between her hands. "Does what I told you about my parents make no difference to you?"

"None at all," he assured her, with a small grunt of satisfaction when he freed the knotted laces. His gaze returned to hers as he loosened the ties, a spark of some undefinable emotion in his eyes. "I would wipe away the sorrows of your past were it within my power to do so, but I will never hold you responsible for events beyond your control. What you told me only makes me realize the gift of your affections is greater than I thought. For years you have not allowed yourself to care for anyone. You resist what you feel for me because you are afraid you will lose me, that I will abandon you as your family abandoned you."

"My family did not abandon me!"

"Nay, they died," he said softly. "Yet the result is the same, is it not? Can you tell me that you never felt alone or abandoned all these years?"

She forced the word from her lips, but it came out as little more than a broken whisper. "Nay."

"You are not alone anymore, Claudia." His hand trapped hers against his face, and he turned his head to place a passionate kiss in her open palm. "I possess no jealous relatives who covet what is mine, and your uncle is more nuisance than threat. I would marry you if you were the bastard daughter of a fishmonger, or the rightful queen of England. I will give you children to cherish, just as I will cherish their mother. And I will never leave you. No matter what happens, you will never be alone again."

She shook her head in an almost frantic motion, afraid to believe him. Afraid that he knew too much of her fear and would use it against her.

"Aye, Claudia. You are mine, and I protect what is mine. Our children will never know the fear you have lived with all these years." He brushed his thumb across her lower lip. "In time I will make you forget your fears and replace them with smiles. I want sleepy smiles when you wake up in my arms each morning. Sensual smiles when you arouse my passions at night. Playful smiles when you tell me I am pigheaded in my business ventures." He kissed the corners of her mouth, gentle, undemanding kisses that melted her resistance. "That is one of the reasons I would marry you, sweetheart. Your smiles make me feel things I have never felt before. They are as addictive as a fine wine, and just as rare. I want them all."

His mouth closed over hers before she could say anything, his kiss deep and possessive. She could taste his power, felt his strength surrounding her, holding her safe. An odd sensation returned, the same deep emotion she felt every time Guy took her into his arms. It was a sense of coming home. Her arms slipped around his neck, warm and welcoming. She was never afraid when he held her. She wanted to hold him forever.

"Slower this time," Guy whispered, breaking away from her mouth. His lips moved along the delicate line of her jaw. "Much slower."

He braced himself on his elbows, then his hands were at her shoulders, lowering her bodice and chemise to her waist. She pulled her arms free of the garments, her eyes locked with Guy's until his lashes lowered and his gaze moved downward. She could feel him looking at her, his gaze as intimate as a caress. Overcome by a surge of modesty, she tried to cover herself. He caught her wrists and pinned them to the bed near her shoulders, exposing her completely to his examination.

"I want to know every part of you," he murmured, his eyes hot and hungry. "Every luscious, beautiful inch of your body." He pressed a kiss against the very center of her chest, moving his head back and forth so his rough cheeks rubbed against the cleft of her breasts. She felt as if he had started a fire inside her heart. She wanted to touch him. With her hands pinned and useless at her sides, she arched her hips toward him.

"Nay, sweet. There is more I must teach you." His lips trailed over her breasts, touching her, kissing her. He circled one breast in an ever-tightening spiral, then took the nipple into his mouth.

Claudia tried to breathe, failed, then tried again with gasping success. He had touched her with lightning. He started to suckle and every emotion seemed to overflow her body. She twisted beneath him, desperate now to hold on to the storm itself. Then he was gone, the carnal kiss and his grip on her wrists at an abrupt end. She opened her eyes and found him standing next to the bed, his hands on the fastening of his breeks, his dark gaze burning into her, branding her as his own.

This time she didn't look away. In fact, she sat up to take a better look at him. She took in the breadth of his shoulders, the way his muscles flexed and strained as he bent down to remove his clothing, then the startling sight of his arousal. He straightened and stood unmoving, letting her look her fill, his hands clenched at his sides. Every part of him looked braced against some invisible force like a warhorse reined hard. His low, seductive voice sounded amazingly controlled. "Take down your hair, Claudia."

Her hands went to her hair, slowing the task when she realized he liked to watch the movements she made as she removed the ribbons that held her coiled braid in place. She started to unplait the braid, but he shook his head.

"The gown," he muttered, his voice huskier. "Remove it."

She felt a blush warm her cheeks, but hastened to obey.

Her hands went to her waist and she pushed the gown and chemise over her hips, then sat back to slide the garments over her legs and onto the floor where she wouldn't be tempted to clasp them over her nakedness. He wanted to look at her. After all the staring she had done, she supposed he deserved an equal opportunity. Still, she hoped he would join her soon. She wanted the warmth of his big body next to hers.

Guy didn't dare move. He held every part of himself tightly leashed except his eyes. His gaze moved freely over Claudia's slender form, feasting on every part of her at once, then slowing to take in more detail. Her breasts were made to fit his hands. Her waist . . . Aye, her waist curved in an exact measure that he knew his hands would encircle just right. Her hips flared in gentle swells for no other reason than to give his hands more soft flesh to touch. He saw the soft triangle of curls between her legs, and his loins tightened. He forced himself to look lower, at her long, shapely legs, watched in fascination as she uncrossed her ankles and lay back against the pillows. She turned to her side, one hand resting on the bed in front of her, then rubbing that spot as if inviting him to join her. She was Eve, inviting him to Eden.

He took one step forward, then another. His legs felt made of lead, his joints as stiff as rusty armor, every muscle savagely controlled to keep himself from ravishing her. He glanced at her face, at her soft eyes and sweet, welcoming smile. She had no idea how much control he was exerting, or she would be on the other side of the room. Nay, out of the chamber entirely. The things he wanted to do to her, she couldn't know any of them. Well, perhaps one or two, he amended, placing his knee carefully on the side of the bed.

Slow . . . slow . . . slow, he reminded himself. Cherish her. Let her touch you.

He took her hands and urged her to sit up, then to kneel before him so they were facing each other. His hands went to her sides, stroking downward to her waist, pausing to take her measure, then moving over her hips. "Touch me, Claudia."

Her hands went to his chest, then moved slowly over his

shoulders. She caught her lower lip between her teeth and bit down on the succulent flesh. It looked delicious. He had to taste her. He lowered his head and brushed his mouth across hers until her lips parted, then caught her lower lip and bit gently. She moaned and clutched at his shoulders.

"Touch more of me," he murmured, urging her hand lower. She stroked his waist and belly with the tips of her fingers until he thought he would go mad. His lips moved in a random line along the slender column of her neck and shoulders, raining kisses over her face, but avoiding her lips. He wanted to concentrate on what she was doing with her hands, on what he was doing with his own. He confirmed the shape of her breasts, finding the fit just as perfect as he knew it would be, delighting in the small sounds she made when he caught a nipple between his fingers and gently squeezed. His voice became almost unrecognizable. "Lower, Claudia."

He was crazed. Did he think she needed more inventive ways to toture him? Somehow she ended up pressing her hand downward, then he released his grip on her wrist to see what she would do.

Her hand drifted lower. His body tightened in anticipation. The abrupt movement made her jerk her hand away.

"Did I do something wrong?" Claudia asked. She leaned back to eye him warily, but her gaze was far from his face.

"Nay. Do not stop." He supposed it was the harsh sound of his voice that made her give him a sharp glance.

Without warning, her fingers wrapped around him. He groaned and his hands fell to his sides. He could survive this. He just needed to concentrate on that thought.

Her grip tightened.

"Easy, love," he managed, wondering at the stranger's voice that came from inside him. He had squeezed his eyes shut to withstand the exquisite pain but opened them now to find Claudia studying her handiwork.

There was no way on God's earth he could survive this.

"You are so soft," she murmured, her voice filled with awe, "yet so hard at the same time." Her fingers tightened around him again, as if to confirm that fact. "Like marble itself, yet not. I have never felt anything like you in my life."

He didn't have enough breath left to groan. Somehow he found her wrist and slowly disengaged her hand. "We must save this particular exploration for another time. At the moment, I have a few caresses in mind that you will find more familiar."

He intended to kiss her thoroughly, to stroke her with his hands until she cried out for him. This time he would remain in complete control. Her arms slipped around his neck and she pressed herself closer. He closed his eyes and drew a sharp breath, wanting nothing more than to feel her breasts crushed against his chest. Her nipples brushed against him in quick darting glances meant to make a man crazy. His arm went around her waist and he lowered her to the pillows, her mouth sweet and inviting as her lips opened beneath his. A dim warning sounded in his head as he settled himself between her legs. This time was supposed to be different. He tried to break away from her lips. "Uhm. Mm. Clau—"

She thrust her tongue into his mouth. Guy knew he was lost. One arm went around her shoulders, the other around her slender hips, crushing her body against his. He couldn't get close enough to her. He wanted to be inside her, to become a part of her.

He forced his mouth away from hers, turning his head away when she sought his lips. It hurt to deny her. He assuaged that ache with the knowledge that his intentions were honorable.

She kissed his neck instead, kisses as delicate as the brush of a butterfly's wings. They made his heart pound hard and heavy all the way to his loins. Her mouth closed over the pulse point at the base of his throat and the kisses turned wildly erotic. They fired his lust as effectively as they stirred a sense of panic. He framed her face between his hands, a gentle restraint that tested his own. He wanted to make love to her for hours, stroke and caress every part of her until she knew the same madness of longing that possessed his body. The craving was insatiable.

He managed just one word, a plea, an endearment, and a curse of his own weakness. "Claudia."

Her hips arched as she positioned her body to accept him. Her small gasp and the slight widening of her eyes said it was nothing she did by intent. She had no more control over the explosive passion they shared than he did. He began to ease inside her, staring into her luminous eyes as he sank into her body. He saw each of her emotions, felt them so profoundly that they were his own, breathless anticipation, a deep sigh of satisfaction, and the tingling awareness that there would be more this time. It went so far beyond the joining of their bodies that he wondered why he ever bothered to bed a woman before Claudia. He was as much a virgin in their lovemaking, as much adrift in this vast, uncharted sea. It would take them a lifetime to learn all its currents and eddies.

He moved slowly inside her and they created their own current, a surging force that flowed between them. That strength gathered within him until he felt as powerful as a king, humbled willingly when he handed that power to Claudia. This was the reason she searched for, the reason he would never let her go. It was the force of love.

It was magic.

He wanted to tell her.

He couldn't speak a word.

Claudia's eyes glowed with a radiance that nearly blinded him. It was like staring into the sun. A tremor shook them both, then another, and then they were clinging to each other. Her cries sounded as wrenching as his own, pleasure so intense that it hurt. It was the most beautiful, most terrifying experience of his life. He poured himself into her in waves that seemed without end, until he wondered what would be left of him. He didn't care. This was worth dying for. Worth . . .

12

Guy awoke with a start. He stared up at the ceiling of his bedchamber and realized it was morning. Late morning. He didn't remember falling asleep, but he was underneath the covers with Claudia fit snugly against his side, her head pillowed on his arm. She felt right there. Odd that he didn't recall going to sleep with her. The last thing he remembered was making love to her, then . . . Good God. He'd passed out. Not only passed out, but then he'd slept through the entire night without stirring. He rarely slept until morning without waking once or twice, and never past dawn.

He scowled at the top of Claudia's tousled head as if she were responsible for his appalling lapse of control. She *was* responsible. No other woman alive could leave him in such a sated stupor. It appeared that she'd managed well enough. Somehow she had them both beneath the covers, and her hair lay unplaited in rich, mahogany waves across his pillows. He pictured himself lying sprawled across the bed like a felled bear while she went about her evening ablutions. He wondered how long she'd stared at him, or if she'd touched him. She was just curious enough, and certainly bold enough to do some clandestine explorations. He silently cursed himself for sleeping through it.

He turned to his side to look at her, careful not to wake her. She stirred and moved closer, nuzzling her face against the center of his chest. A small, contented sound escaped her lips, then her breathing became slow and even once again. He brushed his thumb across her lower lip and let the memories wash over him, every kiss and caress, her passionate response to him. His fingers traced the delicate line of her jaw, still marveling at the softness of her skin. He recalled the remark she'd made about how soft he felt, and his manhood stirred to life again. God, he was insatiable.

He'd never wanted a woman again so soon. The difference lay in the fact that with other women it was nothing more than a physical joining to sate a physical appetite. With Claudia, it was a joining of their souls. And that appetite would never be satisfied.

It was too soon for her, of course. He'd hurt her the first time, but gave her pleasure the second. Best not press his luck. Actually, it felt very nice just to hold her. He drew her closer until she was pressed against the length of him. Her sleep-warmed body seemed to mold itself to the hard planes of his own. A feeling of contentment crept over him as he stroked her back, a sense of relief that came from possessing something he'd searched a long time to find. The first day he saw Claudia, something deep inside him had recognized that this was where she was meant to be, where she belonged. Soon there would be no doubt about whom she belonged to, or where. She would bear his name, and someday bear his children.

The thought of Claudia's soft belly swollen with his seed made his arms tighten around her. She barely moved. The thick fringes of her lashes lay undisturbed against her cheeks, her expression in sleep as innocent as an angel's. Her lips curved into a smile. He wondered what she was dreaming about. Him, he hoped. He wanted to know her so well and so intimately that he knew her very thoughts.

He wanted to tell her that he loved her.

Just admitting it to himself made something feel freer inside him. He would tell her soon, but not too soon. He needed time to gain her trust, her confidence that her heart would be safe in his care, that he would never leave her. She could not love him until she learned to trust him. It would serve no purpose to admit his love until she was ready to return his feelings.

A soft knock at the door interrupted his thoughts. He

kissed Claudia's forehead and decided to ignore it. The knock sounded again, more insistent this time. With an annoyed sigh, he eased Claudia from his side then tucked the covers around her. He couldn't remember the last time he'd been so reluctant to leave his bed. Whoever was at the door was about to be sorry. Wearing nothing but a scowl, he stalked across the room and opened the door just wide enough to find out who dared to disturb him.

Stephen took one look at his baron then fastened his gaze on the ceiling. "Your brother approaches, my lord. The watch spied his pennant and a score of knights on the far crest of the east road. They will arrive well within the hour."

That news only soured Guy's mood. "Only a score? There is no sign of a larger force behind him?"

"Nay, my lord."

"Very well. Tell Cook that we will have a score of hungry guests at our tables. Lord Kenric's men tend to eat as if he doesn't feed them." Guy's stomach rumbled and he looked over his shoulder at the table and his own stale meal. He noticed that Claudia had also found time to have her dinner and found himself distracted for a moment by an image of her sitting naked at his table, eating slowly and sensually while she watched him sleep. He made a mighty vow to stay awake the next time. He shook his head to clear his thoughts. "Inform Evard that I will meet him in the middle bailey. I want you there as well."

"Aye, my lord." Stephen gave him a hesitant look. "Should I ready your horse and lance, Baron?"

Guy rubbed his chin, his tone thoughtful. "Nay, this time I will greet my brother with a sword."

Claudia stopped at the entrance to the great hall. The sight that greeted her made her mouth drop open in surprise. The place was deserted. There was never a time of the day or night when the great hall should be empty. During the day, servants went about the business of meals in endless rounds while soldiers gathered there to relax and pass the time when they weren't on guard duty. At night, the long benches became beds for the kitchen workers. But now the cavernous chamber was so empty that it echoed when she set the wooden bucket down that she carried. Now that she thought about it, she hadn't seen anyone on the upper floors, either, yet that did not seem so strange. This seemed very strange indeed.

She glanced down at the bucket and wondered where to start her search for Lenore. For anyone. Guy must have told Lenore not to disturb her this morning, for she'd slept half the day away. Not so unusual, given the fact that she stayed awake half the night watching Guy sleep, thinking over everything he'd said to her, everything they'd done. It was the most amazing night of her life.

Guy's absence when she awoke hadn't worried her. He'd fallen asleep early enough that she assumed he'd risen early to go about his duties. Uncertain what else to do, she'd dressed and intended to go about her own tasks for the day. Scouring the castle with Lenore for poisoned rats, she was bound to come across Guy sooner or later. Then she would find out if the night before was nothing more than a dream, or indeed as real as it seemed. At the moment, nothing seemed very real. The eerie quiet in the great hall made her shiver. Then she heard a roar, the muffled sound of a crowd as it cheered.

She turned toward the massive double doors that led outside. The crowd roared again as she opened one of the doors and she stepped onto the landing that overlooked the middle bailey. It appeared that the entire castle had gathered there. Soldiers formed a large ring six and seven men deep, while servants, squires, and serfs stood on anything they could find to look over the soldiers' broad shoulders. A few servants stood near Claudia on the steps, and she tugged the sleeve of a man she recognized as the pantler. "What is happening?"

The man craned his neck toward the crowd of soldiers and answered without looking at her. " 'Tis a grudge match.

Lord Guy just drew the first blood, but my money is on the Butcher. He has not lost a fight yet."

"The *Butcher*?" Claudia's gaze flew to the circle of soldiers and she caught a glimpse of Guy as he raised his sword to fend off a crushing blow that sent him to one knee. The sight of who, or more aptly, *what* inflicted that blow made her heart stop beating. It was not a man at all, but a giant. An ogre. An enormous black-haired barbarian. This one came straight from a nightmare.

Guy regained his feet and edged around the circle of men with his back toward her. The barbarian faced her, yet it was a face that made her shudder, marked by a savage scar that ran the length of one cheek, an expressionless mask that showed no hint of mercy. Only animals killed so emotionlessly. Or demons. His sword lashed out with the speed of lightning bolts. Thunder followed when the swords struck together hard enough to shoot sparks.

It seemed obvious that Guy had met his match. Most men as large as the one who fought him seemed clumsy and slow-witted. This one seemed nothing less than lethal. He'd stripped down to his breeks, and the midday sun glinted off his sweaty chest. Even at this distance, she could see the violent scars that marked his body. Guy had stripped to his breeks as well, but his smooth, unblemished back looked beautiful and perfect in comparison. The giant looked intent on changing that state of affairs. He swung his sword high, neatly parried Guy's desperate thrust, then the deadly sword slammed downward. This time Guy dropped to one knee on purpose to brace his sword in a line above his head, his only hope of stopping a blow that should have shattered his skull.

Claudia made her way down the steps in a trancelike state, her gaze fastened on the combatants until they disappeared behind the crowd. She looked around at the rapt faces of those who stood by while this butcher person hacked their baron to pieces. Were they so pressed for sport that they would stand idle while Guy fought for his life?

She muttered a curse and pushed her way forward

through the lines of soldiers who stood around the combatants. A few jabbed at her with their elbows, not wanting to give up their place, then one noticed her and the crowd suddenly parted. She supposed it had something to do with the dagger she held.

The knife was nothing more than the dagger she used at meals. She wondered if it would have any effect on the barbarian. No matter. The dagger might slow him long enough for Guy to act. She would not stand by like these traitors and watch Guy die. She would have glared at his men, but she could not look away from the fight. The Butcher arched his sword high overhead, then changed direction at the last moment to deliver a vicious sideswipe that laid open the belly section of Guy's leather gambeson. Guy staggered backward and his executioner closed in for the kill.

Claudia heard someone scream, a high, almost inhuman sound. The dagger in her hand lifted of its own accord, aimed straight at the barbarian's back. She bared her teeth, feeling little more than a savage animal herself, her gaze intent on the beast who intended to take Guy away from her. She would make him pay dearly.

Nay, she would cut his throat.

Halfway to her target, someone grabbed her from behind. She tried to push away, but a large hand locked around her wrist in a grip so crushing and instantly painful that the dagger dropped out of her hand. She felt the sharp prick of a knife at her own throat and still she struggled. The knife bit deeper. She would have continued her struggles, but at that same moment Guy turned to look at her. The barbarian's sword sliced down toward Guy's unprotected neck and she squeezed her eyes shut.

Guy had watched Claudia make her way to the edge of the crowd and silently cursed the distraction. He didn't want her there. Humiliation was not a sight any man would wish his betrothed to witness. Kenric was very good at inflicting it. If he'd known Claudia would show up, he would have challenged his brother-in-law, Roger Fitz Alan, a knight he'd beaten a time or two in the past. Against Kenric, the only question was how badly would he lose?

Kenric had already delivered several blows that would have maimed or killed him, had the blade of the sword struck him rather than the flat. Guy knew from experience that the longer he fought, the more punishing the blows would become until he conceded the match. Yet he didn't want to look a complete weakling in front of Claudia.

Unaware of Guy's reasons for continuing the match, Kenric started to move his blade closer, warning Guy that he would soon suffer a scratch. Kenric's blade ripped open Guy's gambeson in a strike that should have gutted him. His brother was toying with him. Guy staggered back a step to regain his balance, ready to eat his pride and name Kenric the victor. So much for impressing Claudia with his prowess as a warrior.

Then he heard her scream.

Roger Fitz Alan held her by the waist, a deadly miseriecord pressed to her throat. She struggled against his hold, and the long dagger drew blood. A haze of red clouded Guy's vision.

Kenric had already raised his sword for the next punishing blow. Guy countered the downward swing with enough force to send Kenric's sword flying from his hands, and to create a small commotion where the sword landed as soldiers scrambled out of its path. He didn't stop to gloat over the fact that he'd done what no one else had ever managed. He rushed forward to place the tip of his sword at the base of his brother-in-law's neck.

"Release her."

"I am restraining her for a reason," Fitz Alan said in a calm voice, a spark of defiance in his deep brown eyes. "The wench was intent on murder."

"Release her."

The miseriecord came away from Claudia's neck, and Fitz Alan spread his arms wide. "She was intent on killing one of you. I've seen enough murderous looks to recognize what was in her eyes."

Guy pulled Claudia to his side, his sword still holding Fitz Alan at bay. He tilted her chin up with one finger to examine the damage. His voice sounded strange to his ears. "He hurt you."

Claudia pulled her chin away and her hands searched the front of his gambeson. She glanced up, her expression bewildered. "You are not hurt at all. Not even a nick."

Guy ignored that, his attention on the blood that trickled down her neck. He caught a drop and rubbed it between his fingers. His own blood pounded in his ears, a roar that made his brain feel dulled. He looked again at Fitz Alan. "You hurt her."

Fitz Alan's eyes widened. "Guy. What are you doing?"

"That is what I would like to know," Kenric said from beside him. "Put the sword down, Guy. Are you crazed? He did no more than scratch the wench."

Claudia pleaded with him in softer tones, so shaken that she spoke in Italian. "I am fine, Guy. This man did not mean to hurt me."

That was a lie, but Guy realized she meant to calm him. He closed his eyes, then opened them again very slowly. Kenric was right. He was crazed. He lowered the weapon and looked from Fitz Alan to Kenric, then back again. "This 'wench' is my betrothed, soon to be my wife. No one touches her but me."

Fitz Alan exchanged a cryptic look with Kenric, then inclined his head toward Guy. He even managed to smile. "My apologies, brother. 'Tis not my habit to welcome new members to the family at knifepoint." He bowed to Claudia. "My apologies to you as well, Lady—" Fitz Alan cocked one brow toward Guy. "An Italian lady by her speech. Would this be the Lady Claudia you wrote us about in your missive?"

Claudia stiffened and moved closer to Guy's side. "Addio . . . é tuo fratello?"

"Nay, sweet. Fitz Alan is my sister's husband." His arm

tightened around her and he nodded toward Kenric. "This is my brother, Kenric, Baron Remmington."

Guy watched Claudia's gaze move from Fitz Alan to Kenric. His brother's scowl had its usual effect. Her eyes widened in horror. She shook her head. "But he was trying to kill you!"

"Is that what you thought?" Guy found himself smiling. Relief made him feel light-headed. " 'Twas but a contest."

"A contest?" she echoed, her gaze darting again to Kenric. He felt her shudder. "You risk your life for a contest?"

"My brother would never hurt me," he assured her. "He is simply determined to teach me all he knows of fighting. Everyone knows these contests are something of a tradition whenever we meet."

"I did not know that," she bit out.

He grinned at her, pleased to see her courage return. "I cannot believe you meant to stop it. To enter a sword fight armed with nothing more than a dagger. What possessed you to do something so foolish?"

Guy knew he made a mistake the moment the words left his mouth.

"Your foolish games made me shame myself before your family," she announced, still speaking in Italian. Her chin rose and she gathered her skirts. She looked every inch a queen, chastising a lowly subject. "I will await your apology in our chamber."

Guy just smiled and eyed the saucy switch of her hips as she walked away from him. She'd tried to save him from his own brother. His smile faded.

It occurred to him that Kenric's fearsome exterior was not the only reason for the look of horror when she discovered his identity. Aye, she'd made an endearing fool of herself before Kenric and Fitz Alan. But she also found herself unexpectedly in the company of her own brother's killers. And he was now faced with the prospect of explaining why he intended to marry a traitor's sister. His mouth curved downward.

"*Our* chamber?" Fitz Alan asked dryly. "Clever of you to gain the girl's confidence by seducing her. Willing prisoners are so much more pleasant to have about."

"I suggest you lock the wench away before she learns you have no intention of marrying her," Kenric suggested matter-of-factly. "A woman scorned can make a deadly enemy. That one appears more dangerous than most."

Guy looked around the circle of soldiers. The men closest to them hung on their every word. Others craned their necks to eavesdrop. He wondered when his brothers had grown so thickheaded. "You may both make a habit of discussing family business before your soldiers, but I do not." He nodded toward the great hall. "I suggest we retire to a place more private."

Fitz Alan resheathed his dagger while a squire produced Kenric's clothing in exchange for his sword. Stephen delivered Guy's shirt and tunic as well, and Guy donned the garments with quick, harsh movements. His gaze scanned the crowd for Evard, and he motioned the knight forward with a silent gesture. "Have the steward arrange a bath and meal for my brothers, and whatever else they need to refresh themselves from their journey. I want a bath delivered to my chamber as well."

Evard had the audacity to grin. "Like as not, the water for the bath you ordered upon your return yesterday is still heating."

Guy's eyes narrowed. "That will be *all*, Evard."

"Aye, my lord." Evard bowed low, then turned to carry out his orders.

Guy was tempted to place his boot on Evard's insolent backside. Instead he turned toward Kenric and Fitz Alan. Both eyed him warily. "Now that I consider the situation more fully, it seems best if you avail yourselves of my hospitality while I attend to other matters. I will meet you in the solar in a few hours. There is much we must discuss." He inclined his head in a mocking bow. "Now, if you will excuse me, I have an apology to make."

Guy ignored their looks of disbelief and set off for the great hall. He didn't feel any need to explain his concerns about Claudia, that it just occurred to him that her haughty departure was little more than a disguise to hide her fears. He didn't want her to be afraid ever again. His brothers' timing couldn't be worse. It would not hurt them to cool their heels for a few hours. Left to her own devices, Claudia's imagination could doubtless conjure any number of dire scenarios. She was more important than his family at the moment.

That thought made him pause on the winding stairs that led to his chamber. In all his life, no one had taken precedence over his family. Claudia not only took precedence, somehow she had become the entire focus of his life. He no longer imagined a moment without her in it.

Once he'd worried that his obsession with her would make him weak and vulnerable. Instead he felt new purpose. She filled a void in his life that he'd never known existed. The wealth he'd amassed and the trade empire he'd built meant nothing without someone to share his fortune, someone to confide in who had only his best interests at heart, someone who understood him. Until Claudia, no one could grasp the logic of his interest in trade. She understood what drove him better than any other, and seemed to recognize when he lost sight of his own goals. He could save her from a lifetime crowded with fears, but she could save him from a lifetime of empty successes.

The time had come to give himself over completely to his obsession, without reservation. He found the object of his obsession in his chamber. Claudia sat cross-legged amidst the pillows in front of the fireplace, a green and white tunic spread across her lap. He closed the door loud enough to announce his presence, but she didn't look up from her sewing. Content to study her delicate profile until she acknowledged him, he leaned against the door and waited. The wait lengthened and he turned his attention to the cut of her plum-colored daygown. It clung to her in all the right places, the bodice low enough to tempt his imagination, yet modest enough to be worn in front of others. Her long braid drew his gaze down the trim lines of her back to where the braid curved along her hip. His hands mentally followed the same path and he felt a traitorous quickening in his loins.

"You are here to apologize?" she asked at last.

"Aye. You have my most heartfelt apology, my lady."

Her hands stilled and she turned her head to give him a long, thoughtful look. "I did not think you would do it."

"And risk losing my lady's favor?" He smiled and shook his head. "I think not."

She lowered her lashes. "Perhaps I was a bit hasty in my demand. I acted without thinking. You were right to call me foolish."

"Then I retract my apology and accept yours."

Her mouth formed a pout. "You mock me, sir. Was your apology nothing more than an attempt to humor me?"

"Aye. Did it work?"

Her haughtiness dissolved into a smile. That smile made him feel warm everywhere. "I will not encourage such ungallant behavior."

There were all sorts of ungallant behavior he would like her to encourage. He sat down behind her on the pillows, then stretched out his legs so that she sat cradled between his thighs.

"Is this tunic meant for me?" His arms went around her and he smoothed the fabric of the tunic in her lap, making certain there were no wrinkles at all where the tunic lay across her legs.

She tried to push his hands away, being careful not to jab him with her needle. "Aye, 'tis yours. I took the measurements from another of your tunics, so I am certain this one will fit."

"Is this a dog?" His fingers traced the shape of an animal she'd stitched on the shoulder of the tunic. The emblem happened to lie atop her knee. The pressure of his finger made her leg jerk and he smiled over the discovery that she was ticklish.

"I thought it looked more like a wolf," she said, her voice hesitant. She tilted her head to one side, a clear invitation that Guy accepted. His lips brushed along the smooth column of her neck.

" 'Tis a dog." He traced the emblem again, delighted by the small movements she made to escape his tickling. "See? You made the body too long and narrow to be a proper wolf. And the wolf of Montague should be on a field of blue, not green."

"You do not like it?"

His fingers moved to a series of stripes resting along her inner thigh. "On the contrary, I daresay this will be my favorite tunic."

She giggled and grabbed his hand. "Stop that."

"Why?" He ignored her order. His hand closed over her knee and he gave it a gentle squeeze. Her throaty laughter made him smile. "Are you ticklish?"

"Nay, oh, stop that. Please." She pushed against his hand even as she dissolved into a fit of giggles. "Aye! I will admit it. I am ticklish. Stop!"

He released his hold on her leg. "Hm. I wonder where else you are so sensitive."

Her elbows clamped against her sides. "Nowhere."

"Really?" He chuckled over the blatant lie and tossed the tunic aside along with the sharp needle, then wedged his hands beneath her elbows to test her waist. "You are not ticklish here?"

"Nay. Oh! Ah, ah . . ." Her giggles turned to laughter. She made one last effort to control herself and braced both hands against his legs. "Stop!"

He tickled her mercilessly, his laughter just as loud, her mirth infectious. She twisted and turned until she ended up sprawled across his lap. Her laughter turned to helpless shrieks and his hands finally grew still, one at her waist, the other at her thigh.

She collapsed against the pillows, her taut body suddenly limp. Her eyes sparkled with tears of laughter as she gazed up at him. She laid her hands atop his and gasped for air. "You are—*ruthless.*"

"I like to see you laugh." He stretched out on the pillows next to her, his head propped on his hand, and brushed a stray wisp of hair behind her ear. "You may take your revenge on me later tonight when we are abed. I, too, am ticklish, but in only one place and I shall not tell you where. You must make that discovery on your own."

She turned on her side to face him, then reached out to wedge her fingers beneath his arm. "Perhaps I will make that discovery right now."

He shook his head when she wriggled her fingers. " 'Tis doubtful you will make any such discovery while I am dressed. However, if you wish to undress me right now, I will be happy to place myself at your complete mercy."

"That has a nice sound to it." Her expression turned thoughtful, and she lowered her lashes. "But I do not want to keep you from your guests. They think little enough of my character as it is."

"They thought you were trying to murder me. Or meant to murder Kenric. They know better now." He stroked his fingertips along the soft curve of her cheek. "I am touched that you were so concerned for my safety, yet now I worry that you might someday put yourself in harm's way on my account. Do not be fooled by my poor showing against Kenric. I can take care of myself in any fight."

"You were losing," she pointed out.

"Aye, as every man loses against my brother. He is unbeatable with a sword or lance. 'Tis a fact," he assured her, when she gave him a skeptical look. "Have you never heard of him?"

She shrugged one shoulder. "After Roberto died, I heard a few tales about the man who killed him. Now that I have met your brother, all that seems missing are the horns. He is—frightening."

"He will not harm you, Claudia. I promise. You might even come to like him some day." Her expression said that would be no day soon. He tried a different tack. "He and Fitz Alan will accept you as my betrothed. If anything would ever happen to me, you will always have the protection of my family."

"Do they know who I am?"

"Nay, but they will not hold you responsible for the actions of your brother when they learn the truth."

"I think you overestimate your family's willingness to forgive and forget."

"You will see for yourself," he predicted. "Just be yourself when we join them in the great hall, and you will have them eating from your hand in no time."

She shook her head. "I cannot face them again. Not yet."

"Do not tell me you are turning coward at this late date?" He gave her a look of mock horror. "Here I boasted to my brothers that you have the heart of a lion, that you could scale castle walls and face down a boar without batting an eye. They will think me a liar."

"I think you are spinning a tale right now," she countered. Still, she was smiling. He took heart.

"This afternoon I will meet with my brothers alone. There are matters we must discuss that are best spoken where everyone in the great hall will not strain to hear them. Tomorrow we will have a feast to celebrate their arrival." He watched her face carefully. "You will attend that feast, and take your rightful place at my side."

Rather than argue, she placed her hand on his cheek. "Does it mean so much to you?"

"Aye," he answered. "I would have you show them your courage, Claudia. You have nothing to be ashamed of, and no reason to hide. On the other hand, I can understand the reasons you have to fear and dislike them, and why you would wish to avoid their company. Yet they are my family and will soon be yours. Can *you* forgive and forget, as you would have them do the same?"

She bit her lower lip, then her mouth turned to a sulky

pout. "There are times when I wish you were not so good at reading my thoughts."

"You have a talent for that yourself, my lady." His fingertip traced the outline of her mouth. "Will you help plan the festivities as well?"

"Aye." She released a long sigh. Clearly, it was not an appealing prospect. "If you promise to let me leave the hall as soon as the meal ends. They may be your family, but it will take time before I can accustom myself to the notion that they will be mine. Indeed, I still have difficulty accepting that I will be your wife."

" 'Tis fact," he assured her, his gaze on her lips. She had the most sensual mouth imaginable. His fingertips moved along the neckline of her bodice, caressing her soft skin. "I meant every word I spoke last night, sweetheart."

She shivered under his touch, but did not try to stop his seductive exploration. "What if your brothers do not accept me?"

"They will accept you."

"But what—"

He leaned forward to cut off her objection with a kiss. And then another.

She managed to free her lips when he tried for thirds. "How can you be so sure? You said yourself that Kenric would probably slit my throat when he learns I am Roberto's sister."

Guy frowned over the reminder. What had possessed him to say something so stupid? "I exaggerated. The reason why escapes me at the moment, but rest assured that no one in my family will hurt you."

She lifted her chin to reveal the small cut Fitz Alan made, her expression skeptical. " 'Twould seem they intended an early start on your exaggeration. You are certain they do not know who I am?"

"That was a misunderstanding, as well you know."

She didn't look convinced.

He drew her closer. "Claudia, do you know how your

brother died? The details, I mean, of what really happened that day?"

She drew small circles around the hollow at the base of his neck with her finger. "I know that Roberto tried to kill Kenric's wife, but Kenric slit his throat instead."

He captured her hand and held it against his chest. "Your brother was wounded, sweetheart. There was to be a joust between Kenric and your brother, and Roberto received a mortal wound. There was no hope for recovery, only long hours of suffering until he succumbed to his injury. Kenric ended his life to end his suffering. Roberto confessed his plot before he died."

Guy knew he spoke the truth, even though it was a truth colored by deliberate omissions and a few small rearrangements of the events. Roberto was dead and he could not change that fact. What he sought now was a means to turn Kenric into something less than a monster in her mind. Her thoughtful expression said he might be succeeding.

"Your brother would have died anyway," he pressed. "Kenric did nothing more than shorten his life by a few hours, a day at most."

Her brows drew together in a frown. "I did not know this."

"You will find most tales that concern my brother are not as grim as they sound. And it will not matter who you are to Kenric and Fitz Alan. When they realize my reasons for choosing you, they will support my decision."

She turned her frown in his direction. "Are we back to your cryptic reasons again?"

"Aye." His gaze drifted lower, wondering where he would find the laces on this gown. "I believe we are."

She read his thoughts easily enough and flattened her palm against his chest. "Your brothers will be waiting to meet with you."

"I came here to make an apology," he informed her, as his hands worked to loosen his tunic. He sat up to toss the garment aside, his smile wicked. "I intend to make it a very long apology."

"They are apt to guess the reason for your delay."

"Aye." He stripped away the last of his garments, then leaned back against a pile of pillows. He stretched his legs out in front of him, and crossed them at the ankles. "Does that bother you?"

"Oh, yes," she whispered, and he knew the answer had nothing to do with his brothers.

Claudia was either unaware of her expression, or didn't care that he knew of her interest in his nakedness. Once he had hoped to find a mistress who would look at him with such undisguised longing. He had never dared hope to find lust in a wife. The perfect woman sat before him, and she was his. Life was very good indeed. He propped his hands behind his head. "I am at your mercy, my lady. Do with me as you will."

"You wish to be ravished, Baron?"

" 'Tis my fondest desire."

"I am not so certain how to go about this." She looked him over from head to foot, her voice considering. "I did not realize that a woman could ravish a man. You may need to provide a few instructions, my lord."

"Do you want to touch me?"

"That would be *my* fondest desire." She knelt at his side, then drew her fingertips across his chest. "May I touch you however I wish?"

His pulse gave a leap of excitement. "Aye."

Guy lay unresisting beneath her hands, at least, in spirit. His muscles contracted wherever she touched him. She found the reaction fascinating and tested him thoroughly, delighting in her visible control of his strength. His body's response to more intimate caresses startled her at first, but curiosity soon overcame modesty. She experimented until she discovered certain strokes that made him groan, others that made him shudder. He exerted himself not at all, yet a fine sheen of perspiration covered his body, and his breathing sounded labored.

"Do you want me to stop?"

She brushed her fingers across his belly and he shuddered again, but managed to shake his head. She shifted restlessly. Her skin felt warm and sensitive beneath her gown. More than once she had imagined what it would feel like to receive caresses as intimate as the ones she bestowed. She studied the grim set of his jaw and his pained expression, then drew a line down the center of his chest. "I cannot tell if you are enjoying this, or if you tolerate my explorations just so I may sate my curiosity."

He released a breath so deep that she wondered how long he'd held it. "I want you to know my body as intimately as you know your own, Claudia. Be warned that I intend to know yours just as thoroughly." His heated gaze lingered on her breasts, and they suddenly felt swollen. He could heighten her arousal with a glance alone. "You will undress for me while I watch, then you will lie down among these pillows to await the pleasures I will give you with my hands and mouth. I think I will start with sighs."

Her hands moved to knead the muscles of his chest and belly. "Sighs, my lord?"

"Aye, I will caress your arms and soft, white shoulders, and you will give me little sighs of longing. Then my hands will skim over the sensitive skin along your sides where you are ticklish, and lower to your waist, to the curves of your hips, then down the full, delicious length of your legs. You will start to tremble, but I will massage your feet to relax you a little, just as you rubbed mine. Then you will learn that such a massage is not the least bit relaxing while you lie naked before me. That realization will make you moan."

Her voice was little more than a breathless whisper. "It will?"

Guy nodded, then closed his eyes. "I will work my way up again very slowly, rubbing and massaging every inch of your legs. You will discover that the tender skin behind your knees is more sensitive than you ever imagined, that a few strokes along your inner thighs is enough to make you tremble. It is anticipation that causes a quickening sensation in your belly, the need to be caressed even more intimately, but I will not ease your need so soon in the game."

"This is a game to you?" One hand drifted lower to stroke his thigh. She traced the line between his legs, moving upward until she heard his breath catch.

He swallowed visibly. "Aye, Claudia. 'Tis a most pleasurable game called love-play, one that we will play often."

"What will you do next in our game?"

"Stroke your stomach," he managed. His breath came out in a long hiss when her actions matched his words. There was a dark edge to his voice that made her shiver. "It will no longer be enough just to touch you. I will want to kiss you, to taste where I touch you."

She pressed her lips to his stomach and swirled her tongue over the taut skin. Guy uttered a blasphemous curse that made her blush. "What next, my lord? Would your kisses move higher, or lower?"

His body responded to the question, but his words denied its reaction. "On you, my lips would move higher, along with my hands. A woman's breasts never fail to fascinate a man, and yours are so perfect that they fair make my mouth water. I will brush my thumbs over your nipples until—"

To her amazement, his flat male nipples hardened beneath her thumbs, and she felt a tremor pass through his body. She leaned down to kiss the small bud, then bit him painlessly. A low growl from deep in his chest ended in a tortured moan when she nibbled a path across his chest to inflict more of the torment.

"Claudia." His voice was barely recognizable, and she leaned back to look at him. His arms were still clasped behind his head, but every muscle stood out in rigid relief. His chest heaved with each breath he drew, and his eyes were tightly clenched, as if he suffered some mortal agony. "Please, Claudia. End this game."

She was more than ready to oblige. She just wasn't quite certain how. "Should I take off my gown?"

He shook his head. "No time."

"Then what—"

"Mount me. Now."

"What?" It had never occurred to her that they could make love in such a way. It sounded most intriguing. She eased her leg over his until she straddled his thighs, then rearranged her skirts around them. Every brush of the fabric against his skin made him flinch.

"Hurry, love."

His patience was strained to the very limits, she would wager, along with his control. Still, he didn't touch her, or do anything to hasten her movements. The feel of his bare thighs beneath her made her own skin tingle. She moved higher until her own aroused flesh stroked the length of his. She repeated the seductive movements until he was slick with her desire. Being fully clothed made the intimacies taking place beneath her skirts somehow more intense, more wickedly erotic. She tilted her head back and curled her hips forward to slide against the length of him once more. Guy arched his body at the same moment, freeing himself from beneath her, then surging upward again to seek her opening. She braced her hands against his chest and made small, tentative motions with her hips to help position him, then she sat down. Very slowly.

His eyes opened just as slowly. The look of near-violence in those blue depths made her shudder. His expression would frighten her if she did not have such complete control of him, but he gave her his strength willingly. Somehow she knew that he had never played this particular game with another, never allowed anyone to dominate his will so completely. She sensed that this was much more than a game, that there was a hidden meaning in his intense gaze, something important, yet unspoken.

Then she knew.

He did not touch her because she did not give him permission to touch her. Her earlier explorations continued unhindered because she indicated no desire to see them ended. He would do anything she asked, and nothing against her wishes. It was a game, but a game meant to teach her one thing. He belonged to her. Body and soul.

Tears blurred her vision as she took him fully inside her, and a shadow of concern crossed his features. She leaned down to kiss his beautiful mouth, to murmur words of reassurance. "Our lovemaking is always a source of wonder, my lord. Pray forgive my tears and hold me as you wish."

His arms wrapped around her and he crushed her to his chest for a kiss that tasted of all the restraint still leashed inside him. Yet he did not become the aggressor even then. His hold loosened until his hands moved over her in sweet caresses that guided her movements and taught her how to dominate them both. The first small shivers became tremors deep inside her, and only then did he take control of her. His hands held her hips down hard against him, taking and giving at the same time. Her whispered words of love were lost in the harsh sound of his completion. He called out her name.

13

uy gave his tunic one last tug to make certain the garment was back in place, then he opened the door to the solar. Fitz Alan sat in one of the window embrasures, while Kenric had his hands clasped behind his back as he paced before the fireplace. They both turned at the sound of Guy's voice.

"I trust the two of you had ample time to refresh yourselves?"

"We had ample time to conquer half of Scotland," Kenric drawled. "What kept you?"

"Careful, Baron." Fitz Alan stood up to help himself to another goblet of wine. "You will make the boy blush."

"What kept me is none of your business," Guy told Kenric, then he inclined his head toward Fitz Alan. "And I would thank you to remember that you were already a father at my age."

"Is that the reason you are in such a rush to become a father yourself?" Fitz Alan gave an exaggerated sigh. "Ah, I have a rival. A glass of wine?" he offered, before Guy could voice any more arguments. He filled another goblet without waiting for the answer. "I vow you have the finest spirits. Where is this batch from?"

"Burgundy," Guy answered. He accepted the goblet and took a deep drink, hoping to soothe his irritation. Anger would get him nowhere in this discussion. Still, it annoyed him when these two treated him like a child. Since he was the youngest in his family, the others tended to forget that he held power and responsibilities equal to or greater than their own. Most times he remained good-natured about their teasing. Today would not be one of those times. "Before we go any further, I want to make one thing perfectly clear. I will not have either of you speak of Claudia again as you did in the bailey. My people accept her, and I would not have a few careless words turn them against her."

One dark brow rose as Kenric fixed his silvery gaze on him. "This game you play with the wench will lead to trouble. 'Tis obvious you have taken what you want from her. Put her in the dungeons where she belongs, before she discovers your deception. Or was that exhibition in the bailey a sign she made that discovery already? 'Twas hard to tell who she meant to skewer. At the very least, you need to disarm the girl and set a guard on her."

At first Guy was too stunned by his brother's remarks to say anything. Then he reminded himself, forcefully, that Kenric knew little about Claudia. What he did know came from the message Guy sent, written when she seemed guilty of treachery. Guy set his goblet down and willed his fingers to unclench before he dented the silver. "I do not play any games with Claudia. Soon after I wrote you, it became clear that she did not take part in the plot against me. Indeed, she risked her own life to help free me from Lonsdale. Since then, I found she possesses all the traits I could wish for in a wife. I have every intention of marrying her. We will be wed within the fortnight."

Kenric made a sound of disgust. "Can you not see the obvious? She seduced you into thinking you are in love with her. You were ready to take Fitz Alan's life because he kept the girl from stabbing one of us. She very nearly turned you against your own family." He shook his head. "Take my advice and lock her up before she spreads any more of her poison."

Guy struggled to keep his voice below a shout. "Unlike you, I do not intend to keep my wife a prisoner until I decide she is trustworthy. I have made that decision already."

White-hot anger flared in Kenric's eyes, but died away almost as quickly. He turned to Fitz Alan. "Talk some sense into this fool's head before I decide to use something other than words to open his eyes."

Fitz Alan propped up his leg on the window seat and draped one arm over his knee. He held his goblet by the rim and stared at the blood-red liquid for a long moment as he swirled the wine in a steady circle. "Your brother is right, Guy. This girl has reason to hate every one of us. 'Tis hard to imagine that any affections she shares with you are genuine."

" 'Tis hard to imagine a woman risking her life to protect someone she hates," Guy countered. "This afternoon she drew her dagger with every intention of setting herself against an armed knight more than twice her size. You were a stranger to her, Kenric. She saw her betrothed on the losing side of a sword fight and did not stop to ask questions. A reasonable reaction, as my death seems her greatest fear. Does that sound like an affectionless woman to either one of you?"

"Nay," Kenric answered, "it sounds like a woman who knows she will be at the mercy of your men if you die. In that she seems wise enough to realize there is only one man here who is fool enough to be seduced by her lies."

"Her name is Claudia," Guy informed them through clenched teeth. "Not 'this girl,' or 'the wench,' or—" He gave Fitz Alan a sharp glance. "What do you mean, she has reason to hate every one of us?"

Fitz Alan shrugged. "She is Roberto of Ravenna's sister. Surely that is reason enough." His brows drew together. "And surely you were aware of that fact."

"I knew." Guy raked one hand through his hair. Christ. Kenric's hostility suddenly made sense. Little wonder they were so set against her. "How did you know?"

Fitz Alan gestured toward Kenric. "Your brother learned all he could of Roberto and his family five years ago. We knew he was a part of Baron Lonsdale's family. 'Tis why your message did not take us by complete surprise. Traitors run in that family."

"Why didn't one of you tell me about Lonsdale?" Guy

demanded. "Had I known of his relation to Roberto, I would have negotiated for Halford Hall on a battlefield."

"You were not in England when we made the discovery, and Lonsdale seemed to pose little threat at the time. It was an oversight," Fitz Alan admitted. His tone turned considering. "You do know there is another brother?"

"Aye, Claudia told me about Dante." Guy held up his hands when Kenric and Fitz Alan exchanged a knowing look. "I know he is one of Edward's mercenaries."

The two remained silent a long moment, then Kenric cleared his throat. "Dante Chiavari is not just any mercenary. He is—"

"Then he is alive?" Guy asked, without much enthusiasm. Dante would only complicate matters, yet not even this phantom brother could keep him from marrying Claudia. Kenric nodded and Guy's scowl deepened.

"Aye, as of a few months ago, when the king held court at Remmington. As I was saying," Kenric went on, "he is not part of the pack of mercenaries Edward keeps at his heels these days. Dante Chiavari is the king's Enforcer. If you will not give her up for the simple fact that she is a traitor, then be rid of her because you will find your throat laid open if her brother discovers you hold her here as your mistress."

The king's Enforcer. The words echoed in Guy's mind. Good God. Claudia's brother was the king's personal assassin. How appropriate, in a perverse sort of way. "Are you certain?"

"Aye. Positive. The king once asked my counsel on a matter that involved Chiavari. I cannot break the king's confidence, but I can tell you that Dante Chiavari is even more dangerous than his brother, Roberto."

"Few even know what he looks like," Fitz Alan offered. "He wears a disguise whenever he must present himself at court, the garb of an infidel, complete with a turban and scarf that conceals every feature but his eyes. Green Chiavari eyes." Fitz Alan shook his head. " 'Tis enough to inspire fear in any Englishman with traitorous thoughts on his mind.

They say if you do see his face, it will be the last thing you see in this lifetime."

Guy looked between the two men who had inspired fear in entire countries. "You sound half afraid of him."

"I have no reason to fear him," Fitz Alan answered. "You, however, have cause for concern."

"Perhaps," Guy mused. "Perhaps not. Claudia has not heard from Dante for over a year, nor laid eyes on him since he left Lonsdale. If he had any care for her, he would have taken her away from Lonsdale years ago. Even if he does recall his responsibilities at this late date, he can find nothing to object to in our marriage. Indeed, he should thank me for ensuring his sister's safety, a duty he sorely neglected. As far as I am concerned, she is alone." He looked his brother squarely in the eye, a silent challenge. "I am all Claudia has, and she is all I want."

"I do not want her in this family," Kenric said flatly. "I trust her no more than I would trust one of her brothers. You made a mistake by taking her to your bed, but it is not too late to undo the damage." He gave Guy an equally challenging look. "Marriage is not the solution. She is of no value as a prisoner, and you know as well as I that you can break this false betrothal her uncle forced upon you."

"Just what are you suggesting?" Guy asked in an ominous tone.

Kenric folded his arms across his chest. "She is dangerous. 'Tis probable she plotted your murder with her uncle. Lock her in the dungeons where she belongs."

"Where she will die if we are lucky?" Guy asked sarcastically. Kenric's casual shrug infuriated him. "You may be my brother, but I do not have to—"

"My *lords*!" Fitz Alan held up his hands. "This argument will get us nowhere. Guy, you told us in your missive that you suspected Lady Claudia of treason. Tell us what happened to alter your opinion of her so drastically so that we may better understand your reasoning *before* we judge her," he finished, with a warning glance at Kenric.

Guy considered the request, then gave a reluctant nod. He told them of his escape in greater detail than the missive allowed, of Thomas's report a few days later that confirmed much of what Claudia had told him. He explained her willingness to free him of the betrothal, and her plan to search for Dante in London. Although he hadn't planned to tell them more than a few logical reasons for wanting to marry her, he couldn't seem to keep quiet about the qualities that attracted him most; her courage and resilience, her intelligence and quick wit.

He knew he was making himself sound like a lovesick fool. They would never see Claudia as he did, nor accept her as a part of their family. So he told them more than he had intended, a couched warning that he would choose Claudia over his family if they forced him to decide between the two. He would miss his family sorely, but he could not conceive of his life without Claudia. He was willing to make that sacrifice for her.

A long silence descended over the room when he finished. Kenric stood at one of the windows, staring sightlessly at the cloudless sky. Fitz Alan sat with his legs spread apart on the window seat, his elbows on his knees, while his hands rolled the wine goblet between his palms. His eyes lacked any trace of their usual humor. That was a bad sign. Guy braced himself for the worst.

Then he got angry. Did they trust his judgment so little? Did they truly think him stupid enough to be taken in by a pretty face and sweet lies? By God, Claudia had more faith in him than his own family. They would—

"Perhaps the marriage would not be a complete disaster."

Guy jerked his head around to stare at Kenric, shocked that his brother had spoken the words. He had anticipated some measure of understanding from Fitz Alan. From Kenric he had expected nothing more than stubborn silence.

"I am far from overjoyed at the prospect of welcoming a Chiavari into our family," Kenric went on. "Indeed, I doubt I will ever like the girl. However, 'tis obvious you are set on having her, and I accept your choice. Your instincts have never failed you in the past. I pray they do not fail you now."

Not exactly a vote of confidence, but more than Guy had hoped for. He turned to Fitz Alan. "Will you accept my choice as well?"

"Aye." Fitz Alan released a long sigh. "You are well and truly smitten, Guy. I also recognize a lost cause when I see it. I think you are crazed, but your brother thought the same of me when I asked to marry your sister. I have never regretted my choice, and hope you can always say the same." Fitz Alan stood up and set his goblet aside to offer his hand. "You have my best wishes. When will the wedding take place?"

Guy accepted Fitz Alan's hand and smiled in relief. "I spoke with the priest this morning. We will speak our vows a week from Sunday."

"You will not renegotiate the betrothal contract first?" Kenric asked sharply.

"Nay, but I will contest it," Guy answered. "If Lonsdale forces the issue, I will go to the archbishop himself. I have contacts who would be sympathetic to my cause and trust that my version of events is the truth. The last thing I intend to do is reward Lonsdale with so much as a florin for plotting my murder."

Kenric nodded. "Good. I am glad to see you are not completely witless where the girl is concerned."

"Claudia," Guy corrected.

"Aye, well, whatever her name, 'tis good to see a glimmer of your sensible self. I have hope that you are not as gullible as you seem."

Guy inclined his head in a mocking bow. "Your confidence in my abilities overwhelms me, brother."

"Now, now," Fitz Alan cut in. "There is no need to start an argument when we are in agreement. Let us talk of something more pleasant. The siege on Halford, perhaps?"

"Ugh! These things are disgusting!" Lenore held her nose with one hand, a bucket brimming with rat carcasses in the other.

"Aye," Claudia agreed, "but not as disgusting as were they still alive." She dumped her own bucket into the cesspit then hurried away from the foul-smelling hole.

Lenore tagged right behind her. "Will you teach me to make an oil scented with lavender?"

Claudia gave her a sharp glance.

"The rose oil you taught me to make smells divine and it makes my skin feel so soft," Lenore went on. "Of course, I would never think to use the same scent as your own, but I do like the smell of lavender."

Lightened of her grim load, the maid's face was wreathed again in a sunny smile. She all but skipped alongside Claudia as they made their way back to the keep. Lately Lenore seemed to regard Claudia as some sort of expert on all things feminine. She asked Claudia's opinion of hairstyles, the cut and color of gowns, embroidery patterns, perfume mixtures. It felt rather odd to have anyone ask her opinion of anything, much less to have it held in such high esteem. It was as if Lenore looked up to her as she might an older sister. The attention was so flattering and unexpected that Claudia didn't have the heart to discourage Lenore's overly familiar questions. "Aye, 'tis much the same as the mixture for roses. Best be careful, Lenore, or you will learn so much about scents that the baron will appoint you Montague's perfumer."

Lenore looked startled, then intrigued by the possibility. "There is no perfumer in residence at Montague. Do you truly think I could gain such a position?"

"If you memorize the mixtures I teach you, then aye, I see no reason why not." Claudia turned onto the path that led through the gardens. She trailed her hand along the side of the tall hedges that screened the path from the herb plots. It was a silly thing to do, as hoydenish as the little boys who dragged sticks along the stockade fences. They probably didn't know why they did that, either. Sheer joy of the moment, she supposed.

Despite the fact that she would face her future in-laws in a few hours at the feast, Claudia hadn't felt so lighthearted in years. Memories of the last few days with Guy surrounded her like a soft, warm blanket. Her cheeks all but ached from smiling so much. Her body throbbed with a new awareness of passion. Her heart brimmed with the tender emotions of love. She didn't ever remember being this happy. Guy was such a solid presence in her life that she almost believed nothing could take him away. It would be like stealing the sun from the sky, and no one had yet managed that feat. Aye, he was a man determined to have his way in everything and fully capable of getting what he wanted. Amazingly, he wanted her. In this particular instance, Claudia found no fault with that trait.

Lenore continued to chatter on about flowers and potions. Claudia smiled dreamily and stared at the fluffy clouds above them, lost in her own thoughts. She didn't notice when Lenore stopped talking, or realize that the maid had slowed her pace. A hand reached out as she passed an opening in the hedges and brought her to an abrupt halt. She let out a small shriek.

"Daydreaming, little one?" Guy drew Claudia into his arms, then motioned to her maid. "Your lady will meet you inside, Lenore. Run along now."

Lenore bobbed a curtsy, her head lowered to hide her grin. "Aye, my lord."

"W-what are you doing here?" Claudia asked, still startled by his sudden appearance.

Guy drew her into the small, secluded alcove created by the hedges and tossed the bucket she carried back onto the path. He placed her arms around his waist until her wrists met and their bodies fit together intimately. His wolfish smile made his white teeth gleam in the sunlight. "Tarrying with my lover, of course."

His words stirred an ache to life inside her, spoken so

tenderly that he might have said he loved her in the same enticing tone. His arms went around her and he lowered his head for a kiss. At first she resisted his attemps to deepen the kiss. Anyone might happen upon them. That thought made his embrace all the more wickedly sensual, its forbidden fruit even more tempting. He cupped her breast in his hand and her mouth opened beneath his, her modesty lost to an instant white-hot passion.

Guy came to his senses first. He broke away from her mouth with a reluctant groan and buried his face in the crook of her neck. His hands smoothed over her hips, then he held her tight against the hard proof of his words. "Sweet saints, I cannot get enough of you."

"I thought you well sated this morn, my lord." She slipped her hand between their bodies, endlessly fascinated by the physical manifestation of his desires. Even holding his aroused body through his clothing she felt her own turn to liquid heat. "Should you wish to return to our chamber to prove me mistaken, I should not make an objection."

"I would not make it that far," he muttered. His fingers wrapped around her wrist and he pulled her hand away, slowing the movement when he realized she meant to rake her fingers across him. His forehead dropped to her shoulder. "You delight in torturing me, you wicked vixen."

She looped her arms around his neck and ducked down to place small, measured kisses along his taut lips. "I delight in pleasuring you, my lord, as well you know. 'Tis your own fault. I knew nothing of pleasuring a man until we met. You taught me all I know, and truly deserve everything you get."

"Aye, you have a natural talent for torture." His hands went around her waist, and he brushed his lips against her hair. "This is not quite the clever idea I thought it would be. Just let me hold you for a moment."

"Mm, this is very pleasant, too," she said agreeably, tightening her hold around his neck. "I like it almost as much as when you do more than just hold me."

"Do not fool yourself, love. I am still sorely tempted to

lift your skirts. Sometime after that I would be content to do nothing more than hold you."

She heard the smile in his voice, but it was the casual endearment that made her heart skip a beat. Ever since he first made love to her he had showered her with affection and every endearment but the one she wanted to hear most. Did he want her to speak the words first, or was affection all he felt for her? He encouraged her to be bold in her passions. She decided it was time to be bold with her heart. "I—"

"Ssh." He lifted his head, his expression suddenly alert. "Someone is coming."

He leaned down to right the overturned bucket, then straightened and gave his tunic a brisk tug downward. The garment disguised the condition of his body with limited success. His hands went to her hair to tuck a few stray tendrils back into her braid. "There. Return to Lenore now, sweetheart. I must return to my brothers. I left them contemplating a particularly fine stock of penned sheep, but they have doubtless noticed my absence by now. I will see you in our chamber one hour before the feast begins." He pressed a hard, quick kiss against her lips. "One hour. Remember that, love."

Claudia opened her eyes, her lips still tingling. Guy was gone, as if he had never been there. She knew well enough that he had. Smiling, she leaned down to pick up the bucket. At that same moment, two soldiers passed the alcove. One leaped away from her hiding place, as if the hedges themselves had come to life.

"Lady Claudia!" he exclaimed, one hand clutching the front of his tunic. "You gave me a start."

The other soldier took her sudden appearance in stride. He looked up and down the path, then his gaze returned to her. "Lord Kenric sent us to look for his brother. Do you know where we might find the baron?"

"I, ah, well, I am not certain." She felt her face burn with a fierce blush and could only wonder what the soldiers thought of that telling reaction. "I believe he did mention something about the sheep pens."

"Much thanks, Lady Claudia." Both soldiers bowed politely, then they, too, disappeared around a bend in the path.

Claudia made her way to the keep after a quick check of the garden's sundial. She did not want to miss her appointment with Guy in their chamber, knowing exactly why he wanted her there a good hour early. She felt like the most carnal creature on earth. Guy made her feel too good inside to care.

She continued to smile as she made her way to the solar. That was the last area of the keep that she and Lenore had to check for dead rats. Within a few days, she hoped the rats would all be poisoned and these unsightly carcasses no longer a problem. Even though she hated this task, already she slept better at night. That, too, could have something to do with Guy, of course.

Her secretive smile had a strange effect on everyone she passed on her way to the solar. They all smiled back at her. A few even called out greetings that were downright friendly. Aye, she would like living here, making friends and making her family. Her very own family. Well, hers and Guy's. She pushed those thoughts aside as she entered the solar. There would be better times to think about her future family.

She turned to close the door behind her and called to Lenore over her shoulder. "Did you ever guess there were so many rats in this place? I vow—"

She took a few steps forward, but the sight that greeted her froze the words in her throat and her feet to the floor. Guy's brothers stood before her, or his brother and brother-in-law, to be more precise. Kenric towered above her just a few paces away. Fitz Alan sat across the room, frozen in the act of sharpening his sword with a whetstone. Claudia's hand went to her throat. "Pardon me, my lords. I did not realize—"

"Not so fast." Kenric strode forward and took hold of her arm when she began to back toward the door.

Claudia jerked her arm from his grip, and edged away

from the giant. Unfortunately, that took her further from the door. "Please, my lord. I—I do not like to be touched."

"Very well." He clasped his hands behind his back. "Is that better?"

Claudia nodded. Her arms went around the bucket and she held it in front of her chest, as if that flimsy piece of wood might protect her from these two. She watched Fitz Alan set his sword aside in slow, careful movements, as if he feared startling her. "Lord Guy is on his way to the sheep pens to search for you, my lords. Perhaps you should join him there."

"We have seen all we wish to see of sheep for one day. Indeed, for a lifetime." Fitz Alan smiled. "We came here in search of Guy, but your maid informed us you would arrive any moment. We figured Guy would follow soon enough."

Her glance darted toward the door, but her heart sank when she saw that Kenric now lounged with his back against the sturdy oak. They had her trapped. She forced herself to meet the giant's gaze without flinching. "Is there something you wished to speak with me about, my lords?"

Fitz Alan answered. "As long as you are here, why, yes, I do believe a question or two will come to our minds. Will you have a seat and make yourself more comfortable?"

Claudia shook her head, knowing she could make herself no more comfortable here than she could in a lion's den. Guy had told her the night before that Kenric and Fitz Alan knew of Roberto. He had also related what they told him of Dante, that he was alive and indeed a mercenary for their king. Her joy at that news was overshadowed by her alarm. Dante was still very far away in London, but these two were under the same roof as her. Now they were in the room. Guy's heartfelt vows that they accepted her as his betrothed sounded much more reassuring within the encircling safety of his arms. "What is it you wished to ask me?"

"We would know the reason you mean to lure our brother into marriage," Kenric said baldly.

Amazingly, Claudia found herself smiling. "Your brother

will not tell me his reasons for luring *me* into marriage. Why should I tell you mine?"

Kenric's icy gaze narrowed on her, but she heard Fitz Alan chuckle. "Well said, lady. If you would allow me to rephrase the question, I believe Lord Kenric would like to know what demands you will make for a dower."

"I make no demands of your brother," she informed them primly. "I do not covet his property or possessions any more than he covets mine." Her brows drew together in a frown. "Well, that is not quite true. He does covet Halford Hall, and that is part of my dowry."

Fitz Alan and Kenric exchanged an incredulous look. Fitz Alan spoke first. "Halford is your *dowry?*"

"Did Guy not tell you?" She shrugged her shoulders. " 'Tis of little consequence, as he plans to claim the property by siege. He does not seem to think Baron Lonsdale will vacate the property willingly."

"Aye, but Halford is your dowry?" Kenric asked, sounding suspiciously like an echo.

"That, along with a necklace," she replied. They thought her a greedy pauper, scheming to ensnare their brother in her trap. She couldn't blame them, she supposed. There was little doubt in her mind that Guy would receive the short end of their marriage bargain. He didn't care about her emeralds, and Halford would be his either way. She would have a home and the man she loved. "Guy keeps the necklace in his treasury, if you have a mind to calculate my worth."

"A necklace that Guy of Montague keeps in his treasury?" Fitz Alan asked.

Claudia rolled her eyes. "Do you have trouble understanding what I say? If so, I will speak slower. Your brother and his people understand me well enough, but I tend to forget that my accent can confuse outsiders."

"Outsiders!" Kenric's face turned a dull red. "Lady, I will thank you not to call us outsiders within the walls of Montague."

She inclined her head in a gesture that bordered on insolence. They were entitled to equal measure, she reasoned.

"Tell me about this necklace," Fitz Alan said. "What makes Guy, of all people, think it valuable enough to keep locked in his treasury?"

She never thought she would be so thankful for a dowry Guy found no more than interesting. " 'Tis an emerald necklace with a score of oblong stones about the size of sparrow's eggs. I have not counted the emeralds on the smaller strands, but those are about the size of peas and would measure two yards or so if laid end to end. My brother, Dante, assured me that they are of the finest quality."

Fitz Alan directed his smile at Kenric. "I begin to see the attraction. Our Guy is a merchant to the end. If what she says is true, he's captured himself an heiress."

"You think I would lie to you?" Her chin rose several inches. "I did not encourage your brother to marry me, if you must know the truth. In fact, I did what I could to dissuade him. I find the prospect of entering your family as promising as your thoughts of welcoming me into it. If you wish to put a stop to the marriage, then you are speaking with the wrong person. Guy has assured me that I have no choice in the matter. Now if you will excuse me, there are duties I must attend to before the feast to honor your arrival begins."

Claudia turned and marched resolutely toward the door. She didn't have any idea what she would do if Kenric tried to stop her again, but he moved aside at the last moment and let her pass. She kept on walking once she reached the other side, praying her wobbly knees would not fail her before she reached her chamber.

Kenric closed the door behind Claudia and turned to glare at Fitz Alan. "I compliment you on your skills at diplomacy. The king should arrive at any moment to appoint you ambassador to all hostile territories."

Fitz Alan picked up his sword and tested the newly honed edge with his thumb. A bright spot of blood appeared and he muttered a curse. "The girl is not what I expected."

"Nay, that she is not," Kenric agreed. "It would seem she is everything Guy says she is, more to the point, everything he says she is not. She is indeed courageous, and I would wager my horse that she is not a part of her uncle's plot. I would also wager that she thinks us rude and insufferable."

"That meeting did not go well." Fitz Alan pointed his sword at the floor, then let the tip come to rest there. "Do you think she will tell Guy?"

Kenric shrugged. "If she wishes to turn him against his family, she will repeat every word. If she wants peace between us, she just might remain silent on the matter. 'Twill be interesting to see which way the wind blows."

"Did she make you feel like the lowliest snake on the earth," Fitz Alan asked, "or does that honor belong to me alone?"

Kenric slapped Fitz Alan on the back, his deep laughter reverberating through the room. "Oh, you bear that honor alone, Fitz Alan. I feel no more than a great fool."

14

"**I** am cursed," Guy announced, when he joined Claudia in his chamber. She found herself in his arms for a quick, hard kiss, then he held her at arm's length to look at her. She braced her hands against his chest as his heated gaze continued to wander, his voice distracted as he explained what delayed him. "I was almost to our chamber when I received word that the king's messenger had arrived. 'Twas a six-page missive, and Edward demanded an immediate reply. My God, you look delicious. Where did you find that gown?"

"Lenore," she explained, taking measured steps away from him. Even the resourceful Lenore had amazed Claudia when she produced the gold-colored kirtle with long, pointed sleeves lined in deep burgundy samite. A fitted bliaut made of burgundy brocade shot with gold thread covered all but the front of the gown. The emerald necklace completed her outfit, and the golden kirtle made the stones glow as if they were on fire, but she wore the necklace only to impress Guy's family. She would prove to them that she was neither pauper nor liar. The look in Guy's eyes said he appreciated her efforts to look her best, yet he didn't have time to be appreciative. "The feast should have started an hour ago. I gave your—" Realization sunk in, and the excuse for his delay made her eyes widen. "The king's messenger? Is there any word of Dante?"

Guy frowned. "Aye, the king intends to tell him what happened at Lonsdale, and that you are here now and safe. He gave the messenger several days' head start, and thus me advance warning, for the king feels certain your brother will soon pay us a visit."

"This is wonderful!" Claudia clapped her hands together in delight, feeling as if a great weight had been lifted from her shoulders. When Guy's expression remained somber, another thought occurred to her. "This is awful! What if Dante does not realize you truly intend to marry me? He will be furious. He will—"

"Calm yourself," Guy murmured. He lifted her hand to his lips and pressed a kiss into the palm. "The king will make certain he does nothing rash, but I still intend to be married by the time Dante arrives, so there will be no question about who you belong to."

"I—I do not think Dante will object to our marriage." She made the mistake of stroking his cheek and watched passion flare to life again in his eyes. "If he sees you look at me this way, I think he will insist on marriage."

"We will be married already. There will be no reason for him to insist on a thing already done." Guy bent down for a kiss, but she leaned away from him.

"There is not time for this, Guy. I gave your steward leave to serve refreshments while everyone awaits our arrival. We will dine with drunkards if we tarry here much longer."

"They will be in good company, for I am drunk already with desire." He drew her into his arms and touched the thin, plaited ribbons that crowned her head. "You know it drives me mad to see your hair unbound."

She turned her head to avoid his lips, but still shivered when she felt his hands stroke over her hair, along her back all the way to the rounded curve of her hips. His need for her seemed insatiable, but was it love that fueled his passions, or simply lust? This was not a time to ponder that question. She heard a frantic edge to her voice. "We cannot keep your people waiting any longer."

"Aye, we can," he coaxed. He studied her face for a moment, then released a deep sigh. "But I suppose they would all guess the reason. Is that why you seem so reluctant?"

She nodded, grateful yet disappointed at the same time. "There will be time for us after the feast."

"Nay, I think there will be time for us during the feast." He nuzzled her neck, then playfully bit the lobe of her ear. "The feast will last for hours. Few will notice if we slip away after the first dozen or so courses. There will be entertainments to distract them from our absence." His mouth found hers for a deep, carnal kiss that ended in less than a heartbeat. He turned her away from him, his hands caressing her bottom even as he gave her a gentle nudge forward. "Do not wander within arm's reach of me while I change, or our own entertainments will begin sooner than expected."

Guy strode past her to one of his clothes trunks while she found a seat at the table. As he stripped away his clothing, she debated whether or not to tell him of the encounter with his brothers. He shot her a knowing glance and grinned when he tossed his shirt aside and began to remove his breeks. He had learned already that she liked to watch him undress. She propped her elbows on the table and rested her chin in her hands to enjoy the deliberate display.

The sight of his powerful body would never fail to capture her attention, and thoughts of his brothers were replaced with memories of what Guy's body felt like beneath her hands. In her mind she caressed his broad shoulders and chest, then moved lower to his hard thighs, remembering how the coarse sprinkling of hair on his legs tickled her fingers. She moved to the firm, smooth skin of his hips, and her tongue darted out to wet her lips. Her mouth turned downward into a disappointed pout when he stepped into a pair of dark blue leather breeks.

"Did I whet your appetite, little one?" Whatever he saw in her eyes made him chuckle. He picked up his shirt and slipped it over his head. "Your delightful expression speaks for itself. If you look at me this way throughout the meal, I trow this feast will be the shortest on record."

She blushed at his words, a little embarrassed at how easily he could arouse her. "I shall endeavor to keep my gaze fastened on the food, my lord. Your people will think I have never tasted such succulent delights. I shall think of you with every delicious bite I take."

Guy groaned. "My people will think me struck dumb by the sight of you. If you have an ounce of mercy in your heart, you will refrain from licking your fingers. I warn you now, brazen displays of that sort will be dealt with in a swift fashion."

"Is that a threat?" she asked innocently, "or a request?"

"I shall let you puzzle that out for yourself, my lady." The exaggerated movement of his brows made his thoughts easy enough to read, his wolfish smile an even surer indication. He shrugged into the same pearl-studded blue tunic he had worn the day they first met, then draped the leopardskin sash over one shoulder and fastened it at his hip. Next he strapped on his sword and dagger, the sheaths of both weapons crusted with sapphires.

"Where did you get a leopardskin?" she asked.

Guy stroked the pelt with the backs of his fingers. "This fellow tried to eat me whole, along with the Berber merchant who thought to make him into a pet. The merchant gave me the sash as a token of appreciation for saving his life. He also told me that any man who owns a leopard, or even its pelt, will be blessed with virility and a whole host of manly attributes." His grin took on a wicked edge. "You would know best if he told the truth of the matter."

"Oh, aye," she breathed, "he did not lie, my lord."

He extended his hand. "Come, my sweet. The sooner we attend this feast, the sooner I can work on the scores of children promised me."

Evard met them outside Guy's chamber with a list of contestants who wished to participate in the tournament that would be held tomorrow between Guy's men and Kenric's. As the two men talked, Claudia tried to decide the best way to tell Guy about her meeting with Kenric and Fitz Alan. She did not want to sound as if she complained of them, but they were sure to mention the conversation to Guy. Her grip on his arm tightened. "There is something I should tell you before—"

The words died in her throat as she caught sight of the great hall. On any day of the week the great hall looked a place fit for kings. Decorated for a feast, the extravagance took Claudia's breath away. She had known that the steward planned a hunt theme for the feast, but the result of his staff's work was something straight from a fairy tale. Great leafy branches were fastened to the ribs and crossbeams of the ceiling, every arch and pillar transformed into bushes and trees, and a whole row of slender willows served as a backdrop for the high table. All the linen-draped tables in the hall nearly disappeared beneath fragrant evergreen boughs festooned with gold ribbons. Perched among the greenery overhead were stuffed birds of every sort, most of which Claudia knew were the results of clever reassembly after the cooks harvested what they needed for pies and roasts. There were also stuffed forest animals arranged in lifelike poses, including two deer heads that seemed to peek from a mass of shrubbery at the base of one arch.

The musicians struck up a lively tune on lutes, pipes, and tambours the moment Guy and Claudia stepped into the hall. That only added to the din of laughter and conversation that continued all around them as Kenric's knights and soldiers renewed acquaintances with their counterparts at Montague. As they made their way to the high table, Guy paused now and then to greet his men or Kenric's.

Although he seemed to forget her existence as he spoke to his guests, he kept her hand in his and his thumb stroked over her knuckles. He glanced at her only once, when he stopped to greet Thomas and a knight named Haskins. That brief look said he hadn't forgotten her at all, the expression in his eyes so tender that it made her ache inside. Aye, there were times when she believed that he loved her.

His face became a mask of polite interest as he turned again to the knights, but he squeezed her hand and continued the gentle strokes. That helped calm her, but she couldn't concentrate on his conversation with Thomas or any others. Her gaze went again and again to Kenric and Fitz Alan, who awaited them on the raised dais. She didn't want to concentrate on them, either. Instead she started to count leaves.

"You have outdone yourself again," Fitz Alan said by way of greeting when they reached their table. He and Kenric were also finely dressed, Kenric in all black, Fitz Alan in russet and gold. "I have never feasted in the midst of a forest. Even the servants are dressed as huntsmen and woodland nymphs. You do us great honor, Guy."

"We hope you will enjoy our meager hospitality," Guy said, with exaggerated modesty.

Kenric made a guttural sound that Claudia assumed indicated sarcasm. "Your meager hospitality was enough to make my wife plead to take her along on this journey. She happened to be in the midst of birthing my son at the time." He arched one dark brow in Guy's direction. "Your message arrived at a most inopportune moment."

Guy shrugged an apology. "Your lovely wife and children are welcome here anytime, and I look forward to meeting my newest nephew."

"Tess made me promise another visit when she and the babe are strong enough to travel," Kenric answered. "You will see them soon enough."

Claudia tried to picture Kenric's wife, certain Guy's reference to her as "lovely" was nothing more than a polite lie. She had to be built on the same massive scale as her husband to survive his children. Then she wondered if Guy's sister was as tall and solidly built as her brothers. Gesù, she would be made to feel a dwarf in this family.

Guy led her to the seat at his right, while Kenric and Evard sat at his left. They soon had Guy engrossed in a conversation about the latest intrigues at court. Fitz Alan and

Thomas sat at Claudia's right, but they, too, seemed intent on their own conversation. A group of jugglers entertained the diners, and brightly colored balls seemed to fill the air. Occasionally they threw something more dangerous into the mix, such as daggers or flaming torches. Claudia wasn't in the mood to be entertained. Guy no longer held her hand, and she didn't realize how much that small comfort meant until he took it away. Rather than indulge in a childish bout of self-pity, she found the tree she had looked at before they sat down and resumed her count.

"Is that not right, Claudia?"

She gave Guy a baffled look. "My lord?"

His eyes narrowed with suspicion. "What are you counting?"

"Counting? I do not know what—" She looked at the skeptical arch of his brow and reconsidered her answer. "Leaves."

"Leaves?" Kenric echoed. "Why on earth would you count leaves?"

Everyone at the table waited for her answer. Claudia felt her cheeks burn.

" 'Tis a private matter," Guy said, rescuing her from the awkward silence. "Forget the leaves, Claudia. I have other numbers to occupy your mind. Kenric has license to crenelate one of his properties, and the builder says there are—"

"Why are you telling her this?" Kenric interrupted. He shot a brief, dismissive scowl in Claudia's direction. "Tess fell asleep when I told her of Westford. Your lady will find the matter of even less interest."

Claudia wondered how any woman could sleep in Kenric's presence, for she still felt a stab of fear each time he looked at her. Still, her mood brightened a little at hearing Kenric refer to her as Guy's lady. Perhaps they would accept Guy's choice after all. Not that she had any delusions about them ever liking her.

"You will understand soon enough," Guy told him. He turned to Claudia. "As I was saying, the builder told Kenric that the project will take many months to complete, even though the final structure will not be all that large."

He went on to tell her the numbers and types of craftsmen involved, how much work could be accomplished by each in a day, and the total effort to complete the project. "Kenric's builder says it will take one hundred and fifty days to complete the project at a cost of three hundred florins for the labor," Guy said. With all the facts and figures laid out, he leaned back in his chair and eyed Claudia expectantly. "Is he right or wrong?"

"What are you doing?" Kenric asked Guy. He gave Claudia a sympathetic glance that silenced her own objection. It was the first time Kenric had looked at her with an expression that came anywhere close to kindness. "A team of your clerks could not answer that question with any accuracy in less than an hour. There is no call to embarrass your betrothed with a question she cannot possibly answer."

That show of support dumbfounded Claudia. It took her a moment to remember her own objection. "This is not a good idea, my lord."

"Trust me," Guy murmured. "Tell us the answer."

"You are certain?" she asked, with a glance around them. This time everyone but Guy avoided her gaze, pretending that they were not awaiting her reply. Guy gave her an encouraging smile and she released a small sigh of resignation. "The keep will be completed as the builder says, but only if he employs ambitious heathens." She glanced out over the hall and saw a line of servants file from the kitchens. She forced a smile and clapped her hands together in a silly expression of delight. "Oh, look! Here are the first courses. I vow Guy's cooks are the finest. See how they cooked the savory pies into the shapes of trees and flowers?"

Guy ignored her attempt to change the subject. "I believe an explanation of your answer is in order."

Claudia began to rearrange her spoons on the table as if getting them placed just right was of great importance. "The builder did not take any Sabbaths or holy days into account.

He also assumes that no one will become ill or injured, and that work will continue even on days when it rains or snows."

"If the weather forestalls the work for a day every two weeks, and if the builder allows the workers their holy days and the Sabbath each week to rest, how long will the project take and how much will it cost? Assuming, of course," Guy added, "that the workers are paid the same each week regardless of the weather or holy days."

"One hundred and ninety-four days, three hundred and eighty-eight florins."

"What if the builder allows the workers only a half day's rest on holy days, and they are not paid for their day of rest each Sabbath?"

"When will the work begin?" she asked. "There are more holy days at certain times of the year than others."

"Let us say next week for the sake of argument."

Her brows drew together as she made the calculations. "One hundred eighty-eight days, three hundred thirty-four florins."

Guy turned to Kenric. "You may wish to ask Lady Claudia's opinion about other figures your builder presents before you give your final approval to the plans."

"Is she right?" Kenric demanded.

"Aye." Guy smiled agreeably. "Amazing, is it not?"

Kenric nodded, his expression bemused. "An heiress in more ways than one, it would seem. You intend to involve her in your business ventures?"

Guy ignored the question. "What do you know of Claudia being an heiress?"

"She did not tell you?" Kenric gave Claudia a sharp glance. She tried to warn him with a shake of her head that she had not told Guy about their meeting. Oddly enough, Kenric smiled. "Fitz Alan and I had a short discussion with Lady Claudia about the terms of your betrothal. She happened upon us in the solar, where Fitz Alan and I hid to avoid more tours of animal enclosures whilst you enjoyed a tryst with your betrothed. Did you think we would not hear of your visit to the gardens?"

The two brothers seemed to make an abrupt exchange of moods. Kenric became relaxed and almost jovial, while Guy's face darkened beneath a scowl. "What did you say to her?"

"We made mostly rude remarks that do not bear repeating," Kenric admitted. He leaned forward to look the length of the table. "Would you not agree, Fitz Alan?"

"Aye, extremely rude remarks." Fitz Alan inclined his head toward Guy in a regretful gesture. "Your lady's sweet disposition and good manners reminded us of our own. We made complete asses of ourselves, but we hope you will put in a few words on our behalf if we promise to make her polite apologies."

Guy looked at Claudia. "What did they say to you?"

"They were not all that rude," Claudia assured him, alarmed by the anger in his voice. Her hand came to rest on his arm and that seemed to have a calming effect on him. "They are concerned only for your welfare, Guy. You must admit that your wish to marry me will seem strange to any who hear of it. Even without the troubles between our families, I would hardly seem a likely choice for your bride."

"You are my only choice," he informed her in a terse voice. He looked from Fitz Alan to Kenric. "I thought I made myself clear on that matter."

"We understand your reasons well enough," Kenric said in a quiet voice. "She will make your claim to Halford unbreakable, and her talent with numbers would delight any merchant. 'Tis obvious why you decided to marry her."

"Aye, 'tis obvious," Guy murmured. He lifted Claudia's hand for a kiss, his gaze intent as he looked into her eyes. "Obvious to all but one."

Claudia couldn't decide what to make of that remark.

Someone else decided to scream.

Guy's head jerked around to search for the source of the piercing sound. Claudia's gaze followed, along with everyone else's. One of Guy's knights pulled his wife away from their table just as a large, grayish-brown lump of something furry landed on her trencher. A tangle of greenery followed, loosened by the fur ball's descent from the rafters above them. The greenery on the table rustled and a long, hairless tail snaked out from beneath an evergreen bough. The hunched shape of a rat became visible as it regained its feet, dazed by its fall and the affects of poison. Claudia clapped her hands over her mouth and watched as the poisoned rat mustered enough energy to scurry from beneath the branches. It wove a drunken path down the length of the table as one sword after another appeared and slammed down just inches before or behind it. One close strike sent the rat over the edge of the table, where it attracted the attention of several hounds.

Claudia slipped from her seat and rushed around the table. If the dogs decided to make a meal of the rat, the poison would kill them as well.

"Vattene!" She waved her hands in a frantic gesture and all but one of the dogs scattered, skulking away as if she had denied them a great treat. The one that remained was a large mastiff, its attention focused on the dying rat. The rodent lay on its side now, but managed to snap its sharp teeth in the dog's direction each time the mastiff sniffed too close.

"Bad dog," Claudia tried in English, growing more cautious the closer she came to the animal. The dog looked the size of a small horse, and none too friendly. It turned its huge head toward her for only a moment, just long enough to bare its teeth and give her a growl of warning. That didn't sound promising, but she could not let the dumb beast suffer an agonizing death because of her. She took another small step forward and started to reach for its spiked collar. "Bad doggie. This meal is no good for you."

An arm wrapped around her waist and pulled her backward just as the mastiff lunged forward. Its massive jaws snapped closed just inches from her arm. A booted foot planted itself on the dog's side and a firm shove made it back away. Claudia released a faint, shaky sigh of relief.

"Are you crazed?" Guy demanded. He turned her in his

arms and his gaze moved over her, as if he expected to find an injury of some sort. "That beast could take off your arm in one bite."

"The poison in that rat would kill your dog," Claudia explained. She motioned one of the servants forward to dispose of the rat, then laid her hand against Guy's chest. Her voice dropped to a whisper. "We are making a spectacle of ourselves, my lord. Let us return to the table."

Guy rolled his eyes, but he took her arm and led her back to their seats, lecturing her the entire time. "I swear by all that is holy, you will make me old before my time. Do not dare rescue any more animals with sharp teeth. Every dog in this castle can die of rat poisoning for all I care. Did no one teach you to keep your distance from animals when they are intent on a meal?"

" 'Twas a mistake on my part," she admitted, as she took her seat. "I will not cause you worry again, my lord."

Given Guy's concern for her safety and his gallant rescue, she did not feel all that contrite. She was a little surprised to notice that everyone else at their table seemed to be smiling. Everyone but Guy. He all but growled the order that called Stephen forward to begin serving their meal. Claudia made certain a page refilled all their goblets with wine.

" 'Tis a very bad sign when a woman says she will not give you cause to worry," Kenric remarked to Guy. "Just wait until you have children. They will make the gray hairs your wife gives you seem trivial in comparison."

"I do not see Lady Tess standing on the brink of disaster each time you turn around," Guy muttered.

Claudia's mouth became a thin line, but Kenric burst out laughing. "Then you do not see my wife all that often. Did I tell you where I found her just a week before she birthed Phillip?"

Kenric launched into a story of his wife's escapades that soothed Claudia's temper. This Lady Tess did not sound like such a paragon of perfection after all. That story led to several others, and soon Fitz Alan joined in with tales of his own wife and children.

Claudia listened to the stories, enjoying the easy camaraderie between the brothers. Despite their disagreement over Guy's marriage, it seemed obvious that the family was very close and spent a great deal of time in one another's company. She found herself actually looking forward to meeting Guy's sister and sister-in-law as well as his nieces and nephews. They would be her family, too.

Given the polite smiles Kenric and Fitz Alan sent her way, it seemed just possible that they might accept her after all. They told stories that Guy seemed to have heard several times before, which made her wonder if they told them now for her benefit, to make her feel more a part of their close-knit family. It also sounded as if Kenric's and Fitz Alan's wives were fast friends, and Claudia began to hope that she would someday be their friend as well. How strange it would be to have other women to talk to as equals, women who knew how to run large households and raise children and care for husbands. She smiled and popped a sweetmeat into her mouth, unconsciously licking the tips of her fingers.

Guy's hand found hers beneath the table and he leaned over to whisper in her ear. "I told you the consequences of tempting me." His thumb rubbed the center of her palm, reminding her of more intimate kisses he often pressed there. His voice sent shivers down her spine. "The mummers will appear soon to perform a mock hunt. We can slip away then without much notice. As soon as they appear, say you must consult with the steward about the subtleties that will be served at the end of the feast. Soon after, I will excuse myself and we will meet in my chamber. Agreed?"

Claudia nodded and tried to look as if Guy might be murmuring something inconsequential in her ear. The thought that their wait to be alone would not be a long one gave her an idea. She managed to keep her smile contained as she agreed to the rendezvous. "Aye, my lord."

When Guy leaned away again, she picked up another

sweetmeat and took a small, delicate bite. It didn't matter that she had already eaten her fill. Her tongue darted out to lick her lips as if she were starving. "This sweetmeat is so very delicious, my lord." She offered Guy the remainder of the tempting morsel, holding it daintily between her fingers. "Would you care for a bite?"

"Yea, please," he answered politely. When she held the treat closer, his hand caught her wrist and he took her finger-tips into his mouth along with the sweetmeat. His tongue gave her fingers a hidden caress, then he released his hold on her wrist and drew away from her hand. Rather than press her fingers against her lips as she wanted, she made a conscious effort to return her hand to the table.

Guy swallowed the morsel and his gaze moved lower, lingering on her bodice. "Aye, 'tis been too long since I tasted anything so delicious. An excellent choice, my lady."

That was a rather neat turn of the tables. So much for teasing him, she thought, releasing a wistful sigh as Guy undressed her with his eyes. Where were those mummers?

"Guy tells us your brother may soon visit." Fitz Alan's remark distracted her from Guy's silent seduction. "Do you think he will approve of your marriage?"

Claudia turned to face Fitz Alan just as she heard Guy release his own deep sigh. From the corner of her eye she watched him take a long drink of wine. At least she was not the only one who suffered. "I think he will come to accept my marriage."

"Then you have concerns that he will disapprove?"

"Did you have concerns, and disapprove when Guy told you of his plans?"

"Of course. But now I understand his reasons."

"My brother will likely need convincing as well," she replied. Actually, she wasn't all that sure of Dante's reaction when he received the news. Hopefully, the king would assure Dante that Guy was a noble, honorable man who would make her an excellent husband. Then it occurred to her that the king had no idea that Guy truly intended to marry her. "Oh, dear."

"Pardon me?" Fitz Alan asked.

"What? Oh, 'tis nothing," she assured him, knowing that was a huge lie. She turned to Guy. He had to be warned that Dante's mood was bound to be far from agreeable when he arrived, especially if he heard of the sleeping arrangements but not of their marriage plans. Guy was staring at her already, a strange, speculative look in his eyes. She lowered her voice. "I must speak with you about Dante when we are alone."

"That is not the excuse we agreed upon, Claudia. And 'tis not yet time for the mummers." He leaned back to look at her. "On the other hand, why wait for the mummers?"

Claudia's eyes widened when he lifted her hand and kissed the inside of her wrist. Nay, he all but ate her wrist, the kiss was so carnal. "Guy! What are you doing?"

He just smiled in response, a slow, lazy smile that sent a wave of alarm through her. When he dipped his head for another taste of her wrist, she jerked her hand away. His mouth turned downward, his expression crushed. "You are cruel to deny me, Claudia."

She gave him a warning frown but said nothing. His lopsided grin made her wonder how much wine he had drunk, although she couldn't recall seeing his goblet filled more than once. He had seemed fine just moments ago, but now his hand wavered as he reached for his wine. The goblet was halfway to his mouth when he frowned and set it aside, as if the thought occurred that he had already overindulged.

"Are you all right?" she whispered.

"Aye." He smiled again, but his eyes looked glassy. "Never better, love."

"You are certain?"

For some reason, he found her question extremely funny. His deep, unsteady laughter drew Kenric's attention, then Evard's. She glanced over her shoulder to find Fitz Alan and Thomas staring at them already. She reached for a thick, hearty stew. "Here, my lord. This stew is delicious as well. Try a few bites."

He shook his head, but the gesture looked clumsy, like a big, shaggy dog trying to shed water from its coat. "I am no longer hungry. At least, not for food." He rubbed his forehead. "Nay, I am not hungry for anything." His gaze moved to Claudia and he leaned forward, then back again as if he might see her more clearly from that distance. "You are not smiling, Claudia."

He leaned back even farther and would have fallen over if Kenric had not caught him by the shoulders. Frantic now, Claudia pressed one hand to his forehead. His skin felt cool and dry, much too cool for the warm room. "What is wrong with you, Guy?"

"Nothing is wrong," he mumbled. "I am just a little tired. Perhaps a bit soused as well."

His eyes drifted shut while her own widened in horror. Kenric called out his name and gave him a gentle shake while Claudia felt the slow pulse at his neck, then she looked at his hands. His nailbeds were darker than they should be, almost a blue color.

"Oh, my God." Her hands went to the front of his tunic and she gave him a firm shake. "Guy! Wake up!"

"He has been poisoned," Fitz Alan said in an almost calm voice. He stood up and moved toward Guy. "Thomas, order the gates sealed. No one is to enter or leave the fortress until you receive further word."

Thomas hurried away to carry out the order. An unnatural calm settled over the great hall as two hundred voices suddenly fell silent.

Kenric gave Guy a harder shake than Claudia could manage, and his eyes opened. Guy's gaze went to Claudia and he tried to speak, but his mouth moved ineffectually. What she saw in his eyes terrified her. The pupils were no more than small pinpoints, his face a deathly shade of white. Then his eyes rolled back in his head.

"Guy," she whispered. A fear closed over her so cold that she could barely speak. "Please, Guy. Do not sleep."

"Get her away from him," Kenric snapped. His arms went around his brother as he supported more of Guy's weight on his shoulder. "Evard, check the food and wine. I want to know how he was poisoned, then I want to know what he was poisoned with so we will know how to treat him."

"I can help you," Claudia said, without taking her gaze from Guy's face. She could not seem to let go of his tunic, either. " 'Tis a form of opium, probably in the wine. It works faster that way."

She knew the signs well from her mother's teachings, but she had never thought to encounter an opium poison in England. Yet Guy's ships traveled the world. Did one of his own people poison him?

Rather than worry about where the poison came from, she racked her brain for the cures. It did not occur to Claudia how damning her words sounded until she glanced up and met Kenric's gaze. The icy malice she saw in his eyes made her shudder, even as she shook her head against the silent accusation.

Kenric ignored her denial. "Get her away from him!"

A pair of hands closed over her shoulders. She clung to the front of Guy's tunic, but she was no match for Fitz Alan's strength and he dragged her backward until her hands held nothing but air. "Nay! You must let me help him."

"You have helped enough," Kenric bit out. He motioned to a group of his men. "Help me move him."

Claudia shook her head. None of this seemed real: not Guy's collapse, nor the great hall with all its greenery, or even the smiles Kenric and Fitz Alan had sent her way such a short time ago. Surely she had conjured this all in a dream. A dream that had turned into a nightmare. Aye, this was nothing but a horrid nightmare and she would wake up any moment, just as she awoke from her dream about the rats to seek safety in Guy's arms. Fitz Alan's painful grip on her arms felt very real.

He started to pull her further away from Guy and she strained against his hold. "Please, Guy!"

She knew a moment of hope when Guy struggled to open his eyes. His hand clutched at the front of Kenric's tunic. He even seemed to focus for a moment on his brother, but his words were no more than a harsh whisper. "Guard her. Lock her up if you must."

His eyelids drifted closed again and Claudia felt a darkness settle over her heart, the numbness of disbelief. What she had heard was a mistake. Guy could not believe that she had poisoned him. She had mistaken his meaning, just as Kenric mistook it. Kenric's dark gaze impaled her, what she saw in those merciless eyes almost as frightening as the sight of Guy laying unconscious in his arms. Kenric wanted to kill her. Of that, she had no doubt.

"Aye, brother," Kenric replied, never looking away from Claudia. "I will guard her."

Fitz Alan whispered in her ear what she knew already. "If he dies, lady, your death will be more painful."

15

A small sliver of light flickered beneath the door. Claudia knew better than to stare at it. The light was too tempting, a glimmer of hope that only made her cell that much blacker. The darkness was like a living thing all around her, a blanket chilled by massive stone blocks that formed the foundation of the castle, a place unwarmed by even the smallest shadow of the sun. She had counted the blocks in the walls already, using her fingertips to judge their size and shape, and knew the exact number of steps she could pace in each direction. Those calculations kept her mind occupied for a time. Far too short a time.

Anger over her unjust imprisonment came and went. Terror was a more constant companion. In the long hours since Fitz Alan had escorted her here, she had recalled all she could of opium poisons, which was precious little. If Guy lasted the night that would be a good sign, yet he might lie unconscious for days and still succumb to the poison's effects. She hoped they made him vomit. He had to be purged of as much of the poison as possible before it reached his blood. And he needed to be roused from his stupor however they could manage it.

She had told Fitz Alan what they must do, but doubted he paid her any heed. Why would he listen to anything a murderess said about cures for her victim? She was guilty in everyone's eyes. Perhaps even Guy's.

The darkness gave light to all sorts of memories and imaginings. The stone blocks brought to mind the rough surface of Guy's cheeks, and she recalled how he looked at her when she touched him. There could be no question about his lust for her. It was a palpable thing between them. But lust was a flimsy emotion, one that would not stand the test of an attempted murder when it appeared her doing. Then there were the reasons Kenric gave for Guy's interest in marriage, and Guy's ready agreement that he intended to marry her to gain her dowry and mathematical talents. Guy had all but dismissed those reasons out of hand when she had questioned him. Why would he let Kenric believe them true unless those were the real reasons he meant to marry her?

Her nails scraped harder against the stones until one snapped backward and a knife of pain shot up her finger. With a small cry of distress, she stopped pacing and gave her hand a hard shake. When that brought no relief, she sucked on the injured fingertip and resumed her measured steps. The sting began to lessen and she remembered times when Guy kissed her fingertips for no other reason than to give her pleasure. He always seemed so determined to make her happy, to make her push aside her worries to enjoy each moment they spent together. Surely that was some indication of his affection for her. Her happiness did not affect what he would gain from her through marriage. Why would he go to such lengths to please her unless he truly cared for her?

Aye, his words to Kenric were a plea to keep her safe. Guy knew she would be unjustly accused of this crime, and he had tried to protect her. As soon as he recovered and learned of her whereabouts, he would come here himself to set her free. He would make his brothers kneel before her to beg forgiveness. He would hold her in his arms and murmur sweet endearments while she cried.

If he did not recover . . .

She pushed that thought aside and paced faster. Guy would recover. How could she live without him? How could she live if he thought her guilty of poisoning him?

Her lips curved into a grim smile in the darkness. Those worries would not be a problem. Either would prove her death. Only Guy's trust would save her, and only love would create a trust strong enough to withstand the accusations against her. Even she had to admit that the evidence looked damning. There were no candidates with more motives than herself within the walls of Montague, and none with greater opportunity to commit the crime. Guy's brothers would be sure to point out those facts. He would be a fool to believe in her innocence. Guy was no fool.

She squeezed her eyes closed and pressed her hands to her forehead. These thoughts would make her crazy. How could one night last so long? How could a prison cell seem smaller each time she paced around it?

At least her prison itself was nothing to add new fears. The dungeons at Montague were cleaner than most. Ironically, she was the one who had ordered them cleaned. She and Lenore had found their way to even this remote part of the castle when they laid out their rat bait. She had dreaded the place, but found that most of the cold, dark chambers held casks of wine and foodstuffs. One large wing contained the castle treasury, and two soldiers stood guard there at all times. They were her guards now as well.

If she listened closely, she could hear snatches of the guards' conversations, and that gave her a sense of time. These two arrived several hours ago, so it must be the middle of the night. She should be exhausted. Instead she felt restless and wide awake as she paced in endless circles. The next few hours could well be her last.

"Jack!"

The muffled sound of the guard's voice made her pause by the door to her cell. She leaned closer to the thick oak.

" 'Tis your turn to roll the dice," the same voice called out. "Be quick about your business and get back to the game."

She had hoped to hear some word of Guy, yet dreaded hearing it at the same time. News this soon was not likely to be good. Every hour that passed was another hour he lived. She would have to take comfort from that knowledge. She trailed her fingers along the cold stone walls to count the blocks again, then closed her eyes and counted the number of times Guy had kissed her.

A jingling noise made her turn again toward the cell door, the metallic rattle of keys. Someone was at her door. The guards had no reason to check on her. It could only be Kenric or Fitz Alan, come to tell her the worst.

Her heart sank to new depths as the door slowly swung open. The light from rush torches set outside the chamber flooded the entrance with blinding light, and she blinked several times as her eyes tried to recover from the hours of pitch black. The doorway remained empty, yet she sensed a presence in her cell that was not there before. Her gaze moved along the walls, but the sudden light in the doorway almost blinded her to the darkness. A movement from the corner of her eye made her jerk around toward the doorway again as the large, black silhouette of a man stepped in front of her.

The hairs on her arms prickled at the tangible aura of danger that surrounded him, and she backed away in slow, measured steps. The man was not as large as Kenric. Fitz Alan, perhaps? He wore a cloak, but his features were lost in the dark shadows of the cloak's hood.

"Tutto questo solo per liberar Ti, Claudia."

Her hand flew to her throat. The deep voice sounded so familiar. It was the sound of her father's voice, yet different. Blood began to pound in her ears so hard that she could scarce hear herself speak. "Dante?"

The man threw back his hood and stepped closer until she could see the faint outline of his features, the strong jawline, high cheekbones, the noble line of his nose. He held out his hand. "Aye, 'tis me, Claudia."

Dante. She could scarce believe that he stood before her. Guy had told her he would come, but some part of her had not dared to hope. For five years she had hoped, waited each day in vain for his return. Dante's hands were suddenly on her shoulders, steadying her.

"Do not dare faint on me," he commanded. "We must

be away from this place, and I cannot carry you through the bolthole."

"Why must we—" She pressed her lips together. What made her assume he had gained her release from Kenric or Fitz Alan? Guy's brothers would never willingly free her. Dante was here to help her escape.

So many thoughts crowded her head that she could focus on only one. Dante had finally returned for her. She wrapped her arms around his waist and gave him a fierce hug. He hesitated a moment, then his arms went around her as well. Her voice was little more than a broken whisper. "I thought I would never see you again. Why did you leave me at Lonsdale so long?"

"I thought you were safe there," he said in a quiet voice. "Uncle Laurence liked none of us, but I never thought he would try to harm you. Lonsdale seemed safer than any place I could take you these past years."

"You stopped writing, and I had no idea how to find you. Do you know how worried I was?" She drew away from him just enough to search his shadowy features. "Did you forget me?"

"Never!" His voice was harsh with remorse and his hands went to her shoulders again, as if to impress his words upon her. "I never forgot you, cara. Not even for a day. I do not lead a life you would be proud of, and having you near me now will only endanger your life. Those are the reasons I did not come for you sooner. I have no safe haven to offer you, but I would rather you die in my care than see you in the hands of a Montague."

"The king told you of Guy's message?"

"Aye," he bit out, "and I have learned more since then. This morning I entered the castle disguised as a servant. I was in the great hall during the feast and saw everything, including Baron Montague with his hands all over you, as if he had some right to put them there."

"He intends to marry me," she said, quickly jumping to Guy's defense. She would not voice her own suspicions, for surely Dante had enough for them both. And they could both be wrong. She had to believe in Guy, even knowing that his trust in her was unlikely to be as absolute. "As soon as Guy recovers, he will order me freed."

"He ordered you to this prison. His brothers want to hang you."

"Guy did not order me imprisoned," she argued. "He asked his brothers to keep me safe, but they mistook his words. Kenric and Fitz Alan know Roberto was our brother, and they are here to help Guy take his revenge on our uncle. Can you blame them for thinking me guilty?"

Dante's soft, humorless laugh sent chills up her spine. "I counted on the fact that they would think you guilty."

"W-what do you mean?"

"The poison was my work," Dante admitted. " 'Twas the only way to get you away from him."

She backed away, her eyes wide with horror. If Dante wanted a man dead, he would die. The fragile hopes she had held on to for hours crumbled around her. "*You* murdered Guy?"

Dante caught her by the arms to stop her retreat. "Nay, Claudia. I could not risk that he would play the gallant and ask you to share his cup. The king also made me swear that I would not murder Montague nor any of his men. He will suffer, but he will not die. Not yet, anyway."

She began to tremble. "Guy will live?"

"Have I not just said as much?" He reached beneath his cloak and produced a dark bundle he had tied at his waist. "Put on this cape. We must leave here or all will be lost."

"I cannot." She pushed the bundled cape back into his hands. She gripped her trembling hands together at her waist, her thoughts in turmoil. Dante had done this to her, and far worse to Guy. She wanted to slap him, to beat her fists against his chest until he knew a taste of the pain he had caused her. For one terrible moment, she wished he had never come back into her life. Now she had no choice but to send him away from her again. "I must stay here to undo what you have done. Guy will come for me when he recovers from your poison, and I must tell him what happened. Do not worry. He will not hold me responsible for the deeds of another."

"You are crazed!" Dante raked a hand through his hair. "He will hang you."

"H-he loves me."

Dante shook his head and released a long sigh. "You were deceived, sister. Montague does not love you any more than he trusts you, else you would not be here now."

" 'Tis Guy's brothers who keep me here. Guy will—"

"Your precious Guy awoke hours ago." Dante took her by the shoulders and gave her a small shake. "Guy is your accuser, Claudia. He thinks you poisoned him. If you stay here, he will order you hanged on the morrow."

"Guy will—"

"He will hang you," Dante repeated.

Guy is your accuser. The words rang again and again in her ears. Guy did not consider her innocence for even a night. She closed her eyes, but the wave of pain she expected never came. Instead her hands began to tingle, then her arms and legs. She felt numb everywhere, yet couldn't seem to stop herself from clinging to her own lies. "Guy will come for me."

"Aye, with a rope." Dante shook his head. "You must come away with me. Now."

She had to stay. To be hung? Dante was right. Guy had deceived her. He promised that he would never hold her responsible for the actions of another, yet the taste of her brother's poison had changed his mind on that score. His brothers would do nothing to change his mind. Indeed, she could imagine all sorts of vile accusations that Kenric and Fitz Alan would whisper in his ear to harden his heart against her. She was the outsider here, the most likely suspect, since none knew of Dante's presence. Her lashes fluttered opened and she searched the shadows of her brother's face, trying to see his eyes. "Aye, Dante. I will go with you."

Guy awoke at dawn the next morning. In that instant he felt clearheaded. That seemed strange, as if there was some reason he should not be so alert. He rolled to his side and reached for Claudia. A wave of dizziness hit him at the same time he recalled what happened; the feast, the poison, and the half-remembered nightmare that followed. His physician had fed him some awful brew that made him retch until there was nothing left inside him. His muscles felt weak and useless.

"He is awake again," Kenric said.

Guy's unsteady gaze moved across the room to where Kenric and Fitz Alan sat at his table. They both rose and made their way toward the bed. Guy struggled to sit up. He wasn't nearly as clearheaded as he had thought, and his hand went to his forehead in an attempt to steady himself. "Where is she?"

"There will be time for that later," Kenric replied. He turned toward a trunk and pulled out a tunic and breeks. "The physician says you will not retch again. I will dress you, if you wish."

"I can dress myself," Guy muttered, wondering if he could live up to that claim. He rubbed his throat and looked around for something to drink that would ease its rawness. Given the soreness of his stomach, a drink of anything might do more harm than good.

Kenric tossed the clothes onto the bed. "You must walk again to work the poison from your system."

"Your physician wanted to let blood last night," Fitz Alan added, when Guy held up a hand to ward them off. "He also wanted to pull a few teeth for good measure. We persuaded him to reserve those treatments for morning if you did not improve. If you have wish to save your teeth, 'twould be in your interest to walk with us."

Guy wanted nothing more than to lie back down and sleep. Kenric and Fitz Alan also looked worn, as if they had been awake all night, which Guy supposed they had. Both were still dressed in the clothes they wore to the feast. He pushed back the covers. "I will flatten that charlatan if he comes anywhere near me with tongs." He struggled into the tunic, aware that it should not take so much effort but determined to seem less affected than he was. "Where is Claudia?"

"In the dungeons," Fitz Alan answered. "Here are your boots."

Guy's hands froze on the laces of his tunic, his voice an icy whisper. "She is *where?*"

"The dungeons," Kenric repeated. He glanced at Fitz Alan, then back at Guy. "You said yourself to lock her up."

"I said to *guard* her," Guy shouted. He grabbed the breeks and tried to ignore the way his stomach protested as he bent over. "I wanted you to keep her safe from any who might accuse her of poisoning me. *Christ.* I hoped you two would not be among their number."

A violent wave of dizziness caught him off guard, and he would have fallen over if Fitz Alan had not steadied him. Guy shoved his hand away. "Did either of you stop to think through what you have done?"

"Aye!" Kenric snapped. "We saved you once again from the wench. 'Tis obvious from the piles of dead rats in this place that she knows her craft well. She tried to murder you the very day we arrived. Yesterday she all but succeeded. Had I known you would remain so blind to her guilt, I would have ordered her hung."

Guy grabbed the front of Kenric's tunic, his teeth clenched. " 'Tis fortunate you did nothing so rash, brother. I would have killed you."

"You are not in your right mind." Kenric removed Guy's hands from his tunic with ease.

In his weakened state, Guy could not put up much of a fight. He sighed in defeat. "Aye, 'tis truth. I could not kill you, but I would have been sorely tempted." He sat on the edge of the bed and began to pull on his boots. "Rats are the only creatures Claudia would harm by intent. Did you not stop to wonder why she would become so alarmed at the thought that a mere dog might die of her poison if she planned a similar fate for me?"

Neither Kenric nor Fitz Alan replied. Guy made a sound of disgust. "Did it occur to either of you that Baron Lonsdale might have a spy at Montague? That the poison came from his corner?"

"Aye," Fitz Alan answered. "We ordered the gates closed and the guards on the walls doubled. No one has entered the fortress nor left it." He gave Guy an admonishing look. "We are not quite the fools you believe us to be. Of course there is a possibility that Lady Claudia is innocent. Yet there is also the fact that our thoughts are not cluttered by an infatuation for the girl."

"You were the only one poisoned," Kenric pointed out. "Your squire tasted every flagon of wine brought to our table, yet he and everyone else remained unaffected. That means the poison came from someone who could slip it into your wine without notice, one of us, to be more specific. You know we would not poison you, nor would Thomas or Evard. That leaves Lady Claudia. By all appearances, she is a gentle lady and much devoted to you. Yet is it coincidence that she also hails from a family that favors poison to murder their victims?" Kenric shook his head, making his opinion obvious. "You are bewitched by this woman, made blind by your affections for her. She is not made perfect just because you are in love with her. Nor does that make her free of guilt without a shred of proof to name her innocent. We did what was necessary to protect you, what you would have done yourself, were you in our place."

Looking at matters from Kenric's perspective, Guy knew his brother had a point. Kenric and Fitz Alan had little reason to put any trust in Claudia. Guy scowled and remained silent, not ready to admit the soundness of Kenric's logic. Love did not blind him to the possibility of Claudia's guilt, but he loved her for reasons that made him certain of her innocence. And he knew her far better than his brothers or anyone else would ever know her.

"I appreciate your concern for me," he said in a quiet voice. "I know you think me addled, but in time you will discover I am right about Claudia's innocence. The reason I asked you to guard her is that I am certain there is at least one spy within Montague, perhaps more. By now, 'tis likely Baron Lonsdale knows the two of you are here. He will guess right enough that we intend to lay siege to Halford. He may even fear we intend to march on Lonsdale itself. Kenric, your army alone could take Lonsdale. There is not a fortress in England that could withstand our three forces combined."

He looked between his brothers, seeing realization creep into their expressions. Satisfied, he told them the most damning evidence of all, what the drug prevented him from warning them about yesterday. "At one time, Baron Lonsdale believed my family would not retaliate were I to die under suspicious circumstances within his fortress. He planned to make my murder seem Claudia's doing. Her death at the hands of my men was to sate any need for vengeance. Weigh that against the fact that Claudia is not a fool. You think she would poison me when she knew that she would be judged guilty by you both? Even if she hated me so much that she wished to murder me, why would she do so before we were wed, when in less than a fortnight she would be made a wealthy widow?" Guy shook his head. "She is guilty only if she has a strong wish to die an unpleasant death."

Kenric and Fitz Alan exchanged uneasy glances.

Fitz Alan spoke first. "Your missive did not tell us these details of Baron Lonsdale's plot against you, nor did you inform us of the facts when we arrived. Had we known . . ." He shrugged his shoulders, the unspoken words a silent statement that the knowledge did not prove her innocence in their minds.

"And you accuse me of being blind?" Guy gave both men a look of disgust, then headed toward the door. The room swayed with every step, and he ended up with one hand braced against the wall. He could not even make it across the room by himself, much less to the farthest reaches of the castle. He swallowed his pride and demanded the help he needed. "I am ready for that walk. Our destination will be the dungeons."

Two hours later, Guy clung to the pommel of his saddle and willed the ground to stop shifting beneath him. Beneath his horse, to be more precise. He knew the warhorse stood stock-still, but the world seemed a whirl of motion all around him. His head reeled not only from the effects of the poison, but from the knowledge that Claudia was gone.

He had walked no further than the great hall when Thomas and Evard rushed forward with the news: the soldiers sent to relieve Claudia's guards had found them bound and gagged, the guard at the bolthole as well. Two suffered the same effects of poison as Guy, while the third had been knocked unconscious. None of the three got so much as a glimpse of their assailant. Worse yet, Claudia had disappeared without a trace.

Even as he gave the order that mounted two hundred knights and soldiers, he half expected to awake and find this was nothing more than another drug-induced nightmare. It seemed impossible that she was now beyond his reach, beyond his power to protect. Each time he closed his eyes he pictured her as he last saw her, the look of terror on her face when he succumbed to the poison. He spoke the vilest curse that came to mind.

Only Kenric and Fitz Alan were close enough to hear him. Thomas and Evard rode through the ranks of the other soldiers to pass along Guy's orders. Fitz Alan ignored the curse, looking preoccupied as he strapped a crossbow to the back of his saddle.

"We will find her," Kenric assured him. He glanced over at Guy from his own mount, his face an emotionless mask. "I just hope you are convinced now of her guilt."

Guy scowled and remained silent.

"You must face the truth," Kenric went on. "She went from here willingly. If they meant to kill her, the body would

be in the dungeon. If they drugged her or knocked her unconscious, we would have found signs in the bolthole tunnel.
Even a small man must hunch over to walk through those
tunnels. There were no marks to indicate that they dragged
her through. That means she walked out of Montague of her
own free will."

" 'Tis possible they held a knife to her." Guy knew his
argument lacked conviction. Kenric and Fitz Alan were convinced of Claudia's guilt. He had too little strength to waste
on useless arguments. He would sort everything out with his
brothers after they found Claudia. Until then, he needed
their help to do just that. Already he wondered if he could
lead a search party. Just sitting on his horse required almost
more energy than he possessed.

"They passed beneath no less than a score of soldiers on
the walls," Kenric pointed out. "The guards would have heard
the smallest sounds of a struggle. She did not walk out of the
fortress at knifepoint. She crept out of it."

" 'Tis a clever plan," Fitz Alan added. "First the spy poisons you, knowing we will blame your betrothed and thus
separate the two of you. With every spare soldier standing
guard on the walls, Lady Claudia's escape from the dungeons
was made that much easier." One brow rose as he nodded
toward Kenric. "We should have suspected such a plot and
posted extra guards in the dungeons."

"She was abducted," Guy insisted. "She would not go
willingly with her uncle's men."

"That does seem unlikely," Kenric agreed. He watched
Guy with an expectant air. When Guy remained silent, he
released an impatient sigh. "Have you not yet guessed the
obvious?"

Guy was in no mood for riddles. His head felt filled with
mush, his thoughts so cluttered he could scarce think
straight. It was an effort simply to remain upright on his
horse. "Nay, I have not guessed the obvious. Enlighten me."

Kenric made him wait for his answer while he secured his
broadsword to his saddle. There was a strange look in his gray

eyes when their gazes finally met, a rare, worried expression
that made Guy's stomach clench. "She would leave willingly
with her brother."

Claudia pushed her horse harder to catch up with Dante.
The road widened in this section of the forest, but as fast as
they rode, the low-hanging branches were a constant threat.
She ducked down to avoid an oak branch, then brought her
horse alongside her brother's. She had to shout to be heard
over the noise of their horses and the one that followed them.
"Dante! I cannot keep up this pace. Can we rest?"

Dante shook his head without looking at her, his attention on the road ahead. "Soon, Claudia. Not yet."

She let his horse pull ahead of hers again. The gray palfrey tossed its head in protest and tried to get the bit between
its teeth as it had countless times before. Her arms ached
from the strain of keeping the horse at a steady canter rather
than a flat-out gallop. It wanted to be the leader. Claudia
wanted to be anywhere but on its back.

They had not rested since dawn, and had kept up a gruel-
ing pace since then. She could tell by the direction of the sun
that they rode east, but Dante had not told her their destination. She had thought they would ride south, toward London
or Wales. Perhaps they rode this way to avoid any patrols Guy
might send to look for them. Guy would look first to the west
and Baron Lonsdale. Dante assured her that her escape would
appear the work of their uncle. Guy would never think to
search in this direction until they were safely away from Montague. Safely away from Guy.

A sudden image came to mind of the way Guy smiled at
her when they were alone in their chamber, a sly, seductive
smile that made her heart ache even worse. She looked at the
trees that rushed past her and tried to banish the image from
her mind. She also tried to banish the thought that what she
was doing was wrong, that she should have stayed at Montague. This morning she had voiced that worry and Dante told
her again that Guy intended to hang her today. The words

sounded even less believable in the cold light of day than they had in the dungeons. But why would Dante lie to her? Still, she could not shake the nagging suspicion that he was not being completely truthful.

The night before she thought that nothing would be worse than the uncertainty of not knowing whether Guy lived or died. Today she discovered an equal torment; the uncertainty of not knowing whether Guy wanted *her* to live or die. If she had remained in the dungeons, she might have a rope around her neck at this very moment. Or would Guy's arms be around her as he whispered soft words that everything would be all right? She could almost hear his voice when she closed her eyes.

Her horse nearly plowed into Dante's.

She gasped and pulled hard on the reins, coming to a sliding stop next to him. The man who rode behind them came to a stop as well. Armand was his name, a knight in Dante's hire. She had met Armand in the forest beyond Montague's walls where he awaited with the horses. He was a silent, handsome man who seemed to speak only when Dante questioned him.

Claudia's gaze moved to her brother. Dante looked tired to the bone. He had dark circles under his eyes, and his dark brown hair was tousled, as if he had raked his hands through it repeatedly. She stared hard at his face, trying to decide what had changed since she saw Dante last to make him appear so different. His features were the same, with a few new lines around his eyes and mouth, but it was the eyes themselves that worried her. She looked into their dark green depths and saw . . . nothing. It was like looking at a ghost. Even though he was flesh and blood, what she saw was only a shadow of the man she once knew. The empty depths of his eyes made her shiver.

"The crossroads are just ahead," Dante said. "We will walk the horses to the stream that lies just beyond. Armand, take your horse at least half a mile beyond the stream at a steady canter, then double back through the woods. We will meet you at the crofter's hut."

"Aye, my lord." Armand gave a smooth half-bow from his saddle, glanced at Claudia with an unreadable expression, then spurred his horse forward.

Dante and Claudia walked their horses past a wide clearing where another road intersected theirs. She watched Armand disappear around a bend in the road ahead of them. "Do you think they will search this far for us?"

"Aye," Dante answered.

She waited for him to say something more. He remained maddeningly silent, his gaze alert as he watched the road and woods around them. The road was well worn, but they had yet to encounter any travelers, none who might mention their passing to Guy or his men. She could no longer decide if that was a good thing or bad. If only she could see Guy once more, look into his eyes and ask if he thought her innocent or guilty. Was it worth her life to learn the truth? She made a conscious effort to occupy her mind with less dangerous thoughts. "Where are we going?"

"To a crofter's hut."

"I know that already," she said, with an impatient sigh. "Why are we going there? Should we not go to London, or to your fortress in Wales?"

He gave her an oblique glance. "You ask too many questions."

" 'Tis no crime," she argued. "I would like to know more of my future than the fact that I am bound for a crofter's hut. That seems a reasonable request to me."

"Fine. You will stay at a deserted crofter's hut with Armand for about a fortnight, then we will all journey south to Cheshire. From there you will travel to Wales with Armand and Oliver. I must return to London, but I should join you in Wales by first snowfall." His brows lifted as he gave her a pointed look. "Does that satisfy your curiosity?"

"Who is Oliver, and why will you not stay with me when we reach this hut?"

Dante rolled his eyes. "Oliver is another of my men. He and I have business to attend to that may take as long as a week. Armand will take good care of you until we return."

"You trust this Armand so much that you will leave me alone with him?"

"I have no worries that Armand will try to take advantage of you as Montague did. You will be safe in his care."

Dante's confidence did not make her feel any better about the plan. "What is this business you must attend to?"

His expression hardened. "I have one rule that I expect you to follow, as do all others. My business is my own, and I will not be questioned about it."

She studied his profile, made harsh by his scowl. This was not the man she had envisioned whenever she thought about their reunion. Their parents often teased that Dante wore his heart on his sleeve, his emotions so transparent that any could read them. That was no longer the case. Gone was the lighthearted young man who smiled often and easily. This Dante looked at her with eyes far older than his years. He seemed a stranger. She had changed as well, she supposed. The world had made them both sadder and wiser. "Do you also have business to attend in Cheshire?"

"Aye." He pulled his horse to a halt at the edge of a small stream that ran across the road. "We need to make our horses walk backward. Pull down on the reins and press your heels against the palfrey's flanks." He turned and pointed at a fallen tree at the side of the road a good twenty paces behind them, the trunk fallen so long ago that its bark was covered with soft green moss. "Back the horse up until you reach that felled tree, then I will tell you what to do next."

Claudia followed his instructions and touched her heels to the palfrey's flanks. Amazingly, the horse obeyed the command and began to back up in an oddly gaited pace. "Why are we doing this?"

"Your questions grow bothersome, Claudia." He took his gaze from the road behind him long enough to frown at her. "I do not recall such a curious nature in you. 'Tis only natural,

I suppose. All women are too curious for their own good, and you have grown into a woman since I saw you last."

Rather than argue his views of women, she gave him an exaggerated smile. "What a lovely compliment. I see you learned fine English manners at Edward's court. 'Tis said you hide behind some sort of disguise when you are there, which must make it convenient to dole out such praises. None know who you are to hold you accountable for them."

"What do you know of Edward's court, or my presence there?" he demanded.

The sudden intensity in his eyes made her grip on the reins slacken, and the horse ambled to a halt. She gathered the reins and urged the horse into its backward gait again. "I know only what Guy told me, which is more than you have ever shared about your life at court."

"What did that bastard tell you?"

"He is not a bastard! Guy is kind and—"

"I do not care what you think he is," Dante bit out. "I want to know what he told you."

"Guy told me that you are Edward's best knight," she said in a quiet voice, "that you are so formidable most fear to meet you. He says you wear a disguise so you may mingle unnoticed without it, that you are too modest to appreciate the attention you would receive if all knew your identity."

He digested that for a moment, then smiled another of his dark smiles. "It would seem Baron Montague has a sense of humor."

"Are you telling me he lied?"

"Nay, he did not lie to you. Yet the truths he told you would be open to many interpretations. It would also seem he has a talent for making you believe what he wants you to believe."

Claudia had no patience for his riddles. "What do you mean?"

"He made you believe that he loved you," Dante retorted. "A Montague could no more love a Chiavari than he could fly. If anything, you were little more than a game to him, a challenge to see if he could win your affections. 'Tis a sport to English nobles of his ilk, a means to sate their jaded appetites for a time." He shook his head. "You must put Baron Montague from your mind, harden your heart to him. Accept that you meant nothing more to him than a pleasant distraction, for you will not set eyes upon him again."

Dante's words cut through her like a knife, and she winced as if he had slapped her. "You are wrong. He did care for me."

"I am right," he countered. They had reached the fallen tree and he brought his horse to a halt. "You led a sheltered life at Lonsdale and know little of worldly men and their ways. In this you must trust my judgment. I am your brother and will do only what is best for you, unlike others such as Montague who will tell you lies just to use you."

"I did not lead the sheltered life you seem to think," she informed him. "Uncle Laurence often entertained his friends from court, and what I saw made me stay as far from them as possible. You think Guy is the same as the debauched noblemen you know, yet you have never even met him. That does not strike me as sound judgment, no more than your decision to leave me at Lonsdale all these years."

Claudia wished she could stuff the words back into her mouth. She had not meant to insult Dante, but that was the result. The spark of emotion that finally lit his eyes was one she had no wish to see. The deep, burning anger she saw there frightened her.

"You were not meant to be at Lonsdale so many years," he said in an icy tone. "Laurence agreed to send you to a convent just as soon as I sent the gold every good convent requires to accept a lady into its ranks. I sent that money a year ago. More since to Bishop Germaine, who supposedly made all the arrangements. The letters I wrote you explained everything, but Germaine said those messages must be my last, that you were now cloistered from the outside world."

He studied her face, as if searching for some reaction. Claudia was speechless with shock.

"I told you in the dungeons that I have many enemies," he went on, "men who would not hesitate to make you pay for my crimes against them. A convent was the only place I knew you would be safe, beyond the touch of any man."

She finally managed to find her voice, but she had to struggle not to shout. "Did it ever occur to you that I might have no wish to become a nun? That I might want a husband and children? A family of my own?"

The lines around his mouth hardened. "I will not allow you to marry an English lord or bear an Englishman's children. They would only grow up to be like their father. The world needs no more English bastards. Not from my sister."

"My safety had little to do with your decision to send me to a nunnery." Her anger matched Dante's, the one person she had always trusted without hesitation. He had meant to lock her away in a convent, to abandon her for the rest of her life. "It is the thought of me married to an Englishman that made your decision, yet you are half English yourself and sworn to an English king. Your hatred of this country and its people is misplaced, brother."

"My sword is sworn to England, but my heart is sworn to no man. As for English blood?" Dante shook his head. "Our mother became a Chiavari when she wed, and we can trace our line to the finest houses of the Roman empire. A Chiavari has no need to claim English blood."

Claudia knew her arguments would not change his mind. Whatever had happened to Dante in the years they were apart had changed him beyond her ability to undo. She thought of how she had always disliked her uncle, how he had turned his people against her and made her resent anyone who called themselves English. Guy had taught her that the English were not all the same. His people accepted her. Most had treated her as if she were Guy's baroness already. It struck her that she had never felt lonely at Montague. For the first time in years, she had felt as if she truly belonged somewhere.

Ever since Dante appeared in the dungeons she had allowed herself to rely upon his judgment, too distraught to rely upon her own. Now she realized that was a mistake. She could not put Guy from her mind as easily as Dante seemed to think, no more than she could spend the rest of her life wondering if she should have stayed at Montague. Wondering if Dante had lied to her about Guy's belief in her guilt. Dante could still decide to send her to a convent. She would never see Guy again.

"Hold my horse," Dante ordered, as he dismounted and tossed her the reins. He walked to the side of the road, then around the fallen tree to examine it from all sides. Looking satisfied with whatever he spied on the opposite side of the trunk, he returned to the horses and helped her dismount. "Stay here with your horse. I will return in a moment."

Claudia doubted she could go anywhere. Her legs trembled uncontrollably, unaccustomed to such long hours in a saddle. She held onto the horse's mane with one hand, the reins with the other. Dante remounted and spurred his horse toward the fallen tree. The horse made a graceful leap over the trunk, its hoofbeats muffled as it landed on the other side. Her horse tried to follow. She planted her feet and held the reins as tight as she could to restrain the beast. At last Dante reappeared, this time without his horse. He held a large, leafy branch in one hand and skirted a wide path around her to avoid startling her horse.

"I will jump your horse over the trunk," he said. "Brush out our tracks from the road to the tree, then join me on the other side."

Claudia nodded as he handed her the branch, but her gaze went to the sandy dirt road. Their tracks toward the stream were easy enough to follow. Once she brushed over the tracks that led into the forest, no one would notice that they had left the road at this spot. Even if Guy thought to search in this direction, he would never find her. She would live out her life in her brother's remote fortress in Wales or in some cloistered convent. And she would never know the truth. In her heart she knew the truth, or did she wish so badly to be right that it just seemed like the truth? There was only one way to be certain, and that way would risk her own life and Dante's. If her brother soon abandoned her at this crofter's hut, perhaps only her life and Armand's would be at risk. She owed no loyalty to Armand.

She made her decision as Dante mounted her horse and rode away. Her hands worked at the forked branch to strip away the smaller twigs. The horse jumped over the trunk and she hurried forward to place the branch on the ground in front of the tree. She placed the forked end toward the road with the limb pointing toward the trunk to form a crude arrow.

"Claudia!"

She gave a guilty start and stood up to look over the log. Dante stood in the forest beyond her, holding the reins of both horses. She tried her best to sound innocent. "Aye?"

"Hurry up," he ordered. "We do not have all day."

She nodded then bent over again, as if she were brushing away tracks. Before she could think better of the idea, she reached beneath her cloak and slipped off her emerald necklace, thankful that Fitz Alan had not taken the jewels when he imprisoned her. If Guy or one of his men found the necklace, they would recognize the jewels as her own. "I am almost done, Dante. Have patience," she called over her shoulder. She prayed that no thieves or travelers would stumble across the treasure. Her fate and her future now lay at the edge of a forest road. The glittering pile of stones looked as abandoned and unwanted as she felt in that moment. She turned away from the slim hope they represented and walked into the forest.

Claudia opened her eyes, her gaze unfocused in the dark hut. The only light came from the dying coals of a brazier that sat in the center of the hut's only room. She could just make out Armand's large form on the floor across from her, wrapped in a blanket and turned away from the brazier. The handsome knight snored loud enough to wake the dead.

Claudia sighed and rolled onto her back, trying to find a more comfortable position. The dirt floor that served as her bed offered little comfort, no more than the saddle that served as her pillow. At least she could no longer hear the small noises that had kept her awake until Armand drifted off to sleep and started his nightly serenade of snores and snorts. The fierce noise would surely keep most of the forest creatures at bay. Any sensible animal would be too spooked by the racket to seek shelter or the meager food they had brought into the hut. Not that the walls or door would stop any creature determined to enter. The daub had crumbled from the walls long ago, leaving only woven wattle with gaps wide enough for many a furry creature to wriggle through. The door hung on just one hinge, propped into the crooked doorjamb each night more than closed. The latch hung useless where a missing hasp should be, and the thatched roof provided even less shelter, a good portion of it having collapsed in some past storm or snowfall. Claudia hoped that Armand's snoring would keep bats away as well.

Odd that a man so quiet during the day could become so vocal at night. Each morning at dawn, before Claudia even awoke, Armand left to take his guard post. He climbed halfway up a large oak tree each day to keep watch over the meadows and forest that surrounded them. The woods were not so thick here, probably the result of the woodcutter who once lived in this hut. From his vantage point, Armand could see a rider approach from any direction. So far he had spent three full days in that tree while Claudia tried to keep busy on the ground. She found a few berry bushes almost choked by weeds and picked over by birds, but she managed to salvage a few handfuls of berries for one of their dinners. She had collected so many nuts that she was beginning to feel like a squirrel. Yet on each of those food-gathering excursions, she watched the woods as closely as Armand, and for the same reason.

If only she knew if the arrival of soldiers would be a good thing or bad. Or if they would arrive at all. The doubts wore at her nerves and made her start at every small sound: a bird taking sudden flight through branches overhead, a startled rabbit breaking through the brush, the snap of a twig by some larger, unseen creature.

A thousand times she questioned the wisdom of leaving her necklace in the forest. What good could come of it? Armand's death? Her brother's? Her own? Even if Guy believed she had nothing to do with his poisoning, could she live her life in fear of his family, defying the wishes of her own? Her questions were legion, endless problems with no solutions.

Armand made a snuffling sound as he shifted in his sleep, then steady snores once more when he settled into a new position. She wished he would put half so much energy into a conversation, into answering her questions with something other than, "That is for your brother to answer, my lady." He was unfailingly polite, so excruciatingly courteous and proper that she thought him the rudest man she had ever met. Deathly silence, or answers that told her nothing. One more day with that man and she would—

In the blink of an eye, a hand clamped down over her

nose and mouth. A soft voice whispered in her ear. "Make no sound, or your knight's life will be forfeit."

She nodded her head to indicate that she understood, and fought down panic over her lack of air. The hand lowered so she could breathe but remained firmly in place over her mouth. Just as an arm wrapped around her waist and pulled her to her feet, Armand's snoring came to an abrupt halt.

"My lady?" Armand called out in a soft voice. Claudia heard the soft hiss of metal against metal as he sat up, the dull glint of steel from the sword he held. "Is something amiss, Lady Claudia?"

From behind her, something long and slender extended toward the brazier, a torch that flared to life when it touched the coals.

Armand scrambled to his feet too late. Claudia blinked against the sudden glare of light. She was amazed to see a dozen soldiers step forward from the darkest shadows along the walls of the hut, all with drawn swords, and all pointed at Armand. One glance around him and Armand knew he was hopelessly outnumbered. His gaze went to Claudia as he slowly lowered his weapon to the ground. "You will forfeit your life if you harm this lady."

"I intend her no harm." The voice belonged to Fitz Alan, and Claudia knew he was the one who held her. "Where are the rest of Chiavari's men?"

"There are no others, my lord. Just me."

"You expect me to believe that Dante Chiavari left you alone with his sister?"

"Believe what you will," Armand said, in that polite tone Claudia hated.

"Tie him up," Fitz Alan ordered. His hand came away from Claudia's mouth and he led her outside.

More men stood around the hut, how many she could not tell in the shadowy moonlight. Fitz Alan sent a soldier to fetch their horses, then he released his hold on Claudia's arm and turned to face her.

"We found your necklace, Lady Claudia. Did you mark

the path that led us here, or is this some new trickery of your brother's?"

"I left the marker." Claudia backed up a few steps, glad that Fitz Alan could not see how badly her hands trembled. "Guy is recovered?"

"Aye, recovered and furious with your brother's treachery. He rode off to search for you the morning after your disappearance, so ill he could scarce sit on his horse. He will not be pleased that it took this long to find you."

"Is that why he is not with you?" Claudia asked. "Is he still so ill that he could not continue the search himself?"

Fitz Alan folded his arms across his chest. "You do not know?"

"Know what?" she asked, as her heart began to beat harder.

"Your brother issued Guy a challenge. They are to meet tomorrow morning on the grounds outside Kelso Abbey."

"But Dante said—" Fitz Alan would not know why Dante had issued such a challenge, no more than he would know of Dante's orders not to murder Guy. What was Dante about? Nothing that would improve Guy's health. Of that, she was certain. "You must take me to this abbey."

"That was my plan," Fitz Alan said, a surprising trace of humor in his voice. "I am pleased that you intend to cooperate."

"Is there a reason I should not?"

"Your brother went to great pains to abduct you from Montague," Fitz Alan pointed out. "It seemed you went with him willingly."

"Dante told me that I would be hung if I stayed, that Guy gave those orders himself when the poison wore off."

Fitz Alan said nothing for a long moment. "Your brother is a liar, my lady. Guy did not awake from his stupor until you were long gone from Montague, and he gave no such orders in his delirium."

"Does Guy believe that I participated in my brother's plot?"

Fitz Alan spread his hands and shrugged. "At this point, I would not presume to speculate on the matter. Best you save your questions for Guy."

That answer was no more helpful than any of Armand's. Fitz Alan was the last person she should trust, yet she would still go with him willingly. Assuming that Fitz Alan did not lie about the challenge, she had to reach Guy and Dante before one of them killed the other. "How far are we from Kelso Abbey?"

Towering clouds cast a patchwork of shadows over the wide valley and the army gathered there. The clouds did little to diminish the heat of the day or the sticky haze that blanketed the lush green meadows. Guy waited at the edge of the army's encampment. His warhorse tossed its head to escape a small swarm of flies. Guy ignored the flies, just as he ignored the heat that made sweat pour from his armor-encased body. Through the slits of his helm he watched the gates of Kelso Abbey, high on a hill above them. A lone knight rode through the gates, dressed for battle. His squire followed on the knight's palfrey. They moved at a leisurely pace down the hillside, through a flock of grazing sheep that dodged and darted away from the horses, their bleats of protest at the disturbance too far away from Guy's vantage point to be heard. The knight and squire disappeared as they entered a stand of trees.

The woods spread in a thick ribbon along the banks of a river that ran through the valley. Guy envied the knight the cool shade he rode through. He turned to look at Kenric, but could tell nothing of his brother's mood through the lowered visor of Kenric's helm.

"He was wise to take sanctuary at the abbey," Kenric said, his voice muffled by his visor. "A fool to leave its walls."

Guy's gaze went toward the woods again. "Chiavari has yet to make a foolish move. So far he has made fools of us all. First he steals Claudia from under lock and key, then while I comb the countryside for some trace of him, he is back at

Montague, pinning an issue of challenge to the very door of my chamber. I would like to know how he managed such a feat."

"As would we all," Kenric agreed, "but his luck will soon run out. The word from Fitz Alan's patrol sounded promising. We may yet ground this fox at his own game."

"We have not heard from Fitz Alan for three days," Guy said. "The fox still leads this chase."

Dante and his squire emerged from the woods, and Guy abandoned his conversation with Kenric, his thoughts centered on Claudia's brother. Guy could think of no man he disliked more intensely. Even Baron Lonsdale paled in comparison. So far Dante had proved much more adept at treachery than his uncle. Poisoned, robbed of his betrothed, led on a wild goose chase, and outmaneuvered at every turn. Guy vowed that the man who rode toward him would pay for each of those crimes. Most damning of all, Dante was responsible for Claudia's betrayal. The last five days provided him with plenty of time to surmise what had happened the night of her escape. The plot to poison him did not involve her. Of that much, he was certain. He knew her expressions too well to mistake the look on her face the day of the feast for anything but shock and fear for his safety. He assumed that Dante had not revealed his presence to Claudia until he went to her in the dungeons. Surely Dante told his sister that the poison was not fatal, but somehow he convinced her to go away with him.

Guy recalled the promises he made Claudia, the promises of a besotted fool. He would have renounced his family for her. When faced with her own test of loyalty, she chose her brother. That knowledge ate at him like an acid.

Even worse than knowing she betrayed him was knowing that it didn't matter. He would never again trust her, but he was still determined to marry her. No matter what she did or who she turned to, he would always love her. She was his greatest weakness. His only weakness. He would marry her for that reason alone. In the hands of an enemy, she would be a weapon to use against him. Dante's challenge proved as much.

Guy's gaze narrowed on his nemesis. Dante rode forward from the woods with no sign of hesitation, despite the fact that he and his squire rode toward an army of two hundred mounted knights and soldiers. He was a brave fool, Guy decided. He also looked to be a wealthy one. Sunlight glinted off the gold and silver fittings of his armor, and rare white plumes on his helm and horse's bridle waved in regal splendor with each step the horse took. Over his armor Dante wore a deep red surcoat with a shield the same color, yet he wore no emblems or devices, no coat of arms to proclaim his house or identity. Guy knew the reason why from Claudia. Sworn to no liege lord and branded a bastard, Dante could represent no one in a contest but himself. It seemed fitting that the color he chose was the same as blood. As the king's Enforcer, he had surely spilled more than his share of it.

Guy expected Dante to keep his distance, to rein his horse not far from the edge of the clearing so he could make a run for the abbey and sanctuary at the first sign of trouble. Instead he rode forward until his horse was no more than a length from Guy's. Cocky bastard.

"I have word from your king," Dante said. The slits in his helm formed a cross and his deep voice carried well. Surprisingly, he lacked any trace of the Italian accent that marked his sister's speech. He stripped off a gauntlet, then reached into his surcoat and withdrew a small scroll. He extended the parchment toward Guy. "I will tell you its contents, although I have little doubt that you will wish the message verified."

Without a word, Kenric nudged his horse forward and retrieved the scroll, then backed into position again next to Guy. He broke the scroll and began to read.

"The king wishes us to settle this matter in a peaceful manner," Dante went on. "Before I left London, Edward made me swear that I would not murder you for the wrong done my sister. However, he said nothing about a fair fight to the finish." In a sudden move, Dante threw his gauntlet down on the ground between them. The high-strung warhorses tossed their heads, and all three men tightened their reins to control the animals as Dante delivered his own message. "Thus I challenge you, Guy of Montague."

Guy lifted his visor, wanting to be certain his voice carried the full weight of his warning. "Given my present mood, you would be ill-advised to provoke me into a fight."

"But that is exactly what I intend," Dante answered. "A fight to the death."

The corners of Guy's mouth lifted in a smile that lacked humor. "Why should I accept your challenge, Chiavari? I can kill you now for the wrongs you visited upon me. I made no pledges to Edward that concern your life."

"Perhaps you should read the king's message before you do anything hasty," Dante said, his voice calm.

Guy looked to Kenric, who had also pushed his visor up to read the message. "Well?"

"Edward orders you to abide by the same agreement he made with Dante," Kenric said. "He also makes mention that Dante is Lady Claudia's legal guardian, that her uncle had no right to contract a betrothal agreement." He gave Guy a meaningful look. "The king thinks you might be pleased by this news, seeing as the betrothal was forced upon you. The issue of guardianship makes it invalid."

Guy felt his gut tighten. No betrothal meant he could make no legal claim to Claudia. His gaze went to Dante. Was this challenge simply a means to negotiate the terms of a new betrothal? Now that he held Claudia, Dante must know that he also held all the favor in any bargaining he meant to do. But a challenge to the death? It made no sense. "What do you want from me, Dante?"

The answer came sure and swift. "Your blood."

"I did nothing to dishonor your sister." Guy spoke quietly, even though enough of his men could hear the conversation well enough to repeat it. Unfortunately, he doubted that Dante would be stupid enough to agree to a more private meeting in Guy's tent. "To my knowledge we were betrothed, which made her mine in the eyes of the law and God. You have no need to challenge me, for I treated Claudia with the respect due my betrothed. I intend to make her my wife within the fortnight."

"She will never be your wife," Dante vowed. "Claudia is bound for a convent. You will never see her again, Montague."

The discussion was over. Guy made a small gesture with his hand, and a loud hiss filled the air as two hundred swords left their scabbards. He spoke two words that could well decide his future. "Seize him."

Guy studied Dante over the rim of his goblet. Claudia's brother didn't look the least disturbed by the fact that he was bound hand and foot to the center pole of Guy's tent. His armor and helm were stripped away just moments ago to reveal a face that all of England speculated about. Guy would have recognized him anywhere.

Dante was a masculine reflection of his sister, his profile almost identical. The hair was an exact match in color, as were the eyes. It unnerved Guy to see such familiar features in the guise of a man he hated so thoroughly.

It was the lack of any emotion in Dante's eyes that bothered him the most. He had seen that same look at a few bargaining tables and strove to imitate it himself on occasion. It was the look of an observer, someone who watched everything that went on around him without any noticeable interest in the outcome. Dante had accepted his capture without resistance, hadn't argued when they stripped away his armor and tied him up, and now he didn't show the slightest trace of curiosity about what his fate at Guy's hands might be. Guy knew it was almost impossible to outmaneuver an enemy not knowing how his mind worked. He didn't have a clue how Dante's mind worked. It was frustrating to no end. It was a trait he could not help but admire.

Guy suspected that any demands for answers would only meet with aloof silence. Patience was the key to unlocking such a mind and Guy was very good at waiting. He settled back on his cot and sipped at his wine. The two men stared at each other, Dante bound in what had to be an uncomfortable position, Guy relaxed and at ease. A good hour passed in their silent standoff, and then it was Dante who finally spoke. "This accomplishes nothing, Baron."

Guy tried not to smile over the small victory. "What accomplishes nothing?"

Dante ignored the question. "You cannot kill me, and I will not tell you where she is. Claudia is in a place you will never find."

"You think not?" Guy asked the question as if he truly wanted an answer. "The most likely places to search for her seem to be the west and south. A dullard such as myself would never think to search the east road toward Alstead, nor a hidden path through the forest where the road forks toward the Tyne."

That did not garner the reaction he had hoped for. In fact, it garnered no reaction at all. Dante's features remained impassive, his eyes . . . observant. Nothing more.

"Do you want a chance to spill my blood, Chiavari?"

"Aye."

"I will make a bargain with you," Guy said, his tone thoughtful. "I will accept your challenge, but the terms must differ and we must both agree on them."

"What are your terms?"

"Swords," Guy said, "on foot, without armor or chain mail."

The corners of Dante's mouth lifted in a vague shadow of a smile. "You have a wish to die quickly?"

"Nay, I have no wish to die in any manner at your hands. Nor to slay you," Guy added. "Your death gains me nothing. The fight will not be to the finish, but until one of us draws blood. The contest ends there, with Claudia as the prize. If you win, you can ride out of this valley and go wherever you wish. You have my word that none will follow you, and I will call off my search for Claudia. She will be free to leave these lands as well and I will make no attempt to delay or recapture her, or to see or speak with her before she leaves. If I win, Claudia becomes my wife with your blessings and you will not interfere in our lives again." He folded his arms across his chest. "Those are my terms."

He held Dante's gaze as he waited for an answer, his own unwavering. He wanted Dante to know that he was sincere, that he hid nothing from him and offered a fair bargain. Hopefully that would be enough to convince him of the lie. If Dante agreed to the contest, Guy would win either way. He had made no promises about petitioning the king. If Edward ordered Guy and Claudia to marry, Dante would have no choice in the matter. Not if he wished to remain in the king's employ, or, anywhere in England. Winning the match would only make things that much simpler.

At last Dante nodded. "I agree to your terms."

"Give me the reins," Claudia demanded. "You have my word that I will not try to escape. My only wish is to reach this abbey."

Fitz Alan glanced over his shoulder, a speculative look in his brown eyes. "That is the reason I hold your reins, lady. 'Tis the hottest day of the year and you would run your horse to the ground if I let you have the reins."

"I would not," she muttered. "Can we at least canter for awhile? This meadow is flat, and the road through it well-packed. 'Tis a waste of time to walk the horses through such even ground."

Fitz Alan replied without turning around. "I agreed that we would ride ahead of my patrol to make faster time. Be satisfied with that."

"But I—"

"Look at your horse's neck and tell me we have not pushed the beasts too hard already."

Claudia's gaze went to the lather that covered her palfrey's neck and withers. The animal sounded winded as well.

She glared at Fitz Alan's back, not about to admit that he was right.

"The horses must walk after such a long run," he went on. "Only then can they be put out to pasture."

"What? Surely you do not intend to stop before we reach the abbey!"

Fitz Alan flashed her a smile. "Nay, lady. Why should we stop when the abbey overlooks the next valley? We are almost there."

Her eyes narrowed. "Not an hour ago I asked how much further and you said half a day. Why did you lie to me?"

"Because I knew you would argue about walking the horses if you realized we were so close to the abbey. And I did not exactly lie. If we had to walk from there because you ruined your horse, it would take half a day. You did not ask how long it would take on horseback, if you will recall."

"You knew what I meant," she bit out. "Give me my reins."

Fitz Alan shook his head. "Nay, lady. The horses cannot take another hard run, and we are still an hour away—by foot."

Claudia clenched her jaw and remained silent. Odious man.

Ahead of them was a thick stand of trees bordering the edge of the meadow that turned out to be a sizable forest as they ventured further into it. The scent of pine filled the air, and the screeching racket of birds above them marked their passage through the forest. The ground began to slope downward, and the birds became less vocal. Another sound grew louder, the distant shouts of a great many men and the distinctive ring of metal striking metal.

Claudia's heart went to her throat. " 'Tis Guy and Dante. I must stop them!"

She kicked her horse forward, but Fitz Alan tightened his hold on the reins. "Have patience, Lady Claudia. You must not rush into this fight. If that is a match between Guy and Dante that we hear, 'tis no harmless contest between brothers. They will be bent on blood. A distraction from you could cost one of them their life, and I have seen the effect you have on Guy. 'Tis likely he would be the one distracted. When we reach the clearing, I will signal one of the soldiers to halt the match, and we will arrive without incident."

They reached the clearing even as Fitz Alan shared his plan. Claudia gave him a distracted nod. "Aye, very well, but let us hurry."

Below them were dozens of round tents topped with Montague pennants. Beyond the tents, it looked as if Guy's entire army had gathered to form a large circle around the two combatants. She was still too far away to see the men clearly, but she would recognize Guy at any distance. As in his match with Kenric, he carried no shield and had stripped down to his breeks. His opponent, who could only be Dante, had done the same. What possessed them to shed their armor for such a contest? She shook her head. They were both crazed.

Fitz Alan let out a long, low whistle that made her palfrey's ears twitch. If he hoped for some reaction from Guy's soldiers, the result was disappointing. Not one man turned their way, the sounds of shouts and swordplay too loud to hear Fitz Alan's signal. Given the steep, rocky terrain on the hill below them, they were now forced to let their exhausted horses pick a careful path down the hillside despite Claudia's wish to race toward the crowd of men. She watched the contest with fascinated terror, knowing she could do nothing to stop it from this distance.

From what she could see, Guy and Dante looked evenly matched. They were about the same height and size, and both wielded their swords as if they knew what they were about. Guy parried and backed away from a fierce series of attacks, then turned aggressor and forced Dante to back away from his blows. Dante would parry until he reached the edge of the crowd, then launch another attack of his own. It looked a macabre dance of sorts, the moves graceful and well practiced, the price of a mistake lethal.

"They are testing each other," Fitz Alan said, his gaze also on the match. "That means they have not been at it long. If they are as evenly matched as they appear, this could go on for hours. Do not worry, Lady Claudia. Someone will note our arrival before either of them is hurt."

The words might have been comforting if Fitz Alan had not sounded so worried himself. The horses had walked long enough.

Claudia waited until they were almost at the bottom of the hill. Her chance came when Fitz Alan stood in his stirrups to let out another whistle, his attention focused on any soldier who might respond to his signal. She urged her horse alongside Fitz Alan's and reached for the reins even as she applied her heels to the palfrey's sides. The reins came away in her hand as the palfrey bolted forward.

"Damn it, Claudia. Come back here!"

She had almost reached the tents when Fitz Alan caught up with her. He grabbed the palfrey's bridle and pulled them both to a sliding stop. She was off her horse before it came to a full halt. The path she took through the tents twisted and turned, but she could hear Fitz Alan close behind her, also on foot. An arsenal of longbows stood just ahead, already strung and propped on end to make them easy for soldiers to grab in case of attack. Claudia slowed long enough to yank out the bow closest to the center, which toppled the entire pile. Bows flew in every direction. She glanced over her shoulder and saw Fitz Alan make a graceful leap over one pile, only to catch his foot in another. He tripped and sprawled to the ground just as Claudia smashed into a soldier at the edge of the crowd. Both she and the soldier tumbled forward.

"Mi scusi," she mumbled, as she pushed herself off the soldier to stand up. The momentum of their fall had carried them forward to the inner edge of the crowd. She heard other soldiers call out her name, but ignored them.

Guy and Dante were just a few paces away from her, both so intent on their match that they paid her disturbance no heed. Neither spoke, but Guy made a sound deep in his throat each time his sword lashed out. She sensed something different in this attack of Guy's than the ones she had witnessed from the hillside. This was not an assault to find his opponent's weakness, but to close in on it.

Guy's sword made a series of tightening circles around Dante's blade, ending one circle with an upward thrust, the next downward, then he made a final wide sweep that sent Dante's sword flying through the air. Almost before Dante could react to that loss, Guy slashed his sword in a sideways arc that made Dante throw his shoulders forward and his stomach backward to avoid the blade. Guy's sword missed its mark by no more than a hair's breadth. Thrown off balance, Dante rolled to the ground and somersaulted away from Guy.

"Stop!"

Guy turned instantly at the sound of Claudia's voice, his body still braced for attack, a look of stunned surprise on his face. His eyes widened when he caught sight of her and his sword lowered as he strode forward.

"Montague!"

Dante's shout slowed Guy's pace, then he came to a halt a few feet from Claudia. She remembered Fitz Alan's warning that she would distract Guy if she interfered in the fight, just as she saw a movement from the corner of her eye. Dante was still crouched on the ground, one hand near the cuff of his boot. She knew that he always carried a concealed dagger there. Once Guy turned around, Dante would have a clear aim at his heart. Panic shot through her and she ran toward Guy even as the dagger appeared in Dante's hand. The deadly weapon shot forward in a blur of flashing steel.

17

Claudia stared down at the jeweled hilt that protruded from her chest and thought it strange that she should notice its workmanship. Inlaid emerald chips formed the letter C on the hilt, and intricate etching on the guard spelled out the first half of the Chiavari motto: *For the Good of God.* The side of the guard she could not see would read *No Enemy Unpunished,* the part of the Chiavari motto that Dante chose to live by.

Guy's bellow of rage seemed to come from very far away, even though she knew he stood close by. Weren't those his hands on her waist? She glanced up and caught sight of Dante, his face drained of color. It was good to see an honest emotion on his face, even if it was shocked horror. He kept too much inside him, tried too hard to cut away what was left of his heart. Aye, he needed a reminder that he was human after all, and not some soulless beast who felt no regrets for his actions. This he regretted. She could see it in his eyes. She gave him a gentle smile to tell him everything would be fine.

Why was it so hard to breathe?

She watched in a haze as Guy lowered her slowly to the ground. Dante rushed over as well and crouched down beside her. Guy's fist lashed out and Dante toppled over backward. "Stay *away* from her!"

The icy hatred in Guy's face disappeared the instant his gaze returned to her. He smoothed a few stray wisps of hair from her forehead. "The blade is in your shoulder, Claudia. Painful, I am sure, but not a mortal blow. Hold very still while I pull it free."

"The blade is poisoned, Montague." Dante struggled

against Kenric's hold on him, his arms pinned behind his back. He winced from some unseen pain that Kenric applied. "Free me, for God's sake, or she will die."

Guy spoke in a tone she had never heard before. It was a little frightening. "You have the cure for this?"

"Aye," Dante replied. He called over his shoulder. "Oliver! Bring my kit and a measure of wine."

Guy and Kenric exchanged a look, then Guy nodded. Kenric released his hold on Dante and her brother knelt at her side once more. She smiled up at him. "Hullo again."

"What is wrong with her?" Guy demanded.

" 'Tis the poison," Dante snapped. He glanced up at Kenric. "Bring whatever clean cloths you can find. She will bleed more than usual."

"I want this fouled blade out of her," Guy said, as he reached for the hilt.

Dante smacked his hand away. "Wait for the bandages. Send someone for clean water as well. I must wash this grime from my hands before I touch the wound." He leaned closer to her face as Guy shouted out an order for water. "Can you still see me, cara?"

The look on Dante's face was so tender and caring that her eyes filled with tears. This was the brother she remembered. "Si, Dante. Mi sento mancare."

" 'Tis normal to feel dizzy," he said. "Can you feel me squeeze your hand?"

"Are you holding it?"

Dante scowled.

"Here are the bandages." Kenric's face appeared suddenly, upside down, as he knelt by Claudia's head and leaned forward to look at her. His smile looked upside down, too, or was it a frown? Uncertain, she smiled up at him.

"Hullo."

Kenric ignored the greeting. "Why is she smiling?"

No one answered him. She felt a small pinprick in her shoulder, then a heavy pressure.

"Did you feel that?" Dante asked.

Why would Dante prick her shoulder with a needle? For some reason, that reminded her of the tunic she had sewn for Guy. She had to change the emblem into a wolf before he decided to wear it. "Where did I leave my sewing?" she mused aloud. "Will you help me find my needle and threads, Guy?" While she waited patiently for an answer, she tried her best to focus on his face. Those tears made her vision all blurry. Or was it something else? Why wouldn't he answer her? "There is something I must finish on that tunic I sewed for you. Did I leave my needle on the mantel again?"

Guy's voice sounded strange, as if his throat were constricted somehow. "I will search for your needle, love. Just rest now."

"Nay, Claudia! Do not rest." Dante swatted at her face as she closed her eyes. " 'Tis the poison, cara. You must not sleep."

But she had to sleep. It was so late, and she was so very tired. The last thing she heard was the sound of Guy's voice, ragged now with some unknown emotion. His words sounded hauntingly familiar. "If she dies, you die with her."

The urge to kill flowed swift and hard through his veins. Guy wondered that there could be so much violence in his heart when he had never considered himself a violent man. Watching Claudia's torment only intensified his urge to destroy something. Or someone. She had retched too many times to remember over the past two days, so violently that her wound broke open each time until it was sealed with a red-hot knife. No one had paid any heed to Claudia's frantic assurances that she did not mind a little blood. Dante ended up with the gruesome duty while the others held her down.

Guy would hear those screams in his nightmares for the rest of his life. Each time he looked at Dante, he recalled the smell of burning flesh and the image of soft white skin seared to blackened red. He feared she could survive little more of her brother's cures.

The long hours that Claudia lay unconscious afterward

turned into a full day, then night fell again and Guy still could not bring himself to leave her side, not until he knew if she would live. This was the strongest test of his willpower, to look from the pale oval of Claudia's face to that of Dante's as they kept an endless vigil at her bedside. He could reveal nothing of his inner turmoil, no hint of his fear for Claudia, no telling caresses or words of comfort that would give evidence to his love. There was no doubt in his mind that Dante would use every word and deed against him. The man who watched Claudia for any sign of recovery watched Guy just as closely for a sign of weakness. Guy refused to provide such an easy means for Dante to bargain with him. He trusted Claudia no more than he trusted Dante. When she recovered, he would give her no reason to believe she still controlled his heart. But what would he do if she did not recover?

He tried to content himself with images of Claudia's brother being subjected to every hideous torture imaginable. Strangely, Dante's silent presence provided not only fuel for his rage, but a measure of hope. Guy knew Claudia's emotions so well that her brother's proved equally transparent. Gone was the look of desperate grief in those familiar green eyes, replaced by grim relief. Guy knew then that Claudia would live.

He rolled his head from side to side and tried to ease muscles cramped by hours of tension. An oil lamp set on a campaign chest near the doorway provided the only light in the large tent. The flame sputtered and cast strange, distorted shadows against the linen walls as an evening breeze ruffled the vented canopy. The breeze carried a faint scent of rain, followed by the distant rumble of thunder. A sudden crack of lightning heralded the storm's arrival, and the walls of the tent shuddered before a sudden gust of wind.

Claudia moaned, and Guy clenched his fists against his need to hold her, to reach out for the comfort it would give him just to touch her. Whatever pain caused her brow to furrow eased away, and he sensed that she drifted deeper into sleep rather than unconsciousness. The storm grew louder around them, but she didn't stir.

"When will she awaken?" Guy demanded.

From his seat opposite Guy, Dante rubbed his hands over his face as if to push away the last thoughts of sleep. "Tomorrow, perhaps sooner. The sleeping draught I gave her is not a strong one. There was still too much poison in her to risk anything stronger."

"Too much of *your* poison in her," Guy clarified. The sound of the rising storm covered their quiet conversation. "I find myself growing restless to see you pay for that crime. I may kill you yet, even if she does survive."

"You may try." Dante folded his arms across his chest, but he looked more tired than defiant. "At the moment, I would not put up much of a fight."

"I should do it now, when I will not have to worry that Claudia will throw herself in front of another coward's dagger."

"Aye, you should."

Guy was silent a long moment. "I vow 'tis pointless to goad you. I have never met a man who cares less whether he lives or dies. 'Tis a wonder you are still alive."

"I will live long enough to thwart your plans for my sister," Dante said. "Claudia is all I have left of my family, and yours already murdered one Chiavari. I will not hand you another."

Guy arched one brow. "You think I will allow you to take her away from me again?"

" 'Twas not such a difficult feat the first time." Dante stretched out his arms and yawned. "Once I have her within a convent's walls, she will be safe from you and your family forever."

"You sound very sure of yourself," Guy mused. "I wonder why, when I hold you and your knights prisoner. The only thing that keeps you from chains is the misery you inflicted on your own sister. Once she is recovered, I have no use for you. Few would find it strange to hear that a man such as yourself suffered a fatal accident. Indeed, I feel certain there are many who would be thankful for such news."

"Think well before you murder me, Baron. The men you hold are not the only in my hire, and their orders are clear. My murder signs your own death warrant." A shadowy smile touched Dante's lips. "Aside from that, Claudia would never forgive the death of a second brother at the hands of a Montague, nor will she come to you willingly, knowing it means the death of one or both of us."

"Do you think I care what her thoughts are on the matter?" That wiped the smug expression from Dante's face. Guy forced his own features into a mask of indifference. "A willing wife is not a requirement for marriage. What I want from your sister is her dowry and a healthy heir."

"You care for her more than you would like me to think," Dante said. "I saw you together at Montague. I would say you care for her a great deal."

"I will admit to a certain fondness for every woman I take to my bed. However, being poisoned tends to put a damper on a man's affections. I will take measures to ensure that she does nothing so foolish in the future." Guy waited for Dante to deny Claudia's involvement in his poisoning, to speak of something he knew to be truth. It was an old bargaining tactic. Hearing Dante speak the truth would provide a measure to determine the lies. Unfortunately, Dante did not seem inclined to fall into the trap so easily.

"You would not marry Claudia for Halford alone."

"I should allow Halford to fall into the hands of another, when all know its worth to me? Your uncle demanded four hundred gold florins, and I agreed to his price before he betrayed me. An unwilling bride seems a much more profitable bargain."

"You bastard."

"Nay, there is no question of my legitimacy, Dante. However, your sister tells me there is some question as to your own, and hers as well. She also mentioned your determination to exact vengeance against the man who labeled you bastards. Is that the reason you placed yourself in Edward's hire?"

Dante's eyes narrowed. "What do you know of my work for the king?"

"I know you are Edward's Enforcer," Guy said, "an assassin hired to rid him of those he finds troublesome. Do you find some pleasure in what you do? Or is it the gold Edward pays that attracts you?"

Dante's brows drew together, and he directed a scowl toward Claudia. "I am not such an animal that I hire myself out for murder simply to slake my thirst for blood. Nor do I murder for gold."

"There are many at court who neither seek gold nor remain in that nest of vipers for their own pleasure. They seek Edward's favor, a means to bend a king's will to their own. A king could influence a great many matters, such as the Church's decree that a man is illegitimate. A reversal of such a decision would make you the heir to a very great estate, would it not?"

The corners of Dante's mouth tightened. A small reaction, but telling just the same. Guy had happened upon Dante's weakness, and every man with a weakness had a price. "There is nothing you can do to prevent my marriage to your sister, but I realize you will be a threat to me as long as you remain in England. As I see it, there are two possible solutions to the problem you present. Either I rid myself of you for good, or I take steps to ensure that you are too far from England to cause me any trouble." Guy spread his hands in a congenial gesture. "You know as well as I that your execution would complicate matters. Your exile holds more appealing possibilities."

"Now who sounds cocksure of himself?" Dante scoffed. "Edward values my services too highly to stand idle while you spirit me from his services."

"It would be a mistake to underestimate my influence in matters that involve the king." Guy let that quiet warning sink in for a moment before he continued. "It is within my means to have you leave England willingly, and in my best interest to ensure that you are too busy with your own affairs to interfere in mine. Perhaps you underestimate my influence in Italy as well. The vengeance you seek is within your grasp, Dante."

A flash of lightning turned the walls of the tent an eerie shade of blue. Neither man flinched. They stared in silence at one another, the air charged between them. At last Dante looked away. "You will not bend me to your will, Baron. Nor will you live long enough to see me curry the favor of a Montague. I would sooner slit your throat."

Guy shrugged his shoulders. Better to give Dante time to think the notion over in his mind. Time and patience *would* bend Dante to his will.

Claudia closed her eyes again before either man realized she was awake. The words they had spoken made her want to cry, but her eyes felt dry and bloodshot, as if they could produce sand sooner than tears. The storm outside the tent grew in intensity until it matched the storm that raged inside her heart. Dante wanted her placed in a nunnery. Guy wanted her for nothing more than her dowry. She was a burden to Dante and a possession to Guy, her worth calculated in gold and land.

Guy's presence at her side was but another part of her torture, having him so close, knowing he was almost always nearby. It hurt just to look at him. He would marry her because she would bring him Halford. He had been foolish enough to tell Dante as much. That frightened her most. If she married Guy, someone she loved would die as a result.

The silence between the two men continued, and the summer storm faded to the steady patter of a gentle rain. The pain in her body warred with the pain in her soul, and at last she fell into an exhausted slumber. The next time she awoke, muted rays of morning sunlight streamed through the tent walls and Guy was gone. She was alone with her brother.

Dante sat on a stool pulled up next to the bed, his head

bowed with his fingers laced through his hair. His eyes were closed, and the ravaged look on his face spoke of little sleep.

She tried to speak, but made a small croaking sound instead. Dante lifted his head and slowly opened his eyes. "Do you need the bucket again?"

She considered the somewhat settled state of her stomach and shook her head. "Water."

After the long drink her voice did not sound so harsh. Weak, but understandable. "Why, Dante?"

A look of pain and regret flashed in his eyes. "I would never hurt you on purpose, cara. The dagger was meant for Montague."

"I know that," she assured him. "What I want to know is, why did you challenge him? Why do you hate him so?" She lowered her head and stared at her clasped hands. "What makes you hate him so much that you would lie to me? Your words alone convinced me to leave Montague. Why would you say such horrible things, knowing how much they hurt me?"

"You expected me to leave you there? He thinks you poisoned him, Claudia. The lies I told you would be truth, if you had stayed."

"You are wrong," she whispered. "Guy would have believed in my innocence if I had remained at Montague. Running away only confirmed my guilt in his mind. He will never trust me again."

"His lack of trust does not matter, and he is not worthy of yours. I intend to take you away from here. You will never have to see him again."

"We are his prisoners," she reminded him. "At Montague, his brothers were convinced that he would marry me just to gain Halford and my dowry, but I did not believe them. Now I do. Halford means more to him than you know. He will never let me go."

Dante squeezed her hand. "While I live, Montague will not have you."

The words struck terror in her heart. She would be married to a man who cared nothing for her, and her brother would be dead. She could see that future as clearly as she could see the determination in Dante's eyes, the knowledge that he would die for her. His death would change nothing. "Guy will kill you if he must. He is possessive, Dante. More possessive than any man I have known. There is a stubborn streak in Guy that makes him close his eyes to the consequences of that stubbornness. Once he makes up his mind, there is no changing it. His belief that I betrayed him only makes him more determined to marry me. There is no better vengeance. His control of me will be absolute."

"You think I should leave you to that fate? To know you will spend your life paying for a crime you did not commit?" Dante shook his head. "What kind of monster do you think I am?"

"You misunderstand my meaning, Dante. 'Tis doubtful Guy will beat me, or see me suffer physical harm. He is not a violent man."

"He is a man," Dante bit out. "You will suffer at his hands."

He was right. Guy would make her suffer. Claudia forced herself to look away from Dante before he could read her thoughts. She needed time to sort them out. "I am very tired. Do you mind if I close my eyes and rest for awhile?"

Guy turned away from his tent and walked blindly toward Kenric's. He parted the flap and stepped inside. Kenric and Fitz Alan sat on camp stools, with a chest between them that served as a makeshift table. Loaves of fresh bread from the abbey and a pitcher of thin ale sat atop the chest. Whatever they saw on Guy's face made both men set their morning meal aside. Kenric reached beneath his cot for another wooden goblet and a flagon of wine. He poured a healthy measure for Guy, then spoke in a hushed tone as he offered the drink. "She is dead?"

Guy managed to shake his head. He tilted the goblet and let the numbing liquid flow into him in one long drink. The last swallow was barely past his mouth when he extended the goblet toward Kenric. "More."

Kenric gave him a considering look. "I think not. You spent the past two days in your tent, but I doubt you ate or slept at all during that time. Wine is not the answer to what ails you. Another goblet would see you retching."

"As usual, you are right," Guy admitted. The wine felt sour in his stomach already. He set the goblet down, then took a seat on one of the cots and leaned forward with his hands propped on his knees. "I need a stronger cure than wine for what ails me. Claudia is awake, and 'tis certain she will recover."

"That is indeed news to celebrate," Fitz Alan offered, "but judging by your expression, I suspect a celebration is not what you had in mind."

"I left her for no more than half an hour," Guy said, "just long enough to give orders to the morning patrol. When I returned to my tent I overheard her talking with Dante, asking why he lied to her at Montague. Whatever that bastard told her was enough to make her flee with him."

"You do not know?"

Guy's head shot up and his eyes narrowed on Fitz Alan. "You do?"

"Aye," Fitz Alan answered. "Dante told her that you awoke soon after the feast and knew of her imprisonment, that she would hang by your orders the next morn."

Guy's hands became fists and he pictured them doing serious damage to Dante. "Why didn't you tell me this the day you brought her back?"

"This is the first time I could speak with you outside her brother's presence." Fitz Alan tore apart a loaf of the crusty bread and its rich aroma filled the tent. He tossed half to Guy. "And this is the first time you asked. On the ride to the abbey, Lady Claudia told me that Dante's sudden appearance in the dungeons and the tale he told her both came as a great shock. Locked in the bowels of the castle, 'tis not hard to imagine how true Dante's words rang in her ears. He is her brother. She had no reason not to believe him, although she claims to have had doubts about his story from the start. According to the lady, 'twas fear for her brother's safety as much as her own that made her flee."

"And the necklace?" Guy asked, almost afraid of the answer. "Was it left as a trap of some sort?"

"How could it be? Dante hid her well. Without the marker, we never would have found her. One does not set a trap, then leave a lone knight to guard the bait. It appears that Lady Claudia left the marker just as she claimed, with the hope that we would find her. She thought Dante rode off to attend to the king's business, that she risked only her life and the knight's by leading us to her. She had no idea that Dante came here to challenge you."

"I see." Guy saw a great many things, all with more clarity than he appreciated. He pictured Claudia in his dungeons, imagined her desperate fear and uncertainty. Dante only confirmed her worst fears. How incredibly arrogant he was to think she could survive such a test of loyalty. She had not left him until she heard that he had condemned her, damning words that came to her from the only other person in the world she trusted. Dante had lied to her, and now she thought he had lied to her as well, that he would marry her for no other reasons than to gain control of Halford and of her. Little wonder she thought him heartless. Dante was right. He did not deserve her trust, did not deserve anything she would give him. Somehow he had to undo the damage. What if it was too late?

He stood up abruptly and strode from the tent without a word to his brothers. Outside he stopped just long enough to give orders to two soldiers, then they fell into step behind him. The sound of Dante's voice as he neared his own blue-and-white-striped tent fired his anger to the boiling point.

"I cannot deny the possibility, Dante."
"When will you know for certain?"
Claudia hesitated. She still felt groggy from the effects of

the draught Dante had given her, but the direction of his latest round of questions made her instantly alert. "Why?"

"I am understandably curious. If you carry a child, then a journey to Wales is out of the question. We will find a place more civilized until you deliver the child."

She breathed a sigh of relief. For an awful moment she had suspected more devious reasons for his curiosity. There were several poisons that could loosen a child from its mother's womb, and Dante would know of them all. The thought that she might carry Guy's child filled her with awe and fear in equal measure. She had no idea what would become of her own life, much less any child she might bring into it.

"It still seems a bad jest," Dante went on. "If I had any idea that a Montague would defile my sister, I would have put you in a convent years ago."

"He did not defile me." She would never think of the most wondrous experiences in her life as being defiled. The most intimate aspects of her relationship with Guy had nothing to do with Halford or her dowry. He had truly cared for her, perhaps he even loved her a little. "There was no sin in anything that took place between us. We are betrothed."

"You *were* betrothed. I will not allow—"

"I do not think you are in a position to allow or disallow anything," Guy announced. He stepped through the flap of the tent and his expression made her wonder how much he heard of their conversation. He looked furious. "There are two guards who will escort you to a place where you may break your fast, Dante. I will send them word when you may return to your sister." He leaned his head toward the tent's opening. "Leave us."

Dante scowled. "I will not—"

"Please," Claudia whispered. "I will be fine."

"Are you hungry?" Dante asked.

"Nay, just a little thirsty."

Guy reached for an ewer of water. "See to your meal, Dante. I will see to Claudia's needs."

With one last scowl directed at Guy, Dante left them.

Guy turned his attention to pouring a goblet of water, and Claudia took the opportunity to study him. He appeared as disheveled as Dante, his clothes so wrinkled that she wondered if he had slept in them. The dark shadows around his eyes bespoke little or no sleep for days. When he finally turned toward her, his gaze held no trace of his anger with Dante. After seeing nothing but scowls or frowns since her return, the blatant longing in his expression startled her so much that she stared openly at his face.

He cleared his throat. "You look—much better."

She wondered how awful she looked before if he thought this was better. Then she recalled how often he had watched her retch. So much for vanity. "You look tired, my lord."

"Aye, well, I am not that tired."

Why did he seem so ill at ease? If she didn't know better, she would suspect he was nervous about something. He glanced down at the goblet and surprise flickered in his eyes, as if he had forgotten what was in his hand. "Would you like a drink of water?"

Had she not already requested as much? When she nodded, he took a seat next to the cot and supported her shoulders while she drank, careful not to jar her injured side. His gentleness surprised her. He held her as if he feared she would break.

He set the goblet aside when she finished, but did not release his hold on her. Instead he lifted her hand and pressed a kiss against her palm, then turned his head to trap her hand against his cheek.

"I failed to protect you, Claudia. You have my promise that I will not be so careless in the future." He eased her against the pillows and sat back, then carefully turned her hand to trace the delicate lace of blue veins on the inside of her wrist. "I failed to trust you as well."

The words reminded her of others he had spoken, his promise to Dante that he would not give her another opportunity to poison him. His touch also reminded her of other times. It took a considerable effort to push those thoughts aside. "Why should you trust or protect me, Baron? You think I poisoned you."

"Nay, Claudia." He pressed another kiss on her wrist, then cradled her hand between his. "I know you would never do anything to harm me, love."

"I heard you tell Dante otherwise."

"What I said was meant to prod Dante into telling me the truth. I never thought you poisoned me. Not even for a minute. Ask my brothers. They thought me crazed to believe in your innocence when you seemed the only one who could be guilty."

"They were quick enough to find me guilty. If you had died, your brothers would have hung me." A shudder passed through her as she recalled the night in Montague's dungeons, the look on Kenric's face when he ordered her there. "I do not think I would trust anything they told me."

"My brothers do not know you so well, and yours made certain I could not defend you. Kenric and Fitz Alan realize their mistake. They will not act against you ever again. Once we are wed—"

She pulled her hand away. "Why are you doing this, Baron? Is this another of your odd punishments, to force a marriage between us so you may watch me suffer each day?"

He winced as if she had slapped him. "I will do everything within my power to make you happy in our marriage, Claudia."

"Dante will find a way to kill you if we marry. Do you think that will make me happy?"

"I will deal with your brother."

"Aye," she whispered, "I heard that as well."

Guy opened his mouth to reply, then closed it again. He found the goblet he had set aside, then stood up and returned the cup to its place on the chest. His movements looked stiff and precise, and he stared down at the goblet as if it held some great interest. He seemed to speak more to himself than to her.

"Until today, I did not know of the lies that convinced you to leave Montague. In my mind, you knew from Dante that I would recover, that your safety would be my first concern when I awoke. Yet I also knew that you had waited five years for Dante's return. By all appearances, it seemed you chose your brother over me." He raked a hand through his hair and his hand came to rest along the back of his neck. "That is the reason for much of what you heard. Jealousy, and anger over a betrayal that never took place. Your brother's lies are as noxious as his poisons."

He glanced at her, and the mixture of hope and pain in his eyes cut her to the quick. She lowered her lashes to escape his penetrating gaze, but she could not escape his words.

"You have but to ask and there is nothing I will deny you, nothing I will do against your wishes. Except in matters that concern your brother. He thinks you will suffer at my hands, but he is the one who would make you suffer. Do not ask me to stand aside so he may hurt you more than he has already."

He would marry her to protect her from Dante? She didn't know what to believe. The silence weighed heavily between them. At last Guy moved closer to the tent opening.

"I can see that you are tired. I will let you rest now."

"Guy." She could barely speak around the constriction in her throat, but the whispered word made him stop in midstride. "I would hear from your own lips that Halford is not the reason you wish to marry me."

"Did you forget so soon, love?" He spoke the words so tenderly that they sounded like a caress. "I can take Halford any time I please, and our marriage will make no difference in the outcome."

Her eyes widened. In the turmoil of everything that had happened the past few days, she had managed to forget that Guy planned to take Halford by siege, no matter who owned it. No one could sell him a thing he already possessed. Halford had nothing to do with the reasons he would marry her, yet he did not set the notion of marriage aside even when he thought she had betrayed him. If her suspicions were right, her flight from Montague had wounded him far deeper than she ever imagined. And that was a pain she knew only too well. "I am sorry, Guy. For everything."

He grasped the tent flap and made to leave. At the last moment, he turned and spoke to her in a low, tortured voice. "I do not want your apologies, Claudia. I want your forgiveness."

18

For the next two days, Claudia fell asleep whenever Guy entered his tent, or else he found her asleep already. It frustrated him to no end. That was selfishness on his part, he knew. She needed a great deal of rest to recover from her wounds. Dante had injured her physically, but Guy had broken her heart. Each time he looked into Claudia's eyes, he saw a sadness so deep that it hurt.

It was the wounds he could not see that worried him most. Whenever he did manage to exchange a few words with her, she said nothing more of her brother's treachery. Despite her silence, he sensed her frustration with Dante and interrupted more than one quiet conversation between the two. No matter how he prompted, she would not share what she and Dante discussed, using sleep to evade his questions. Those unspoken refusals to confide in him bothered him most. Had Dante managed to steal her away from him after all?

"Your mood turns fouler by the day," Kenric remarked. He had shared his tent with Guy the past few nights, and they were there now to break their fast for the day. "Yet Lady Claudia grows stronger each day. She will be recovered enough by the end of the week to journey up to the abbey for a marriage, if that is your wish."

"Aye, 'tis my wish. I spoke with Abbot Gregory two days ago, and he has agreed to marry us," Guy said. "Claudia still seems reluctant to speak of the matter. I believe Dante is doing his best to convince her that we should not wed."

"You may be sure of that," Kenric said. "He makes his hatred of us known to all. Yet you do not need his permission, nor Lady Claudia's, for that matter. The abbot will agree to perform the ceremony without anyone's consent when he learns you consummated your union with the lady. While you hold her, you have the right to wed her. If you let Dante leave here with Claudia, you have no rights whatsoever. Her future will be his to decide. If you have a mind to wed the lady, do so now while you hold her brother prisoner."

" 'Tis not that simple," Guy said. "Dante is single-minded when it comes to revenge. He will not listen to any offers I make about Italy, even though I know it is his fondest desire to seek his vengeance there. Every offer I make him meets with silence or insults. He makes it clear that he does not intend to let our marriage stand unchallenged. I would have to kill him to be certain of my own life."

"Then do so."

Guy rolled his eyes. "You oversimplify the situation. Do you honestly think that Claudia would ever forgive me if I murdered her brother to accomplish our marriage?"

"Aye." Kenric grinned. "If you will recall, my own wife proved very forgiving after I killed her brother."

"Stepbrother," Guy corrected, "and Gordon MacLeith was the lowest slime ever to walk the earth. He was no blood relation to Tess, and certainly not the last of her immediate family. Dante is a different matter entirely."

"Then challenge him to another contest," Kenric suggested. "I watched him fight and can show you his weaknesses. You will win the match, and he will be forced to give his blessings to the marriage."

Guy shook his head. "Dante cannot be trusted to keep his word. He is a man who survives on lies."

"You cannot kill him, you cannot trust him, and you are likely to forfeit your own life if you marry his sister," Kenric summarized. "There is only one way you can defeat such an enemy."

"Aye," Guy agreed, "I know what I must do. A wise man once said you must hold close to your friends, and hold your enemies even dearer."

Kenric looked satisfied. "Good. Do you intend to hold him in your own dungeons, or would you rather he be a guest in mine, where he is less likely to smuggle messages to his sister?"

"You miss the meaning of the proverb, brother. I must gain the trust of a man who trusts no one, and make him believe he can capitalize on my greatest weakness. That will not happen if I lock him in my dungeons." A grim smile twisted Guy's lips. "Nay, I must be far more devious in my methods to outwit a Chiavari. I must become his best friend."

Guy would rather become the best friend of a snake. Not that he saw much difference between the two, other than the fact that Dante was much more dangerous than any snake. And not that he had any real intention of becoming the man's friend. If his plan worked as he hoped, it wouldn't take Dante long to see through his ruse. That improved his mood considerably.

He left Kenric's tent and turned toward his own with long, determined strides. The sun shone clear and bright this morning with the promise of another insufferably hot day. Guy had almost reached his destination when his nemesis and soon-to-be best friend emerged from the tent.

Dante glanced over his shoulder, then walked toward Guy, his face blank and expressionless as ever. Guy forced a smile. "Good morn, Dante. How fares your sister today?"

"She continues to improve. You cannot see her."

Guy's smile disappeared. "I intend to do just that."

"She is taking a bath."

"And you left her alone?" Guy started toward his tent. "She is so weak she will drown. What possessed you to leave her alone?"

Dante grabbed Guy's arm and brought him to a halt. " 'Tis but a sponge bath, Montague. She asked for privacy and will not appreciate your ogling while she bathes."

Guy opened his mouth to inform Dante that Claudia

happened to like the way he ogled her, then thought better of the idea. He was no longer so certain of her appreciation. Beside which, discussing his lust for Claudia was hardly the quickest path toward a friendship with her brother. "Aye, well, I suppose not." He glanced toward the woods at their right. " 'Tis another day fit for little but seeking shade. Will you walk with me to the river? There is a spring along the banks where the water flows as cold as ice."

Dante's hand went to his belt, to the empty sheath where his dagger should be. "I am not thirsty."

"Have you something better to do?"

"Aye, I must speak with my squire."

"Excellent," Guy said. "I would very much like to meet this squire who bears such a striking resemblance to a knight I faced in tournament three years ago. Perhaps they are related."

Dante turned and started toward the woods. "I am thirsty after all. Are you coming, Baron?"

"Aye." Guy's mouth curved into a genuine smile, but he said nothing more until they reached the river. The monks from Kelso Abbey had placed a hollowed trough into the bank where the spring flowed. Another log held the end of the trough off the ground a few feet from the river's edge, and the result was a small waterfall of clean spring water. Guy followed the well-worn path down the embankment, then cupped his hands beneath the trough and drank his fill. He glanced up to where Dante still stood at the top of the embankment, his gaze watchful as he scanned the woods and clearing around them.

"Not thirsty after all?" Guy asked.

"What is your game, Montague?"

"Game?" Guy repeated innocently. It occurred to him that a man might drown without notice in this secluded spot, or succumb to foul play made to look a drowning. Dante looked wary enough to be thinking the same. "Surely you do not think I would try to drown you, Dante. That would seem a little obvious, don't you think, when half the camp and your squire saw us walk together this way?" Guy cupped his hand for another drink of water, then wiped his mouth on his sleeve. "Murder is your business, not mine. You have my word that I intend you no harm."

"You could not drown me if you tried," Dante said, as he made his way down the path. "I am an excellent swimmer, and that sword you wear would weigh you down like a stone once I dragged you into deep water."

Guy resisted the urge to glance at the river where the water flowed swift and deep past the spring's embankment. When he looked up again, Dante was smiling. "Have no fear, Montague. I have much to lose by your murder, and as you say, a drowning today would be too obvious."

Guy leaned over for another drink, but not before he made sure that Dante saw his scowl. "I would have you cured of this need to murder me on any day."

At that, Dante laughed out loud. Guy glanced up in surprise. He decided that a smile made Dante look almost human. Not quite, but a fairly good imitation. "You seem in an unusually good mood today."

"Aye, that I am, Baron. Claudia will be better in a few days, which means you and I will soon part company. 'Tis entertaining to watch you consider every way you might do away with me, or at the very least, remove me from your life on some permanent basis. It must frustrate you to no end to know that you can act on none of them. You cannot kill me, nor marry my sister without dire consequences." He held up his hands and looked around the clearing. "Is this another of your plans, Baron? If all else fails, try to sway my mind with jovial camaraderie?" He shook his head. "You English are such a simple lot."

Guy dried his hands on his tunic, then folded his arms across his chest. "And you are a fool."

Dante's smile faded a little, but he simply shrugged. "I think not, Baron."

"Aye, you are. Half of England would sell their eyeteeth to be in your position at this moment. You are such a bigoted fool that you will not open your eyes to see what is within your grasp."

"Would you care to explain yourself?"

Guy ignored the question. "What do you want most in this world? Why do you continue to act as the king's henchman when the deeds you carry out must haunt you each night?"

Dante remained silent. There wasn't a trace of any emotion on his face now, nothing but the cold stare of a man who cared little about what his future might hold.

Guy knew better than to be fooled by that disguise. "Aye, you would see your parents' murderer face justice, and take back what is rightfully yours. Is that not the way of it?"

Dante gave him a curt nod.

"In the meantime, you would sell yourself to a king who will keep you dangling for at least a dozen years before you can act on your vengeance, rather than see your sister marry a man who wants nothing more than to make her happy."

"You have a strange way of making her happy," Dante countered. "She cries herself to sleep each night, and refuses to speak at all whenever your name is mentioned."

"And who bears the greatest fault for her sorrow?"

Dante placed both hands on his chest. "You think *I* am to blame?"

"You think you are not?" Guy bit out. "It was your lies that destroyed Claudia's trust in me, your lies that made me believe she betrayed me. In time, I think she will forgive me, but I cannot be certain if she will ever again open her heart, to me or anyone else. She trusted us as she trusted no others, and we both betrayed her." He gave Dante a look of disgust. "By all appearances, you want nothing more than to destroy what is left of her heart."

"You are in love with her," Dante said, in an incredulous tone. He took a step backward, as if staggered by the revelation. "It isn't Halford you want, but Claudia."

Guy summoned up the best affronted tone he could manage. "Men in my position do not marry for love. I knew from the start that Halford was part of Claudia's dowry. 'Tis the only reason I decided to marry her."

"You are very good, Baron." Dante pointed his finger at Guy, as if giving him credit for the deception. "I never guessed. All this time I thought—"

"There was nothing for you to guess," Guy said in a clipped voice. "I will marry Claudia no matter what you do or say, yet you would see her suffer each day of her marriage, wondering if that will be the day you murder me. Did you know that the thought of my death was her greatest fear before you came to Montague, that I would die somehow and she would be alone again?"

"I thought you did not care how she felt about anything."

"I would not have her unhappy."

"Is that so?" There was a knowing gleam in Dante's eyes. "You claimed to have no care if she came to you an unwilling bride. Pray tell, how do you intend to make an unwilling bride happy?"

"You twist my words," Guy said moodily. " 'Tis obvious you taught the talent to your sister as well."

"I twist nothing, Baron. Halford cannot be worth so much that you would court certain death to possess it. Your own words make plain the reasons you insist on a marriage. You were wise to try to hide your feelings." He spread his hands in an expansive gesture. "This information makes my plans much less complicated."

"Do you honestly believe I will allow her to leave with you? The life you lead makes her an easy target for any of your enemies."

"I would protect her," Dante insisted.

"Truly? Is that the reason you are so determined to put her in a convent? Because you are so certain you will live a long and healthy life as a hired assassin?" Guy made a sound of disgust. "Where do you think her fear stems from? You are all that remains of her family, and I would not lay favorable odds that you will live beyond a handful of years in Edward's hire. The offer I made you does not come from any sense of generosity on my part, but from a need to put a few of Claudia's fears to rest. I offered you the chance to let your sister live her life in peace. At the same time, you could greatly increase the likelihood that you will live to see a few gray hairs. The only way I can hope to regain Claudia's trust is to make certain she no longer has any need to worry about you."

Dante's brows drew together and a wary light came to his eyes. "What are you talking about?"

"I am talking about the fact that I have more power than you can possibly imagine." Guy knew from experience that the bargain was all but made. He closed in for the kill. "If you want this Lorenzo brought to justice, then I have more influence in Italian matters than the kings of England and Scotland combined. There are Italian merchants, noblemen, clergy, and officials by the score who owe me favors. And I can buy the favors of as many more. I all but hit you over the head with the fact that I am willing to negotiate for anything you wish in this world if you will but strike me a fair bargain in return. Instead you sneer and spew insults, and inform me that you would rather make your own life and Claudia's a living misery."

Guy clenched his hands beneath his arms. He would much rather use his fists to beat sense into Dante than mere words. "Aye, Dante. You are the greatest fool I have ever known. Only a fool as great as you would fail to realize that I will use every means within my power to make certain your plan to ruin Claudia's life does not come to pass. Your own life I could care less about, but I will not see you drag her down with you on this path to hell that you chose for yourself. Be glad that you have little care whether you live or die. If you do not come to your senses and accept my offer, any sane man would tremble at what I have in store for you."

Guy turned on his heel and stalked away, aware that Dante stared after him in bemused silence. He didn't start to smile until he turned onto the path that took him beyond Dante's sight.

Upon his return to camp, Guy headed straight for his tent. He didn't bother to announce his arrival, but simply pushed aside the flap and strode inside. Claudia whirled around to face him, dressed in a russet-colored gown with a small white sling around her left arm to keep her injured shoulder immobile. He was so surprised to see her out of bed that he stopped in his tracks.

"You brought my clothes," she said, as her hand skimmed over the skirt of her gown. She still looked a little pale, but much healthier than when he last saw her. The night before she could barely keep her eyes open and dozed off the moment he tried to discuss their marriage. Today she gave him a tentative smile. "I thought I would be forced to borrow a tunic and breeches from one of your squires or a robe from one of the monks in yon abbey. What made you think to bring my clothes here?"

"I knew I would find you here, or wherever Dante thought to hide you." He dismissed the subject with a shrug. There were far more important matters on his mind than her wardrobe. "Why have you avoided me these past two days?"

Her gaze moved from one side of the large tent to the other. "I have been right here the entire time. How could I avoid you?"

"By falling asleep, or pretending to sleep, each time I come near you." His hand swept out to indicate her appearance. "Last night you were too exhausted even to sit up in bed and talk to me, yet today you seem fit enough to bathe and dress yourself. That seems an unusual improvement over so few hours."

"Well, as to that . . ." She turned around and treated him to a view of her back. Her bare back. The gown she wore gaped open to the waist and she wore no chemise beneath it. His body reacted immediately to the sight of so much creamy flesh. "I could not manage the laces. Would you mind helping me?"

The sight alone drew him forward, the request for help

no more than an added incentive. His hands went to the laces that trailed from the gown's waist, but he did not tighten them. "First tell me why you will not talk to me."

"I am talking to you now," she said, in an overly bright tone.

He pushed her braid aside, then trailed his fingers down the length of her spine, pleased to feel her shiver. "You know what I mean."

"And you surely know how ill the poison made me." Her voice sounded unsteady, and he continued to brush his fingertips over her velvety skin in light, erotic strokes. "I was very tired from the ordeal."

Her soft sigh made him smile. For the past few days he had started to wonder if her brother had poisoned more than her body, if Dante's words had somehow hardened her heart against him. The realization that his touch still had the same effect on her eased his worries considerably. He leaned down and pressed a kiss along the slender column of her neck. "I am glad to find you so recovered, for we have much to discuss."

"I know." She sounded defeated. He wrapped his arms around her waist and held her close, careful of her injured shoulder. She leaned her head against his shoulder and released another sigh, but there was nothing sensual about the sound. It was the sound of sadness.

His cheek came to rest against her hair. "Everything will work itself out, Claudia. I will not let Dante take you away from me."

She stiffened in his arms and tried to step away, but he held her fast. "I cannot stay with you, Guy. What you want was never meant to be. I see that now."

Guy drew a deep, shuddering breath. "Is there no hope that you will forgive me?"

She spoke in such a hushed voice that he had to lean closer to hear her. "I forgave you two days ago."

"Sweet saints, I worried that it would take you much longer." He felt as if the weight of the world had been lifted from his shoulders, and closed his eyes for a silent prayer of thanks. He brushed his fingers over the soft velvet of her cheek, and knew she felt none of the relief that coursed through him. "What is it, love? Why didn't you tell me sooner?"

She held his hand to her cheek, and tilted her head until it rested in his palm. "Because nothing will change the fact that I cannot marry you."

"Aye, you can and you will." He wanted nothing more than to hold her tight against him. He settled for a small but passionate kiss behind her ear.

Her grip on his hand tightened. "Please, Guy. If you have any care for me, do not force a marriage between us. I—I could not live with myself if you or my brother died because of me. If we marry, one of you is sure to die. Dante vowed as much."

"I intend to change his mind on that score."

"You do not know him," she said, a frantic edge to her voice. "I do not know him anymore. He will not listen to anything I try to tell him. You are a Montague. That alone is reason enough to make him hate you. His promise to the king protects you now, but he will only goad you into another challenge. Failing that, he will make certain some illness or accident befalls you in such a way that all may suspect him, but none can prove him responsible for the deed." She gave him a knowing look over one shoulder. "Your brothers will know who to blame, and soon enough we will all find ourselves dead."

He wanted to shake her for such morbid thoughts, and knew well enough who put them there. He should have pushed Dante into the river when he had his chance. "My brothers will never make the same mistake they made at Montague," he assured her. "They know now that you would give your life to spare mine. Already they have pledged any support I need to make you my wife. As for Dante, I will see that he does not interfere with our marriage." The way she stiffened in his arms made him scowl. "Much as he might tempt me otherwise, your brother will not die at my hands. If he does not show sense soon and agree to our marriage, I will make his life as miserable as he would make yours."

That did nothing to relax her tensed body. "What will you do to him?"

He pictured Dante chained to the wall of his dungeon, then on one of his ships, also in chains, with the ends of the earth as its destination. For Claudia's sake, he hoped Dante chose Italy, where he could slake his need for vengeance on Lorenzo. "Several ideas come to mind, but I have not yet decided. Until I can work out the details, he will remain my prisoner."

"You expect me to agree with this plan?"

" 'Tis only a plan that Dante will enact if he refuses my latest offer," he told her. "Your brother holds the key to his own freedom."

"And when he refuses your offer?"

"I expect you will disagree with anything I decide upon until you recall that Dante would prefer that you be imprisoned in a convent for the rest of your life, that he would do his best to make you a widow and very possibly carry out his blind vindictiveness on any child I might give you." His fingers caught a stray wisp of hair near her temple, and he rubbed the silky lock between his fingers. He took a deep breath to savor the scent of roses. "Given time, I believe your anger over my decision will fade to pity for your brother. You will grieve for him, but you will know that he left me no other choice."

"I have tried everything I know to make him realize you will not be swayed from your decision, yet he is as stubborn as you, my lord."

"Aye, that he is," Guy admitted. "Over the past five days I have tried every reasonable tactic and a few truly desperate ones to settle this matter in some manner that would allow you to see him on occasion. So far, Dante refuses to consider a truce, and he seems determined to make an enemy of me. If he does not change his mind on that score, he will pay the price."

"Am I to have no choice in this matter?" she asked. "Just as Dante would give me no control over my future, now you will decide my fate?"

His harsh expression dissolved. He turned her in his arms to look into her eyes. "Do you really want the choice of which man's life to ruin? Do you want to bear the burden of deciding your brother's fate, or would you rather decide mine? You are my heart, Claudia. I might live without you, but I would never be whole."

A sudden gust of wind ruffled the walls of the tent, as if the earth itself sighed to see her look so sad. Tears shimmered in her eyes as she lifted her hand to stroke his cheek. "How can such beautiful words sound so cruel?"

"The truth is seldom kind, my love." He cupped her face in his hands and brushed away her tears with his thumbs. "I know you love your brother, flawed as he is, and I think you love me as well. In my mind it would be crueler to make you decide between us than to make the decision for you."

He sensed her lingering indecision, and knew he was deliberately tearing her heart in two. He had already laid his own heart bare to her. If he was wrong about her love, he had just handed her the weapons to destroy him. There was no other way. The merchant in him had tried to bargain with the devil. The warrior had brought an army to show the force behind his words. If she were not injured, he would use all the sensual skills of a lover to seduce her into his arms. Yet he wanted to possess not only her body, but her very soul. He wanted her to know that he would use every means known to win those treasures. Most of all, he wanted her trust.

"If I thought Dante might have any reasonable amount of concern for your safety and welfare, I would not do this," he went on. "Yet I know what your life would be like in his care, the dangers he would expose you to through his enemies. You do not deserve to pay for the mistakes he made in his life, nor do I. You have my promise that I will be as lenient with Dante as possible under the circumstances, but I must be certain that he will never again be in a position to interfere with our lives."

She lowered her lashes, and her thoughts were concealed from him. He held his breath and waited. If she insisted on the matter, he would put the choice in her hands. He could not force her to stay with him. Not if he wanted her love. And he wanted that very badly. He had an awful feeling she would choose that miserable cur of a brother out of some misguided sense of loyalty. If Dante refused his latest bait, how could he possibly let her go?

"What about the king? What will Edward do when he learns you hold Dante prisoner?"

He simply stared at her, trying to absorb the fact that she would let him decide her fate. She trusted him. She did love him, and nothing her brother said or did had changed that fact. He wanted to shout his relief, to crush her to his chest and hold her there always, to—

"The king?" she prompted.

"Oh. Aye, well . . ." He cleared his throat and tried to concentrate on her question. He would much rather hear that she loved him. "Your brother thinks his connection to the king will protect him, but he does not comprehend my own. Edward will object to my plans for Dante, but in the same breath he will list a reason or two why I am due a favor. Thus Edward will let me know which debts he considers paid, and in exchange he will turn a blind eye to the matter."

"The king owes you money? I thought him a wealthy man."

"The king is very wealthy," he agreed, "but most wealthy men owe debts of some sort or another, and even kings have their price."

"You bought a *king*?"

"You miss my meaning," he said, chuckling at the idea. "I did not give the king a sack of gold and say, 'You now owe me five hundred florins, your majesty.' A king's debts are incurred with much more subtlety. In the course of my trade, I travel to the courts of many kings and noblemen, as do the men who represent me. On occasion I am privy to information of interest to Edward that he would not learn from another; a king with designs on Edward's holdings in Normandy, a nobleman with designs on his daughter, a cousin with designs on his throne. It is my duty to inform my sovereign and liege lord of any threat, and a wise lord does not let a vassal's duty go unrewarded. There are also debts incurred of a more monetary nature, but a king needs the eyes and ears of a faithful subject far more often than he needs gold."

"No wonder you believe anyone can be bought."

She did not sound the least awed by the power he held. That was another reason he loved her. He had legions of men in his hire who would follow his orders without question, people who would agree with anything he said simply to gain his favor, or cower before him to appease his anger. Claudia would always stand proudly, even defiantly, at his side. His equal in all things. He looked into the gemlike brilliance of her eyes, and knew that he had found his match.

"You are the only one in this world who is priceless to me."

"You made some mention of your heart," she said. The beginnings of a shy smile touched her lips. " 'Tis a fine treasure you give me. Do you think my own heart will be fair compensation?"

"Aye," he murmured, as he lowered his head. He captured her lips for a long, satisfying kiss. " 'Tis more than a fair trade."

"I love you, Guy."

It seemed he had waited a lifetime to hear those words, and held very still as they washed over him like a gentle balm. His throat constricted, and he could not return the words of love that welled up inside him. She seemed to sense his distress, and she twined her good arm around his neck, then she pulled him closer to offer another taste of her sweetness. He accepted the offer without hesitation, as a starved man would enter a feast. His hands moved of their own accord, encircling her waist, then drifting lower to explore the enticing shape of her hips. Somehow he managed to resist the urge to enfold her in his arms, to feel her soft body pressed against the hard contours of his own. The sling around her left arm reminded him that he would hurt her if he gave in to those urges. The sensual things she did to his mouth made it hard to hold onto that thought. She ravished him with her kisses, and he let her, knowing that her frantic urgency had as much to do with desire as the need to reassure herself that he wasn't going anywhere, that he would be with her always. He returned her kisses with the same urgency.

His resolve weakened, and he made himself picture what her shoulder had looked like just a few short days ago, the image that would be branded forever into his memory just as surely as she would forever wear the brand of Dante's knife. After all the upheaval in her life of late, she needed gentle comforting, to be held for no reason but quiet companionship. She felt very companionable in his arms, all warm, womanly curves. He delighted in the seductive caresses along his neck, the provocative way she rubbed her hand across his chest, then he panicked when her hand charted a steady course downward. She was deliberately trying to seduce him.

She was about to succeed.

He grabbed her hand and dragged it back to his chest. "Nay, love. Not this time."

"I need you." Her voice was a husky whisper, the measured kisses along his neck blatantly carnal, yet somehow sweet and innocent at the same time. They drove him mad. "Make love to me, Guy. Please. Make me forget everything but what I feel when I am in your arms."

Guy heard himself groan. "You would feel a great deal of pain as well, vixen. I will do nothing that will hurt you."

"Then kiss me," she said, as she worked her way toward his mouth. "Just one more kiss. Or two."

Or three, as it turned out. Guy tried to recall what it was like to have a will of his own, how he could resist the charms of any other woman, only to succumb so easily to the one in his arms. Already his mind raced to think of ways he could make love to her without touching her shoulder or putting any pressure on her wound. He was perverse even to consider the notion. Her kisses turned his blood to liquid fire. A voice from the opening of the tent turned it to ice.

"Your mauling does my sister's injury no good, Montague."

Claudia gasped and whirled to face her brother. She made a small, squeaking sound, then grasped the forgotten laces of her gown and dangled them toward Guy. " 'Tis not what it seems, Dante. I could not lace my gown alone, and asked Guy for his help. Then, well, one thing led to another, and I asked him to kiss me."

Guy ignored the frantic motions she made behind her back toward the laces. Instead he draped his arms around her waist and clasped his hands together in front of her, his hold on her casually possessive. "You have no need to explain anything we do to anyone, Claudia."

The two men stared across the tent at each other, the air charged with a silent challenge. At last Dante unclenched his hands and clasped them behind his back. "He is right, Claudia. What the two of you do together is no longer my business."

"What did you say?" Claudia sounded incredulous.

Even Guy doubted what he heard. Had he happened upon Dante's price at last?

"I thought to speak with my sister first," Dante went on, as if he hadn't heard her, "but as you are both here I may as well save myself the distasteful task of saying this twice." His gaze returned to Guy. "You were right to call me a fool. As you said, all that I wish is within my grasp. I am ready to accept your offer."

"What are your terms?" Guy asked, without hesitation.

"Your word that I can leave here," Dante said, "that you will interfere in my life no more than you want my interference in your own."

Guy eyed him warily. "And the rest?"

"I have no other demands at the moment. 'Tis enough to know that you are in my debt." A cynical smile touched Dante's lips. "Make no mistake, Montague. The day will come when I will collect that debt."

Guy knew exactly what that debt would entail. Yet helping Dante regain his birthright would also mean helping him leave England, hopefully for good. Guy thought it an excellent bargain. Claudia did not seem inclined to agree.

"You would sell me?" she asked Dante, her voice a bare whisper. "Is that all I am to you, goods to be bartered for favors?"

A look of pain flashed through Dante's eyes, then disappeared just as quickly. His voice turned brisk and efficient. "A long time ago I promised you a home and security, a place where you would always be safe. Consider that promise fulfilled, Claudia."

She turned to look up at Guy, her own pain reflected in her eyes, but he gave her a reassuring smile. He held everything he had ever wanted within his arms, within his power to possess. His gaze didn't waver from her as he sealed his bargain with Dante. "Agreed."

19 ❧

That afternoon, Guy and Dante mounted their horses for the ride to Kelso Abbey. There they would sign the marriage contracts and make arrangements for the ceremony that would take place the next day. Guy lifted Claudia's hand for a brief kiss. "You are certain you would rather remain here?"

Claudia nodded, still stung by the selfish way Dante had bartered her. She wanted no more of her brother's company. "My signature is not required on the contracts, and the journey sounds tiring. I would rather stay here and rest."

" 'Tis another day as hot as the last. You will be overcome by the heat if you remain in my tent all afternoon." Guy nodded toward Kenric and Fitz Alan, who stood a few paces behind her. "My brothers will take you to the river. There is a shallow bend about a quarter mile upstream where you can rest in the shade along the banks, or go a-wading if you wish. The water is cool and refreshing."

The thought of spending the afternoon with Guy's brothers was only slightly more appealing than spending the afternoon with her own. She didn't trust any of them. The promise of an escape from the unbearable heat swayed her decision. "Very well."

"I will meet you there in a few hours," he said, his concern for her quiet mood plain to see. He gave her hand a gentle squeeze as she stepped away from his horse, then he turned in the saddle and urged his horse forward.

Dante followed Guy without a word to Claudia. She decided that it would be a relief to see him leave tomorrow, for his presence only reminded her of the kind, considerate brother she once knew. This Dante was a stranger who cared only for what he could gain by bargaining her life away. He looked well pleased with himself when Guy released his knights, Oliver and Armand, and allowed them to pack for their journey. They intended to leave at dawn, before the ceremony took place. Claudia tried to convince herself that she was glad. She did not want her brother to cast his dark shadow over her wedding day.

Kenric gave orders to have their own mounts made ready as she watched Guy and Dante ride away. Fitz Alan led a palfrey forward a few moments later.

"Lady Claudia?" Kenric prompted. When she glanced at him, he nodded toward the palfrey. "I will help you mount, if you wish."

With her left arm in a sling, she had little choice. Kenric lifted her by the waist as if she weighed no more than a feather, and even helped rearrange her skirts when she swung her leg over the saddle to ride astride. Modesty be hanged. She had no wish to fall off the beast with her shoulder so far from healed.

Once they were all mounted, Kenric set a plodding pace, probably due to her injury as well. There was no pressing need to reach their destination, and Claudia tried to enjoy the cool shade of the woods they passed through. Fitz Alan tried to keep up a one-sided conversation about the unusually hot weather, then gave up when his remarks met with silence.

The trail forked, and Kenric took the path that led upriver. When they finally reached the bend, Claudia had to admit that the place looked inviting. A dark blue ribbon of water ran swift and choppy along the opposite shore, but closest to them the river flowed over a wide, shallow sandbar where the current gentled and sunlight sparkled on the clear waters. Kenric and Fitz Alan hobbled their horses while Claudia made her way to the river's edge.

A large tree had lost its tenuous hold on the eroded riverbank and tumbled onto the submerged sandbar, so long ago that its bark was washed away and the wood weathered to smooth silver. She kicked off her slippers and carefully gathered her skirts with one hand, then waded up to her ankles to find a seat on the log. The cool water felt delicious.

"This sun will turn your fair skin bright pink," Fitz Alan warned, as he took a seat on part of the log that remained on shore. He started to pull off his boots.

Claudia wriggled her toes into the sand and watched a school of minnows dart away. With all the reasons she had to dislike and distrust Guy's brothers, there was a sense of strength and protectiveness about them that set her at ease. She did not want to be at ease with them. "This pale English sun is no threat to my complexion."

Fitz Alan shrugged, then waded further into the river until the sheath that held his sword started to drag in the water. He unbuckled his sword belt and placed the weapon on top of the tree trunk, then waded to where the sandbar started to fall away into the dark blue depths of the river. Claudia glanced back at the riverbank where Kenric still stood, his shoulder propped against the trunk of another large tree that leaned toward the river. She wondered if he had any worry that his weight would make the tree topple into the water. His expression revealed nothing but boredom. Aye, this would be a very pleasant place but for his presence and Fitz Alan's.

She looked again at Fitz Alan. He was bent over with his hands in the water as if to wash them, but he looked stuck in the awkward position and did not move so much as a muscle. Curiosity finally loosened her tongue. "What are you doing?"

"Fishing," he whispered.

Kenric gave a snort of laughter. "Ian Duncan is the only man I know who can catch fish that way."

"What way?" Claudia asked.

"With his hands," Kenric answered. "Fitz Alan thinks his face irresistible, even to fish. See how he smiles down at them? He thinks to seduce a fat trout into his arms."

Claudia giggled. Even Fitz Alan's smile grew broader. "Abbot Gregory told me this river is filled with fat trout, and I have practiced this technique several times since Ian showed it to us."

Kenric made another sound that Claudia assumed had something to do with humor. "Have you ever caught anything?"

"Nay, but I—" Fitz Alan's eyes moved in erratic directions to follow the progress of something only he could see.

Claudia stood up and craned her neck toward Fitz Alan, careful to hold her skirts above water. "Is it a fish?"

Fitz Alan didn't answer. She glanced over her shoulder and saw that Kenric also looked interested in this development. A flurry of motion turned her attention back to Fitz Alan. His hands chased beneath the water to capture the unseen fish. There was a great splash as Fitz Alan's hands flew upward, then a shimmering arc of water as he threw the fish toward shore. Startled, Kenric started to back away, then stood rooted in place when the fish landed at his feet. His shoulders relaxed visibly, then he bent down to pick up Fitz Alan's trout. It was nothing but a long, flat river rock. He gave Fitz Alan a disgusted look and tossed the rock back into the water. Fitz Alan doubled over with laughter.

"Indulge your humor," Kenric drawled. " 'Tis the only thing you are like to catch, other than leeches between your toes."

"Leeches?" Claudia sat down abruptly and drew her feet out of the water. She inspected each toe thoroughly, her one-armed balance on the log precarious at best.

" 'Tis doubtful there are any leeches where you sit," Kenric assured her. "The creatures tend to—"

He fell silent, and then they all heard the unmistakable whirring sound of an arrow in flight, punctuated by a loud *twang* when it struck the tree just inches from Kenric's head. There was a loud splash from Fitz Alan's direction just as Kenric lunged forward. He grabbed Claudia by the waist and kept going, amazingly sure-footed considering his size and Claudia's added weight as he raced along the fallen log. She heard the sounds of more arrows just as they reached the end of the log, and Kenric leaped into the river, taking her with him.

A stab of pain shot through her shoulder and took her breath away, even as the water closed over her head. She broke the surface again, sputtering and shaken, but Kenric's steel grip around her waist guided her closer to the fallen log where Fitz Alan already waited.

Water lapped at Kenric and Fitz Alan's shoulders, but the submerged branches of the tree kept the trunk above the waterline even in this deeper part of river. Claudia pointed her toes downward as far as they could stretch to find the riverbed, and her hand grasped at a branch made slippery by algae. The current was much swifter here, and she found herself thankful that Kenric kept a firm grip around her waist. They ducked beneath the meager shelter of a large forked branch that protruded upward from the trunk. Kenric and Fitz Alan peered cautiously from their hiding place to search the riverbanks.

"There," Fitz Alan said, as a score of men emerged from the forest.

All the soldiers wore muted greens and browns to blend with the woods around them. Half carried deadly longbows, while the others held swords. Claudia clapped her hand to her cheek when she saw who led them. " 'Tis my uncle, Baron Lonsdale!"

Kenric and Fitz Alan exchanged a silent glance, then their gazes scanned the riverbanks all around them, searching for a means to escape. Their swords were useless against the longbows. They would be dead before they came within a sword's length of any Lonsdale soldier.

"If he had more men, there would be no reason to hide them," Kenric mused. "There must be more somewhere nearby with the horses, but I doubt it is a large force. I do not think he would risk bringing any more than a score or so of soldiers this close to our camp."

"Aye, but we rode too far upstream," Fitz Alan said.

"Even the watch will not hear our signal through these woods."

Kenric's gaze followed Fitz Alan's toward the river. His mouth became a grim line. "Do not consider it, Fitz Alan. Even if she can swim, she has skirts and a lame shoulder to contend with."

"We could cut the skirts away," Fitz Alan suggested.

Kenric shook his head. "We would be lucky to make it ourselves, and we are healthy. For this you will need your sword."

Fitz Alan uttered a curse as he looked toward the middle of the fallen log, where his weapon still lay. He began to work his way toward his sword, careful to keep his head below the log, where Lonsdale's soldiers could not see him.

"What was your plan if I could swim?" Claudia asked.

Kenric kept his attention focused on Fitz Alan, sounding distracted as he answered. "We could make our way to the deepest part of the river where the water runs swiftest, then dive beneath the surface and swim underwater as far as we could, hopefully around that next bend. The terrain that Lonsdale's soldiers would be forced to follow is rough and clogged with brush. We would have a good head start on them by the time we reached the path further downstream that leads to our encampment."

His grip on her waist tightened and her head jerked in Fitz Alan's direction. Another volley of arrows filled the air as Fitz Alan reached up to snatch his sword. With the weapon safely retrieved, he flattened himself against the trunk and began to ease himself into deeper water again. Lonsdale made a gesture, and two archers ran along the bank to position themselves where they would have a better shot at Fitz Alan.

Kenric swore under his breath, then called out to her uncle. "What do you want?"

"The girl," Lonsdale answered. "Give us my niece and we will let you go."

The two archers released their arrows just as Fitz Alan

reached water deep enough to swim. He ducked beneath the surface an instant before the arrows struck the trunk where his head had been. He emerged again next to Kenric, and worked his way beneath the branches that offered protection from archers on both sides. Claudia breathed a sigh of relief.

"You must swim downstream to get help," she told them. She summoned up her strongest voice to cover her fear. "I am not afraid to stay here alone. My uncle will not hurt me."

Both men stared at her in incredulous silence. Kenric found his voice first. "The uncle who ordered his men to shoot arrows at all of us, who intended to murder Guy and hang you for the deed? This is the uncle who will not hurt you?"

Claudia gave an exasperated sigh. "I meant that he will not hurt me until he thinks himself safely away from here, if he intends to hurt me at all. He surely has some plot to ransom me to Guy or Dante, and for that he needs me alive."

"We will not leave you here." Kenric's voice brooked no argument.

" 'Tis only a matter of time before he moves his archers in closer where they will have a clear shot at us all," Claudia protested. "He will kill you both if you stay."

"We will take our chances," Fitz Alan said.

Kenric shifted her to his side so he could draw his sword. "Aye, these are not the worst odds we have faced."

She thought them crazed. "You have the means to save yourselves. Why will you not leave while you can?"

They both looked at her as if she should know the answer, but Kenric enlightened her. "We would not leave any lady in such danger, Claudia. Least of all a member of our family. You insult us by suggesting we do so."

Claudia opened her mouth to voice another argument, then promptly closed it again. They considered her a part of their family?

Kenric grinned. "I thought that might silence you."

"Guy will return in an hour or two," said Fitz Alan. " 'Tis possible we can hold them off until then."

"Nay, they will not wait." Kenric looked toward the bank at their left. "We must draw them into the water, tempt them to take a shot from this side. The river runs deeper over there and we might have a chance to—"

The woods behind Lonsdale's soldiers erupted with shouts. More soldiers rushed forward, only these wore the blue and white colors of Montague and carried shields to protect them from the wild volley of Lonsdale arrows. The archers dropped their bows and drew their swords, just as Claudia saw Guy and Dante emerge from the woods with Guy's soldiers.

"Christ," Fitz Alan swore, "he has but six men at his side."

"Come with me. We can attack Lonsdale's men from behind." Kenric was already moving to the side of the trunk and shallower water. He stopped when the water reached their waists, then loosened his hold on Claudia. "Can you keep your balance if we leave you here?"

Claudia braced her good hand against the trunk. "Aye."

"Good. Stay crouched down. We will take care of the archers on the left. Do not give the ones on the other side of this log anything to aim at."

With that, Kenric and Fitz Alan made their way through the water toward shore. They moved slower than Claudia expected, careful to make no sudden moves that would draw the attention of the archers who had already turned to join the attack on Guy's soldiers. The archers realized their mistake too late to face the new threat from the river. Kenric and Fitz Alan made short work of them, then moved ashore and found new targets to attack.

Claudia peeked over the trunk and saw that Lonsdale's soldier no longer paid her any heed. They were well occupied fighting off their attackers. She looked for her uncle but didn't see him anywhere. Then she spied Guy. He was running toward her, but had to stop to fight off a Lonsdale soldier. That one fell an instant before another attacked him from behind. Guy turned just in time to stop the death blow aimed at his skull. The near miss made Claudia's heart skip several beats, but it soon became obvious that this soldier would fall as well. She released a shaky sigh of relief.

The sound of a great many hoofbeats mingled with the sounds of the battle. Another force of Guy's men arrived, this one much larger than the first. Guy started toward her again, but stopped abruptly. He glanced to his left and right, then suddenly sprinted along the bank, heading upstream. The brush and bushes grew thicker there and he disappeared behind a wall of greenery.

Claudia wondered if he had spied a Lonsdale soldier trying to escape in that direction, perhaps even her uncle. Several loud shouts turned her attention back to the fight taking place in front of her. Guy's men had the Lonsdale soldiers surrounded, and those still standing threw down their weapons at the sight of heavily armed reinforcements. Dante glanced over his shoulder then started toward her as well, and just like Guy, he came to a sudden stop. "Claudia! Behind you!"

The warning came too late. Just as she glanced over her shoulder, a dark figure emerged from the water. She caught only a glimpse of faded blond hair and piercing blue eyes, then her uncle grabbed her by the waist and pressed a knife to her throat, using her as a shield.

"I will have safe passage, along with those of my men still standing," Lonsdale shouted to the men on shore. "Throw down your weapons!"

Dante was the first to comply. He flung his sword aside with a look of contempt. " 'Tis like you to hide behind a woman's skirts, uncle. I am surprised your old friend the bishop is not here as well. He is just as adept at using my sister to fill his coffers. Did you think I would not learn of her whereabouts?"

"She was to go to the convent after I struck a bargain with Baron Montague for Halford Hall. No harm would have come to her if Montague had kept his word, and you would never have known that she had stayed at Lonsdale longer than planned. I will compensate you for the inconvenience this caused you."

Claudia heard more than a trace of fear in her uncle's voice. He was a desperate man, driven to desperate measures. If he somehow managed to escape with her, she would not survive long in his care. His hold on her turned painful, for he had no concern for her injured shoulder. A small whimper escaped her lips.

"You are a poor liar, uncle." Dante drew a dagger from inside his tunic and drew the flat of the blade through his fingers. He tilted his head to one side and looked up from the dagger, as if he had just come to a decision. " 'Tis time to pay for your crimes."

"I will slit her throat," Lonsdale shouted. "I swear I will!"

"Do you think I will let you walk away from here?" Dante shook his head, answering his own question. "You must kill me first, uncle."

Lonsdale backed up a step, then another pair of arms were suddenly wrapped around them both. Claudia watched in wide-eyed terror as Lonsdale's dagger moved away from her throat to waver in front of her face. His hand trembled with his effort to return the blade to her neck, his wrist in the steely grip of a large, familiar hand. Lonsdale's hold on her waist loosened just as Guy shouted his orders. "Get away from him, Claudia. Now!"

Ducking her head to avoid Lonsdale's dagger, she twisted and turned, then fell forward into the water. Unmindful of the throbbing pain of her fall, it took only a moment to right herself. She struggled to her feet and stumbled through the water to put distance between herself and her uncle. Afraid to turn her back on Lonsdale, she whirled around in the water just in time to see Guy standing behind him, struggling to take the knife from Lonsdale's hand. Then in a blurring flash of silver another dagger appeared, this one embedded in Lonsdale's throat. Lonsdale sank to his knees, a look of stunned disbelief on his face. Claudia turned away from the gruesome sight.

"Did he hurt you?" Guy demanded, even as he swept her into his arms, jarring her shoulder in the process. He cursed, loud and fluently.

" 'Tis nothing. I am fine."

That did nothing to ease Guy's scowl. He headed resolutely toward the shore. His men had the situation well in hand, but Guy motioned Kenric closer with a small movement of his head. "Find out where their horses are and send out a patrol to round up any more of his men."

"Aye," Kenric answered. "One of the wounded already made mention that another score of soldiers await them in the next valley. Fitz Alan and I will arrange a small surprise for them."

"Excellent. Claudia and I will return to camp. We will meet you there." Guy started to walk toward his horse.

"Montague, hold!" The words stopped Guy in his tracks and he turned around. Dante gave his sister a worried look. "You were not injured, cara?"

"Nay, I was not injured." Claudia's eyes narrowed on her brother. "But you could have skewered Guy with that dagger you threw. If Baron Lonsdale had moved just inches in either direction, Guy would be dead."

The look in Dante's eyes took on a decided chill. "There was no possibility of that, I assure you."

"Can you, Dante?" She wanted to believe him. Could she ever believe in him again? "Can you assure me that you will never try to take Guy's life, and swear to me that you speak the truth?"

"This is not the time or place to argue." The censure in Guy's tone surprised her as much as the admonishing look he gave her. "You two can discuss this later, in my tent."

"I think not." Dante resheathed his sword in one smooth, efficient stroke. "My men are ready to leave, and I have tarried here too long already. The papers I signed at the abbey mean you are no longer my responsibility, Claudia. I wish you well in your marriage."

Without another word, Dante pivoted on his heel and

strode toward Armand and Oliver, who waited with his horse. Claudia looked away from her brother.

"Call him back," Guy said.

Claudia shook her head. "He is the one who forced me to choose. My loyalties are with you."

"I did not ask you to choose between us, I asked you to—"

"Please, Guy. I do not wish to speak of him." She did not mean to sway him with tears, but they filled her eyes anyway. "Let Dante go. He brought us nothing but trouble."

Guy's mouth became a straight line. "You will not thank me for indulging your stubbornness, for the time will come when you regret those words."

The time came sooner than Claudia imagined. A company of soldiers rode with them when they returned to camp, and Guy indicated that he did not want to speak in front of them. She tried her best to push Dante from her thoughts, but failed at that task as surely as she failed to contain her speculations about everything else that had happened at the river. After a warning look from Guy, she managed to hold her questions until they reached his tent and Guy gave his squire orders that they were not to be disturbed.

He smiled at her obvious impatience to be alone with him. "You have a few questions?"

"A few?" She pushed a damp lock of hair off her forehead in a restless gesture. "How did you get behind Uncle Laurence in the water? How did you know he attacked us in the first place? What made you leave the abbey so soon, and why did you try to rescue us with so few men?" She paused to take a breath. "Did you know your brothers would not leave me, even when they could save themselves? Why did—"

He held up one hand for silence. "Claudia, please. I can only answer one question at a time. Turn around and I will unlace you while I explain."

"You wish to undress me? Now?" She looked at her soaked gown. "Oh. I suppose I should change clothes."

"Aye, and I intend change your bandage as well," he said, "but you are right to be wary."

His eyes drank in the sight of her slender curves, and she knew that the wet gown clung to her in all the places she wanted him to touch her, which was everywhere. His clothes were soaked as well. The damp garments revealed an endless display of sleek, hard muscles that would flex beneath her touch when she kissed and caressed him. She couldn't wait to get started. She saw how closely he watched the movement of her tongue when she wet her lips, so she did it again, this time to whet his appetite.

He cleared his throat. "I need to check your injury to make certain there is no further damage. Did Dante leave any of that salve?"

She nodded, then pointed to a trunk and a small jar that sat on top of it.

"Good. Now turn around." She obeyed the order and his hands went to the laces. He worked slowly, careful not to pull too hard. On more than one occasion, she felt his fingers brush against the skin he bared. "To answer your first question, I was still on shore when I saw Lonsdale swim around the end of the fallen tree. I knew he intended to hold you hostage to gain his own freedom, and knew just as well that I would never reach you before he did. Instead I made my way along the bank and entered the river upstream, then floated beneath the surface and came up behind him. You know what happened from there."

"Aye, Dante nearly murdered you!" She recalled again her awful terror when she saw the knife slice through the air, without knowing which man it would strike.

Guy unknotted the sling and eased it from her shoulder, supporting her left arm so it would not drop unexpectedly. "Dante had a clear target, and this time no one rushed forward to throw herself in front of his dagger. He told me himself that I was his first failure, that no other man he marked for death still lived."

"He has become a monster," she whispered.

"Perhaps," he agreed, "but I believe there is a tortured soul in there somewhere, one capable of more emotion than he would have you know."

"What do you mean?"

"He signed the marriage contracts because he wants you to be happy. I doubt he would ever admit it, but I think he also came to terms with the fact that I can keep you safe whereas he can offer you nothing but a life fraught with danger. And I would wager half my gold that you hurt his feelings when you accused him of trying to murder me."

"He no longer has any feelings," she countered, "and he only signed the marriage contracts because he wants you in his debt."

"You are wrong, Claudia. If that were his only reason, he would demand payment of that debt right away. At the very least, he would demand that a debt of some sort be put in writing. Once you are my wife, he knows that I am bound to that debt by nothing but my word. Given the decided lack of friendship between us, 'tis a risk few men would take."

She considered that for a moment. "But he tried to kill you the very day I arrived. I heard you both threaten to kill each other while I lay ill."

"I believe he had a change of heart." Guy eased the gown off her shoulders, and she felt his heated gaze touch her as surely as any caress. He sucked in his breath when she pushed the gown over her hips and it fell in a damp puddle at her feet.

"You may be right," she mused. "Perhaps I did misjudge him. I did not take time to consider what Dante must have felt when he realized that a man he thought of as his enemy had succeeded where he failed. He said the words himself when he agreed to our marriage, that you would give me the home and security he had always promised." She stepped away from the gown and made her way to the small trunk placed next to his cot, trying her best to seem unaware of her nudity.

"I, ah—That is—"

She glanced up at him and realized he did not have the vaguest idea what they were talking about.

"Dante?" she prompted.

"Aye. Dante." His distracted gaze returned to her face and he gave her a sheepish grin. "Do not fret, love. We have yet to see the last of your brother. 'Tis a certainty the king will want me to present my new wife at court, and there is a good chance we will see Dante there as well. Edward tends to keep your brother close at his side these days."

He moved closer to draw a line down the curve of her back, moving lower and lower until she shivered. "You have dimples in the most surprising places."

She felt a blush spread from her cheeks all the way to her breasts, and hastily turned around. "When do you think we will—"

She found herself staring at the front of his breeks. The garment looked strained at the seams by his hard erection. Her mouth felt suddenly dry. Perhaps she was rushing things a bit. She snatched up one of his tunics that lay across the cot and held it up in front of her with one hand, then sat abruptly on the cot to cover more of her nakedness. "You wished to change my bandage?"

He nodded, but made no move toward her.

"There are fresh bandages in the trunk," she said, "and the salve is there on its top."

Guy strode forward to reach for the small jar. Water dripped from his sleeve, and he took a moment to strip off his tunic. Claudia eased most of the wet bandage off her shoulder until only the square patch that covered the wound itself remained.

"Here, let me take care of that for you." He knelt beside her and removed the bandage, then started to remove the patch. "It came away easier than I expected. I feared it would be stuck to the wound. The welt on your shoulder does not look so red and swollen today, but it still looks far from healed. Perhaps your foray into the cool river water actually did the injury more good than harm."

He worked the ointment into the seared wound, his hands so gentle that his tender ministrations did not bother her in the least. The sure knowledge that he would be just as gentle in their lovemaking eased away her worries.

"To answer the last of your questions," he went on, "it was your brother who made certain we knew of your peril. Apparently he did not trust you alone with my brothers, and he ordered his men to follow you this afternoon, but to remain out of sight. Armand rode to the abbey to warn us when he saw Lonsdale's soldiers enter the woods, while Oliver sent the nearest patrol to meet us. A larger force of my men set out as soon as they received word, but we had the situation almost in hand by that time."

"That would be about the time a Lonsdale soldier nearly split your skull while you were busy dispatching his companion?"

"Aye, that would be the time." His grin disappeared when the tunic dropped from her fingers. He turned away to unroll the fresh bandage and kept his gaze averted as he handed her a new patch. "Hold this in place, and I will wrap the bandage around your shoulder."

"Be sure to bind it tight," she said. "If the bandage is secure, my shoulder scarce bothers me. Even when I undertake a strenuous activity."

"There is no strenuous activity you must undertake today."

Her hand brushed along his cheek to caress a muscle that twitched along his jaw. She waited until he met her gaze, her voice warm and inviting. "There is one I would like to undertake."

"Nay, do not tempt me." He tried to drape the tunic around her, with little success. She kept tugging it away.

"You must finish tying the bandage in place, Guy."

He tried his best to fulfill her request, but she stroked her fingers through his hair as he went about the task. That seemed to distract him mightily. "We will not make love, Claudia. Stop your teasing."

" 'Tis not teasing," she murmured, as her fingertips began to explore his chest. "I need you no less now than I did this morn. Indeed, with all that happened this day I would find great comfort in your arms."

"I will hold you all you wish, comfort you all you wish, but I will not make love to you. 'Tis too soon." He stared at her breasts. "I feel a sinner just thinking about—"

She pressed her fingers against his lips, and even managed to turn that into a caress. "There is no sin in anything we do. If you will recall, my brother agreed to our marriage. That means we are once more betrothed."

Guy tied the bandage in place, and made certain it was tied securely. "There is sin in every thought you put into my head." He caught her hand in his and placed a kiss in her palm, then against the sensitive skin of her wrist, then worked his way up her arm. Their gazes met, and she saw her own desire reflected in his eyes. "The first time I saw you standing on the steps of a chapel, I thought you looked like some heavenly vision. I am beginning to think you are no saint after all, my lady."

Claudia smiled and did her best to prove him right on that account.

Epilogue ❧

"**Y**ou might have warned me." Claudia kneaded her fingers into Guy's back and knew he did not deserve the soothing massage. Not that she believed the story that he had strained his muscles in his most recent contest with Kenric. Guy just liked to have his back rubbed. Because she liked to rub his back, she decided not to challenge his story. Besides, she would need ministrations of her own after this trying day with his family. "You *should* have warned me. I felt a fool."

Guy lay amidst the pile of pillows in front of the hearth. He glanced over his shoulder and gave her a devilish grin. "And ruin the surprise? I waited months to see that expression on your face when Tess and Helen rode through the gates. It was worth every second."

"I gaped at your sisters a good hour after they arrived. You knew I had braced myself to meet giants, and you even encouraged me to think Kenric's wife would look every bit as fierce as her husband. Your sister, Helen, is no more than half an inch taller than me, and every bit as pretty as you are handsome. Yet it was Tess who left me dumbfounded. She is so small and delicate that she looks half fairy or sprite. Then there is all that gold hair, and those unusual eyes. They are the color of violets." Claudia shook her head. "It will take time to accustom myself to the fact that she is married to that brute you call a brother."

"Give yourself a few days," Guy said. "Soon you will wonder how you ever thought them anything less than perfect for each other. They are very much in love."

"Aye," she agreed, " 'tis obvious by the change in your brother whenever she is near him. I did not know Kenric could smile so much. I found it hard not to stare at him as well, yet Lady Tess seemed to catch me each time I did." She stopped rubbing his back and leaned closer. "Do you think your sisters will ever learn to like me?"

"They like you already," he said surely.

"I am not so sure." Her hands worked at her task again. "They seem very close. It does not appear that they need another friend."

She felt him stiffen, but his voice sounded unconcerned. "No one can have too many friends, my love. Just be yourself around them, and give them time to know you better. Helen mentioned already that I made an excellent choice of brides. She thinks you are very nice."

"Lady Tess thinks me rude. She frowned at me several times during dinner, quite pointedly, I might add. I have no idea what I did to offend her."

"She thinks you covet her husband," Guy quipped.

Claudia tilted her head to look down at his face. His eyes were closed, but she could see no trace of teasing in his content expression. "Why would she think such a thing?"

Guy's lips curved into a smile. "Tess thinks all women covet her husband, that they cannot help but be drawn to his handsome face."

"Kenric's face? We are speaking of your brother?"

"Aye, Tess thinks her husband irresistible to all women. It will take her time to realize you are well satisfied with your own."

"You jest with me." She could not imagine that any woman would think Kenric irresistible.

Guy shot her an indignant look. "You are not satisfied with your husband, my lady?"

She pressed one hand to her forehead and affected a pout. "Alas, my lord, you have found me out. I am cursed with a husband who but towers over other men rather than make them look the size of ants. And his face is far more suited to some dull, heroic statue than a barbarian's nightmare." She bit her lower lip and looked thoughtful. "Yet he does have one or two qualities I find appealing."

"Such as?" he prompted.

She leaned back until her palms rested against the backs of his knees. "All women wish for a husband who can be brought instantly awake at any time of the night when they feel in need of . . . a little companionship." She smoothed her hands higher and wished she had asked him to remove his breeks before she started this massage. Still, she felt his body tense beneath hers. "Aye, a man so ticklish behind his knees is quite handy to have about in such circumstances. Once he is awake, 'tis no great chore for a wife to trail her hands along his hard thighs to see if there are other parts of him so sensitive to her touch."

He shifted beneath her and rolled over to lie on his back. Desire warmed his eyes already. "I assure you, lady, that your husband possesses parts that are especially sensitive to his wife's touch."

She wriggled her hips to test that theory and was rewarded with a deep sound of pleasure. "There is one other matter that piques my curiosity, my lord. Do you think my husband can produce children as handsome as those made by his brothers?"

"Sweet Claudia, it pains me to see you so perplexed by this." His grin turned wicked as he pressed the source of his pain against her soft core. At the same time, his hands disappeared beneath her skirts to start a slow, smooth caress toward her thighs. "I see that I must work on the answer to this question right away."

She splayed her hands against his chest and her lips curved into a secretive smile. "Your work is done, my lord. We will know the answer come spring."

For a moment his seductive expression did not change, then his eyes widened in surprise. "You are certain? We have made a child?"

"You need not sound so surprised," she teased. " 'Tis rare

you give me rest from my wifely duties. Babes are most often the result."

"Your wifely duties could be called wifely demands on more than a few occasions, love." His hands reached her hips, then suddenly stilled. " 'Tis said a man must not spend his lust on a woman who is breeding."

"You think I will stand idle while you spend your lust on one who is not?" She pinched the taut skin of his belly to emphasize her point.

"Ouch! Cease your scowls, vixen." He caught her hands and brought them to his lips. "I would become a monk rather than have you entertain ideas of making me a eunuch. My lust belongs to you alone, as well you know, but we must both have a care for the child." He sat up and eased her off his lap. "How long after a child's birth must a woman wait before she can make love?"

"How long . . ." She stared at him in amazement. "You think to leave me untouched until spring?"

He raked a hand through his hair in an abrupt gesture of frustration. "I know little of babes and breeding, Claudia. What if I hurt you?"

"You did not hurt me last night," she reasoned. She braced her hands on either side of his hips and pressed an innocent kiss at the base of his neck, then rubbed her body against his chest in a purely seductive caress. The sound of his indrawn breath made her smile. "Or the night before, or the night before that."

"True," he admitted. "That seemed to cause no harm."

" 'Tis a certainty your brothers are well versed in such matters." She placed small, tempting kisses at the corners of his mouth. "Somehow I feel certain they did not deny their wives as long as you would deny me."

"Aye, that does seem unlikely." His arms went around her and his lips captured hers for a long, deep kiss. She was sitting astride his lap again by the time it was done. "I shall be sure to ask their opinion on the matter. Tomorrow."

His head lowered for another kiss, but an insistent

pounding on their door made him stop just a breath from her lips. He swore under his breath.

"They will go away," she assured him, trying her best to distract him from the racket.

He caught her wrists and gave her a wry smile. "There are matters afoot that may need my attention."

"What matters?" she asked, as he strode toward the door.

She sat up and straightened her skirts while she waited for a reply, but he pretended to ignore her. Guy opened the door no more than a crack, but Claudia heard the clear sound of Evard's voice on the other side.

"News from London, my lord! 'Tis as you expected. The king himself put a reward on Dante's head. Two hundred pieces of silver, dead or alive."

Guy pushed his way into the hallway and the door slammed behind him. Claudia stared after him in stunned silence. A cold knot of dread tightened in her stomach when he reappeared moments later, his mouth set in a grim line. "You heard?"

She gave a mute nod.

He crossed the room in long strides and lifted her in his arms, then placed her on the bed. "Trust me, Claudia. 'Tis not as dire as it sounds."

"The king has a price on Dante's head." She looked up at him and tried to blink back tears. "This is not dire?"

"Nay, 'tis no more than an inconvenience." His hands went to the unfastening of his breeks and he soon stood naked before her.

Her eyes widened. "What are you doing?"

"I would not have you upset in your condition. It does the babe no good, nor yourself." He gently pushed on her shoulders until she lay back against the pillows. "You made your peace with Dante in the missive you sent him right after our return to Montague, yet you fret for weeks before you received his reply. The subject of your brother does nothing but upset you. I intend to take your mind off Dante, and turn your thoughts to something more pleasant."

Claudia gave an exasperated sigh and sat up again, even as Guy's hands worked at the laces of her bodice. "I am not so pliable as you would like to think. Do you expect me to simply ignore such news?"

"Aye." He gave her a firm nod and eased her gown and chemise off her shoulders. This time he used the pressure of his kiss to urge her to lie down again, his lips holding hers captive as he pushed her clothing over her hips. His kiss turned carnal.

She bit his tongue.

"Ow! You play too rough, little cat." He lifted his head. "I would rather hear you purr."

"What is it you are not telling me?"

"Nothing, love." His hand stroked over her stomach, then gave her breast a more intimate caress. "I cannot feel any change in you yet. Are you sure you carry our child?"

She tried to ignore the heat that his touch unleashed inside her. "The truth, Guy. Why are you so certain that I need not worry about Dante?"

"Do you trust me?" He murmured the words close to her ear.

She managed to nod.

"Then put your fears to rest when I tell you that your brother is safe." His tongue darted out and he released a gentle puff of breath that made her toes curl. The sound of his voice vibrated deep inside her. "He is in a place where none will think to search for him."

His hands moved over her body insistently, expertly, knowing just how to increase her need for him. Resistance flowed out of her, replaced with a burning need to return the pleasure he bestowed. Her hands began their own explorations, fanning the flames of her own desire. He moved quickly to take her. She shook her head, trying one last time to deny him until he answered her questions. "Where is he, Guy?"

It was too late. His hand moved between her legs and her

head fell back on the pillow as she gave herself over to the magic of his touch. His voice held the satisfied tone of a victor. "Open for me, love."

She obeyed without question, just as she trusted him without question. He had accomplished his goal before he even moved inside her, for her thoughts were far from fear or worries. The beauty of their lovemaking never failed to amaze her, the astonishment that they could join their hearts and bodies so completely that even their souls seemed to touch. And the incredible calm after the storm that made any worries seem very far away.

Cradled against her husband's chest, Claudia tried her best to stay awake. She meant to ask him again about Dante, to sit up and demand that he tell her everything. Soon she would do just that. For the moment, she was loath to miss the simple pleasures of listening to the steady sound of his heartbeat, feeling his hand move in gentle strokes along her back, the deeper pleasure of being held in his arms and knowing he would hold her there always.

Until she met Guy, these were pleasures she never dreamed possible in her life. In his arms she found the home she always longed for and a love deeper than any she imagined. Within the year they would become a family in every sense of the word. Her lips curved into a smile and her eyes drifted shut. Guy's voice came to her in a soft whisper.

"Montague." He placed a gentle kiss against her forehead. "Dante is within the walls of Montague, my love."

About the Author

Elizabeth Elliott took a turn off the corporate fast track to write romances on the shores of a lake not far from Woebegone. In her spare time, she works as a free-lance writer/consultant in the software industry. At home with her husband and sons, she is currently writing her next novel.